ONYX

A LUX NOVEL
BOOK TWO

Other books by Jennifer L. Armentrout:

The Lux Series:
Obsidian: A Lux Novel, Book One
Onyx: A Lux Novel, Book Two
Opal: A Lux Novel, Book Three

The Covenant Series:
Daimon
Half-Blood
Pure
Deity
Apollyon

Single Titles:
Cursed

ONYX

A LUX NOVEL
BOOK TWO

JENNIFER L. ARMENTROUT

Entangled Publishing, LLC
2614 South Timberline Road
Suite 109
Fort Collins, CO 80525
Visit our website at www.entangledpublishing.com.

Edited by Liz Pelletier
Cover design by Liz Pelletier

Print ISBN   978-1-62061-011-4
Ebook ISBN   978-1-62061-012-1

Manufactured in the United States of America

First Edition August 2012

The author acknowledges the copyrighted or trademarked status and trademark owners of the following wordmarks mentioned in this work of fiction: Oreos, Pac-Man, Super Mario Bros., Wii, Coke, Expedition, Barbie, Rubik's Cube, Infiniti, X-Men, Snack Pack, Prius, Pop-Tart, Google, Pepto-Bismol, Mac, Yukon, Windex, Rolex, Dumpster, Jetta.

Dedicated to book lovers and book bloggers everywhere, those large and small.

Chapter 1

Ten seconds passed between when Daemon Black took his seat and when he poked me under my shoulder blade with his trusty pen. Ten whole seconds. Twisting around in my seat, I inhaled the unique outdoorsy scent that was all him.

Daemon pulled his hand back and tapped the blue cap of his pen on the corner of his lips. Lips I was well familiar with. "Good morning, Kitten."

I forced my gaze to his eyes. Bright green, like the stem of a freshly cut rose. "Good morning, Daemon."

Unruly dark hair fell over his forehead as he tilted his head. "Don't forget we have plans tonight."

"Yeah, I know. Looking forward to it," I said dryly.

As Daemon leaned forward, his dark sweater stretched over broad shoulders. He tipped his desk down. I heard the soft inhales from my friends Carissa and Lesa, felt the eyes of everyone in class watching us. One corner of his lips curved higher, as if he were secretly laughing.

The stretch of silence became too heavy. *"What?"*

"We need to work off your trace," he said, low enough that only

I could hear. Thank God. Trying to explain what a trace was to the general populace was not something I wanted to get into. *Oh, you know, just alien residue that rubs off on humans and lights them up like a Christmas tree and becomes a homing signal to an evil alien race. Want some?*

Uh huh.

I picked up my pen and considered poking him with it. "Yeah, I figured as much."

"And I have this really fun idea of how we can do it."

I knew what his "fun idea" was. Me. Him. Making out. I smiled, and the green of his eyes heated.

"Liking the idea?" he murmured, and his gaze dropped to my lips.

An unhealthy amount of excitement had my entire body humming, and I reminded myself that his sudden turnaround had more to do with the effect of his bizarre alien mojo on me than it did with me as a person. Ever since Daemon healed me after the battle with the Arum, we were connected, and while that seemed to be enough for him to jump into a relationship, it wasn't for me.

It wasn't *real*.

I wanted what my parents had. Undying love. Powerful. True. A whacked-out alien bond couldn't do that for me.

"Not in this lifetime, buddy," I said finally.

"Resistance is futile, Kitten."

"So is your charm."

"We'll see."

Rolling my eyes, I faced the front of the classroom. Daemon was a total babe, but he was stab-worthy, which, at times, zeroed out the babe part. Not always, though.

Our ancient trig teacher shuffled in, clutching a thick wad of papers while he waited for the tardy bell.

Daemon poked me with his pen. Again.

Squeezing my hands into fists, I debated ignoring him. I knew better. He'd just keep poking me. Turning around, I glared at him.

"*What*, Daemon?"

He moved as fast as a cobra striking. With a grin that did funny things to my stomach, he glided his fingers along my cheek, plucking a tiny bit of fuzz out of my hair.

I stared at him.

"After school…"

I started to get all kinds of crazy ideas as his grin turned wicked, but I wasn't playing his game anymore. I rolled my eyes and whipped back around. I would resist my hormones…and the way he got to me like no one else.

A slight tic of pain throbbed behind my left eye the rest of the morning, which I totally blamed on Daemon.

By lunch, I felt like someone had sucker punched me in the head. The steady noise of the cafeteria and the mix of disinfectant and burned food made me want to run from the room.

"You going to eat that?" Dee Black gestured at my untouched cottage cheese and pineapple.

Shaking my head, I pushed my tray over, and my stomach roiled as she dug in.

"You could eat the football team under the table." Lesa watched Dee with obvious envy sparkling in her dark eyes. I couldn't blame her. I'd once seen Dee eat an entire package of Oreos in *one sitting*. "How do you do it?"

Dee shrugged dainty shoulders. "I guess I have a fast metabolism."

"What did you guys do this weekend?" Carissa asked, frowning as she wiped her glasses with the sleeve of her shirt. "I was filling out college applications."

"I was making out with Chad all weekend." Lesa grinned.

Both girls looked at Dee and me, waiting for us to share. I guessed the whole killing-a-psycho-alien-and-almost-dying thing probably wasn't something to throw out there.

"We hung out and watched stupid movies," Dee answered, giving me a slight smile as she tucked a shiny black curl behind her ear. "It was kind of boring."

Lesa snorted. "You guys are always boring."

I started to smile, but a warm tingle skated across the nape of my neck. The conversation around me faded and a few seconds later, Daemon dropped into the seat to my left. A plastic cup full of strawberry smoothie—my favorite—was set in front of me. I was more than a little shocked to be receiving any present from Daemon, much less one of my favorite treats. My fingers brushed his as I took the drink, and a jolt of electricity danced along my skin.

I yanked my hand back and took a small sip. Delish. Maybe it would make my tummy feel better. And maybe I could get used to this new gift-giving Daemon. Much better than the other douchebag version of him. "Thank you."

He smiled in response.

"Where're ours?" Lesa quipped.

Daemon laughed. "I'm only at the service of one person in particular."

My cheeks flamed as I scooted my chair over. "You are not servicing me in any way."

He leaned in, closing my newly gained distance. "Not yet."

"Oh, come on, Daemon. I'm right here." Dee frowned. "You're about to make me lose my appetite."

"Like that will ever happen," Lesa retorted with an eye roll.

Daemon pulled a sub out of his bag. Only he could skip fourth period early to get lunch and not end up in detention. He was just so... *special*. Every girl at the table, besides his sister, was staring at him. Some of the guys were, too.

He offered his sister an oatmeal cookie.

"Don't we have plans to make?" Carissa asked, two bright spots coloring her cheeks.

"Yep," Dee said, grinning at Lesa. "Big plans."

I wiped a hand over my damp, clammy forehead. "What plans?"

"Dee and I were talking in English about throwing a party the week after next," Carissa jumped in. "Something—"

"Huge," Lesa said.

"Small," Carissa corrected, eyes narrowing on her friend. "Just something with a few people."

Dee nodded, and her bright green eyes glimmered with excitement. "Our parents are going to be out of town Friday, so it works out perfectly."

I glanced at Daemon. He winked. My stupid heart skipped a beat.

"That's so cool that your parents are letting you have a party at your house," Carissa said. "Mine would stroke out if I even suggested something like that."

Dee shrugged one shoulder and looked away. "Our parents are pretty cool."

I forced my expression blank as a pang hit me in the chest. I truly believed Dee wanted her parents alive more than she wanted anything else in this world. And maybe even Daemon, too. Then he wouldn't bear the weight of being responsible for his family.

During the time we'd spent together, I'd figured out most of his bad attitude was because of all the stress. And there was his twin brother's death…

The party became the topic of discussion at the table for the rest of the lunch period. Which was kind of cool scheduling, since my birthday was the following Saturday. But by Friday, the party would be all over the school. In a town where drinking in a cornfield was the height of excitement on a Friday night, no way was this going to stay a "small" party. Did Dee realize that?

"You okay with all of this?" I whispered to Daemon.

He shrugged. "Not like I can stop her."

I knew he could if he wanted, which meant he didn't have a problem with it.

"Cookie?" he offered, holding a cookie full of chocolate chips.

Upset tummy or not, there was no way I could refuse that. "Sure."

His lips tipped up one side and he leaned toward me, his mouth inches from mine. "Come and get it."

Come and get...? Daemon placed half the cookie between those full, totally kissable lips.

Oh, holy alien babies everywhere...

My mouth dropped open. Several of the girls at the table made sounds that had me wondering if they were turning into puddles under the table, but I couldn't bring myself to check out what they really were doing.

That cookie—those lips—were right *there.*

Heat swept over my cheeks. I could feel the eyes of everyone else, and Daemon...dear God, Daemon arched his brows, daring me.

Dee gagged. "I think I'm going to hurl."

Mortified, I wanted to crawl in a hole. What did he think I was going to do? Take the cookie from his mouth like something straight out of an R-rated version of *Lady and the Tramp*? Heck, I kind of wanted to, and I wasn't sure what that said about me.

Daemon reached up and took the cookie. There was a gleam to his eyes, as if he'd just won some battle. "Time's up, Kitten."

I stared at him.

Breaking the cookie in two, he handed me the larger piece. I snatched it away, half tempted to throw it back in his face, but it was...it was chocolate chip. So I ate it and loved it.

Taking another sip of my smoothie, I felt unease skitter along my spine like I was being watched. Glancing around the cafeteria, I expected to find Daemon's alien ex-girlfriend giving me her trademark bitch look, but Ash Thompson was chatting with another boy. Huh. Was he a Luxen? There weren't many their age, but I doubted Ash in all her supremeness would be smiling at a human boy. My gaze moved away from their table, scanning the rest of the cafeteria.

Mr. Garrison stood by the double doors to the library, but he was staring at a table full of jocks who were making some intricate designs with their mashed potatoes. No one else even remotely looked in our direction.

I shook my head, feeling foolish for being weirded out over nothing. It wasn't like an Arum was going to bum-rush the high school cafeteria. Maybe I was coming down with something. My hands shook a little as I reached for the chain around my neck. The obsidian was cool against my skin, comforting—a herald of safety. So I needed to stop freaking out. Maybe that was why I was lightheaded and dizzy.

It surely had nothing to do with the boy sitting beside me.

. . .

There were several packages waiting for me at the post office and I only barely squealed. They were advanced reader copies from other bloggers passing them along for review. And I was, like, whatever. Sure evidence I was coming down with mad cow disease.

The trip home was torturous. My hands felt weak. My thoughts were scattered. Gathering my mail close to my chest, I ignored the way the skin on the back of my neck tingled as I climbed the porch steps. And I also ignored six feet and then some of boy leaning against the railing.

"You didn't come straight home after school." Annoyance colored his tone. Like he was my own screwed-up, super-hot version of the Secret Service and I'd managed to evade him.

I dug out my keys with my free hand. "Obviously I had to go to the post office." I pushed open the door and dropped the pile on the table inside the foyer. Of course, he was right behind me, not waiting for an invite.

"Your mail could've waited." Daemon followed me into the kitchen. "What is it? Just books?"

Grabbing the OJ from the fridge, I sighed. People who didn't heart books didn't understand. "Yeah, it was *just* books."

"I know there probably aren't any Arum around right now, but you can never be too careful, and you have a trace on you that will lead them right to our doorsteps. Right now, that's more important than your books."

Nah, books were more important than the Arum. I poured myself a glass, too tired to get into it with Daemon. We hadn't mastered the art of polite conversation yet. "Drink?"

He sighed. "Sure. Milk?"

I gestured at the fridge. "Help yourself."

"You offered. You're not going to get it for me?"

"I offered orange juice," I replied, taking my glass to the table. "You picked milk. And keep it down. My mom's asleep."

Muttering under his breath, he grabbed a glass of milk. As he sat beside me, I realized he was wearing black sweats, which reminded me of the last time he'd been in my house dressed like that. We'd gotten into it. Our argument had turned into a steamy make-out session straight from one of those cheesy romance novels I read. The encounter *still* kept me up late at night. Not that I'd ever admit it.

It was so hot, Daemon's alien mojo had blown most of the lightbulbs in the house and had fried my laptop. I really missed my laptop and my blog. Mom promised me a new computer for my birthday. Two more weeks…

I fiddled with my glass, not looking up. "Can I ask you a question?"

"Depends," he replied smoothly.

"Do you…feel anything around me?"

"Other than what I felt this morning when I saw how good you looked in those jeans?"

"Daemon." I sighed, trying to disregard the girl in me that screamed, *HE NOTICED ME!* "I'm being serious."

His long fingers idly traced circles on the wooden table. "The back of my neck gets all warm and tingly. Is that what you're talking about?"

I peeked up. A half smile played across his lips. "Yeah, you feel it, too?"

"Whenever we're near."

"It doesn't bother you?"

"Does it bother you?"

I wasn't sure what to say. The tingling wasn't painful or anything, just weird. But what it symbolized did bother me—the damn connection we knew nothing about. Even our hearts were beating the same.

"It could be a...side effect of the healing." Daemon watched me over the rim of his glass. I bet he'd look hot with a milk mustache. "Are you feeling well?" he asked.

Not really. "Why?"

"You look like crap."

Any other time his comment would've started a war in this house, but I just set my half-empty glass down. "I think I'm coming down with something."

His brows furrowed. The concept of being sick was foreign to Daemon. The Luxen didn't get sick. Like, ever. "What's wrong with you?"

"I don't know. I probably got alien cooties."

Daemon snorted. "Doubtful. I can't afford for you to be sick. We need to get you outside and try to work your trace off. Until then, you're a—"

"If you say I'm a weakness, I will hurt you." Anger pushed down the nausea in my stomach. "I think I proved that I'm not, especially when I led Baruck away from your house and *I* killed him." I struggled to keep my voice low. "Just because I'm human doesn't mean I'm weak."

He sat back, brows inching up his forehead. "I was going to say that until then, you're *at risk*."

"Oh." My cheeks flushed. Whoops. "Well, then, I'm still not weak."

One second Daemon was sitting at the table and the next he was beside me, kneeling down. He had to look up slightly to see my face. "I know you're not weak. You've proven yourself. And what you did this weekend, tapping into our powers? I still can't figure out how that happened, but you're not weak. Ever."

Whoa. It was hard to stick to my resolve of not caving to the ridiculous notion of us being together when he was actually...*nice*, and when he stared at me like I was the last piece of chocolate in the whole world.

Which made me think of that damn chocolate chip cookie in his mouth.

The side of his lips twitched as if he knew what I was thinking and was fighting a smile. Not that little smirk of his, but a real smile. And suddenly he was standing, towering over me. "Now I need you to prove you're not weak. Get off your butt and let's work off some of that trace."

I groaned. "Daemon, I'm really not feeling well."

"Kat..."

"And I'm not saying that to be difficult. I feel like hurling."

He folded his muscular arms, stretching his Under Armour shirt across his chest. "It's not safe for you to be running around when you look like a damn lighthouse. As long as you carry the trace, you can't do anything. Go anywhere."

I pushed up from the table, ignoring the rolling in my stomach. "I'll get changed."

Surprise widened his eyes as he stepped back. "Caving in so easily?"

"Caving in?" I laughed without feeling. "I just want you out of my face."

Daemon chuckled deeply. "Keep telling yourself that, Kitten."

"Keep using your ego steroids."

In a blink of an eye, he was in front of me, blocking my exit. Then he prowled forward, head lowered and eyes full of intent. I backed up until my hands found the edge of the kitchen table.

"What?" I demanded.

Placing his hands on either side of my hips, he bent forward. His breath was warm against my cheek and our eyes locked. He moved a fraction of an inch closer, and his lips brushed my chin. A strangled gasp escaped the back of my throat, and I swayed toward him.

A heartbeat later, Daemon pulled back, chuckling smugly. "Yeah… not my ego, Kitten. Go get ready."

Dammit!

Giving him the finger, I left the kitchen and went upstairs. My skin still felt clammy and gross and it had nothing to do with what happened, but I changed into a pair of sweats and a thermal. Running was the last thing I wanted to do. Not like I expected Daemon to care I wasn't feeling well.

He only cared about himself and his sister.

That's not true, whispered an insidious, annoying voice in my head. But maybe that voice was correct. He had healed me when he could've left me to die and I had heard his thoughts, heard him begging me not to leave him.

Either way, I had to swallow the urge to puke and go for a fun jog. Some sixth sense knew this wasn't going to end well.

Chapter 2

I lasted twenty minutes.

With the uneven terrain of the woods, the brisk November wind, and the boy next to me, I couldn't do it. Leaving him halfway to the lake, I speed walked all the way back to the house. Daemon called out to me a couple of times, but I ignored him. Within a minute of reaching my bathroom, I threw up—the clutching-the-toilet, on-my-knees, tears-streaming-down-my-face kind of hurling. It was so bad I woke up Mom.

She hurried into the bathroom, pulling my hair back. "How long have you been feeling sick, honey? A few hours, all day, or just now?"

Mom—ever the nurse. "On and off all day," I moaned, resting my head against the tub.

*Tsk*ing under her breath, she placed her hand against my forehead. "Honey, you're burning up." She grabbed a towel and ran it under the tap. "I should probably call in to work—"

"No, I'm okay." I took the towel from her, pressing it against my forehead. The coolness was wonderful. "It's just the flu. And I feel better already."

Mom clucked over me until I got up and took a shower. Changing into a long sleep shirt took an absurd amount of time. The room did a Tilt-a-Whirl on me as I climbed under the covers, and I squeezed my eyes shut and waited for Mom to return.

"Here's your phone and some water." She placed both on the table and sat beside me. "Open up." Prying one eye open, I saw a thermometer shoved at my face. I obediently opened my mouth. "Depending on how high your temperature is, we will determine if I'm staying home," she told me. "It's probably just the flu, but…"

"Mmm," I groaned.

She gave me a bland look and waited until the thing beeped. "One hundred and one. I want you to take this." Pausing, she handed me two pills. I downed them, no questions asked. "The temp isn't that bad, but I want you to stay in bed and rest. I'll call and check on you before ten, okay?"

I nodded and then snuggled down. Sleep was all I needed. She folded up another damp cloth and placed it over my forehead. I closed my eyes, almost certain I was approaching stage one of a zombie infection.

A weird fog entered my brain. I slept, waking up once to check in with Mom, and then again past midnight. The night shirt was damp, clinging to my feverish skin. I went to push the blankets off and noticed they were across the room, covering my cluttered computer desk.

Cold sweat dotted my forehead as I sat up. My thumping heart echoed in my head, heavy and erratic. Two beats at once, it seemed. My skin felt stretched tight over my muscles—hot and prickly. I stood, and the room spun.

I was so hot, burning up from the inside. My insides felt as if they'd melted into goo. My thoughts ran into one another, a never-ending train of nonsense. All I knew was that I needed to *cool down*.

The door to the hallway swung open, beckoning me. I didn't know where I was going, but I stumbled down the hall and then downstairs. The front door was like a beacon, promising relief. It would be cold outside. Then I would be cold.

But it wasn't enough.

I stood on the porch, the wind blowing my damp shirt and hair back. Stars lined the night sky, intensely bright. I lowered my gaze and the trees lining the road shifted colors. Yellow. Gold. Red. Then they turned a muted shade of brown.

I was dreaming, I realized.

In a daze, I stepped off the porch. Pieces of gravel poked at my feet, but I kept walking, the moonlight leading the way. Several times the world felt like it turned upside down, but I pushed on.

It didn't take me long to reach the lake. Under the pale light, the onyx-colored water rippled. I moved forward, stopping when my toes sunk through loose dirt. Prickling heat scorched my skin as I stood there. Burning. Sweltering.

"Kat?"

Slowly, I turned. Wind whipped around me as I stared at the apparition. Moonlight sliced his face in shadows, reflecting in his wide, bright eyes. He couldn't be real.

"What are you doing, Kitten?" Daemon asked.

He seemed fuzzy. Daemon was never fuzzy. Fast and blurry sometimes, yes, but never fuzzy. "I…I need to cool down."

Understanding shot across his face. "Don't you dare go into that lake."

I moved backward. Icy water lapped at my ankles and then my knees. "Why?"

"Why?" He took a step forward. "It's too cold. Kitten, don't make me come in there and get you."

My head throbbed. Brain cells were definitely melting. I sunk farther down. Cold water soothed the burning in my skin. It washed over my head, stealing my breath and the fire. The burn eased, nearly fading. I could stay under here forever. Maybe I would.

Strong, solid arms surrounded me, pulling me back to the surface. Frigid air rushed me, but my lungs were seared. I dragged in deep gulps, hoping to extinguish the flames. Daemon was pulling me out of the blessed water, moving so fast I was in the water one second and standing on shore the next.

"What's wrong with you?" he demanded, grasping my shoulders and giving me a light shake. "Have you lost your mind?"

"Don't." I pushed at him weakly. "I'm so hot."

His intense gaze drifted down to my toes. "Yeah, you're hot. The whole wet white shirt… It's working, Kitten, but a midnight swim in November? That's a little daring, don't you think?"

He wasn't making sense. The reprieve was over, and my skin was burning again. I stumbled from his hands, back toward the lake.

His arms were around me before I took two steps, turning me around. "Kat, you can't get in the lake. It's *too* cold. You're going to get sick." He brushed back the hair plastered to my cheeks. "Hell—sicker than you already are. You're burning up."

Something in what he said cleared a bit of the haze. I leaned into him, pressing my cheek into his chest. He smelled *wonderful*. Like spice and man. "I don't want you."

"Uh, now is not the time to get into *that* conversation."

This was just a dream. I sighed, wrapping my arms around his taut waist. "But I do want you."

Daemon's arms tightened around me. "I know, Kitten. You aren't fooling anyone. Come on."

Letting go, my arms hung limply at my sides. "I…I don't feel good."

"Kat." He pulled back. Both hands were on my face, holding my head up. "Kat, look at me."

I wasn't looking at him? My legs gave out. And then there was nothing. No Daemon. No thoughts. No fire. No Katy.

· · ·

Things were hazy, disjointed. Warm hands kept the hair back from my face. Fingers smoothed over my cheek. A deep voice spoke to me in a language that was musical and soft. Like a song, but…more beautiful and comforting. I sunk into the sound, lost for a little while.

I heard voices.

Once, I thought I heard Dee. "You can't. It'll just make the trace worse."

I was moved around. Wet clothing stripped away. Something warm and soft slid over my skin. I tried talking to the voices around me, and maybe I did. I wasn't sure.

At some point, I was wrapped in a cloud and carried somewhere. A steady heart beat under my cheek, lulling me until the voices faded and cool hands eventually replaced the warm ones. Bright lights intruded. I heard more voices. *Mom?* Mom sounded worried. She was talking to… someone. Someone I didn't recognize. *He* had the cool hands. There was a prick in my arm, a dull pain that radiated to my fingers. More hushed voices, and then I heard nothing.

There was no day or night, but this weird in-between where a fire raged in my body. Then the cool hands were back, pulling my arm out from underneath the covers. I didn't hear Mom as I felt the prick again on my skin. Heat swept *inside* me, rushing through my veins. Gasping, I arched my back off the bed, and a strangled scream escaped the back of my throat. Everything burned. A fire raged inside me ten times worse than before, and I knew I was dying. I had to be…

And then there was a coolness in my veins, like a rush of winter's air. It moved quickly, dousing the flames and leaving a trail of ice in its wake.

The hands moved to my neck, tugging something up. A chain… my necklace? The hands were gone, but I felt the obsidian *humming*, vibrating above me. And then I slept for what felt like an eternity, not certain I was ever going to wake up.

• • •

Four days of being in the hospital, and I had next to no recollection of any of it. Only that I woke up Wednesday in an uncomfortable bed, staring at a white ceiling and feeling fine. Great, even. Mom had been by my side, and it took a hefty amount of bitching to get released after I spent all day Thursday telling anyone who came within a block of my door that I wanted to go home. I'd obviously had a bad case of the flu, not something serious.

Now Mom watched me with shadowed eyes as I downed the glass of orange juice from our fridge. She was in jeans and a light sweater. It was odd seeing her out of her scrubs. "Honey, are you sure you're feeling well enough to go back to class? You can take today off and go back on Monday if you want."

I shook my head. Missing three days of classes already earned me the truckload of homework Dee had dropped off last night. "I'm fine."

"Honey, you were in the hospital. You should take it easy."

I washed out the cup. "I'm okay. Really, I am."

"I know you think you're feeling better." She fixed my cardigan which I'd apparently buttoned wrong. "Will—Dr. Michaels—may have cleared you to go home, but you scared me. I've never seen you so sick. Why don't I give him a quick call and see if he can check on you before he goes in for his rounds?"

Even more bizarre was that my mom was now referring to my doctor on a first-name basis—their relationship had taken a trip into serious land, it seemed, and I'd missed it. Grabbing my backpack, I stopped. "Mom?"

"Yes?"

"You came home in the middle of the night Monday, right? Before your shift ended?" When she shook her head, I was even more confused. "How did I get to the hospital?"

"Are you sure you're feeling okay?" She placed her hand on my forehead. "You don't have a fever, but… Your friend brought you to the hospital."

"My friend?"

"Yes, Daemon brought you in. Although, I'm curious how he knew you were so sick at three in the morning." Her eyes narrowed. "Actually,

I'm very curious."

Oh, crap. "So am I."

Chapter 3

I'd never been more eager to get to trig in my life. How in the hell had Daemon known I was sick? The dream I had about the lake couldn't have been real. No way. If it was…I was going to…I didn't know what I'd do, but I was sure my flaming cheeks would be involved.

Lesa was the first to arrive. "Yay! You're back! How are you feeling? Better?"

"Yeah, I'm doing okay." My eyes darted to the door. A few seconds later, Carissa came in.

She tugged on a strand of my hair as she passed, smiling. "I'm glad you're feeling better. We were all worried. Especially when we stopped by to visit and you were completely out of it."

I wondered what I'd done in front of them that I couldn't remember. "Do I even want to know?"

Lesa giggled, pulling out her textbook. "You mumbled a lot. And you kept calling out for someone."

Oh, no. "I did?"

Taking pity on me, Carissa kept her voice low. "You were calling out for Daemon."

I dropped my face in my hands and moaned. "Oh, God."

Lesa giggled. "It was kind of cute."

A minute before the tardy bell rang, I felt an all-too-familiar warmth on my neck and glanced up. Daemon swaggered into class. Textbook-less as usual. He had a notebook, but I don't think he ever wrote anything in it. I was beginning to suspect our math teacher was an alien, because how else would Daemon get away with not doing a damn thing in class?

He passed by without so much as a look.

I twisted around in my chair. "I need to talk to you."

He slid into his desk chair. "Okay."

"In private," I whispered.

His expression didn't change as he leaned back in his chair. "Meet me in the library at lunch. No one really goes in there. You know, with all those books and stuff."

I made a face before flipping to the front of the class. Maybe five seconds later, I felt his pen poking me in the back. Taking a deep, patient breath, I faced him. Daemon had his desk tipped forward. Inches separated us. "Yes?"

He grinned. "You look a lot better than the last time I saw you."

"Thanks," I grumbled.

His gaze flickered around me, and I knew what he was doing. He was looking at the trace. "Know what?"

I cocked my head to the side, waiting.

"You're not glowing," he whispered.

Surprised, I let my jaw fall slack. I'd been shining like a disco ball on Monday and now I didn't have a trace? "Like, at all?"

He shook his head.

The teacher started the class, so I had to face the front again, but I wasn't paying attention. My mind was stuck on the fact I wasn't glowing anymore. I should be—no, I *was* ecstatic, but the connection, it was still there. My hope that it would fade along with the trace was total bunk.

After class, I asked the girls to let Dee know I'd be late for lunch.

Since they'd overheard part of the conversation, Carissa was full of giggles and Lesa launched into her fantasy about doing it in the library. Something I didn't need to know. Or think about. But now I was, because I could *so* picture Daemon getting into that sort of thing.

Morning classes dragged. Mr. Garrison gave me the usual untrustworthy glance throughout biology after his eyes widened upon seeing me. He was like the unofficial guardian of the Luxen living outside of the alien colony. The non-glowy version of me seemed to get as much attention as the glowy version. Probably had more to do with the fact he wasn't too happy that I knew what they really were.

The door opened just as he went for the projector, and a boy walked in, wearing a vintage Pac-Man shirt—which was made of awesome. A low murmur went through the classroom as the stranger handed Mr. Garrison a note.

He was new, obviously. His brown hair was artfully messy, like it was styled that way on purpose. Good looking, too, with golden-colored skin and a confident grin on his face.

"It seems we have a new student," Mr. Garrison said, dropping the note on his desk. "Blake Saunders from…?"

"California," the boy supplied. "Santa Monica."

Several *ooh*s and *ahh*s followed that. Lesa sat up straighter. Yay. I'd no longer be the "new kid."

"All right, Blake from Santa Monica." Mr. Garrison scanned the classroom, his gaze stopping on the empty seat beside me. "There's your seat and your lab partner. Have fun."

My eyes narrowed on Mr. Garrison, not sure if "Have fun" was a thinly veiled insult or a secret hope the non-alien boy would distract me from the alien one.

Appearing oblivious to the curious stares, Blake took his seat next to me and smiled. "Hi."

"Hi. I'm Katy from Florida." I grinned. "Now known as 'no longer the new kid.'"

"Ah, I see." He glanced up to where Mr. Garrison was wheeling the projector to the middle of the classroom. "Small town, not many faces, everyone stares kind of thing?"

"You got it."

He laughed softly. "Good. I was beginning to think something was wrong with me." He pulled out a notebook, his arm brushing mine. A static charge shocked me. "Sorry about that."

"Totally okay," I told him.

Blake gave me one more quick grin before turning his gaze to the front of the classroom. Fiddling with the chain around my neck, I sneaked a quick peek at the new boy. Well, at least bio now had some eye candy. Couldn't go wrong with that.

• • •

Daemon wasn't waiting at the double doors to the library. Shouldering my bag, I entered the musty-smelling room. A young librarian glanced up and smiled as I looked around. The back of my neck was warm, but I didn't see him. Knowing Daemon, he was probably hiding so no one would see His Coolness in a library. I passed a few underclassmen at the tables and computers eating their lunches, and then roamed around until I found *him* back in the nosebleed section—Eastern European culture. A basic no-man's-land.

He was lounging in a cubicle beside an outdated computer, hands shoved into the pockets of his faded jeans. A wavy lock of hair covered his forehead, brushing against thick lashes. His lips curled into a half smile.

"I was wondering if you were ever going to find me." He made no move to clear up any space in the tiny 6x6 hole.

I dropped my bag outside the walls and hopped up on the desk opposite him. "Embarrassed someone would see you and think you're capable of reading?"

"I do have a reputation to maintain."

"And what a lovely reputation that is."

He stretched out his legs so that his feet were under mine. "So what did you want to talk about"—his voice lowered to a deep, sexy whisper—"in private?"

I shivered—and it had nothing to do with the temperature. "Not what you're hoping."

Daemon gave me a sexy smirk.

"Okay." I gripped the edge of the desk. "How did you know I was sick in the middle of the night?"

Daemon stared at me for a moment. "You don't remember?"

His eerie eyes were way too intense. I dropped my gaze...to his mouth. Wrong move. I stared at the map of Europe over his shoulder. Better. "No. Not really."

"Well, it was probably the fever. You were burning up."

My eyes snapped back to his. "You touched me?"

"Yes, I touched you...and you weren't wearing a lot of clothes." The smug stretch of his lips spread. "And you were soaked...in a white T-shirt. Nice look. Very nice."

Heat crept over my cheeks. "The lake...it wasn't a dream?"

Daemon shook his head.

"Oh my God, so I did go swimming in the lake?"

He pushed off the desk and took one step forward, which put him in the same breathing space as me...if he actually needed to breathe. "You did. Not something I expected to see on a Monday night, but I'm not complaining. I saw a lot."

"Shut up," I hissed.

"Don't be embarrassed." He reached out, tugging on the sleeve of my cardigan. I smacked his hand away. "It's not like I haven't seen the upper part before, and I didn't get a real good look down—"

I came off the desk swinging. My knuckles only brushed his face before he caught my hand. Wowzers, he was fast. Daemon pulled me up against his chest and lowered his head, eyes snapping with restrained anger. "Don't hit, Kitten. It's not nice."

"*You're* not nice." I tried pulling back, but he kept my wrist secured in his hand. "Let me go."

"I'm not sure I can do that. I must protect myself." But he dropped my hand.

"Oh, really, that's your reason for—for manhandling me?"

"Manhandling?" He pressed forward until my lower back was against the cubicle desk. "This isn't manhandling or whatever the hell that is."

Visions of me against the wall at my house and Daemon kissing me danced in my head like sugarplums. Parts of my body tingled. Oh, so not a good sign. "Daemon, someone is going to see us."

"So?" He gently picked up my hand. "Not like anyone is going to say a thing to me."

I drew in a deep breath. His scent was on my tongue. Our chests touched. Body said yes. Katy said no. I *wasn't* affected by this. Not by how close we were or how his fingers were sliding under the sleeve of my cardigan. It wasn't *real.* "So my trace has faded, but this stupid connection hasn't?"

"Nope."

Disappointed, I shook my head. "What does that mean, then?"

"I don't know." His fingers were completely under my sleeve, smoothing up my forearm. His skin—it hummed like electricity. There was nothing like it.

"Why do you keep touching me?" I asked, flustered.

"I like to."

God, I liked it, too, and I shouldn't. "Daemon…"

"But back to the trace. You know what that means."

"That I don't have to see your face outside of school?"

He laughed, and it rumbled through me. "You're no longer at risk."

Somehow, and I really haven't a clue how, my free hand was against his chest. His heart beat was fast and strong. So did mine. "I think the not-seeing-your-face part outweighs the safe part."

"Keep telling yourself that." His chin brushed my hair and then slid over my cheek. I shivered. A spark passed from his skin to mine, humming in the charged air around us. "If that makes you feel better, but we both know it's a lie."

"It's not a lie." I tipped my head back. His breath was a warm stroke against my lips.

"We're still going to be seeing each other," he murmured. "And don't even lie. I know that makes you happy. You told me you wanted me."

Hold your horses. "When?"

"At the lake." He slanted his head, and I should've pulled back. His lips curved knowingly against mine, and he let go of my wrist. "You said you wanted me."

Both of my hands were on his chest. They had a mind of their own. I claimed no responsibility for them. "I had a fever. Lost my mind."

"Whatever, Kitten." Daemon gripped my hips, lifting me onto the edge of the desk with an ease that was disturbing. "I know better."

My breath was coming in short gasps. "You don't know anything."

"Uh huh. You know, I was worried about you," he admitted, moving forward, easing my legs apart. "You kept calling out my name, and I kept answering, but it was like you couldn't hear me."

What were we talking about? My hands were on his lower stomach. His muscles were hard underneath the sweater. I slid my hands to his sides, totally meaning to push him away. Instead, I gripped and pulled him forward. "Wow, I must've been really out of it."

"It…scared me."

Before I could respond or even give thought to the fact that my sickness actually scared him, our lips met. My brain clicked off as my fingers dug through his sweater, and…and oh, God, his kisses were deep, scorching my lips as his hands tightened on my waist, pulling me against him.

Daemon kissed like he was a man starving for water, taking long, breathless drafts. His teeth caught my lower lip when he pulled away, only to come back for more. A heady mix of emotions warred inside me. I didn't want this, because it was just the connection between us. I kept telling myself that, even as I slid my hands up his chest and circled them around his neck. When his hands inched under my shirt, it was as though he reached deep inside me, warming every cell, filling every dark space within me with the heat from his skin.

Touching him, kissing him, was like having a fever all over again. I was on fire. My body burned. The world burned. Sparks flew. Against his mouth, I moaned.

There was a *POP!* and *CRACK!*

The smell of burned plastic filled the cubicle. We pulled apart, breathing heavily. Over his shoulder I saw thin strips of smoke wafting from the top of the ancient monitor. Good God, was this going to happen every time we kissed?

And what in the hell was I doing? I'd decided I wasn't going to let this happen with Daemon, which meant no kissing…or touching. The way he'd treated me when we first met still stung. The pain and embarrassment lingered in me.

I pushed him. *Hard.* Daemon let go, staring at me like I'd kicked his puppy into traffic. Looking away, I wiped the back of my hand over my mouth. It didn't work. Everything about him was still around me, *in* me. "God, I don't even *like* this—kissing you."

Daemon straightened, coming to his full height. "I beg to differ. And I think this computer tells a different story, too."

I shot him a dirty look. "That—that will never happen again."

"And I think you've said that before," he reminded me. When he saw my expression, he sighed. "Kat, you enjoyed that—just as much as I did. Why lie?"

"Because it's not real," I said. "You didn't want me before."

"I did—"

"Don't you dare say you wanted me, because you treated me like I was the Antichrist! You can't just undo that because there's a stupid connection between us." I sucked in a sharp breath as an icky feeling spread through my chest. "You really hurt me then. I don't think you even know. You humiliated me in front of an entire lunch room!"

Daemon looked away, dragging his fingers through his hair. A muscle popped out in his jaw. "I know. I'm…I'm sorry for how I treated you, Kat."

Shocked, I stared at him. Daemon never apologized. Like, ever. Maybe he really… I shook my head. His apology wasn't enough. "Even now, we're all the way hidden in the library, as if you don't want people to know you made a mistake that day and acted like a dick. And I'm supposed to be okay with that now?"

His eyes widened. "Kat—"

"I'm not saying we can't be friends, because I want to. I do like you a lo—" I cut myself off before I said too much. "Look, this didn't happen. I'm going to blame aftereffects of the flu or that a zombie ate my brain."

His brows furrowed. "What?"

"I don't want this with you." I started to turn, but he caught my arm. I glared at him. "Daemon…"

He looked at me straight on. "You're a terrible liar. You do want this. Just as badly as I do."

My mouth opened, but no words came out.

"You want this as badly as you want to go to ALA this winter."

Now my jaw was on the floor. "You don't even know what ALA is!"

"The American Library Association midwinter event," he said, grinning proudly. "Saw you obsessing over it on your blog before you got sick. I'm pretty sure you said you'd give up your firstborn child to go."

Yeah, I kind of did say that.

Daemon's eyes flashed. "Anyway, back to the whole you-wanting-me part."

I shook my head, dumbfounded.

"You do want me."

Taking a deep breath, I struggled with my temper…and my amusement. "You are way too confident."

"I'm confident enough to wager a bet."

"You can't be serious."

He grinned. "I bet that by New Year's Day, you will have admitted that you're madly, deeply, and irrevocably—"

"Wow. Want to throw another adverb out there?" My cheeks were burning.

"How about irresistibly?"

I rolled my eyes and muttered, "I'm surprised you know what an adverb is."

"Stop distracting me, Kitten. Back to my bet—by New Year's Day, you'll have admitted that you're madly, deeply, irrevocably, and *irresistibly* in love with me."

Stunned, I choked on my laugh.

"And you dream about me." He released my arm and folded his across his chest, cocking an eyebrow. "I bet you'll admit that. Probably even show me your notebook with my name circled in hearts—"

"Oh, for the love of God…"

Daemon winked. "It's on."

Spinning around, I grabbed my backpack and hurried through the stacks, leaving Daemon in the cubicle before I did something insane. Like throw common sense aside and run back to tackle him, pretending that everything he'd done and said all those months ago hadn't left a raw mark on my heart. Because I'd be pretending, right?

I didn't slow until I was standing in front of my locker on the other side of the school. I reached inside my backpack and pulled out my binder full of art crap. What a hell of a day back. I'd dazed out in half of my classes, made out with Daemon, *and* blew up another computer. Seriously. I should've stayed home.

I reached for the handle on my locker. Before my fingers could touch it, the locker swung open. Gasping, I jumped back, and my art binder fell to the floor.

Oh my God, what just happened?

It couldn't be… My heart rate went into cardiac arrest territory.

Daemon? He could manipulate objects. Opening a locker door with his mind would be a piece of cake for him, considering he could uproot trees. I looked around the thinning crowds, but I already knew he wasn't there. I hadn't felt him through our creepy alien bond. I backed away from the locker.

"Whoa, watch where you're going," a teasing voice intruded.

Sucking in a sharp gasp, I whipped around. Simon Cutters stood behind me, clenching a ragged backpack in his meaty fist.

"Sorry," I croaked, glancing back at the locker. Had he seen that happen? I knelt to pick up my artwork, but he beat me to it. Epic awkwardness ensued as we tried to pick up the papers without touching each other.

Simon handed me a stack of craptastic drawings of flowers. I had no artistic talent. "Here you go."

"Thanks." I stood, shoving my binder into the locker, ready to flee.

"Wait a sec." He grabbed my arm. "I wanted to talk to you."

My eyes dropped to his hand. He had five seconds before my pointy-toed shoe ended up between his legs.

He seemed to sense this, because he dropped his hand and flushed. "I just want to apologize for everything that happened homecoming night. I was drunk and I…I do stupid things when I'm drunk."

I glared at him. "Then maybe you should stop drinking."

"Yeah, maybe I should." He ran his hand over his closely cropped hair. Light reflected off the blue and gold watch around his thick wrist. Something was engraved on the band, but I couldn't make it out. "Anyway, I just didn't—"

"Yo, Simon, what are you doing?" Billy Crump, a beady-eyed football player who only seemed to notice my boobs when he looked in my direction, sidled up next to Simon. He was closely followed by a rabid pack of teammates. Billy grinned as his gaze zeroed in on me. "Hey…what do we have here?"

Simon opened his mouth, but one of the guys beat him to it. "Let me guess. She's trying to get on your jock again?"

Several guys chuckled and elbowed one another.

I blinked at Simon. "Excuse me?"

The tips of Simon's cheeks turned ruddy as Billy lurched forward, dropping his arm over my shoulder. The scent of his cologne nearly knocked me out. "Look, babe, Simon ain't interested in you."

One of the guys laughed. "Like my mama always said, why buy the cow when the milk's for free?"

A slow rush of fury inched through my veins. What the hell was Simon telling these douchebags? I shrugged out from underneath Billy's arm. "This milk isn't for free and wasn't even for sale."

"That's not what we hear." Billy fist-pumped a red-faced Simon. "Isn't that right, Cutters?"

All of Simon's friends' eyes were on him. He choked out a laugh and stepped back, swinging his backpack over his shoulder. "Yeah, man, but not interested in a second glass. I was trying to tell her that, but she wouldn't listen."

My mouth dropped. "You lying son of a—"

"What's going on down there?" Coach Vincent called from the end of the hallway. "Shouldn't you boys be in class by now?"

Laughing, the guys broke apart and headed down the hall. One of them spun around, motioning a "call me" hand signal while another made a rather obscene gesture with his mouth and hand.

I wanted to slam my fist into something. But Simon wasn't my biggest problem. I faced my locker again, wincing as my stomach dropped to my toes. It had opened by itself.

Chapter 4

Mom was gone, already having started her shift in Winchester earlier that day. I'd been hoping she'd be home so I could chat with her for a little while and forget about the whole locker incident, but I'd forgotten it was Wednesday—also known as Fend For Yourself Day.

A dull ache had taken up residency behind my eyes, like I strained something, but I wasn't sure if that were possible. It had started after the whole locker incident and didn't show signs of stopping.

I threw a load of clothes into the dryer before realizing there were no dryer sheets. Fail. Going to the linen closet, I rummaged around, hoping to find something. Giving up, I decided that the only thing that was going to make today better was the sweet tea I'd seen in the fridge that morning.

Glass shattered.

I jumped at the sound and then hurried to the kitchen, thinking someone had broken the window from outside, but it wasn't like we had a lot of visitors out here unless it was a Department Of Defense officer bum rushing the house. At that thought, my heart tripped up a little as my gaze went to the counter below an opened cupboard. One of the tall, frosted glasses was in three large pieces on the counter.

Drip. Drip. Drip.

Frowning, I looked around, unable to figure out the source of the noise. Broken glass and water dripping... Then it struck me. My pulse sped up as I opened up the fridge.

The jug of tea was on its side. Lid off. Brown liquid ran across the shelf, spilling down the sides. I glanced at the counter. I'd wanted tea, which requires a glass and, well, tea.

"No way," I whispered, backing up. There was no way the act of wanting tea had somehow caused this.

But what other explanation could there be? It wasn't like there was an alien hiding under the table, moving crap around for fun.

I checked just to be sure.

This was the second time in one day that something had moved on its own. Two coincidences?

Numb inside, I grabbed a towel and cleaned up the mess. The whole time I was thinking about the locker door. It had opened before I reached it. But it couldn't be me. Aliens had the power to do that kind of stuff. I didn't. Maybe there had been a minor earthquake or something—a minor earthquake that only targeted glasses and tea? Doubtful.

Weirded out to the max, I grabbed a book off the back of the couch and sprawled out. I needed a serious distraction.

Mom hated that there were books everywhere. They weren't really *everywhere*. Just wherever I was, like the couch, recliner, kitchen counters, laundry room, and even the bathroom. It wouldn't be like that if she caved and installed a wall-to-ceiling bookcase.

But no matter how I tried to get into the book I was reading, it wasn't working. Half of it was the book. It had insta-love, the bane of my existence. Girl sees boy and falls in love. Immediately. Soul mate, breath stealing, toes curling, love after one conversation. Boy pushes girl away for some paranormal reason or another. Girl still loves boy. Boy finally admits love.

Who was I kidding? I sort of loved all that angst. It wasn't the book. It was me. I couldn't clear my head and fully immerse myself in the characters. I grabbed a bookmark off the coffee table and shoved it in the book. Dog-eared pages were Antichrist of book lovers everywhere.

Ignoring what was happening wasn't working. It just wasn't in me to run from my troubles like this. Besides, if I was honest with myself, I knew I was more than a little freaked out by what was happening. What if I was imagining I was moving things? The fever could've killed off a few brain cells. I dragged in air so fast my head swam. Could a person get schizophrenia from being sick?

Now that just sounded stupid.

Sitting up, I pressed my head to my knees. I was fine. What was happening… There had to be a logical explanation for it. I hadn't closed the locker door all the way and Simon's lumbering steps had jarred it open. And the glass—left on the edge. And there was a good chance that Mom had left the cap on the tea loose. She was always doing stuff like that.

I took several more deep breaths. I was okay. Logical explanations made the world go around. The only fault in that line of thought was the fact I lived next door to *aliens*, and that was *so* not logical.

Pushing off the couch, I checked the window to see if Dee's car was out front. Pulling on my hoodie, I headed next door.

Dee immediately pulled me into the kitchen. There was a sweet, burned smell.

"I'm glad you came over. I was just about to come get you," she said, dropping my arm and rushing over to the counter. There were several pots scattered across the countertop.

"What are you doing?" I peered over her shoulder. One of the pots looked like it was filled with tar. "Ew."

Dee sighed. "I was trying to melt chocolate."

"With your microwave hands?"

"It's an epic fail." She poked at the gunk with a spatula. "I can't get the temp right."

"Then why don't you just use the stove?"

"Pfft, I loathe the stove." Dee pulled the spatula up. Half of it had melted. "Whoops."

"Nice." I shuffled over to the table.

With a wave of her hand, the pots flew to the sink. The tap turned on. "I'm getting better at this." She grabbed some dish soap. "What were you and Daemon doing at lunch?"

I hesitated. "I wanted to talk about the whole lake thing. I'd thought I…dreamed that."

Dee cringed. "No, that was real. He got me when he brought you back. I was the one to place you in dry clothes, by the way."

I laughed. "I was hoping that was you."

"Although he did volunteer for the job," she said, her eyes rolling. "Daemon is so helpful."

"That he is. Where…where is he?"

She shrugged. "No clue." Her eyes narrowed. "Why do you keep itching your arm?"

"Huh?" I stopped, not even realizing I was doing that. "Oh, they took my blood in the hospital to make sure I didn't have rabies or something."

Laughing, she tugged up my sleeve. "I have some stuff that you can put—holy crap, Katy."

"What?" I glanced down at my arm and sucked in a breath. "Yuck."

My entire inner elbow looked like a fleshy strawberry. All that was missing was a leafy green cap. The raised splotches of red skin were speckled with darker dots.

Dee ran a finger over it. "Does it hurt?" I shook my head. It just itched like crazy. She dropped my hand. "All you did was get your blood taken?"

"Yeah," I said, staring at my arm.

"That's really weird, Katy. It's like you had some kind of reaction to something. Let me get some aloe. That might help."

"Sure." I frowned at my arm. What could've done this?

Dee returned with a jar of the cool gunk. It helped with the itching, and after I tugged my sleeve back down, she seemed to forget about it. I hung out with her for the next couple of hours, watching her destroy one pot after another. I laughed so hard my stomach hurt when Dee leaned too close to a bowl she was heating and accidentally set her shirt on fire. She'd raised one brow at my larger chest as if to say she'd like to have seen me avoid the same mistake, sending me into another fit of giggles.

When she ran out of chocolate and plastic spatulas, Dee finally admitted defeat. It was after ten, and I said good-bye as I headed home to get some rest. It had been a long first day back at school, but I was glad I'd headed over and ended it hanging with Dee.

Daemon was crossing the road just as I shut the front door behind me.

In less than a second, he was on the top step. "Kitten."

"Hey." I avoided his extraordinary eyes and face, because, well, I was having a real hard time not recalling what his mouth had felt like on mine earlier. "Where, um, so what have you been doing?"

"Patrolling." He stepped onto the porch, and even though I was busy staring at the crack in the wood floor, I could feel his gaze on my face and the heat from his body. He stood close, too close. "Everything is all quiet on the western front."

I cracked a smile. "Nice reference."

When he spoke, his breath teased the loose hair around my temple. "It's my favorite book, actually."

My head jerked toward his, narrowly missing a collision. I hid my surprise. "I didn't know you knew how to read the classics."

A lazy smirk appeared, and I'd swear he managed to get closer. Our legs touched. His shoulder brushed my arm. "Well, I usually prefer books with pictures and small sentences, but sometimes I step out of the box."

Unable to help it, I laughed. "Let me guess, your favorite kind of picture book is the one you can color in?"

"I never stay in the lines." Daemon winked. Only he could pull that off.

"Of course not." I looked away, swallowing. Sometimes it was too easy to fall into the easy banter with him, too damn easy to imagine doing this with him every night. Teasing. Laughing. Getting in way over my head. "I've got…to go."

He swung around. "I'll walk you home."

"Um, I live *right there*." Not like he didn't know that. Duh.

That lazy smirk spread. "Hey, I'm being a gentleman." He offered his arm. "May I?"

Laughing under my breath, I shook my head. But I gave him my arm. The next thing I knew, he scooped me up into his arms. My heart leaped into my throat. "Daemon—"

"Did I tell you I carried you all the way back to the house the night you were sick? Thought that was a dream, eh? Nope. Real." He went down one step as I stared wide-eyed at him. "Twice in one week. We're making this a habit."

And then he shot off the porch, the roar of the wind drowning out my surprised squeal. The next second, he was standing in front of my door, grinning down at me. "I was faster the last time."

"Really," I said slowly, dumbfounded. My cheeks felt numb. "You…going to put me down?"

"Mmm." Our eyes met. There was a tender look in his that warmed and frightened me. "Been thinking about our bet? Wanna give in now?"

And he totally ruined that tender moment. "Put me down, Daemon."

He placed me on my feet, but his arms were still around me, and I had no idea what to say. "I've been thinking."

"Oh, God…" I murmured.

His lips twitched. "This bet really isn't fair to you. New Year's Day? Hell, I'll have you admitting your undying devotion to me by Thanksgiving."

I rolled my eyes. "I'm sure I'll hold out until Halloween."

"That's already passed."

"Exactly," I muttered.

Laughing under his breath, he reached forward, tucking a strand of hair behind my ear. The back of his knuckles brushed my cheek and I pressed my lips together to stop a sigh. Warmth blossomed in my chest, having nothing to do with the simple touch.

It had everything to do with the ache in his gaze. Then he pivoted around, tipping his head back. Moments passed in silence. "The stars… They're beautiful tonight."

I followed his gaze, a little thrown off by his sudden change in topic. The sky was dark, but there were a hundred or so bright dots glimmering against the inky night. "Yeah, they are." I bit my lip. "Do they remind you of your home?"

There was a pause. "I wish they did. Memories, even bittersweet ones, are better than nothing, you know?"

A knot formed in my throat. Why had I asked him that? I knew he didn't remember anything about his planet. I tucked my hair back again and stood beside him, squinting at the sky. "The Elders—do they remember anything about Lux?" He nodded. "Have you ever asked them to tell you about it?"

He started to respond, then laughed. "It is that simple, right? But I try to avoid the colony as much as possible."

Understandable, but I wasn't entirely sure why. Daemon and Dee rarely talked about the Luxen that remained in the colony hidden deep within the forest surrounding Seneca Rocks. "What about Mr. Garrison?"

"Matthew?" He shook his head. "He won't talk about it. I think it's too hard on him—the war and losing his family."

Tearing my gaze away from the stars, I looked up at Daemon. His profile was harsh and haunted. Christ, they'd had a tough life. All of the Luxen. War had turned them into refugees. Earth was practically a hostile planet to them, considering how they had to live. Daemon and Dee couldn't remember their parents and had lost their brother. Mr.

Garrison had lost everything and God only knew how many of them shared the same tragedy.

The knot was growing bigger in my throat. "I'm sorry."

Daemon's head swung toward me sharply. "Why would you apologize?"

"I…I'm just sorry for everything…you guys have had to go through." And I meant it.

He held my gaze for a beat and then looked away, laughing under his breath. There was no humor in the sound, and I wondered if I'd said something wrong. Probably. "Keep talking like that, Kitten, and I…"

"You what?"

Daemon backed off my porch, his smile secretive. "I've decided to go easy on you. I'll keep New Year's Day as the deadline."

I started to respond, but he was gone before I could, moving too fast for my eyes to track.

Placing my hand against my chest, I stood there and tried to make heads of what just happened. For a moment, a crazy moment, there had been something infinitely more than mad animal lust between us.

And it scared me.

I went inside and eventually was able to push Daemon to the back of my mind. Grabbing my cell, I went from room to room until I got a signal and called Mom, leaving her a message. When she called back, I told her about my arm. She said I probably bumped it on something, even though it didn't hurt and it wasn't bruised, either. She promised to bring me home a salve, and I felt better just hearing her voice.

I sat on my bed, trying to forget about all the weird stuff and focus on my history homework. There was an exam on Monday. Studying on a Friday was the height of lameness, but it was either that or I fail. And I refused to fail. History was one of my favorite subjects.

Hours later, I felt the weird warmth that was becoming increasingly familiar creep across my neck. Closing the textbook, I hopped off the bed and crept toward the window. The full moon lit everything in a pale, silvery glow.

I tugged up the sleeve of my shirt. The skin was still patchy and red. Did being sick have anything to do with the locker, the glass of tea and the connection to Daemon?

My gaze moved back to the window, drifting over the ground below. I didn't see anyone. A yearning sparked in my chest. I pulled the curtain back farther and pressed my forehead against the cool glass. I couldn't understand or explain how I knew, but I did. Somewhere, hidden in the shadows, was Daemon.

And every part of my being wanted—*needed*—to go to him. The ache that had been in his eyes... It was so much, going beyond him and me. More than what I undoubtedly could wrap my head around.

Denying that desire was one of the hardest things I'd ever done, but I let the curtain slip free and went back to my bed. As I opened my history text again, I focused on my chapter.

New Year's Day? Wasn't going to happen.

• • •

I was having one of those days where I wanted to start throwing things because only breaking crap would make me feel better. My limit for acceptable weirdness in my daily life had been maxed out.

On Saturday, the shower turned on before I even got in it. Sunday night, my bedroom door opened as I walked toward it, smacking me right in the face. And this morning, to top it all off, I'd overslept and missed my first two classes, plus my entire closet emptied itself onto my floor as I debated what to wear.

Either I was turning into an alien, about to have one crawl its way out of my stomach, or I was crazy.

The only good thing about today was that I'd woken up without that itchy rash on my arm.

The whole way to school, I debated what to do. These things couldn't be brushed aside as a coincidence any longer, and I needed to get over myself and confront them. My new outlook on not being a bystander in life meant I had to face the fact that I'd *really* changed. And I needed to do something about it before I exposed everyone. Just thinking about that possibility left a bitter taste in my mouth. There was no way I could go to Dee, because I'd promised Daemon not to tell anyone that he'd healed me. I had no other option but to saddle him with another one of my problems.

At least that was how it felt. When I first moved here, I'd been nothing but problems for him. Making friends with his sister, asking way too many questions, almost getting myself killed…twice. Plus discovering their big secret, and all the times I'd ended up with a trace.

I frowned as I slid out of my car and slammed the door behind me. No wonder Daemon had been such a douche canoe those months. I *was* trouble. So was he, but still.

Late for bio and out of breath, I raced down the nearly empty hall, praying that I'd be safely in my seat before Mr. Garrison strolled in. As I reached for the heavy door, it swung open with a powerful rush and slammed against the wall. The noise echoed down the corridor, drawing the attention of a handful of other late students.

Blood drained from my face, inch by inch, as I heard the startled gasp from behind me and knew I was busted. A million thoughts ran through my numb brain and none of them was worth a damn. Closing my eyes, fear settled like sour milk in my stomach. What was wrong me? Something was—something was really bad.

"These damn drafty hallways," Mr. Garrison said, clearing his throat. "They'll give you a heart attack."

My eyes snapped open. He straightened his tie while he clenched his brown suitcase tightly in his right hand.

I opened my mouth to speak and agree. Agreeing would be a good thing. Yes, damn drafty hallways.

But nothing came. I just stood there like a damn fish. Gaping and gaping.

Mr. Garrison's blue eyes narrowed, and his scowl deepened until I thought it would leave a permanent mark on his face. "Miss Swartz, shouldn't you be in class?"

"Yes, sorry," I managed to croak.

"Then please, don't just stand there." He spread his arms and ushered me inside. "And that is a tardy. Your second."

Unsure of how I earned my first tardy, I shuffled into class, trying to ignore the giggles from the other students who'd apparently heard my ass getting chewed out. My cheeks flooded with color.

"Skank," Kimmy said from behind her hand.

Several more giggles erupted from her side of the class, but before I could say anything, Lesa shot the blonde a look. "That's real funny coming from you," she said. "You *are* the same cheerleader who *forgot* to wear her undies during the pep rally last year, aren't you?"

Kimmy's face turned blood red.

"Class," Mr. Garrison said, eyes narrowing. "That's enough."

Passing Lesa a grateful smile, I took my seat next to Blake and yanked out my textbook while Mr. Garrison began reading off the attendance, making small swipes with his favorite red pen.

He skipped my name. I was sure it was on purpose.

Blake nudged me with his elbow. "Are you doing okay over there?"

I nodded. There was no way I was going to let him think that Kimmy was the reason my face had gone albino white. And besides, Kimmy calling me a skank probably had something to do with Simon, which wasn't even worth my anger right now. "Yeah, I'm perfect."

He smiled, but it looked forced.

Mr. Garrison flipped off the lights and launched into a stimulating lecture on tree sap. Forgetting about the boy beside me, I started replaying the door incident over and over again in my head. Had Mr. Garrison really believed it had been a draft? And if he didn't, what was stopping him from contacting the DOD and handing me over?

Unease squirmed in my belly. Was I going to end up like Bethany?

Chapter 5

Carissa was waiting for me by my locker after biology. "Can I just go home?" I asked as I switched my textbooks.

She laughed. "Having a bad day?"

"You could say that." I thought about elaborating for a second, but what could I tell her? "I was running late this morning. You know how that just screws your day up from there."

We headed down the hall, chatting about the party on Friday and what we were going to wear. I really hadn't put much thought into it, figuring I'd just wear jeans and a shirt.

"Everyone is dressing up," she explained, "since we don't get a lot of reasons to actually wear something nice around here."

"We just had homecoming." I groaned, knowing I didn't have anything dressy.

Carissa launched into the routine conversation about what colleges I was going to apply to. She was hoping I would send an application into WVU. Most of the students were applying there.

"Katy, you really need to start applying," she insisted as she grabbed a plate of what appeared to be Salisbury steak. "You're going to run out of time."

"You know, I hear it from my mom every day. I will when I decide where I want to go." Problem was I had no idea where I wanted to go or what I wanted to do.

"You don't have forever," she said, quick to remind me.

Dee was already at our table, and I launched into my own tirade the moment I sat down. "So I can't wear jeans to the party? I have to wear a dress?"

"Huh?" Dee blinked and looked at me.

"Carissa told me I had to wear a dress on Friday night. I didn't really plan for that."

Dee picked up her fork and pushed the food around on her plate. "You should wear a dress. We get to be pretty princesses for the night and dress up for the party."

"We're not six."

Lesa snorted and repeated, *"Pretty princesses?"*

"Yes, pretty princesses. You can borrow one of my dresses. I have enough." Dee poked at her green beans.

Something was not right with her. She wasn't eating and was now suggesting I could wear one of *her* dresses. "Dee, I don't think I'd fit in one of your dresses."

She turned her angelic face to mine, lips turned down at the corners. "I have plenty of dresses you can wear. Don't be silly."

I stared at her, dumbfounded. "If I wore one of your dresses, I'd look like a tightly packaged sausage."

Dee's gaze darted over my shoulders, and whatever she was going to say died on her lips. Her eyes widened and face paled. I was afraid to turn around, half expecting to find a set of DOD officers strolling through our school cafeteria in black suits.

The picture in my brain was equally hilarious and frightening.

I slowly twisted in my seat, preparing myself to be thrown on the floor and handcuffed, or whatever it was they did. It took me a moment to find what Dee was utterly transfixed by, and when I did, I was confused.

It was Adam Thompson—the nice twin as I liked to refer to him and he was Dee's… friend? Boyfriend?

"What's going on?" I asked, swiveling around.

Her gaze darted to me. "Can we talk later?"

In other words, it wasn't something she could say in front of the others. I nodded and glanced behind me. Adam was getting food, but I noticed someone else.

Blake stood by the doors to the cafeteria, scanning the crowds for someone. His gaze found our table and his hazel eyes settled on me. He smiled, flashing a set of ultra-white teeth, and waved.

I gave him a little wave back.

"Who's that?" Dee asked, frowning.

"His name is Blake Saunders," Lesa said, eyeing her lunch. She poked it with her fork as if she expected it to jump off her plate and run away. "He's a new kid in our biology class. I found out he's living with his aunt."

"Did you go through his personal files or something?" I asked, amused.

Lesa snorted. "I overheard him talking to Whitney Samuels. She was giving him the third degree."

"I think he's coming over here." Dee turned to me, her expression unreadable. "He's cute, Katy."

I shrugged. He was very cute. Blake reminded me of a surfer, and that was hot. And he was human. Bonus points there. "He's nice, too."

"Nice is good," Carissa said.

Nice was great, but…I glanced at the table in the back. Daemon wasn't sitting with us today. He seemed to be in a heated discussion with Andrew. There was also no Ash. Strange. My eyes bounced back to Daemon.

He looked up at that exact moment. The smirk on his face faded. A muscle in his jaw popped. He looked…*pissed*. Whoa. What'd I do now?

Dee kicked me under the table, and I twisted back around.

Standing beside me was Blake. A nervous smile was on his face as his eyes flickered over the table. "Hey."

"Hi," I said. "Want to sit?"

Nodding, he took the empty seat beside me. "Everyone is still staring at me."

"Ah, it should fade in a month or so," I told him.

"Hi," Lesa chirped. "I'm Lesa with an *e*, and this is Carissa and Dee. We're Katy's cool friends."

Blake laughed. "Nice to meet you. You're in bio, right?"

Lesa nodded.

"So where are you from?" asked Dee, her voice surprisingly tight. Last time I'd heard that tone was when Ash had shown up at the diner with Daemon before school started.

"Santa Monica." After another round of *aah*s, he grinned. "My uncle was getting tired of the city, so he wanted to get as far away from it as possible."

"Well, this is as far as you can get." Lesa grimaced after taking a bite of her food. "I bet lunch was better in Santa Monica."

"Nah, it's also questionable there."

"So how are you adjusting to your classes?" Carissa folded her hands on the table, as if she were going to do an interview for the school newspaper. All she needed was a pen and paper.

"Okay. It's a much smaller school than my old one, so I've been able to find my way around easily. The people are nicer here, except for the whole staring thing. How about you?" He turned to me. "Since you're still technically new?"

"Oh no, I hand over new-kid status completely to you. But it's pretty cool around here."

"Not much happens, though," Lesa added.

The conversation moved easily. Blake was super friendly. He answered every one of our questions and was quick to laugh. Turned out he had gym with Lesa and art with Carissa.

Every so often, he'd glance at me and smile, revealing a set of straight white teeth. It had nothing on Daemon's smile—whenever he decided to grace our world with its presence—but it was nice. And it was also drawing the attention of the other girls. Their eyes kept darting back and forth between us. My cheeks were growing hotter by the second.

"We're having a party Friday night." Lesa flashed me a quick grin. "You're more than welcome to come. Dee's parents are letting us have it at their house while they're away this weekend."

Dee stiffened with the fork halfway to her mouth. She didn't say anything, but I could tell she wasn't happy with the invite. What was her deal? Half the school appeared to be invited.

"That sounds cool." Blake glanced at me. "You're going?"

I nodded, twisting the lid on my water.

"She doesn't have a date," Lesa added with a sly look.

My mouth gaped. Real smooth move there.

"No boyfriend?" Blake sounded surprised.

"Nope." Lesa's eyes sparkled. "You have a girlfriend you left back in California?"

Dee cleared her throat as she found the food on her plate to be of extreme interest.

Mortified, I wanted to hide under the table.

Blake chuckled. "No. No girlfriend." He turned his attention back to me. "But I'm surprised you don't have a boyfriend."

"Why?" I asked, wondering if I should be flattered. Like my awesomeness was just so extreme that I couldn't be single?

"Well," Blake said, leaning in toward me. When he spoke, it was right in my ear. "That guy over there. He's been staring at you since I sat down. And he doesn't look happy."

Dee was the first to look. Her lips formed a tight smile. "That's my brother."

Blake nodded as he leaned back. "Did you guys date or something?"

"No," I said. Every muscle in my body demanded that I take a look-see. "He's just…Daemon."

"Huh," Blake said, stretching. He nudged my arm. "So no competition there?"

My eyes widened. Boy, he was bold. His hotness level went up ten points. "Not likely."

A slow smile crept over Blake's lips. He had a fuller bottom one. Looked totally kissable. "Good to know, because I was wondering if you wanted to grab something to eat after school?"

Whoa. I glanced at Dee, who looked just as surprised as I did. I had every intention of finding out why she was acting so weird over Adam and then talking to Daemon about the weird stuff that had been happening.

Dee misinterpreted my hesitation. "We can get together tomorrow after school."

"But—"

"It's okay." Her look seemed to say, *Go out, have fun. Be normal.* Or maybe that was my wishful thinking, because she didn't seem very pleased with Blake's interest in me. "It's fine," Dee adds.

I could wait one more day to talk to Daemon. I glanced over at Blake and our eyes locked. I found myself nodding.

Blake's smile remained on his face the rest of the lunch. Toward the end, I caved and had to look because I could still feel him. Blake had been right. Daemon *was* staring. Not at me, but at the boy next to me. There wasn't anything friendly in the hard line of his jaw or his sharp jewel-toned eyes.

Daemon's gaze slid to mine. There was a flutter deep in my chest. I tried to draw in a breath, but I felt pierced. My lips tingled.

There was definitely no competition there.

• • •

Blake and I decided to go to the Smoke Hole after school. We took separate cars, and the wind was howling when we got there, tearing at the bare branches of the trees surrounding the parking lot as we rushed inside.

His cheeks were flushed under his tan as we grabbed a seat near the crackling fireplace. "I don't think I'm ever going to get used to the wind here. It's brutal."

"Me, too," I said, rubbing my chilled hands over my arms. "And I've been told to expect a lot of snow come winter."

Interest lit up his eyes, making the specks of green stand out. Nowhere near as bright as Daemon's, though. "Perfect snowboarding weather, then. Do you snowboard?"

I laughed. "I'd kill myself in two seconds. I went skiing once with my mom and it wasn't pretty."

Blake grinned and then shifted his attention to the waitress taking our orders. Surprisingly, I wasn't nervous. There wasn't a tipsy feeling in my stomach when our gazes met. My skin didn't feel stretched too thin. And I wasn't sure what that meant. It seemed so...*normal.*

He told me about surfing while we waited for my slice of cheese pizza and his cup of chili. I told him the closest I'd come to surfing was watching the guys down in Florida. I didn't have that kind of coordination, and he tried to convince me it wasn't that hard.

I laughed. A lot. We took our time eating. With him, I wasn't thinking about aliens from outer space or the looming threat of the DOD or Arum. It was the most relaxing hour I'd spent in a long time.

Toward the end, he was ripping a napkin into tiny pieces while he grinned at me. "So, you have a blog?"

Surprised, I nodded and figured I'd get my geekdom out of the way. "Yeah, I love books. I review them on the blog." I paused. "How did you know?"

Blake leaned forward and whispered, "I looked you up. I know, kind of a nerdy thing to do, but I found your blog. I like how you write your reviews. Very witty. And you're passionate about it."

Flattered and completely won over by the fact he actually read my reviews, I smiled. "Thank you. The blog is really important to me. Most people don't get it."

"Oh, I totally do. I used to blog about surfing."

"Really?"

He nodded. "Yep, I miss the surfing and blogging—the whole connecting with people all around the world that shared the same passion. It's a pretty awesome community."

This guy was perfect. He didn't make fun of me like Daemon had over the whole blog thing. Cool points for Blake. I took a sip of my drink as I glanced out the window. Dark, thick clouds blanketed the sky. "When I first saw you, I had you pegged for a surfer. You have that look."

"What kind of look is that?"

"You just have the surfer-boy look going on. The hair, the tan—it's very cute."

"Cute?" He arched a brow.

"Okay, it's pretty hot."

He grinned. "I like the sound of that."

He had one of those personalities, much like Dee, where I couldn't help but feel comfortable around him. A welcome change from the pins-and-needles feeling I got around Daemon.

When we left the diner close to five, I couldn't believe how much time had passed. The wind whipped at my hair, but I was still buzzing too much from my afternoon with Blake to care about the fact I hadn't bought a jacket yet.

Blake nudged me with his elbow. "I'm glad you came with me."

"So am I." I twirled my keys as we stopped by his truck.

"I don't normally put myself out there." He leaned against the hood of his truck, crossing his ankles. "You know, just asking like that in front of an entire table of strangers."

Brisk wind cooled my warm cheeks. "You seemed pretty confident."

"I am when I want something."

Pushing off the hood, he moved to stand in front of me. Oh God.

Was he going to kiss me? I totally loved the easy afternoon we'd just spent, but, well…I just didn't feel right leading him on. I didn't know what was going on with Daemon, if anything really *was* going on, but I knew it wasn't fair to pretend I was completely free. I had feelings for Daemon; I just wasn't sure what they meant.

Blake leaned toward me, and I froze.

Above him, the branches shook and groaned under the force of the wind.

There was a loud *crack*, and my head jerked up. One of the thick branches broke under the weight of the wind. Panic leaped into my throat as it spiraled down to where Blake stood. There was no way he could move fast enough, and the size of the branch promised major damage.

Static rushed over my skin, crackling between the layers of my clothing. I felt the tiny hairs on the back of my neck raise. Heart racing, I shot forward and I thought I screamed *Stop*, but it was only in my head.

And the branch stopped…in midair, suspended by nothing.

Chapter 6

The branch hung there, hovering as if it were tethered by an invisible string. My breath pawed at my chest, not quite making it out. I stopped the branch—*I* did that. Panic and power rushed through me, leaving me dizzy.

Blake was staring at me, his eyes wide with what? Fear? Excitement? He stepped to the side and lifted his gaze. The rush of power left me at once. The heavy branch crashed, cracking the pavement like it would've done to Blake's skull. My shoulders slumped as I dragged in air. Sharp, slicing pain erupted behind my eyes and I winced.

"Wow…" Blake ran a hand through his spiky hair. "That would've killed me."

I swallowed, unable to speak. Shock rippled through me, lapping at my sides. I felt and recognized the warmth tingling across the nape of my neck, but I couldn't move. This little "event" had sapped me of energy, and my head…it throbbed something fierce—a kind of scary pain that signaled something was very wrong.

Oh, God, was this it? Was I having an aneurysm?

"Katy…it's okay," Blake said, stepping forward as his eyes darted behind me.

A warm, strong hand curled around my arm. "Kat."

I sagged at the sound of Daemon's voice. Turning to him, I lowered my head, shielding my face with my hair. "Sorry," I whispered.

"Is she okay?" Blake asked, sounding worried. "The branch—"

"Yes. She's fine. The falling branch scared her." Each word sounded like he spoke it through gritted teeth. "That's all."

"But—"

"See you later." Daemon started walking, taking me along with him. "Are you okay?"

I nodded, staring straight ahead. Everything seemed too bright for a cloudy day. Too real. The whole afternoon had been perfect. Normal. And I'd ruined it. When I didn't answer, Daemon took my keys from my numb fingers and opened the passenger door.

Blake called out my name, but I couldn't bring myself to look at him. I had no idea what he must be thinking, but I knew it couldn't be good.

"Get in," Daemon said almost gently.

For once, I obeyed without question. When he climbed in on the driver's side and moved the seat back, I snapped out of it. "How…how are you here?"

He didn't look at me as he turned the ignition and pulled out of the parking space. "I was driving around. I'll have Dee and Adam get my car."

Turning in my seat, I saw Blake by his car. He was still standing there like we'd left him. Knots twisted my insides. I felt sick. Trapped by what I'd done.

"Daemon…"

His jaw worked. "You'll pretend like nothing happened. If he brings it up, you'll tell him that he moved out of the way. If he even suggests that you…that you stopped that branch, you laugh it off."

Understanding seeped in. "I need to act like you did in the

beginning?"

He nodded curtly. "What just happened back there never happened. Do you understand me?"

Close to tears, I nodded.

Silence ticked away the minutes. Halfway home, the headache eased up and I felt almost normal, except it was like I had pulled an all-nighter. Neither of us spoke until he pulled into the driveway of my house.

Daemon yanked the keys from the ignition and sat back. He faced me, eyes sheltered by a long wave of hair. "We need to talk. And you need to be honest with me. You don't seem surprised you just did that."

I nodded again. He was furious, and I couldn't blame him. I'd possibly exposed them all to a human—a human who could go to the press, who could talk at school, and who could catch the attention of the DOD. They'd find out that the Luxen had special abilities. They'd learn about me.

We went inside my empty house. The central air was blowing heat from the vents, but I was shivering uncontrollably as I sat on the recliner. "I was planning on telling you."

"You were?" Daemon stood in front of me, hands clenching and unclenching at his sides. "When, exactly? Before or after you did something that puts you at risk?"

I flinched. "I didn't plan on this happening! All I wanted was to have a normal afternoon with a boy—"

"With a boy?" he spat, eyes flaring an intense green.

"Yes, with a normal boy!" Why did that sound so surprising? I took a deep breath. "I'm sorry. I did plan on coming to you tonight, but Blake asked me to grab something to eat with him and I just wanted one freaking afternoon with someone like me."

His frown went so deep I thought his face would crack. "You have friends who are normal, Kat."

"It's not the same thing!"

Daemon seemed to get what I wasn't really saying. For a second, his eyes widened and I'd swear there was a flicker of pain in them, but then it was gone. "Tell me what's been happening."

Guilt shot through me, pulling behind it spiky barbs that dug in deep. "I think I did get alien cooties, because I've been moving things… without touching them. Today, I opened the door to Mr. Garrison's classroom without touching it. He seemed to think it was a drafty hallway."

"How often has this been happening?"

"On and off for around a week. The first time it was my locker door, but I thought it was a fluke, so I didn't say anything. Then I thought about wanting a glass of tea, and the glass flew out of the cabinet and the tea started pouring itself in the fridge. The shower turned itself on, doors opened, and a couple of times, clothes flew from my closet." I sighed. "My room was a mess."

A snicker escaped. "Nice."

My hands balled into fists. "How can you think this is funny? Look at what happened today! I didn't mean to stop the branch! I mean, I didn't want it to hit him, but I didn't consciously stop the damn thing. The whole healing-me thing—it *changed* me, Daemon. If you haven't guessed it yet, I couldn't move things before. And I don't know what's wrong with me. I get a splitting headache and feel exhausted afterward. What if I'm dying or something?"

Daemon blinked and was suddenly beside me, sitting on the arm of the chair. Our legs touched. His breath stirred my hair. I shrank back as my heart rate picked up. "Why do you have to move so fast? It's… wrong."

He sighed. "Sorry, Kitten. For us, moving fast is natural. It's actually more effort to slow down and appear 'normal,' as you put it. I guess I just forget I have to pretend around you."

My heart ached. Why did everything I say lately come out as a criticism?

"You're not dying," he said.

"How do you know?"

His eyes latched onto mine. "Because I'd never let that happen."

He said it so strongly that I believed him. "What if I'm turning into an alien?"

A look crossed his face, like he wanted to laugh, and I could get why. It did sound absurd. "I don't know if that's possible."

"Moving stuff with my mind shouldn't be possible."

He sighed. "Why didn't you tell me when this first happened?"

"I don't know," I said, unable to look away. "I should've. I don't want to put you guys at risk. I swear I'm not doing it on purpose."

Daemon leaned back. His pupils turned luminous. "I know you aren't doing anything on purpose. I wouldn't have thought that."

My breath caught as he held my gaze with his strange eyes. The prickly feeling was back, spreading over my skin. Every inch of me became painfully aware of him.

He was silent for a moment. "I don't know if it was a product of my healing you those times or when you connected with us during Baruck's attack. Either way, it's obvious that you're using some of my abilities. I've never heard of this happening before."

"Never?" I whispered.

"We don't heal humans." Daemon paused, pursing his lips. "I've always thought it had something to do with exposing our abilities, but now I'm wondering if it's more than that. If the real reason is because we…change humans."

I swallowed. "So I *am* turning into an alien?"

"Kitten…"

All I could think about was the movie *Alien* and that thing crawling out of the dude's stomach, except mine would be a glowing ball of light or something. "How do we stop this?"

Daemon stood. "I want to try something, okay?"

My brows rose. "Okay."

Closing his eyes, he let out a long breath. His form flickered and faded. A few seconds later, he was in his true form, radiating a powerful red-white light. He was shaped like a human, and I knew he would be warm to touch. It was still strange seeing him like this. It drove home the point—the one I forgot sometimes—that he wasn't from this planet.

Say something to me, his voice whispered in my thoughts.

In their true form, Luxen don't speak out loud. "Uh, hi?"

His chuckle tickled inside me. *Not aloud. Say something to me, but not out loud. Like what happened in the clearing. You spoke to me then.*

When he'd been healing me, I'd heard his thoughts. Would it happen again? *Your light is really pretty, but it's blinding me.*

I heard his ghost inhale. *We can still hear each other.* His light dimmed, and he was standing in front of me again, solid, eyes troubled. "So my light was blinding you, huh?"

"Yeah, it was." I fiddled with the chain around my neck. "Am I glowing now?" It usually happened when they went into their true form, leaving a faint trace behind.

"No."

So that had changed, too. "Why can I still hear you? You act like I shouldn't."

"You shouldn't, but we're still connected."

"Well, how do we get unconnected?"

"That's a good question." He stretched idly as his gaze roamed across the room. "You have books everywhere, Kitten."

"That's really not important right now."

One hand outstretched. A book flew off the arm of the couch and into his hand. As he turned it over, his brows rose and his gaze moved over it quickly. "His touch kills? Really, what is this stuff you're reading?"

I shot from the chair, snatching the book away and holding it close to my chest. "Shut up. I love this book."

"Uh huh," Daemon murmured.

"Okay, back to the important stuff. And stop touching my books." I set it back where I'd left it. "What are we going to do?"

His gaze settled on me. "I'll figure out what is happening with you. Just give me some time."

I nodded, hoping we had enough time. There was no telling what I'd accidentally do next, and the last thing I wanted was to expose Dee and the others. "You do realize this whole thing is why you…"

He arched a brow.

"It's why you suddenly like me."

"I'm pretty sure I liked you before this, Kitten."

"Well, you had one hell of a way of showing it."

"True," he admitted. "And I've already said I'm sorry for the way I treated you." He took a fortifying breath. "I always liked you. From the moment you first flipped me off."

"But you didn't start to want to spend time with me until after the first attack, when you healed me. Maybe we were already starting to, like…morph together or whatever."

Daemon frowned. "What is it with you? It's like you need to convince yourself I can't possibly like you. Does doing that make it easier to tell yourself you don't have feelings for me?"

"You treated me like a red-headed stepchild for months. I'm sorry if I have a hard time believing that whatever you feel is real." I sat on the couch. "And it has nothing to do with what I feel."

His shoulders tensed. "Do you like that guy you were with?"

"Blake? I don't know. He's nice."

"He was sitting with you today at lunch."

My brow arched. "Because there was an open seat and it's a free world where people can pick where they want to sit."

"There were other seats open. He could've sat anywhere else in the cafeteria."

It took me a few seconds to respond. "He's in my bio class. Maybe he just felt comfortable with me, because we're both sort of new."

Something flickered across his face, and then he was standing in front of me. "He kept staring at you. And obviously he wanted to spend time with you outside of school."

"Maybe he likes me," I said, shrugging. "Lesa invited him to the party on Friday."

Daemon's eyes darkened to an evergreen. "I don't think you should be hanging around him until we know what's up with you moving stuff. You doing that thing with the branch was only one instance. We can't have a repeat of that."

"What? I'm not supposed to date or hang out with anyone now?"

Daemon smiled. "Anyone human, yes."

"Whatever." I shook my head, standing. "This is a stupid conversation. I'm not dating anyone anyway, but if I were, I wouldn't stop just because you said so."

"You wouldn't?" His hand shot out, tucking back a strand of hair behind my ear. "We'll just have to see about that."

I stepped sideways, keeping distance between us. "There's nothing to see."

Challenge filled his eyes. "If you say so, Kitten."

Folding my arms, I sighed. "This isn't a game."

"I know, but if it were, I'd win." He flickered out and appeared by the entrance to the foyer. "By the way, I've heard what Simon has been saying."

Heat swept over my face. Another problem, but less important in the grand scheme of things. "Yeah, he's being a douche. I think it's his friends. He actually apologized to me, and then when his friends showed up, he told them I was trying to get with him."

Daemon's eyes narrowed. "That's not okay."

I sighed. "It's no big deal."

"Maybe not to you, but it is to me." He paused, his shoulders squaring. "I'll take care of it."

Chapter 7

I didn't get much sleep that night, so trig the next day sucked worse than normal. There was a six-foot-three alien behind me. Not talking to me, just breathing softly against the back of my neck. And no matter how far I scooted up, I could still *feel* him. I was hyperaware of him— when he moved, when he wrote something down, when he scratched his head.

Halfway through class, I debated making a run for the door.

It was also day two of no pen pokes.

On the other hand, Simon kept glancing over his shoulder throughout class. Needing a distraction, I glared at his head. A slow flush crept over the back of his neck. He could feel me drilling holes into his head. Ha. Jerk-face.

Brown hair curled against the faintly flushed skin. He normally kept it cut close to the skull. I supposed he was in need of a haircut, since most boys around here didn't let their hair grow more than an inch or two. The dull gray shirt he wore stretched over his broad shoulders as he tensed under my stare. He glanced over his shoulder at me.

I arched a brow.

Simon turned back stiffly, and his shoulders rose as he took a deep breath. Annoyance flared and my fingers burned. The tool had half the school thinking I was easy. My attention fell back to the book in front of him.

The heavy English text flipped off the desk, smacking Simon right in the face.

My mouth dropped open as I sat back. *Holy crap…*

Jumping up, he stared at the book now lying on the floor as if it were some kind of creature he'd never seen before. Our teacher's eyes narrowed as he searched for the source of the disruption.

"Mr. Cutters, is there something you would like to share with the class?" he asked in a tired, bored voice.

"W-what?" Simon stuttered. He looked around frantically, and then his eyes settled on the book. "No, I knocked my book off the desk. Sorry."

He let out a loud sigh. "Well, then pick it up."

There were a few scattered chuckles from the other students. Simon was beet red as he swiped the book off the floor. He placed it in the middle of his desk and continued staring at it.

After the class settled down and the teacher turned back to the chalkboard, Daemon poked me with his pen. I twisted around.

"What was that?" he whispered, eyes narrowed. There was no mistaking the amusement in the tilt to his lips, though. "Very bad kitty…"

• • •

Blake arrived to bio minutes before the bell. He was wearing a vintage Super Mario Bros. shirt today. "You look…"

"Like crap?" I supplied, resting my cheek on my fist. I had no idea how to prepare myself for seeing him after the branch issue. Playing it cool wasn't something I was particularly skilled at.

"I was going to say tired." His eyes narrowed as he watched me. "Are you okay?"

I nodded. "Look, about yesterday? I'm sorry I freaked out. The branch—"

"Scared you?" he said, eyes locked onto mine. "It's no big deal. It shocked me, too. It all happened quickly, but I'd swear that branch stopped." He tilted his head to the side. "Like it was suspended for a few seconds."

"I…" What was I supposed to say? *Deny. Deny. Deny.* "I don't know. Maybe the wind caught it or something."

"Yeah, maybe. Anyway, the big party is coming up."

I smiled faintly, relieved at the change in topic. Would it be that easy? Damn. I was a better liar than Daemon gave me credit for. "You coming?"

"I wouldn't miss it for the world."

"Good." I toyed with my pen, remembering what Daemon had said about not hanging out with Blake. Screw that. "I'm glad you're coming."

Blake's smile was infectious. We chatted for a little while about the party, waiting for class to begin. A couple of times, his hand brushed mine. I doubted it was on accident. And I liked that. There wasn't anything forcing him to do it, except that maybe he *wanted* to touch me. He seemed to like me all on his own, and that made him a thousand times more attractive. And, well, that boyish smile of his helped. I could see him shirtless, surfing the waves. He was totally dateable.

Taking a deep breath, I did something I rarely ever did. "You can stop by my place first, before the party, if you want?"

His lashes lowered, fanning his golden cheeks. "That sounds cool. Like a date?"

I flushed. "Yeah, kind of. I guess you can say that."

Blake leaned in, his breath surprisingly cool on my cheeks. Minty. "I'm not sure I like the 'kind of' thing. I like the idea of calling it a date."

My gaze flicked up, meeting his. The little specks of green in his eyes were nowhere near as vibrant as Daemon's—why was I even thinking about him? "We can call it a date."

He sat back. "Sounds better."

I smiled, glancing down at my notebook. A date—not dinner-and-the-movies kind of date—but a date nonetheless. We exchanged numbers. I gave him directions. Excitement bubbled through me. I snuck a look at him. He was watching me with a crooked smile on his face.

Oh, the party just got a whole lot more interesting.

I refused to think about what Daemon would do when he saw me arrive with Blake. A small part of me wondered if I'd asked Blake just to find out.

• • •

Curled up on my couch after school on Thursday, Dee toyed with a ring on her finger and kept her voice low due to Mom sleeping upstairs. "The new boy seems to really have the hots for you."

I plopped down beside her. "You think so?"

Dee smiled, but it was off. "Yeah, I think so. I'm surprised you're actually okay with him coming to the party. I really thought…"

"You thought what?"

Her gaze skittered away. "I just thought there might be something between you and Daemon."

"Oh, no, there's nothing between us." Besides a whacked-out alien bond and all our secrets. I cleared my throat. "Let's not talk about your brother. What's up with Adam?"

Crimson swept across her pale cheeks. "Adam and I have been trying to spend more time together, you know? Everyone expects us to be together, and there is a part of me that likes him. The elders know that since we're both eighteen already, we're coming of age."

"Coming of age?"

She nodded. "Once we reach eighteen, we're old enough to be

mated."

"What?" My eyes bugged. "Mated? Like, marrying and making babies?"

"Yeah." She sighed. "We usually wait until we're done with school, but knowing that we're getting close, Adam and I are trying to decide what we want to do."

I was still stuck on the whole mating thing. "Do the elders tell you who you can be with?"

Dee frowned. "Not really. I mean, they want us with another Luxen and to reproduce as soon as possible. I know that sounds messed up, but our race is dying off."

"I get that, but what if you didn't want to have kids? What if you fell in love with another boy or…a human?"

"They would outcast us." She faded and then was standing on the other side of the coffee table. "All of them would turn their backs on us. That's what they would've done to Dawson if he…if he were still alive and with Bethany. And I know he would still be with her. Dawson loved Beth."

And her brother's love had ultimately led to their deaths. I lowered my gaze, feeling for the remaining siblings. "Would they force you to leave or something?"

She shook her head. "They'd make us want to leave, but we can't, not without the DOD's permission. It's a lot of pressure."

No doubt. I had to worry about what college to pick. Not about getting knocked up as soon as possible. And Daemon really wanted to risk all of that to be with me? He had to be on crack. "What happened with you and Adam?"

Stopping in front of the TV, she ran her hands through her curly hair. "We had sex."

"Come again?" Up until five seconds ago, I was positive Dee wasn't even attracted to Adam.

Dee's small hands fluttered to her sides. "Yeah, shocking, huh?"

I blinked. "Yeah, that's shocking."

"I didn't know how I felt about him. Like, I totally respect him, and he's good looking." She started pacing again. "But we've only been friends, really. Or at least, I've only let him be a friend to me. I don't know, but anyway, I decided I wanted to see if we, you know, could even do it. So, I told him that we should try to have sex. And we did."

Wow, that sounded real romantic. "And how was it?"

Her cheeks flushed again. "It was...it was good."

"Good?"

Dee appeared beside me, sitting on the couch, hands twisting together. "It was more than just good. A little awkward at first—okay, a whole lot of awkward at first, but things...worked out."

I didn't know if I should be happy for her or not. "So what does all of this mean?"

"I don't know. That's the problem. I like him, but I don't know if I like him because I'm supposed to or if it's real." She flopped onto her back, one arm hanging off the couch. "I don't even know what love is. Like, I thought I loved him when we were doing it. But now? I don't know."

"Damn, Dee, I don't know what to say. I'm glad it was...good."

"It was great." She sighed. "Want to know how great it was? I want to do it again."

I laughed.

One jade-colored eye opened. "But now I have all these...knots in my tummy. I can't stop thinking about him, wondering what he thinks."

"Have you tried talking to him?"

"No. Should I?"

"Uh, yeah, you just did it with him. You should probably call him."

Dee sat up, her eyes wide. "What if he doesn't feel the same?"

It was strange seeing Dee like this, having such a...human reaction. "I think he probably feels the same."

"I don't know. We were just friends and nothing more. We didn't even want to go to homecoming together." She was on her feet again. "But I'm not sure if he felt that way because of me and how I'd acted.

Maybe he's always felt more for me."

"Call him." That was the best advice I could give, since I had no experience in any of this. "Wait. Did you guys use protection?"

Dee rolled her eyes. "I'm so not ready for a baby Dee. We totally used protection."

Relief flooded me. She hung around a little longer then left to go call Adam. I was still shocked that Dee had sex. It was such a big step, even for…aliens. At least it was great. But to have sex just to find out if you liked someone? Where was the romance in that? Of course, who was I to judge? I asked one guy to go out, I was pretty sure, just to see if another noticed. Yeah, I was totally not the go-to person for relationship advice. Poor Dee.

Mom woke up and we ordered pizza before she had to leave for work. While waiting, we chilled on the couch like we used to, before Dad died.

Mom handed me a cup of steaming cocoa. "Don't forget I have you all day Saturday until I go into work, so don't make any plans."

I smiled, wrapping my hands around the warm cup. "I'm all yours."

"Good." She threw her slipper-covered feet onto the coffee table. "I wanted to run something by you."

Taking a sip, I raised my brows.

She crossed her ankles and then re-crossed them the other way. "Will wants to do dinner with us on Saturday, for you birthday."

"Oh."

A faint smile curved her lips. "I told him I wanted to check with you first and make sure you were okay with it." She paused, crinkling her nose. "You are the birthday girl and all."

"I'll only turn eighteen once, right?" I grinned. "It's okay, Mom, we can do dinner with *Will*."

Her eyes narrowed.

I took another drink of cocoa. "Should I dress up for this? Since he is a doctor and all. Oh! Are we going to a fancy dinner and will we talk politics and current events?"

"Shush it." She smiled, though, settling back. "I think you'll like him. He's not stuffy or overbearing. He's really like…"

My heart did a funny thing. "Like Dad?"

Mom smiled sadly. "Yeah, like Dad."

Neither of us spoke for a few minutes. Mom had met Dad her first year of nursing residency at the hospital in Florida. He'd been a patient, having fallen off the deck and broken his foot, trying to impress some girl. But according to my dad, the moment he'd looked into Mom's eyes, he couldn't even remember the other girl's name. They'd dated for six months, got engaged, and married within the year. I came shortly thereafter, and there hadn't been two people more in love than them. Even when they'd argued, love fueled their words.

I'd give anything to have that kind of relationship.

I finished off the rest of my cocoa and wiggled closer to Mom. She lifted her slender arm and I snuggled in, inhaling the apple-scented body lotion she always wore during autumn. Mom had this habit of changing her perfumes and lotions with the seasons.

"I'm happy you met him," I said finally. "Will sounds like a really nice guy."

"He is." She kissed the top of my head. "I like to think your father would approve."

Dad would approve of anyone who made Mom happy. I'd been there the day hospice had told us it wouldn't be much longer. Standing outside their bedroom, I'd heard him tell Mom to love again. That was all he wanted.

I closed my eyes. That kind of love should've been able to beat sickness. That kind of love should've conquered anything.

Chapter 8

I readjusted the thin black straps for the third time and finally gave up. No matter how many times I tugged on it, the neckline of the dress wasn't coming up any higher. I couldn't believe it fit me. Aw hell, it fit a little too well, emphasizing the vast difference between Dee's body and mine. My boobs just might come out and say hello tonight. The dress clung to my bust and had a cinched empire waist before it billowed in soft waves to end before my knees.

I kind of looked hot.

But I needed to cover those babies up. I whipped open the closet door. I knew I had a red cardigan that wouldn't look too bad with this dress, but I couldn't find it in the mess. It took me a few minutes to realize that it was in the dryer.

"Holy crud." I moaned and headed downstairs in a flurry of black and tapping heels.

Thank God Mom had already left for work. She'd either stroke out or applaud the dress. Either one would've been embarrassing. I headed down the hallway, nervous and nauseous. I could hear the car doors outside, the laughter as I pulled out the cardigan, shook it, and slipped it on. What if I did something stupid? Like lift a TV in front of an entire house full of classmates?

Just then there was a knock on the door. Taking a deep breath, I backtracked to the front door and swung it open. "Hey."

Blake stepped in, holding a half dozen roses in his hands. His eyes drifted over me. "Whoa, you look really great." He smiled as he held out the flowers.

Blushing, I took the roses and inhaled their clean scent. Giddiness swept through me. "Thank you, but you didn't have to."

"I wanted to."

Ah, the key word again: *want*. "Well, they're beautiful. And you look really nice, too." And he did, dressed in a dark V-neck sweater with a collared shirt on underneath. I stepped back, holding the roses close. No one had ever given me flowers before. "Would you like something to drink before we head over?"

Blake nodded and followed me into the kitchen. Options were limited, so he settled on one of my mom's wine coolers. He leaned against the counter, looking around as I found a vase for the roses. "You have books everywhere. It's really cute."

I smiled as I set the roses on the counter. "My mom hates it. She's always trying to pick them up."

"And you just put them right back, huh?"

I laughed. "Yeah, sounds right."

He moved forward, wine cooler in one hand. His gaze dipped and he reached out, picking up the silver chain. His knuckles brushed the swell of my chest. "Interesting necklace. What kind of stone is this?"

"Obsidian," I told him. "A friend gave it to me."

"It's really different." He let it drop. "It's cool."

"Thanks." I placed my fingers on it, trying to push away the images of Daemon it brought along with it. I searched for something to say. "Thanks for the flowers again. They're really pretty."

"I'm glad you like them. I was worried I'd look like a nerd for giving them to you."

"No. They're perfect." I smiled. "Are you ready to go over?"

He finished up the wine cooler and rinsed it before tossing it in the trash. Mom would've loved him for that—well, not the underage-drinking-of-her-wine-cooler part. "Sure," he said. "But I kind of have some bad news. I can only stay for half an hour tops. We have some family coming in last minute. I'm really sorry."

"No," I said, hoping the disappointment wasn't audible. "It's okay. We didn't give you much notice."

"Are you sure? I feel like such a tool."

"Of course. You're not a tool. You did bring me roses."

Blake grinned. "Well, I want to make it up to you. Can you do dinner with me tomorrow night?"

I shook my head. "I can't tomorrow. Spending the day with my mom."

"How about Monday?" he asked. "Do your parents let you out on a school night?"

"It's just my mom, but yes, she does."

"Good. There's this little Indian restaurant I saw in town." He inched closer. There was a slight scent of aftershave that reminded me of the conversation I'd had with Lesa about how boys smelled. Blake smelled good. "You game?"

"Sure thing." I glanced around, biting my lip. "You ready to head over now?"

"Yep, if you do one thing."

"Which is?"

"Well, two things." Another step closer and his shoes were touching mine. I had to tip my head back to meet his eyes. "Then we can go over."

I felt a little dizzy, staring in his eyes. "What are the two things?"

"You've got to give me your hand. If this is a speed date, we've got to make it believable." He dipped his head, still holding onto my gaze. "And a kiss."

"A kiss?" I whispered.

His lips spread in a crooked smile. "I need you to remember me when I leave. In that dress, you're going to have guys all over you."

"I don't know about that."

"You will. So? Is it a deal?"

My breath slowed in my lungs. Curiosity filled me. Would kissing him be like kissing Daemon? Would the world burn or just simmer? I wanted to find out, needed to discover if I could forget the boy next door in a simple kiss.

"Deal," I murmured.

His hand found my cheek, and I closed my eyes. Blake whispered my name. My mouth opened, but there were no words to be spoken. There was just anticipation and the need to lose myself. At first, his lips brushed across mine lightly, testing my response, and the gentle nature of the kiss was disarming. I placed my hands on his shoulders, and they tightened when he swept his lips over mine again.

His kiss deepened, and I felt like I was swimming in raw emotions. It was elating and yet confusing at the same time. I kissed him back, and his hands dropped to my waist, pulling me closer. I waited breathlessly in between kisses for something—anything—other than the restlessness stirring inside me. Then all at once, I felt frustration, anger, and sadness—which were nothing I was searching for.

Blake broke contact, breathing heavily. His lips were ripe, swollen. "Well, I will definitely remember you when I leave."

I lowered my chin, blinking. Nothing had been wrong with that kiss, other than it was lacking something. It had to be me. Stress. With everything happening, I was thinking too much into things. And kissing him was just too fast. I felt like one of those girls in the books I read, delving into a guy headfirst without even thinking about it. Practical Katy still lived inside me, and she wasn't happy with what I'd done. And it was more than that. A stirring of sour guilt poked at me, telling me that my heart hadn't been in that kiss because of someone else.

"Just one more thing," he said, and his hand found mine. "Ready?"

Was I? Confliction tore through me. Maybe if Daemon saw me

happy with Blake, he wouldn't feel compelled to pursue our unreal connection. I felt sick. "Yes. I'm ready."

Outside, there were numerous cars lining the driveway and all the way down to the empty house at the beginning of our road. "Holy crap, I thought this was supposed to be a little party?"

Dee had really outdone herself. She'd dug up numerous paper lanterns and strung them along the porch. Through their windows, thick candles spread throughout flickered softly. A warm, pleasant cider-and-spice smell floated outside and tickled my nose, reminding me how much I loved the smell of autumn.

People were everywhere inside, packed on the couch, surrounding two guys in a Wii death match. Several familiar faces were crowding the staircase, laughing as they drank from red plastic cups. Blake and I couldn't go two feet without bumping into someone.

Dee weaved in and out of the crowd, playing the hostess. She looked beautiful in her delicate white dress that highlighted the darkness of her hair and the emerald color of her eyes. When she saw our hands joined together, she barely hid her surprise…or disappointment.

Feeling like I was doing something wrong, I pulled free and gave her a tight hug. "Wow. The house looks great."

"It does, doesn't it? I'm a natural." She looked over my shoulder. "Katy…?"

My cheeks burned. "He's my—"

"Date," Blake inserted, catching and squeezing my hand. "I have to bail soon, but I wanted to escort her to the party."

"Escort her?" She glanced at him, then back to me. "Okay. Well, I'll go…check on some stuff. Yeah." Then she floated away, back stiff.

I tried to not let her disappointment get to me. She couldn't seriously want me to be with her brother. One of them had already gone down that path with a human and look what happened.

A huge amount of suspicious noises were coming from the dark corners of the large house, distracting me from my thoughts. I then briefly saw Adam, who appeared to be stalking Dee through the crowd. I made a mental note to ask her how her call with him had gone.

"Want to get a drink?" Blake asked. When I nodded, he led me toward the dining room, where we could see several bottles. There was even a punch bowl. Spiked, no doubt.

"We had parties like this back home," Blake said, handing me a red plastic cup. "In beach houses, though, and everyone smelled of sea and suntan lotion."

"You sound like you miss it."

"I do sometimes, but hey, change isn't too bad. It makes life interesting." He took a sip and coughed. "What did they put in this? Moonshine?"

I laughed. "God only knows around here."

Wild giggles came from the kitchen. We turned just in time to see Carissa rush from the room, an annoyed look on her face as she bolted to where Dee was in the doorway. "Dee, your friends are crazy."

"They're your friends, too," Lesa commented dryly, coming up behind Dee. She saw Blake and me and came to a stop. Then she bumped me with her hip. "Yay."

Carissa folded her arms over her chest. "My friends would not do *that* with whipped cream."

I busted into laughter at the horrified look on Dee's face and the curious one that crossed Lesa's. Blake smiled at me, as if he liked the sound of my laugh.

"What?" Dee screeched and took off toward the kitchen.

"I have to see this," muttered Lesa, following quickly behind the flurry of white.

I glanced over at Carissa, whose cheeks were as red as my sweater. "You're kidding, right?"

She shook her head emphatically. "You have no idea what Donnie and Becca are doing in there."

"Aren't they the two who planned to get married after graduation?"

"Yep. And I can tell you they have not waited for marriage for most things."

I giggled. "Awesome."

Carissa shuddered. "I'm not trying to be a prude, but who acts like that in public or at a friend's house? I mean, come on. It's disgusting." She took a deep breath, her dark eyes flicking up. "Hi, Blake, sorry about that."

"It's okay. Whipped cream should only be used on pies."

I had to look away to stop from laughing. It was kind of gross, but I still found it entertaining. Not sure what that said about me. And who was I kidding? Last Friday I'd been getting all hot and heavy in a library.

At the reminder, my stomach knotted again and my gaze darted around the room.

We were briefly interrupted by a group who wanted to talk to Carissa about her older brother, who was away at college. I'd forgotten that she had older siblings. Mental note number two: pull head out of ass.

Blake must've made a lot of friends quickly, because most of the kids were talking him up. And a lot of girls kept stealing looks at him. This filled me with an obscene amount of glee. I leaned into Blake's arm, mostly for show, and then I stayed there, liking the way the bulge of muscles in his upper arms felt against my chest.

He didn't seem to mind. The hand on my back bunched into the silk of my dress, and he stopped mid-sentence to lean down and whisper, "I really wish I were staying,"

I turned my head, smiling. "Me, too."

His hand slid across my back, curving around my waist. I liked this—whatever this was. It seemed natural to be close to a guy, to be flirting, having fun. Kissing. It all felt *easy*. We stayed like that after Carissa drifted away, and then it was time for him to leave.

I walked him to the door, his arm still around my waist. "We still on for dinner?" he asked.

"You bet. I'm actually—" My back was to the stairs, but I still knew the second *he* came down. The air changed, grew heavier and warm.

The nape of my neck tingled.

Blake frowned. "You're actually…what?"

My heart sped up. "I'm…I'm looking forward to it."

He started to smile, and then he glanced up. His eyes widened slightly, and I knew Daemon was there. I didn't want to turn around, but it seemed unnatural not to.

And it was like being struck by lightning. I hated his effect on me, but at the same time it thrilled me. Nothing was *easy* about it.

Daemon was dressed casually compared to the rest of us but still looked better than any guy in the room. He had on a pair of old, distressed blue jeans and a shirt that bore some long-forgotten band name. He absently tucked a strand of dark hair behind his left ear and flashed a wolfish grin at something someone said. Those magnetic eyes shimmered under the dim light of the candles. This was the first time I'd really seen Daemon around anyone other than his family or a friend or two outside of school.

Daemon had this effect on others, no matter their gender. It was obvious that people wanted to be around him, but at the same time, it seemed like they were afraid to come too close. They were drawn to him, like I was, whether they liked it or not. People approached but stopped just a few feet from him. But the whole time, he had his eyes fixed on me.

In that second, I completely forgot the boy with his hand on my waist.

Daemon stopped in front of us. "Hey there…"

Blake's hand pressed into me as he leaned around. "I don't think we got the chance to introduce ourselves the other night at the diner. My name is Blake Saunders." He offered his free hand.

Daemon glanced at Blake's hand before returning his gaze to me. "I know who you are."

Oh, geez. I twisted toward Blake. "This is Daemon Black."

His smile faltered. "Yeah, I know who he is, too."

Laughing under his breath, Daemon straightened. At his full

height, he was a good head taller than Blake. "It's always nice to meet another fan."

Yeah, Blake had no idea what to say to that. He shook his head slightly and faced me. "Well, I need to get going."

I smiled. "All right. Thanks for…everything."

He smiled a little as he leaned in, wrapping his arms loosely around me. Acutely aware of Daemon's intense stare, I placed my hands on Blake's back and leaned up, pressing my lips against his smooth cheek.

Daemon cleared his throat.

Blake laughed softly in my ear. "I'll call you. Behave."

"Always," I said, letting go.

With one last grin tossed in Daemon's direction, Blake sauntered out the door. Had to give it to the boy, he held his own—sort of—against Daemon.

I faced him, scowling as I started fiddling with the obsidian around my neck. "You know, you couldn't have been much more of a jerk if you tried."

He arched a brow. "Thought I told you not to hang out with him?"

"Thought I explained that just because you say I can't doesn't mean I won't."

"You did?" His gaze followed the obsidian, and then he lowered his head. "You look really nice tonight, Kitten."

My stomach hollowed. Must ignore—must ignore. "I think Dee has her hands full, but she did a great job decorating the house."

"Don't let her fool you into believing she did all of this herself. She recruited me from the moment I got home."

"Oh." Surprise shot through me. I couldn't picture Daemon stringing paper lanterns without lighting them on fire and then throwing them. "You both did a great job."

Daemon's gaze dipped again, and I shivered under his intense scrutiny. Why, oh why, did Blake need to bail early, leaving me behind with Daemon? "Where did you get this dress?" he asked.

"Your sister," I told him blandly.

He frowned, looking half disgusted. "I don't even know what to say about that."

"Say about what, babe?"

Daemon stiffened. Tearing my gaze from him, my eyes locked with Ash's. Holding my stare, she smiled sweetly and wrapped a thin arm around his narrow waist. She leaned into him, as if she were all too familiar with the lines of his body. And she was. They'd been dating on and off for a while.

Oh, this was fabulous. He'd just given Blake the stink eye and now Ash was leeched to his side. And God, I *didn't* like that at all. Irony was such a bitch.

"That's a cute dress. It's Dee's, right?" Ash asked. "I think she got it when we went shopping together, but it usually looks looser on her."

Oh, that felt like a jellyfish sting. An unreasonable emotion crept up my spine the longer she stood there, in her skintight sweater dress that ended an inch below her butt. "I think you forgot some jeans or the bottom part of your dress."

Ash smirked, but then turned her attention back to Daemon. "Babe, you rushed off so fast. I had to search the entire upstairs for you. Why don't we go back to your room and finish what we started?"

The punched-in-the-gut feeling nearly doubled me over. I had no idea where it was coming from or why I felt that way. It wasn't reasonable. I didn't like Daemon—*I didn't*. He could make out with the Pope for all I cared, and I'd just kissed Blake. But that hot feeling was there, stealing through my veins.

Daemon stepped out of Ash's embrace while scratching a spot above his heart. He caught my eyes, and I raised my brows expectantly. He wanted to be with me? Yeah, seemed like it…in between whatever he was doing with Ash.

I turned away before I said something that would embarrass me later. Dee's high-pitched giggle followed my steps. Daemon spoke, but it was lost in the crowd of people. Needing air and distance, I stepped out onto the crowded front porch.

I couldn't figure out what was going on. There was no way I was jealous. That *so* wasn't what I was feeling. And I had a date coming up with a hot, normal human boy. There was no way I cared that Daemon and Ash were doing whatever.

Then it struck me as I headed down the steps. Oh my God, I *did* care. I cared—*I cared* that he'd been upstairs with Ash doing things that…I couldn't even wrap my brain around without wanting to do physical damage. My head spun. Images of Ash kissing him sucked the air out of my lungs. What was wrong with me?

Dazed, I started walking. At some point, I kicked off my heels and tossed them aside. I kept walking, my feet bare against the cold grass and gravel. I didn't stop until I stood beside the empty house at the end of the road. Taking several gulps of fresh, clean air, I tried to get control of my overexposed emotions. Part of me knew what I was feeling was ridiculous, but it still seemed like the world had stopped spinning. I felt like I wanted to explode and everything was hot and cold at the same time.

My breath shuddered in my chest. I squeezed my eyes shut and swore. What I was feeling wasn't right. The last time I'd been this jealous was when all the bloggers went to a book conference last year and Mom wouldn't let me go. Hell, this was worse. I wanted to scream. I wanted to run back in there and pull out every strand of Ash's hair. Jealousy I had no right to coursed through my veins, blinding any rational thought trying to tell me I was being stupid. But my blood was boiling. My palms were sweaty and they felt foreign and cold. My entire body was shaking.

I stood there, lost in my swirling emotions and messed-up thoughts until I heard the sound of feet crunching over grass. The figure moved out of the dark shadows and a stretch of moonlight bounced off a gold and blue watch.

Simon.

My stomach sunk all the way to my toes. What in the hell was he doing here? Had Dee invited him? I hadn't told her what had happened between us, but there was no doubt she had heard the rumors.

"Katy, is that you?" He staggered to the side and leaned against the house. Fully visible, he had a swollen-shut eye that was an ugly shade of violet. Bruises marred his jaw. A lip was split.

I gaped. "What happened to your face?"

Simon lifted a flask to his mouth. "Your boyfriend happened to my face."

"Who?"

He took a drink, wincing. "Daemon Black."

"He's not my boyfriend."

"Whatever." Simon inched closer. "I came here to talk...to you. You've got to call him off."

My eyes widened. When Daemon said he'd take care of the problem, he hadn't been screwing around. Part of me felt bad for the dude, but it was overshadowed by the fact he and his friends had half the school calling me a skank.

"You've got to tell him I didn't mean anything that night. I'm... sorry." He lurched forward, dropping the flask. Jesus. Daemon must've put the fear of God in him. "You've got to tell him I set everyone straight."

I stepped back as the wave of alcohol and desperation crashed into me. "Simon, I think you should sit down or something, because—"

"You've got to tell him." He grabbed my arm with damp, beefy fingers. "People are starting to talk. I can't...have that kind of shit being said about me. Tell him or else."

The hairs on the back of my neck rose. Fury tore through me like a speeding bullet. I wouldn't be pushed around or threatened. Not by Simon or anyone. "Or else what?"

"My dad's a lawyer." His hand tightened as he swayed. "He'll—"

A couple of things happened next.

He pitched toward me, too close, and my heart sped up. A horrible cracking sound deafened my ears. Four of the five windows we stood next to trembled and then cracked. A large, jagged fracture streaked down the middle of each window, and then small ones spread out until the entire windows shuddered under the unseen force and exploded, sending shards of glass raining down on us.

Chapter 9

Simon yelped as he lurched from the falling glass. "What the hell?"

Struck by absolute horror, I stood motionless. Simon shook his arms and more glass fell away from his clothes. Little pieces slid through my hair, some falling out and others getting stuck in the tangled waves. My arm felt like someone pinched me, and I knew Dee's dress was torn. The other window shuddered. I didn't know how to control it. The pane continued to tremble violently. There was another loud *crack*.

Backing up, Simon glanced from the windows and then to me. His glassy eyes were wide. "You…"

I couldn't catch my breath. There was a faint reddish-white glow creeping into my vision. The remaining window on the second floor vibrated.

Face pale, he stumbled over his own feet, falling to the ground. "You're…you're glowing. You—you freak!"

I was glowing? "No! It's not me. I don't know what's happening, but it's not me!"

He scrambled to his feet, and I took a step toward him. He threw up his hand and wobbled. "Stay away from me! Just stay away from me."

Unable to do anything, I watched him stagger around the house. A car door opened and an engine roared to life. A distant part of my brain told me I needed to stop him, because he was obviously too drunk to drive.

But then the top window exploded.

Cringing, I shielded my face as glass rained down, pinging off the ground and me. My breath sawed in and out of my chest until the very last piece of glass landed. I stood there, mortified and frightened by what I'd done. Not only did I expose my freak-o abilities again, I'd almost turned Simon into a pincushion. Man, I was so screwed.

Minutes passed before I straightened and picked my way around the shattered glass, making my way into the heavy tree line. A fine sheen of cold sweat dotted my forehead and residual fear kept hitting me low in the stomach. What had I done? When my house came into sight, I felt the familiar tingle along my neck. Branches and leaves crunched, and I turned.

Daemon's steps slowed as he spotted me. He pushed a low-hanging branch aside as he neared. "What are you doing out here, Kat?"

Several moments passed before I could speak. "I just blew up a bunch of windows."

"What?" Daemon moved closer, eyes widening. "You're bleeding. What happened?" He paused. "Where are your shoes?"

I glanced down at my feet. "I took them off."

In the blink of an eye, Daemon was beside me, knocking off tiny pieces of glass. "Kat, what happened?"

Lifting my head, I sucked in a sharp breath. Full-blown panic squeezed my chest. "I was walking and I ran into Simon—"

"Did he do this to you?" His voice was so low it sent shivers through me.

"No. No! I ran into him, and he was upset about you." I paused, my eyes searching his. "He said you beat him up?"

"Yeah, I did." No apology in his voice.

"Daemon, you can't beat up guys because they talk badly about me."

"Actually, I can." His hand clenched at his side. "He deserved it. I'm not going to lie. I did it because of what he was saying. It was bullshit."

I had no idea what to say. Ha. Me. Speechless.

"He knows what he did—what he tried to do—and to spin that around on you?" Daemon eye's flitted to the shadows seeping among the trees. "I'm not going to let some punk-ass human talk about you like that, especially *him* or his friends."

"Wow," I murmured, blinking rapidly. Sometimes I forgot how protective Daemon could be…or how downright scary. "I don't think I'm supposed to say thank you, because that seems wrong, but, um, thanks."

"Anyway, that's not important. What happened?"

Taking several deep breaths, I let the words come out in a rush. When I was done, Daemon wrapped an arm around me, tugging me against his chest. I didn't resist him, pressing my face into him and clutching his sides, feeling safer in his embrace than I did any place else. And I couldn't blame the connection for that. Even before it was formed, his arms had always been a sanctuary of sorts.

"I know you didn't do it on purpose, Kitten." His hand pressed a soothing circle against my back. "Simon was drunk, so there's a good chance he won't even remember. And if he does, no one will believe him."

Hope sparked. "You think?"

"Yes. People will think he's crazy." Daemon pulled back, lowering his head so we were eye level. "No one will believe him, okay? And if he starts to talk, I'll—"

"You'll do nothing." I shimmied free, drawing a deep breath. "I think you've already scarred the boy for life."

"Obviously not," he muttered. "What were you thinking back there? You were upset. Why?"

Heat infused my cheeks, and I started walking toward my house.

Daemon let out a long, suffering sigh. He was right beside me. "Kat, talk to me."

"I can make it back home without your help, thank you very much."

He held a branch out of the way so I could pass under it. "I would hope so. It *is* right there."

"Shouldn't you be making out with Ash right now anyway?"

He stared at me like I'd grown two heads. I recognized my mistake immediately.

"That's what all of this is about?"

"No. It had nothing to do with you—or her."

"You're jealous." He sounded smug. "I'm so going to win this bet."

I stomped forward. "Me? Jealous? You've lost your mind. I wasn't the one trying to scare off Blake."

He grabbed my arm, stopping me just as my porch came into sight. "Who cares about Ben?"

"Blake," I corrected.

"Whatever. I thought you didn't like me?"

My hand curled in the air. There was no breaking his hold. "You're right. I don't like you."

Anger flared in his eyes. "You're lying—blushing cheeks and all."

The worst case of verbal diarrhea happened. "You were kissing me a few days ago and now you were having *fun* with Ash? Is this what you normally do? Jump from one girl to the next?"

"No." He dropped my arm. "That's not what I do. I *don't*."

"Yeah, I hate to break it to you, but you are doing it." And so had I. What was I doing? I couldn't be mad at him when I had done the same thing, but I was. It was ridiculous. "God, I am being such a whiny girl. Just forget I said anything. You can do whatever you want and I don't have any right—"

Daemon cursed, dropping my arm. "Okay. You have no idea what was going on between Ash and me. We were only talking. She was messing with you, Kat."

"Whatever." I whirled around, walking again. "I'm not jealous. I don't care if you and Ash make alien babies together. I don't care. And honestly, if it weren't for this stupid connection, you wouldn't even enjoy kissing me. You probably already don't."

Daemon was suddenly in front of me. I took an involuntary step back. "Do you think I didn't enjoy kissing you? That I haven't thought about it every second since then? And I know you have. Just admit it."

In the pit of my stomach, tight coils thrummed. "What is the point of this?"

"Have you?"

"Oh, for crap's sake, yes, I have. I do! Do you want me to write it down for you? Send you an e-mail or a text? Will that make you feel better?"

Daemon arched a brow. "You don't need to be sarcastic."

"And you don't need to be here. Ash is waiting for you."

He cocked his head to the side in exasperation. "Do you really think I'm going to go to her?"

"Uh, yeah, I do."

"Kat." He shook his head, his voice a soft denial.

"It doesn't matter." I took a deep breath. "Can we just forget this? Please?"

Daemon smoothed a finger over his brow. "I can't forget this and neither can you."

Frustrated, I turned on my heel and stalked toward my house. I half expected him to stop me, but after a few successful steps away I realized he wasn't going to. I had to fight turning around to see if he still stood there. I'd made enough of a fool of myself tonight. Kicked a hissy fit over Ash and Daemon, stormed out of the party, and nearly decapitated Simon. All of this before midnight.

Awesome.

Chapter 10

Turning eighteen wasn't as exciting as I'd thought it would be when I was a kid, but some pretty cool stuff happened. I made it most of the day not worrying over what had happened last night. Blake called to chat, and I received a shiny new laptop already set up with everything installed.

Before I did anything else, I logged into my blog and wrote a quick "I'm Back!" post. A huge chunk of my life that had been missing returned. Mom had to pull me away from the laptop pretty quickly, though. I spent the rest of the day traveling a great distance with Mom to meet Will at the nearest Olive Garden.

Will was the touchy, feely sort.

I wasn't sure how to feel. Not once did he take his hand off my mother's during dinner. It was cute, and he was charming and handsome, but it was just weird to see her with another dude. Weirder than I'd thought it would be. But he did give me a gift card to the local bookstore. Bonus points there.

The customary ice-cream cake was different this year. Will joined us at home for it.

"Here," he said, taking the knife from Mom. "If you run it under hot water, it's easier to use."

Mom beamed up at him like he'd just discovered the cure for cancer. They chatted while I sat at the table, trying not to roll my eyes.

Will placed a slice in front of me. "Thank you," I said.

He smiled. "No problem. I'm just glad you're completely recovered from the flu. No one wants to be sick on their birthday."

"I second that," Mom said.

She didn't take her eyes off him until it was near the time for her to get ready for her shift in Winchester. Will remained in the kitchen with me, finishing off the last of his cake while the silence between us grew to an awkward level of epic proportions.

"Have you been enjoying your birthday so far?" he asked, dangling the fork from his long fingers.

I swallowed the last of the crunchy part, which was the only section of the ice-cream cake I'd eat. "Yeah, it's been really nice."

Will picked up his glass, tipping it toward me. "Well, let's toast to many more in the future," he said. I picked up mine, clanging it off his. He smiled, crinkling the skin around his eyes. "I plan on being here to share them with you and your mother."

Unsure of how to feel about him being here a year from now, I set my glass down and bit my lip. Part of me wanted to be happy for Mom, but the other part felt like I was betraying Dad.

Will cleared his throat, inclining his head to the side as he watched me. Amusement flickered in his eyes that were so pale, they were almost gray like mine. "I know you probably don't like the sound of that. Kellie told me how close you were to your father. I can understand your reluctance to having me around."

"I'm not reluctant to the idea," I said honestly. "It's just different."

"Different isn't bad. Neither is change." He took a drink, glancing toward the door. "Your mom is a great woman. I thought that from the moment she came to work at the hospital, but it was the night you were attacked that things went from a professional working relationship to something more. I'm glad I could be there for her." He paused, his smile spreading. "Strange how something good can come from something horrible."

My brows furrowed. "Yeah…that is strange."

His smile tipped higher, almost condescending. Mom returned, ending his totally weird attempt at bonding with me…or marking his territory. He stayed right up to the moment she left for work, sucking up her time. I went to the window, seeing them kiss before they got into separate cars. Gross.

With the sun setting outside, I wrote a quick review for Monday and then a longer one for Tuesday. The longer one was because I couldn't stop gushing. I think I had a new book boyfriend and his name was Tod. Yumtastic.

I settled on one of those usually annoying stations on the TV that played only music on a blank screen. Stopping on a channel that offered hits from the eighties, I turned it up loud enough I couldn't hear my own thoughts. There was laundry that needed to be done and a kitchen that could use a good scrubbing. It was too late to get the dead plants out of the flower bed. Gardening was something that always helped clear my thoughts, but autumn and winter sucked for it. I changed into a pair of comfy sleep shorts, little reindeer-covered socks that reached my knees, and a long-sleeve thermal.

I looked like a hot mess.

Running through the house, I gathered all the clothes, sliding at times on the hardwood floors. I dumped a load into the washer and started singing along to one of the songs. *"In touch with the ground. I'm on the hunt. I'm after you."*

I scooted out of the laundry room and skipped down the hallway, arms flaying around my head like one of the hot pink puppets from the movie *Labyrinth*. *"A scent and a sound, I'm lost and I'm found. And I'm hungry like the wolf. Something on a line, it's discord and rhyme — whatever, whatever, la la la — Mouth is alive, all running inside, and I'm hungry like the — "* Warmth spread down my neck.

"It's actually, '*I howl and I whine. I'm after you*,' and not blah or whatever."

Startled by the deep voice, I shrieked and whipped around. My foot slipped on a section of well-cleaned wood and my butt smacked on the floor.

"Holy crap," I gasped, clutching my chest. "I think I'm having a heart attack."

"And I think you broke your butt." Laughter filled Daemon's voice.

I remained sprawled across the narrow hallway, trying to catch my breath. "What the hell? Do you just walk into people's houses?"

"And listen to girls absolutely destroy a song in a matter of seconds? Well, yes, I make a habit out of it. Actually, I knocked several times, but I heard your…*singing*, and your door was unlocked." He shrugged. "So I just let myself in."

"I can see that." I stood, wincing. "Oh, man, maybe I did break my butt."

"I hope not. I'm kind of partial to your butt." He flashed a smile. "Your face is pretty red. You sure you didn't smack that on the way down?"

I groaned. "I hate you."

"Nah, I don't think you do." His gaze went over me, down to my toes. His brows inched up. "Nice socks."

I rubbed my backside. "Do you need something?"

He leaned against the wall, shoving his hands into his jeans. "No, I don't need something."

"Then why did you break into my house?"

He shrugged again. "I didn't break in. The door was unlocked and I heard the music. I guessed you were the only one here. Why are you doing laundry and singing eighties songs on your birthday?"

Now surprise smacked me upside the head. "How…how do you know it's my birthday? I don't even think I told Dee."

Daemon looked entirely too smug for his own good…or mine. "The night you were attacked at the library and I went to the hospital with you? When you were giving them your personal information, I overheard you."

"Really," I said, staring at him. "And you remembered?"

"Yep. Anyway, why are you doing chores on your birthday?"

I couldn't believe he'd remembered. "I'm obviously that lame."

"That *is* pretty lame. Oh, listen!" His glittering eyes slid in the direction of the living room. "It's 'Eye of the Tiger.' Do you want to sing along to that? Maybe jog up the stairs and pump your fists in the air?"

"Daemon." I shuffled past him carefully, went into the living room, and picked up the remote, turning the song down. "Seriously, what do you want?"

He was directly behind me, forcing me to take an uneasy step back. Being that close to him did funny, bad things to me.

"I came over to apologize."

"What?" I was shocked, awed, and shocked some more. "You're going to apologize again? I don't even know what to say. Wow."

Daemon frowned. "I know it seems like a huge surprise to you that I do have feelings and therefore do feel bad at times for things that I may have…caused."

"Hold up. I have to record this. Let me grab my phone." I turned, scanning the tables for the basically unusable shiny object that never got clear reception out here.

"Kat, you're not helping. I'm being serious. This is…hard for me."

I rolled my eyes. Of course apologizing would only be hard for him. "Okay. I'm sorry. Want to sit? I have cake. Cake should sweeten your disposition a little."

"Nothing can soften me. I'm as cold as ice."

"Hardy-har-har. It's made of ice cream and has the yummy crunchy middle part?"

"Okay, that may work. The crunchy middle part is my favorite."

I fought the grin that tugged at my lips. "Okay, then come on."

We went to the kitchen in awkward silence. I grabbed a hair tie off the counter and tugged my hair back. "How big of a piece do you want?" I pulled the cake out of the freezer.

"How big of a piece are you willing to part with?"

"As big as you want." I grabbed a knife out of the drawer and sized up what I thought would be a suitable piece for him.

"Bigger." He hovered over my shoulder.

I moved the knife to the side.

"Even bigger."

I rolled my eyes and moved it a couple of inches.

"Perfect."

The knife refused to cooperate when I tried to cut off half of the cake. It got an inch down and wouldn't go any farther. "I hate cutting these freaking things."

"Let me try." He reached around and our hands brushed as he took the knife from me. Electricity danced over my skin. "You need to run it under hot water. Then it cuts right through it."

Stepping aside, I let him take over. He did the same thing Will had done earlier, and the knife went through the cake. The button-down shirt he wore pulled across his shoulders as he leaned over and ran the knife under hot water again before cutting a smaller piece. "See? Perfect," he commented.

Chewing on my lip, I grabbed two clean plates and placed them on the counter. "Do you want something to drink?"

"Milk is always good if you've got some?"

Getting the milk, I poured two tall glasses. I grabbed the silverware and motioned toward the living room.

"You don't want to eat in here?"

"No. I don't like eating at the dinner table. It seems so formal."

Daemon shrugged and followed me into the living room. I sat down on the couch, and he took a seat on the other end. I poked the cake, not really hungry at all. My stomach was full of knots.

He cleared his throat. "Nice roses. Brad?"

"Blake." I hadn't thought a second about Blake since Daemon showed up in my hallway. "Yeah, they're nice, aren't they?"

"Whatever," he grumbled. "So why are you spending tonight by yourself? It's your birthday."

I scowled at his blatant reminder. "My mom had to work, and I just didn't feel like doing anything." I poked at the cake some more. "It's not as bad as it sounds. I've spent many of them by myself."

"I guess you probably would have preferred I hadn't stopped by then, huh?"

Looking up, I watched as he stabbed his cake with his fork until he parted the ice cream away from the cookie middle. He took a bite of the crunchy part. "I really did come to apologize for last night."

I sat the plate aside and pulled my legs up underneath me. "Daemon—"

"Wait." He held up his fork. "Okay?"

Sitting back, I nodded.

He glanced down at his plate, his jaw clenching. "Nothing happened between Ash and me last night. She was just…messing with you. And I know that's hard to believe, but I'm sorry if it…hurt you." Daemon drew in a deep breath. "Contrary to what you think about me, I don't jump from girl to girl. I do like you, so I wouldn't mess around with Ash. And I haven't. Ash and I haven't done anything for *months*, before you even came around."

There was a peculiar fluttering in my chest. Never in my life had I had such a hard time figuring myself out as I did when it came to Daemon. I understood books. I did not understand boys—especially alien boys.

"Things are complicated between Ash and me. We've known each other since we came here. Everyone expects us to be together. Especially the elders, since we're 'coming of age.' Time to start making babies." He shuddered.

It was official. I liked the sound of that even less the second time around.

"Even Ash expects us to be together," Daemon went on, stabbing his cake. "And all of this? I know it's hurting her. I never wanted to do that." He paused, struggling for the right thing to say. "I never wanted to hurt *you*, either. And I've done both of those things."

Two bright red spots blossomed across his cheeks. I ran my hand over my leg and looked away. I didn't want him to know that I saw him blush.

"I can't be with her the way she wants—the way she *deserves*." He stopped, exhaling. "Anyway, I wanted to apologize for last night."

"So do I." I bit my lip. "I shouldn't have snapped at you like I did. I guess the whole window thing freaked me out."

"What you did last night with the windows. Well, that was one hell of a display of power that you have no control of." He glanced at me, lashes lowered. "I've been thinking about it. And I keep thinking of Dawson and Bethany. That evening they returned from hiking, and he was covered in blood. I think she may have gotten hurt."

"And he healed her?"

"Yep. I don't know more. They…they died a couple of days later. I guess it's like two photons splitting, separate but the same. That explains how we can sense each other." He shrugged. "I don't know. It's a theory."

"Do you think whatever is happening with me will stop?"

He scooped up the last of his cake and then placed his plate on the coffee table. "We may get lucky. What you're doing might fade over time, but you need to be careful. No pressure, but it's a threat to all of us. I'm not trying to be…cruel. It's the truth."

"No, I understand. I could expose you all. I've almost done it several times."

He leaned back against the couch in a lazy, arrogant sprawl that made my toes curl. "I'm checking around to see if anyone has heard of this happening. I have to be careful, though. Too many questions will give way to suspicion."

I fingered the necklace as Daemon turned to the television and smiled. An eighties hair band played, screeching about a love lost and found, to only be lost again.

"After seeing your dance skills earlier, you would have blended right in with the eighties," he said.

I rolled my eyes. "Can we not mention that again?"

He grinned as he turned to me, a sly look on his face. "You were this close to having 'Walk Like an Egyptian' down."

"You're a douche."

Daemon laughed. "Did you know I had a purple Mohawk?"

"What?" I laughed, not even able to imagine that, especially around these parts. "When?"

"Yep, purple and black. It was before we moved here. We were living in New York. I guess I went through this phase. Pierced nose and all," he said, grinning.

I busted out laughing, and he shoved a throw pillow at me. I picked it up and placed it in my lap. "You were a skater boy, huh?"

"Something like that. Matthew was with us. He became our guardian of sorts. He had no idea what to do with me."

"But Matthew—he's not that much older."

"He's older than he looks. He's around thirty-eight."

"Wow. He's aging well."

Daemon nodded. "He arrived at the same time we did, in the same area. I guess he thought he was responsible for us, being the oldest out of everyone."

"Where did you guys…?" How in the world would I say this? Coming up empty, I winced. "Where did you all land?"

Reaching over, he picked a piece of lint off my thermal. "We landed near Skaros."

"Skaros?" I scrunched up my face. "Uh, is that even on Earth?"

"Yes." He smiled slightly. "It's actually a small island near Greece. It's known for this rocky region where a castle once stood. I'd like to go back one day. It's kind of like our birthplace, I guess."

"How many of you landed there?"

"A couple dozen, or at least that's what Matthew has told us. I don't remember anything from the beginning." His lips pursed. "We stayed in

Greece until we were around five, and then we came to America. There were twenty or so of us, and as soon as we arrived, the DOD was there."

I couldn't imagine what that must've been like for him and the others. To be so young, to be from a different world, and then to be thrust right into the hands of a foreign government had to be scary. "How did all of that go?"

He glanced at me. "Not very good, Kitten. We didn't know that humans were aware of us. All we did know was there were Arum around, but the DOD came as a huge surprise to us. Apparently they knew about us from the moment we got here. They rounded up hundreds who had arrived in America."

I twisted toward him, clutching the pillow to my chest. "What did they do with you guys?"

"They kept us in a facility out in New Mexico."

"No shit." My eyes went wide. "Is Area 51 the real deal?"

He eyed me, amusement creeping into his eyes.

"Wow." I let that one sink in. All those crazies trying to get into the compound had good reason. "I thought the whole Area 51 thing had been around a while."

"My family and friends arrived fifteen years ago, but that doesn't mean the Luxen didn't come before that." He laughed at my expression. "Anyway, they kept us there for the first five years. They— the DOD—had been assimilating the Luxen for years. We learned a lot about humans during that time, and when we were…deemed ready to fully assimilate, they let us go. Usually with an older Luxen who could take care of us. Since Matthew had a relationship with us, we were placed with him."

I did a quick calculation in my head. "But you guys would've been only ten years old. Did you live with Matthew until recently?"

"Believe it or not, we mature differently than humans. At ten I could've gone to college. We develop a lot faster, our brains and whatnot. I'm actually smarter than I act." Another fleeting grin graced his face. "Matthew lived with us until we moved here. At fifteen, we were pretty much adults. The DOD set us up with a house and money."

Well, that probably explained part of our national debt. "But what about people asking questions—looking for your parents?"

Daemon glanced at me sidelong. "There's always an older Luxen we can pass off for our parent, or we can morph into an older version. The morphing thing we try to avoid because of the trace."

Shaking my head, I settled back against the couch. Running their own lives since they were fifteen, with just Matthew checking in on them. I shouldn't be so shocked. My own life was sort of that way, with my mom working so much since Dad died.

Daemon was watching me in his intense way when I looked at him. "Do you want me to leave?"

There was the opening—my chance to tell him to go. "No. You don't have to. I mean, I'm not doing anything and if you have nothing to do, you can stay or whatever…" Or I needed to just shut up.

His eyes held mine a moment, and a swelling developed in my chest, threatening to consume me whole. His gaze moved to my shiny red laptop sitting on the coffee table. "I see someone got something for her birthday."

I grinned. "Yeah, Mom got it for me. I've been without since…well, since then."

He scratched his cheek. "Yeah, I didn't apologize for that, did I?"

"No." I sighed. Back to awkward conversation. And not only that, I was remembering just how I'd lost my last laptop.

Daemon cleared his throat. "That's never happened before, the whole blowing-stuff-up part."

My cheeks heated as I stared at my laptop. "Same here."

His gaze focused on the TV again. "It happened with Dawson, in a way. It was how Bethany found out." There was a pause and I held my breath. He rarely talked about his brother. "He was making out with her and lost control. Turned full Luxen while kissing her."

"Yikes. That had to be…"

"Awkward?"

"Yeah, awkward."

Silence fell between us, and I couldn't help but wonder if we were thinking the same thing. How it had felt to be kissing…touching. Skin uncomfortably hot, I searched for something safe to talk about. "Dee said you guys had moved a lot. How many different places?"

"We stayed in New York for a while, then we moved to South Dakota. And if you think nothing goes on here, you haven't lived in South Dakota. Then we moved to Colorado before coming here. I was always the one who provoked the change in scenery. It's like I was looking for something, but none of those places had it."

"I bet New York was your favorite place."

"Actually, it's not." A bit of his teeth showed in his slight smile. "It's here."

Surprised, I laughed. "West Virginia?"

"It's not that bad. There are a lot of us here. More so than any other place. I have friends who I can be myself with—a whole community, really. That's important."

"I can understand that." Clutching the pillow to my chest, I rested my head on it. "Do you think Dee is happy here? She makes it sound like she can't leave. Like, ever."

Daemon shifted, bringing his legs onto the couch. "Dee wants to pave her own way in life, and I can't blame her for that."

Paving her own way had ended up with her having sex with Adam. I wondered if she still had dreams of going to college overseas.

He stretched as if he were trying to rid himself of some sort of tension that had suddenly settled over him. I scooted away, giving him more room. "If you haven't noticed yet, there are more males than females. So the females are paired off very quickly and protected above all."

I made a face. "Paired off and mated? I understand it—you guys need to reproduce. But Dee can't be forced to do that. It's not fair. You should control your own lives."

He glanced at me, deep shadows in his eyes. "But we don't, Kitten."

I shook my head. "It's not right."

"It's not. Most Luxen don't push for anything different. Dawson did. He loved Bethany." Daemon exhaled raggedly. "We were against it. And I thought he was stupid for falling for a human. No offense."

"None taken."

"It was hard for him. Our group was upset with him, but Dawson… he was the strong one." Daemon smiled as he shook his head. "He didn't cave, and if the colony had discovered the truth, I don't think they would've changed him."

"Couldn't he have left with her, snuck past the DOD? Maybe that's what happened?"

"Dawson loved it here. He was big on hiking and outdoors. He was into the whole rustic-living thing." Daemon glanced at me. "He'd never leave, especially without telling Dee or me. I know both of them are dead." He smiled again. "You would've liked Dawson. Looked just like me but a much better guy. Not a douchebag, in other words."

A lump formed in my throat. "I'm sure I would've, but you're not bad."

He arched a brow.

"Okay, you're prone to moments of great dickdom, but you're not bad." I paused, holding the pillow tight. "Do you want to know what I honestly think?"

"Should I be worried?"

I laughed. "There's a really nice guy under the jerk. I've seen glimpses of him. So while I probably want to beat the crap out of you most of the time, I really don't think you're a bad guy. You have a lot of responsibility."

Daemon tilted his head back and chuckled. "Well, I guess that's not too bad."

I shrugged. "Can I ask you a question and you tell me the truth?"

"Always," he swore.

I reached around my neck and pulled at the dainty chain. The obsidian came into view, and I held it in my hand. "The DOD is a bigger concern than the Arum, aren't they?"

His lips thinned, but he didn't lie. "Yes."

I ran a finger over the wire twisted at the top of the crystal. "What would they do if they knew I was moving things like you?"

"They'd probably do the same thing they'd do to us if they knew." Daemon reached out and cupped my hand that held the obsidian. He laid his finger over mine, stopping my movements. "They'd lock you up…or worse. But I'm not going to let that happen."

My skin tingled where it made contact with his. "But how can you live like this? Like, just waiting for them to find out there's more to you guys?"

His fingers curled around mine, enclosing the pendant until we both held it in our hands. "It's all I've known—it's all any of us have known."

I blinked away the sudden rush of tears. "That's really kind of sad."

"It's our life." He paused. "But don't worry about them. Nothing will happen to you."

Our faces were only inches apart. His hand was still around mine. Something struck me then. "You're always protecting others, aren't you?"

He squeezed my hand and then released it. Leaning against the couch, he reached one arm back and rested his head against his curved elbow. He didn't answer my question. "This hasn't been a very birthday-friendly conversation."

"It's okay. You want more milk or anything?"

"No, but I would like to know something."

I frowned and stretched out my right leg in the small space he didn't occupy. He was rather large, so it didn't leave a lot of room. "What?"

"How often do you run through the house singing?" he asked seriously.

I kicked at him, but he caught my toes. "You can leave now."

"I seriously love these socks."

"Give me back my foot," I ordered.

"It's not so much the fact that they've got reindeers on them or that they go all the way up to your knees." As if that were some kind of great distance. "But it's the fact they're like mittens on your feet."

Rolling my eyes, I wiggled my toes. "I like them like that. And don't you dare knock them. I will kick you off this couch."

He raised a brow and continued to inspect them. "Sock mittens, huh? Never seen anything like it. Dee would love them."

I pulled at my foot, and he let go. "Whatever. I'm sure there're cornier things than my socks. Don't judge me. It's the only thing I like about the holidays."

"The only thing? I figured you're the type of person who wants the Christmas tree to go up on Thanksgiving."

"You celebrate Christmas?"

Daemon nodded. "Yes. It's the human thing to do. Dee loves Christmas. Actually, I think she just loves the idea of presents."

I laughed. "I used to love the holidays. And yeah, I was real big on the Christmas tree when Dad was alive. We'd put it up while watching the parade on Thanksgiving."

"But?"

"But Mom is never home on the holidays now. And I know she won't be this year; since she's new at the hospital, she'll get the shaft." I shrugged. "I'm always alone on the holidays, like some sort of old cat woman."

He didn't respond but watched me intently. I think he sensed how uncomfortable it made me to admit, because he changed the subject. "So, this Bob guy…"

"His name is Blake, and don't start, Daemon."

"Fine." His lips tipped up. "He's not an issue anyway."

My brows furrowed. "What's that supposed to mean?"

Daemon shrugged. "I was kind of surprised when I was in your bedroom while you were sick."

"I'm not sure I want to know about what."

"You had a poster of Bob Dylan on the wall. I expected the Jonas Brothers or something."

"Are you serious? No. Not a fan of pop music. I'm a huge fan of Dave Matthews and older stuff, like Dylan."

He looked surprised, but then he launched into a discussion about his favorite bands, and we were surprised that we had the same tastes. We argued over which Godfather movie was the best and what reality show was the stupidest. Hours went by, and I learned more about Daemon. And there was that different side of him, the one I'd glimpsed a few times in the past. He was relaxed, friendly, and even playful without making me want to bash him upside the head. We did argue over a few things, a bit heatedly, but he wasn't a jerk.

It all suddenly felt *easy*, and that scared the crap out of me. It was past three a.m. by the time I'd realized how long we'd been talking. I pulled my tired gaze off the clock and looked at him. His eyes had drifted shut and his chest rose and fell evenly.

Daemon looked so…peaceful. Not wanting to wake him, I pulled the afghan off the back of the couch and carefully spread it over him. I grabbed a smaller quilt and tucked it around my legs. I could've woke him, but I didn't have it in me. And yeah, there was a teeny, tiny part of me that didn't want him to leave. I didn't know what that meant for me. And I didn't put too much thought into that. Not right now. Not when I was sure my brain would take an obsessive turn into boy land.

"Thank you," he murmured lazily.

My eyes widened. "I thought you were asleep."

"Almost, but you're staring at me."

I flushed. "I am not."

Daemon pried one eye open. "You always blush when you lie."

"I do not." I felt the flush spread down my neck.

"If you keep lying, I think I will have to leave," he threatened halfheartedly. "I don't feel like my virtue is safe."

"Your virtue?" I huffed. "Whatever."

"I know how you get." His eyes closed.

Smiling, I snuggled down in my corner of the couch. We never did change the channel.

Sometime later I remembered something he had said earlier. "Did you find it?" I asked sleepily.

His hand slipped over his chest. "Find what, Kitten?"

"What you were searching for?"

Daemon's eyes opened and held mine. The swelling was back in my chest, spreading through my body. There was a spike of something—excitement?—in my lower stomach as the silence stretched out for what felt like an eternity. "Yeah, sometimes, I think I did."

Chapter 11

When I woke up on Monday morning, I wasn't sure exactly how things were going to play out when I saw Daemon in class. He'd cleared out of the house while I was still asleep and I hadn't seen him when I hung out with Dee on Sunday, which consisted of watching her suck face with Adam. Guess that phone call went well.

Spending time with him Saturday night hadn't really changed anything between Daemon and me. At least, that was what I kept telling myself. It was just a good moment in a long string of bad ones. And I had bigger and better things to think about. I had a date with Blake after school.

But my thoughts kept straying back to Daemon, and a deep fluttering started in my stomach when I thought about us side by side on the couch.

Warmth tingled over my neck while Carissa was telling me about a romance book she was reading. I kept my eyes glued to her, but I was well aware of the fact that Daemon was there.

He took his seat behind me. A second later, something I'd oddly missed in a messed-up way happened. Daemon poked me in the back with his pen.

Lesa's brows arched, but she wisely said nothing as I twisted around. "Yes?"

His half grin was all too familiar. "Reindeer socks today?"

"No. Polka dots."

"Sock mittens?"

"Regular," I said, fighting a stupid grin.

"I'm not sure how I feel about that." He tapped his pen on the edge of his desk. "Regular socks just seem so boring after seeing the reindeer socks."

Lesa cleared her throat. "Reindeer socks?"

"She has these socks that have reindeers on them and are kind of like a mitten for the toes," he explained.

"Oh, I have a pair like that," Carissa said, grinning. "But mine have stripes on them. Love them in the winter."

I passed Daemon a smug look. My socks *were* cool.

"Am I the only person who is wondering how you saw her socks?" Lesa asked.

Carissa punched her on the arm.

"We live next door to each other," he reminded her. "I see lots of things."

I shook my head frantically. "No, he doesn't. He hardly sees anything."

"Blushing," he said, pointing at my cheeks with the blue cap of his pen.

"Shut up." I glared at him, fighting a grin.

"Anyway, what are you doing tonight?"

Butterflies filled my stomach. I shrugged. "I have plans."

He frowned. "What kind of…plans?"

"Just plans." I turned around quickly and focused on the chalkboard.

I knew Daemon's gaze was fixed on the back of my head, but all in all I was feeling kind of good about things. Definite progress had been made when it came to Daemon. We'd spent hours together without killing each other or submitting to wild monkey lust. My new laptop was divine. Simon wasn't in class to blame me for getting his ass kicked or to tell people he saw me go all supernatural on the windows. And I had a date tonight.

That last bit made me swallow. I really had to come clean with Blake. It wasn't fair to him...or to Daemon. I wasn't ready to suddenly believe Daemon, but I couldn't go on pretending there wasn't *something* there.

Even if it might only be alien flu.

• • •

"Here." Blake grinned, sliding his dish over. "Try some of this."

I kept my expression in check as I twirled my fork in the noodles. "I don't know about this."

He laughed. "It's really not that bad. It smells kind of funny, but I think you'll like it."

After a small bite, I decided it wasn't horrendous. I glanced up, smiling. "Okay. Not bad."

"I can't believe the first time you're eating Indian food is in West Virginia."

I ran my hand over my jean-clad leg. The small candle on the side of the table flickered. "I'm not very food adventurous. I'm a steak-and-hamburger kind of chick."

"Well, we have to change that, because you don't know what you're missing." Blake winked. It totally looked cool coming from him. "Thai is my favorite. Love the spices."

The slim redheaded waitress swung by and refilled our glasses. She kept smiling coyly at Blake. I couldn't blame her. Blake was one of the few guys who could pull off the sweater and button-down shirt look.

I tried some more of the noodles. I was having fun, but as I pushed the food around the plate, I felt a weird tug in my stomach. I was having a great time with him, but...

"So I heard something at school today," Blake said after the waitress left.

Slumping against the seat, I bit back a string of curses. God only knew what he'd heard. Rumors about me were flying like UFOs. "I'm afraid to even ask."

He looked sympathetic. "I heard that Daemon beat up some guy because of you."

We'd made it this entire time without bringing up Daemon. I slumped a little in my booth. "Yeah, he kind of did."

Both his brows rose in surprise as he leaned forward. "You going to tell me why?"

"You haven't heard the rumors?"

He ran a hand through his messy spikes. "I hear a lot of things, but I don't believe them."

It was the last thing I wanted to do, but I figured he'd hear the not-so-true parts sooner or later. Hell, he might've already. So I told him about my homecoming date from hell.

Anger flashed in his hazel eyes, and when I'd finished, he sat back. "I'm glad Daemon did pummel the dick, but that's kind of an extreme reaction for someone who's just a 'friend.'"

"Daemon can be…"

"An asshole," Blake suggested.

"Yeah, that, but he's kind of protective of…um, Dee's friends." I squeezed my fork, feeling all kinds of awkward. "And so he got a little mad over what Simon was saying. He's really not that bad. Just takes a little bit to get used to."

"Well, I can't blame him for that, but he really is…*protective* of you. I thought he was going to break my hand for touching you at the party."

Sliding the plate back to him, I rested my chin on my hand. I needed to tell him the truth. Soon. But I didn't want to spoil dinner. I was being a total chicken, but I rationalized it was okay if I at least told him by the end of the evening. Heck, I wasn't even sure what I was going to say. *No, I'm not dating Daemon, but I can't stop thinking about how we combust every time we're near, so it's probably best if you don't get too close?* I sighed. "Enough about Daemon. It must be hard loving surfing so much and being so far from a beach."

"It is," he agreed. A distant look crept into his eyes. "Surfing is probably the only thing that clears my mind. When I'm out there on the waves, I don't think about anything. My brain is officially empty. It's just the waves and me. It's peaceful."

"I can understand that." Silence stretched out for a long moment. "It's the same thing when I'm gardening or reading. It's just me and what I'm doing, or the world I'm reading, and nothing else."

"Sounds like you do it to escape."

I didn't respond because I hadn't really thought of it that way, but now that he said it, I did use those things to escape. Discomfited, I idly separated the noodles on my plate into groups. "What about you? Are you trying to escape?"

Several seconds passed before he answered. "That's the funny thing about trying to escape. You never really can. Maybe temporarily, but not completely."

I nodded absently, struck by the depth of what he said. It was the truth. After I finished a book or potted a plant, Dad was still dead, my best friend was still an alien, and I was still attracted to Daemon.

Blake started talking about plans for Thanksgiving break next week. He'd be out of town for most of it, visiting family. I glanced up, my gaze sweeping the small restaurant. Warmth jolted down my spine.

Oh, holy hell to the no. I couldn't believe it. This was not happening.

Behind the tall partition walls, a dark head moved through the tiny rows. I fell back against the seat, wholly aware of *him* and horrified. This was my date—*my date*. What was he doing here?

Daemon navigated around the clusters of tables with a grace I envied. Women stopped eating or ceased mid-conversation as he passed. Men scooted back to give him more room. He had a profound effect on everyone who saw him.

Frowning, Blake twisted around, and his shoulders stiffened as he faced me. "Overprotective type…?"

"I don't…even know what to say," I mumbled helplessly.

"Hey guys." Daemon slid into the seat next to me, which left very little room. The whole left side of my body was pressed against his, tingling and warm. "Am I interrupting?"

"Yes," I said, mouth agape.

"Oh, sorry." Daemon didn't look sincere. Or make any attempt to leave.

A half smile formed on Blake's lips as he sat back and folded his arms. "How are you doing, Daemon?"

"I'm doing great." He stretched, draping his arm along the back of our booth. "How about you, Brad?"

Blake laughed softly. "My name's Blake."

Daemon's fingers tapped off the back of the booth, brushing my hair. "So what were you guys up to?"

"We were having dinner," I said and started to scoot forward, but Daemon's fingers hooked around the back of my turtleneck, fingers gently sliding against my skin. I shot him a death glare and ignored the goose bumps peaking my skin.

"And I think we were just about done," Blake said, his eyes centered on Daemon. "Weren't we, Katy?"

"Yeah, we just need our check." Very discreetly, I lowered my hand under the table, found Daemon's thigh, and pinched. Hard.

He tugged me back, causing my knee to hit the table. "What were you planning to do after dinner? Was Biff taking you to a movie?"

Blake's easy grin started to falter. "Blake. And that would be the plan."

"Hmm." Daemon's gaze flicked up, and a second later, Blake's glass tipped over.

I gasped. Water sloshed over the table, spilling into Blake's lap. He jumped up, letting out a curse. The movement shook the table again. His plate of spicy noodles slid—well, flew—onto the front of Blake's sweater.

My jaw dropped. Holy mountain mama, Daemon had taken my date hostage.

"Jesus," Blake muttered, hands at his sides.

Grabbing napkins, I turned to Daemon. My look promised a vengeful death as I handed Blake the napkins.

"That was really strange," Daemon said, smirking.

Red-faced, Blake glanced up from patting his crotch dry. For a moment, his eyes fixed on Daemon and I swore he was going to come across the table. And then his eyes shuttered. Quietly and with stiff, jerky movements, he brushed off the brown noodles. The waitress rushed to Blake's side with several more napkins.

"Well, anyway, I'm actually here for a reason." Daemon picked up my glass and took a drink. "You're needed at home."

Blake halted his movements. "Excuse me?"

"Did I speak too fast, Bart?"

"His *name* is *Blake*," I snapped. "And why am I needed at home? Right now, at this very moment?"

Daemon met my eyes, his stare heavy and intense with meaning. "Something has come up and you need to check it out now."

Something obviously meant alien business. Unease crawled down my spine. Now his sudden appearance made sense. For a few minutes, I was really beginning to believe it had been pure, primal jealousy that drove him to go all stalker on us.

And as much as it ticked me off to do this, I knew I had to leave.

Turning to Blake, I winced. "I'm *really*, really sorry about this."

Blake's gaze darted between us as he picked up the check. "It's okay. Things happen."

I felt like a tool, which seemed fitting, since I was sitting next to the biggest wiener ever. "I'll make it up. I promise."

He smiled. "It's all right, Katy. I'll take you home."

"That won't be necessary." Daemon smiled tightly. "I got this, Biff."

I wanted to face-palm myself. "Blake. His name *is* Blake, Daemon."

"It's okay, Katy," Blake said, lips thin. "I'm a mess."

"Then it's solved." Daemon stood, allowing me to scoot out.

Blake took care of the check, and we headed outside. I stopped by his car, aware of Daemon's intense stare. "I am so, so sorry."

"It's okay. You didn't knock the stuff on me." He paused, brows narrowing as he stared hard at something over my shoulder. Two guesses what—or *who*—that was. Pulling his cell out of his back pocket, he checked the display before shoving it in his jeans. "Although that was the craziest thing I've ever seen. But anyway, we'll make up for it when I get back from break, okay?"

"Okay." I started to give him a hug but halted. The front of his sweater was stained and moist looking.

Laughing, Blake leaned in and placed a quick, dry kiss on my lips. "I'll call you."

I nodded, wondering how one person could single-handedly ruin everything within a minute. It was a talent. With a wave, Blake was gone, and I was alone with Daemon.

"You ready?" Daemon called, holding open the passenger door.

I stalked over to the car and climbed in, slamming the door behind me.

"Hey." He frowned from outside the car. "Don't take your anger out on Dolly."

"You named your car Dolly?"

"What's wrong with that?"

I rolled my eyes.

Daemon jogged around the front of the car and slid in. The moment he closed the door behind him, I twisted in my seat and punched him in the arm. "You are such a jerk! I know you did the glass and plate thing. That was *so* wrong!"

He held up his hands, laughing. "What? It was funny. The look on Bo's face was priceless. And the kiss he gave you? What was that? I've seen dolphins give hotter kisses than that."

"His name is Blake!" I punched his leg this time. "And you know it! I can't believe you acted like that. And he doesn't kiss like a dolphin!"

"From what I've seen, he does."

"You didn't see the last time we kissed."

His laughter died off. *Uh oh.* He turned to me slowly. "You've kissed him before?"

"That's none of your business." My cheeks flushed, giving me away.

Anger sparked in his magnetic eyes. "I don't like him."

I gaped at Daemon. "You don't even know him."

"I don't need to know him to see that there's something…*off* about him." He turned the key and the engine rumbled to life. "I don't think you should be hanging out with him."

"Oh, this is rich, Daemon. Whatever." Staring straight ahead, I hugged my elbows and shivered. I was so angry my head was two seconds from spinning.

"Are you cold? Where's your jacket?"

"I don't like jackets."

"Did they do something terrible and unforgiveable to you, too?" He turned on the automatic temperature setting. Warm air blasted out of the vents.

"I find them…cumbersome." I sighed loudly. "What was so freaking imperative that you had to go stalker-mode and find me?"

"I wasn't stalking you." He sounded offended.

"Oh, you weren't? Did you use your alien GPS system to find me?"

"Well, yeah, sort of."

"Argh! This is so wrong." I seriously doubted Blake would be calling me again. Not that I blamed him. If I were him, I wouldn't be. Not when a psychotic alien was shadowing me. "So what's the deal?"

Daemon waited until we pulled onto the highway. "Matthew has called a meeting of the minds, and you should be there. It has to do with the DOD. Something's happened."

Chapter 12

We got back to his house before the rest of them showed up, and I was trying to keep calm as I settled into the recliner in the corner. Daemon wasn't panicking, but he didn't know what was going on yet. Outside, several car doors slammed shut. I wrapped my arms around my waist, and Daemon moved to my side, sitting on the arm of my chair.

Ash and the Thompson boys were the first to come in. Adam smiled at us before sitting next to Dee. She offered him the bag of popcorn she'd been scarfing and he dug in. Andrew took one look in my direction and rolled his eyes. "Anyone have a clue why she's here?"

I loathed Andrew.

"She needs to be here," Mr. Garrison said, closing the door behind him. He moved to the center of the living room, all eyes on him. Outside of school, he always dressed down in jeans. "I want to keep this little get-together short."

Ash smoothed a hand over her purple tights. "The DOD knows about her, right? We're all in trouble?"

My breath caught. I wasn't mad at the scornful tone in her voice. A lot was at stake if the DOD found out about me, about them. "Do they,

Mr. Garrison?"

"As far as I know, they don't know about you," he said. "The elders called a meeting tonight because of the increase in DOD presence here. It appears something has caught the DOD's attention."

I sank back against the chair, relieved. But then it hit me. I may be off the hook, but *they* weren't. I glanced around the room, not wanting to see any of them in trouble. Not even Andrew.

Adam stared at a buttery piece of popcorn. "Well, what did they see? No one's done anything wrong."

Dee sat the bag of popcorn aside. "What's the deal?"

Matthew's ultra-bright blue gaze circled the room. "One of their satellites picked up the light show from Halloween weekend, and they've been out to the field, using some sort of machine that picks up on residual energy."

Daemon scoffed. "The only thing they're going to find is a burned patch of ground."

"They know we can manipulate light for self-defense, so from what I've gathered, that's not what caught their attention." Mr. Garrison glanced at Daemon, frowning. "It's the fact that the energy was so strong it disrupted a satellite's signal and they weren't able to snap any pictures of the event. Nothing like that has ever happened before."

Daemon kept his expression blank. "I guess I'm just that awesome."

Adam laughed under his breath. "You're so powerful you're disrupting signals now?"

"Disrupted only the signal?" Mr. Garrison barked a short laugh. "It destroyed the satellite—a satellite designed to track high-frequency light and energy. It zeroed in on Petersburg, and the event *destroyed* the satellite."

"Like I said, I'm that awesome." Daemon's smile was smug, but I was filling with anxious energy.

"Wow," Andrew murmured. Respect gleamed in his eyes. "That's pretty awesome."

"As awesome as that is, the DOD is very curious. The elders believe they will be here a while, monitoring things. That they've *been* here." He glanced at his wristwatch. "It's imperative that everyone is on their best behavior."

"What do the other Luxen have to say about this?" Dee asked.

"They aren't too concerned at this point. And they have no reason to be," Matthew said.

"Because it was Daemon who caused such a disruptive burst of energy and not them," Ash said, and then she gasped. "Does the DOD suspect we have more abilities?"

"I think they want to know how it's possible that he was able to do something like that." Matthew studied Daemon. "The elders told them there was a fight between our kind. No one implicated you, Daemon, but they already know you're strong. You can be expecting a visit from them soon."

He shrugged, but fear spiked in me. It hadn't been Daemon who'd taken out Baruck, so how could he explain what happened? And would the DOD guess the Luxen were far more powerful than they realized, capable of almost anything?

If so, my friends—and Daemon—were in danger.

"Katy, it's very important that you're careful when hanging around the Blacks," Mr. Garrison continued. "We don't want the DOD suspecting that you know anything you shouldn't."

"Speak for yourself," Andrew muttered.

I shot him a look, but Daemon responded before I could. "Andrew, I'm going to knock the—"

"What?" Andrew exclaimed. "I'm just telling the truth. I don't have to like her because you're infatuated with the stupid human. None—"

Daemon was across the room in a flash. Fully enveloped in intense reddish-white light, he snatched Andrew up and slammed him into the wall with such force the pictures around them rattled.

"Daemon!" I shrieked, rising to my feet at the same time Mr. Garrison shouted.

Ash jumped from her chair, gasping. "What are you doing?"

Grabbing her snack, Dee sighed and sat back. "Here we go. Popcorn?"

Adam took a handful. "Honestly, Andrew needs his ass kicked. The DOD being here isn't Katy's fault. She has just as much to lose as we do."

His sister whirled on him. "So you're taking her side now? A human's?"

"This isn't about sides," I said, keeping an eye on the boys.

Both were in full Luxen mode. So was Matthew. Nothing but a male-shaped form of intense bluish light, he grabbed Daemon and yanked him off Andrew.

Ash glared at me for a long moment. "None of this would be happening if you hadn't shown up here. You would've never gotten the original trace on you. The Arum would've never seen you, and this whole messed-up chain of events would've never happened!"

"Oh, shut up, Ash." Dee threw a handful of popcorn at her. "Seriously. Katy risked her life to make sure the Arum didn't know where we lived."

"That's great and dandy," Ash snapped back. "But Daemon wouldn't have gone all Rambo on the Arum if his precious human wasn't in danger every five seconds. This is her fault."

"I'm not his precious human!" I took a deep breath. "I'm just his... his friend. And that's what friends do. They protect each other."

Ash rolled her eyes.

I sat down. "Well, it's what human friends do, at least."

"And it's what the Luxen do," Adam said, staring at his sister. "Some just forget that."

With a disgusted sigh, she spun around and headed for the door. "I'll wait outside."

Watching her go, I wondered if she'd find a reason to blame me for everything, even those gaudy purple tights of hers. But in a way, this situation *was* my fault. It had been my bizarro output of energy that had drawn the DOD here. My chest ached.

Mr. Garrison finally broke the boys apart. Andrew flickered into his human form, eyes narrowed on a still-iridescent Daemon. "Dude, that was just wrong. Knock me around all you want, but I'm not going to be okay with her."

"Andrew," Mr. Garrison warned.

"What?" He backed off, though. "Do you really think she can hold her own against the DOD if they question her? Because of how close she is to Dee and *you*, they *will* ask her questions. And you, Daemon, are you planning to do a repeat of your brother? Wanna die for her, too?"

Daemon's light flared brighter, and I knew he was going to charge Andrew again. This was ridiculous. Without thinking, I shot across the room and wrapped my fingers around his glowing wrist. It was strange to touch him like this. Warmth and electricity shot up my arm. The back of my neck tingled.

"That was a low blow," I said to Andrew, because someone needed to. "He doesn't even deserve your ass kicking, Daemon."

"She's right," Adam said. Until then I hadn't realized he'd moved, but he was on the other side of Daemon. "But if you want to put him out of commission for the next week after that comment, I'll help."

"Gee, thanks, *brother*." Andrew scowled.

Tense silence followed, and then Daemon's light faded and he settled back into his human form. He glanced down to where my hand curved around his wrist, and then his gaze flicked up, meeting mine. Charged air passed from his skin to mine, shocking me with a *crack*. I let go of his wrist and stilled under his intense stare.

"This is the kind of display we cannot afford." Mr. Garrison drew in a deep breath. "I think that's enough for this evening. Both of you need to cool down and keep in mind that they are here. We need to be careful."

They left after that, including Dee. She wanted to spend time with Adam and also make sure he didn't end up mauling Andrew, which left

Daemon and me alone. I should've left, but after Andrew's thoughtless comment, I needed to know that Daemon was okay.

I followed him into the kitchen. "I'm sorry about what Andrew said. That was wrong."

Daemon's jaw worked as he grabbed two cans of Coke, handing me one. "It is what it is."

"Still not right."

His eyes searched my face in a way that made me feel exposed to the core. "Are you worried about the DOD being here?"

I hesitated. "Yeah, I am."

"Don't be."

"Harder said than done." I played with the tab on the can. "It's not me I'm worried about. They think you're responsible for what happened—the crazy energy thing. What if they think you're…a danger?"

Daemon didn't answer for several moments. "It's not just me, Kitten. Even if I had done that, it's never been about me. It's about all the Luxen." He paused, lowering his gaze. "You know what Matthew believes?"

"No."

A cynical grin pulled at his full lips. "He believes that one day, probably not in our generation, but some day, my kind and the Arum will nearly outnumber yours."

"Really? That's kind of…"

"Scary?" he said.

I tucked my hair back. "I don't know if it's scary. I mean, the Arum thing is, but your kind—the Luxen—freaky powers aside…you're not very different from us."

"What about the fact we're made of light?"

I smiled a little then. "Well, besides that."

"It got me thinking," he said, "that if some of our kind believes this, how come the DOD isn't worried?"

He had a good point. And I was trying not to let my fear for him take over, but my brain was throwing out all kinds of wild scenarios. All of them ended with him being taken in by the DOD. "What happens if they think you are a threat? And don't beat around the bush about it."

"When I was at the compound before, there were Luxen who didn't assimilate." The muscle in his jaw started ticking. "Mostly they didn't want to be kept under the thumb of the DOD. Others I guessed were viewed as a threat because they asked too many questions. Who really knows?"

My mouth felt dry. "What happened to them?"

Several moments passed before Daemon answered. Each second that went by, the unease in my stomach grew. Finally, he nodded. "They killed them."

Chapter 13

Horror rolled through me. The extreme emotion triggered the static that rushed over my skin so fast I couldn't stop it. The burst of energy smacked around the room. I dropped the unopened can of soda as wood scrapped over tile.

A chair flew out from under the table, slamming into my knee with such force that my leg collapsed under me. I yelped in pain and buckled over.

Daemon strung together a truckload of f-bombs and appeared next to me, grabbing me a second before I hit the floor. "Whoa, there, Kitten."

Pushing the hair out of my face, I lifted my head. "Holy crap…"

He helped me stand up, easing a shoulder under my arm for support and pulling me close. "Are you okay?"

"I'm peachy." I wiggled out of his embrace and tentatively placed my weight on my leg. Wet warmth trickled down my leg. I rolled up my jeans, finding blood. "Great, I'm a natural disaster."

"I might have to agree with that."

I shot him a dark look.

With a cocky grin, he winked. "Come on, get up on the table and let me look at that."

"I'm fine."

He didn't argue with me about it. One second I was standing—er, hobbling—and then air rushed me and I was sitting on the table. My mouth dropped open. "What...how did you do that?"

"Skill," he said, placing my foot on the chair. His fingertips brushed against my skin as he rolled my pants above my knee. Electricity danced along my leg, and I jerked. "Wow, you really are a disaster."

"Ugh, it's bleeding all over the place." I swallowed at the sight. "You're not going to heal me, are you?"

"Uh, no, because who knows what would happen then? You might turn into an alien."

"Ha. Ha."

Daemon quickly grabbed a clean towel and dampened it. He came back, not quite meeting my eyes. I reached for the cloth, but he knelt and started to gently blot at the blood. He was careful not to touch my skin this time.

"What am I going to do with you, Kitten?"

"See? I didn't even want to move the chair and it flew at me like a heat-seeking missile."

Daemon shook his head as he continued to dap at the blood. "When we were younger, things like this would happen all the time, before we could control the Source."

"The Source?"

He nodded. "The energy in us—we call it the Source, because it links us back to our home planet, you know? Like the source of it all. At least, that's what our elders say. Anyway, when we were kids and learning how to control our abilities, it was crazy. Dawson had this habit of moving furniture, like you. He'd go to sit down and the chair would fly out from under him." He laughed. "But he was young."

"Great. So I'm operating at the level of a toddler?"

Daemon's lustrous eyes met mine. "Basically." The dark graphic shirt strained against his chest when he laid the bloodied towel aside and leaned back. "Look, it's stopped bleeding already. Not that bad."

I glanced down and saw the fresh gash on my knee. Other than looking gross, it was salvageable. "Thank you for cleaning it up."

"No problem. I don't think you'll need stitches." He lightly brushed his fingertips around the cut.

I jerked at the contact. Little tingles shimmed up my leg. Daemon's hand stilled as he lifted his head. His eyes went from a cool green to liquid fire within seconds.

"What are you thinking about?" he asked.

Sliding into his arms, kissing him and touching him—things I shouldn't think about. I blinked. "Nothing."

Daemon rose slowly, holding my gaze. My whole body tensed as he neared and placed his hands on either side of me. Then he bent over the chair between us, resting his forehead against mine. He inhaled deeply and it came out in an unsteady rush. When he spoke, his voice was rough. "Do you know what I've been thinking about all day?"

With him, it was anyone's guess. "No."

His lips brushed the skin of my cheek. "Finding out if you look as good in striped socks as you do in reindeer ones."

"I do."

His head slanted and his smile was lazy, arrogant. Predatory. "I knew it."

I shouldn't let this happen. There was a whole slew of complications: his attitude, the connection between us, and my new kindergarten-age abilities. Funny, the fact Daemon was an alien was the complication I considered the least important.

And then there was Blake. That is, if Blake ever spoke to me again, which was debatable. But due to Daemon's interruption at dinner, I didn't get to talk to Blake. Irony was a bitch.

Knowing all of that, I still didn't pull away. And neither did he. Oh no, he was moving closer. His pupils started to glow and his breath seemed to have stalled in his chest.

"Do you have any idea what you do to me?" he asked gruffly.

"I'm not doing anything."

Daemon shifted his head just enough that our lips brushed once… and then twice before he increased the pressure. This kiss…it was nothing like the other times, which seemed to be angry and challenging. As if we'd kissed to punish each other. But this was gentle and soft, feather light. Infinitely tender. Like the kiss we'd shared in the clearing the night he'd healed me. Light swept through me as we kissed, but soon the kisses, they weren't enough. Not when a slow fire was burning under my skin—and under his.

Cupping my cheeks, he exhaled a soft groan, and his lips scorched mine as he deepened the kiss until we both were breathless from its intensity. Daemon moved as close as he could with the chair between us. Gripping his arms, I held onto him, wanting him closer. The chair prevented all but our lips and hands from touching. Frustrating.

Move, I ordered restlessly.

It trembled under my foot, and then the heavy oak chair slid out from under me, dodging our leaning bodies. Unprepared for the sudden void, Daemon lurched forward, and I was unable to carry the unexpected weight. I collapsed backward, bringing Daemon along with me.

The full contact of his body, flush against mine, sent my senses into chaotic overdrive. His tongue swept over mine as his fingers splayed across my cheeks. His hand slid down my side, gripping my hip as he urged me closer. The kisses slowed and his chest rose as he drank me in. With one last lingering exploration, he lifted his head and smiled down at me.

My heart skipped a beat as he hovered over me with an expression that tugged deep in my chest. He moved his fingers back up, along my cheek, trailing an invisible path to my chin.

"I didn't move that chair, Kitten."

"I know."

"I'm assuming you didn't like where it was?"

"It was in your way," I said. My hands were still curled around his arms.

"I can see that." Daemon smoothed a fingertip over the curve of my bottom lip before taking my hand, pulling me up. Letting go, he watched me carefully and waited. Waited for…

What had happened slowly sank in beyond the fog in my brain. I'd just kissed him. Again. And right after he'd taken over my date with another guy—the guy I should be kissing. Or not. I didn't know anything anymore.

"We can't keep doing this." My voice shook. "We—"

"We like each other," he said, stepping forward, grasping the edges of the table on either side of me. "And before you say it, we were attracted to each other before I healed you. You can't say that's not true."

He leaned in, his nose brushing my cheek. A shudder rolled through me. His lips pressed against the spot under my ear. "We need to stop fighting what we both want."

Air caught in my throat. I closed my eyes as his fingers inched down my turtleneck, clearing a path for his lips to meet my wildly beating pulse.

"It's not going to be easy," he said. "It wasn't three months ago and it won't be three months from now."

"Because of the rest of the Luxen?" My head tipped back, my thoughts swimming at his touch. There was something wicked in those hot little kisses he dropped all over my throat. "They'll outcast you. Like—"

"I know." He let go of my turtleneck and slid his hand around the nape of my neck as his body pressed against mine. "I've thought about the repercussions—it's all I've thought about."

Part of me had been yearning to hear him say that. A secret I'd kept close to my heart—the same heart that was jumping in my chest. I opened my eyes. His were glowing. "And this has nothing to do with the connection or Blake?"

"No," he said, and then sighed. "Yes, some of it has to do with that human, but it's about us. About what we feel for each other."

I was attracted to him on a level that was nearly painful. Being around him had every cell in my body burning, but this was *Daemon*. Caving to him was like saying the way he'd treated me was okay. And more importantly, it required blind faith in the theory that our feelings were real. And when they turned out not to be? It would be heartbreak, because I would seriously fall for him—fall more than I already had.

Wiggling down, I dipped under his arms. A dull ache shot through my injured leg as I backed up. "Is this like a 'I didn't want you until someone else wanted you' type of thing?"

Daemon leaned against the table. "That's not what this is."

"Then what is it, Daemon?" Tears of frustration built in my eyes. "Why now, when three months ago you couldn't stand to breathe the same air as me? It's the connection between us. It's the only thing that makes sense."

"Dammit. Do you think I don't regret acting like such a douche to you? I've apologized." He stood there, towering over me. "You don't get it. None of this is easy for me. And I know this is hard for you. You have a lot to deal with. But I have my sister and an entire race counting on me. I didn't want you to get close to me. I didn't want another person to care about, to worry about *losing*."

I sucked in a breath, and he went on. "It wasn't right how I acted. I know that. But I can do better than that—better than Benny."

"Blake." I sighed, limping away from him. "I have a lot in common with *Blake*. He likes that I read a lot—"

"I do, too," Daemon challenged.

"And he also blogs." Why did I feel like I was grasping at straws?

Daemon caught a piece of my hair and wrapped it around his finger. "I have nothing against the Internet."

I knocked his hand away. "And he doesn't like me because of some stupid alien connection or because some other guy likes me."

"I don't either." His eyes flashed. "You can't keep pretending. It's wrong. You'll break that boy's poor little human heart."

"No, I won't."

"You will, because you want me and I want you."

Deep down, I did want to be with him. And I wanted him to *want me*, not because we were the same atom split or because someone else liked me. Shaking my head, I went for the door. "You keep saying that…"

"What does that mean?" he demanded.

I squeezed my eyes shut briefly. "You say you want me, but that's not enough."

"I show you that I do, too."

Facing him, I cocked an eyebrow. "You do not."

"What was that?" Daemon gestured at the table, and I flushed. People eat at that table… "I think I showed you that I like you. I can do it again if you're not clear on what that was. And I've brought you a smoothie and a cookie to school."

"You stuck the cookie in *your* mouth!" I threw my hands up.

He smiled at that, like it was a good memory. "The table…"

"Humping my leg like a dog in heat every time I'm around you doesn't prove you like me, Daemon."

Daemon clamped his mouth shut, and I could tell he was fighting back laughter. "Actually, that's how I show people I like them."

"Oh. Fine. Whatever. None of this matters, Daemon."

"I'm not going anywhere, Kat. And I'm not giving up."

Not that I really believed he would. I reached for the door but he stopped me. "Do you know why I met you that day in the library?" he asked.

"What?" I faced him.

"The Friday you came back after being sick?" He ran a hand through his hair. "You were right. I picked the library because no one would see us together."

My mouth snapped shut and a sick feeling leached up my throat, causing it to burn. "You know what, I've always wondered if your ego was so big you didn't want to eat crow."

"And as always, you jump to the wrong assumption." His eyes pierced mine. "I didn't want Ash or Andrew to start giving you a bunch of crap because of me like they did with Dawson and Beth. So if you think I'm embarrassed of you or not ready to make my intentions very public, then you better get that idea out of your head. Because if that's what it takes, then it's on."

I stared at him. What in the hell was I supposed to say to that? Yeah, a part of me had believed it. How many people would kick a chick out of the cafeteria like he had and then start wooing her? Not many. And then I remembered the lump of spaghetti hanging off his ear, heard Daemon's amused laughter from the day that felt so long ago.

"Daemon…"

His smile was really starting to concern me. "I told you, Kitten. I like a challenge."

Chapter 14

Lesa practically pounced on me the moment I sat down in class. "Did you hear?"

Half asleep, I shook my head. I'd had a hell of a time going to bed last night after everything with Daemon. The fluttering my stomach was doing had to be a consequence of no breakfast.

"Simon is missing," Lesa said.

"Missing?" I didn't pay attention to the warm tingling on my neck or when Daemon sauntered into class. "Since when?"

"Since this past weekend." Lesa's eyes flicked up behind me and widened. "Wow. Now that's even more unexpected."

Something smelled sweet and familiar. Confused, I twisted around. A single rose in full bloom, a vibrant red, brushed against the tip of my nose. Tan fingers held the green stem. My eyes lifted.

Daemon stood there, his eyes glittering like green tinsel. He patted me on the nose with the rose again. "Good morning."

Dumbfounded, I stared at him.

"This is for you," he added when I didn't say anything.

Every single person in class was staring as my fingers wrapped around the cool, damp stem. Daemon sat down before I could say anything. I sat there, holding the rose until the teacher walked in and started calling off names.

Daemon's throaty chuckle warmed my chest.

Cheeks flaming, I placed the rose on my desk, and I honestly don't think I took my eyes off it. When Daemon had said he wasn't giving up, I had no idea he was going to go all balls-to-the-wall right off the bat. Why would he? Maybe he just wanted to have sex with me. And that had to be all, right? Hatred turned to lust. He'd been so against me months ago and now he wanted to be with me, going against the wishes of his race? Maybe he had a secret drug habit.

The light caught the moisture on the rose.

I looked up, catching Lesa's gaze. She mouthed, *Nice*.

Nice? It was nice and sweet and romantic and about a thousand other things that had my heart doing backflips. Sneaking a peek at Daemon over my shoulder, I watched him scribble along a blank piece of notebook paper. His brows were lowered in concentration. Thick, sooty lashes hid his eyes.

They lifted and his lips spread into a grin.

I was in so much trouble.

• • •

Cops were everywhere over the next couple of days, asking students and teachers questions about Simon. Daemon and I ended up being some of the first people they talked to. As if we were a modern-day Bonnie and Clyde, plotting to take out jocks everywhere. Well, the fact that Daemon had beaten the crap out of Simon didn't look good. But the cops didn't treat us like suspects. After my first and only questioning with them in the principal's office, I determined that two of the state troopers were aliens. And I also got the distinct impression they suspected I knew their secret.

I wondered if someone had let the alien out of the bag. Ash was the most likely suspect, especially since Daemon had become the bearer of gifts. One day he brought me a pumpkin spiced latte—my favorite—then an egg and bacon breakfast croissant, glazed doughnuts on Thursday, and a lily on Friday. He did nothing to hide his intentions.

Part of me actually felt bad for Ash. She'd spent her whole life expecting to be with Daemon. I couldn't even imagine what she was thinking—if she was mourning the final downfall of their relationship or if it was just that she'd lost something she'd believed was hers. If I ended up being found in a ditch somewhere, my bets would be on Ash or Andrew. Adam had left the dark side and was now sitting with Dee at lunch. They literally couldn't keep their hands off each other…or our food.

Each night, Daemon soaked up my time. Keeping an eye on me was what he claimed to be doing, waiting to see if I was attacked by a chair again. In his world, that translated into time suckage that involved every possible way he could get close to me. Like, really, will-breaking, body-tingling close.

Blake…well, Blake spoke to me in class. He texted a few times at night, and I always had to wait until Daemon decided to leave before I could call him back, but there had been no talk of another date.

Daemon had been successful with the scare tactics, which he was unabashedly proud of.

Saturday afternoon, I was in a marathon review-writing spree when someone knocked on my front door. Finishing up my last sentence— *Mesmerizing debut, heart-stopping action, and swoon-worthy romance,* The Hidden Circle *is a forget-your-homework, don't-feed-your-kids, and quit-your-job one-sit read*—before shutting my laptop.

As I neared the door, I felt the tingling on my neck. Daemon. I tripped over the upturned corner of the area rug and took a second to straighten the ribbed sweater that had ridden up before I snatched open the front door.

Familiar feelings of anxiety slid through me. What did he have up his sleeve today? In other words, how much more could he possibly complicate my life? My no-kiss policy had remained strong since Monday. But strangely, even as innocent and clandestine as our meetings were, there was still a level of intimacy that couldn't be denied.

Daemon was changing.

I was used to the sarcastic and rude Daemon. In an odd way, that version was easier to deal with. We could trade insults all day. But this Daemon…this one who wouldn't give up was kind and gentle, funny and—dear God—*thoughtful.*

Daemon waited on the porch, his hands shoved deep into the pockets of his jeans. He had been gazing into the distance but pivoted around the moment I pushed open the door.

He brushed past me and into the hallway. The scent of him, a mixture of the outdoors and sandalwood, followed. It was a heady aroma, all completely his.

"You look nice today," he commented unexpectedly.

I glanced down at my gray hoodie and tucked a tangled strand of hair behind my ear. "Uh, thanks." I cleared my throat. "So…what's up?"

His excuse for spending time with me was always the vague "Watching out for you," so I wasn't expecting anything different today. "I just wanted to see you."

"Oh." Well, hell…

He chuckled deeply. "I thought we could take a walk. It's nice outside."

Glancing back at my laptop, I debated. Spending time with him wasn't something I should be doing. It just encouraged his…not-so-bad behavior.

"I'll behave myself," he said. "I promise."

I laughed at that. "All right, let's go."

It was brisk outside, nowhere near as cold as it would become once the sun set. Instead of heading toward the woods, he steered me in the direction of his SUV. "Exactly where are we going to take a walk?"

"Outdoors," he said dryly.

"Well, I think I figured that part out."

"You ask a lot of questions, you know."

"I've been told I'm very inquisitive."

He leaned forward and whispered, "I think I figured that part out."

I made a face at him, but I was intrigued. I climbed into the passenger's seat. "Have you heard anything about Simon?" I asked after he'd backed out of the driveway. "I haven't."

"I haven't either."

An array of golden, red, and brown leaves blurred as Daemon flew down the highway. "Do you think an Arum had anything to do with his disappearance?"

Daemon shook his head. "I don't think so. I haven't seen any, but we can't be too sure."

An Arum taking Simon wouldn't make any sense, but kids around here didn't disappear without it having something to do with the Luxen and Arum. I glanced out the window at the familiar scenery. It didn't take me long to realize where we were going. Confused, I watched Daemon pull the SUV off the road and park along the entrance to the field the kids partied in.

The same place we'd fought Baruck.

"Why here?" I asked, climbing out. Dead leaves of various colors littered the ground. With each step, my feet sunk an inch or two through the leaves. For a while, the only sound we heard was the rustling of our feet wading through the colorful sea of leaves.

"This place might hold a lot of residual energy from our fight and from Baruck's death." He stepped around a fallen tree limb. "Watch out, the branches are scattered everywhere."

I moved around one particularly gnarly-looking one. "This might sound messed up, but I've wanted to come back here. I don't know why. Crazy, huh?"

"No," he said quietly. "It makes sense to me."

"Is it the whole energy thing?"

"It's what's left over." Daemon bent and pushed another fallen limb out of the way. "I want to see if I feel anything. If the DOD has been out here to check it out, it might be good to be in the know."

We walked the rest of the way in silence. I was following slightly behind him, careful of the rough terrain. I felt a peculiar stirring in me as soon as it came into view. The ground was covered in leaves but the trees were still bent, looking even more grotesque as they twisted toward the ground. I stopped at the edge and tried to find the spot where Baruck had last stood.

I pushed the dead foliage with my foot. Soon, the scarred ground came into view. The soil seemed to remember what had happened that night and refused to let go of the memory.

This spot was like a sick gravesite.

"The ground will never heal," Daemon said softly from behind me. "I don't know why, but it took on his essence and nothing will grow from this spot." He took over, pushing back the leaves until the area was uncovered completely. "Killing at first used to bother me."

I tore my eyes away from the burned patch of ground. What little sun that peeked through the clouds caught the auburn tint in his dark hair.

Daemon smiled tightly. "I didn't like it, taking a life. I still don't. A life is a life."

"It's something you have to do. You can't change it. It only wreaks havoc on you to dwell. It bothers me knowing that I've killed…two of them, but—"

"You aren't wrong for what you did. Never think that." His eyes met mine for a second, and he cleared his throat. "I don't feel anything."

I shoved my hands into the front pocket of my hoodie, curving them around my cell phone. "Do you think the DOD found anything?"

"I don't know." He crossed the small distance between us, stopping when I had to tilt my head back to see him. "Depends on if they're using equipment I'm not familiar with."

"And if they are, what does that mean? Is it something to be worried about?"

"I don't think so, not even if the levels of energy are higher."

He reached out, smoothing back a strand of hair that had escaped my ponytail. "It doesn't really tell them anything. Have you been experiencing any outbursts recently?"

"No," I said, not wanting him to worry needlessly. Today I'd blown the light in my room. And I'd moved my bed about three feet.

His hand lingered on my cheek for a moment longer, and then he captured my hand, bringing it to his lips, placing the lightest kiss against the center of my palm. A hot shiver went up my arm. Peering through his dark lashes, he burned me with one smoldering look.

My lips parted and my heart fluttered in my chest like the many leaves that fell to the ground around us. "Did you bring me out here just to get me completely alone?"

"That may have been a part of my master plan." Daemon's head lowered and his hair fell forward, brushing my cheek. The slant of his mouth tilted and an exhilarating heartbeat later, his lips pressed against mine and my heart swelled.

I jerked back, breathing heavily. "No kissing," I whispered.

His fingers tightened around mine. "I'm trying not to."

"Then try harder." I slipped my hand free and took a step back, shoving my hands back into the pocket of my hoodie. "I think we should head home."

He sighed. "Whatever you want."

I nodded. We started back to the car in silence. I stared at the ground, at war with what I wanted and what I needed. Daemon couldn't be both.

"So I was thinking," he said after a few moments.

I glanced at him warily. "About what?"

"We should do something. Together. Outside of your house and not just walking around." He stared straight ahead. "We should go out to dinner or maybe a movie."

My stupid heart started jumping again. "Are you asking me out?"

He laughed under his breath. "That's what it sounds like."

The trees were starting to thin out. Large bales of hay came into view. "You don't want to take me out on a date."

"Why do you keep telling me what I don't want?" Curiosity colored his tone.

"Because you can't," I told him. "You can't want any of this with me, not really. Maybe with Ash—"

"I don't want Ash." His features hardened as he stopped, facing me. "If I wanted her, I'd be with her. But I'm not. She's not *who* I want."

"Neither am I. You can't honestly tell me that you'd risk every Luxen around here turning their backs on you for me."

Daemon shook his head in disbelief. "And you have got to stop assuming you know what I want and what I would do."

I started walking again. "It's just the challenge and the connection, Daemon. Whatever you feel for me isn't real."

"That's ridiculous," he spat.

"How can you be sure?"

"Because I know." Daemon appeared in front of me, eyes narrowed. He thumped his hand off his chest, directly above his heart. "Because I know what I feel in here. And I'm not the type of person to run from anything, no matter how hard it is. I'd rather face-plant against a brick wall than live for the rest of my life wondering what could've been. And you know what? I didn't think you were the type to run, either. Maybe I was wrong."

Stunned, I pulled my hands out and brushed my hair back. Knots formed in my stomach—the good warm and twisty kind. "I don't run."

"You don't? Because that's what you're doing," he argued. "You pretend what you feel for me isn't real or doesn't exist. And I know damn well you don't feel anything for Bobby."

"Blake," I corrected him automatically. Walking around him, I headed for the car. "I don't want to talk—"

We came to a standstill at the edge of the woods. Two giant black SUVs were parked on either side of Daemon's, blocking him in. Two men stood beside one, dressed in black suits. Unease rolled through me like a chilled, dark wave. Daemon moved in front of me, hands at his sides. Tension tightened his muscles. I didn't have to ask to know who they were.

The DOD was here.

Chapter 15

One of the Suits stepped forward, eyes trained on Daemon. "Hello, Mr. Black and Miss Swartz."

"Hey, Lane," Daemon answered in a monotone voice, apparently knowing the one guy. "I wasn't expecting you today."

Unsure of what I should do, I nodded and remained quiet, trying to make myself as small as possible.

"We got into town a little early and saw your car." Lane smiled, and it gave me the creeps.

The other Suit's eyes bounced to me. "What were you guys doing out here?"

"There was a party here last night, and we were looking for her cell phone." Daemon grinned at me. "She lost it and we're still looking for it"

The cell phone felt like it was burning a hole in my pocket now.

"So I can meet you guys later," Daemon continued. "Once we find the…"

The passenger door of one of the Expeditions opened and a woman stepped out. She had icy blond hair pulled back in a tight bun, revealing sharp features that would've been pretty on someone who didn't look like she might tase me. "Underage drinking?" The woman smiled. It reminded me of the kind painted on Barbie. Fake. Plastic. Wrong somehow.

"We weren't drinking," I said, going along with everything. "He knows better. His parents are like mine. They'd kill him."

"Well, I was hoping to catch up with you, Daemon, and we could get an early…dinner." Lane motioned toward his Expedition. "We only have a few hours. I hate to cut your cell phone search-and-rescue short."

For a moment, I thought he'd protest, but he turned to me. "It's okay. I can take her home and meet up with you guys."

"That won't be necessary," the woman cut in. "We can take her back, and you guys can catch up."

My pulse was all over the place, and I glanced at Daemon for help. A muscle popped in his jaw as he stood by, silent and helpless. I knew then there was nothing he could do. Forcing a smile, I nodded. "That's cool with me. I just hope it's not going out of your way."

Daemon's right hand clenched.

"It's not out of the way," she replied. "We love the roads back here. Fall colors and all. Ready?"

I looked at Daemon as I headed toward the SUV. His hawklike gaze followed my steps. I murmured my thanks as she opened the back door. Getting in, I seriously hoped I didn't end up on a missing person's flyer.

Daemon was getting into his own car, but he stopped and glanced back at me. I'd swear I heard his voice in my head. *It'll be okay.* But it couldn't have been him. Maybe it was wishful thinking, because for a moment, fear trickled like ice water through my veins. What if this was the last time I saw him—saw anyone? What if they'd discovered I knew the truth?

What if they knew what I could do?

Now I wished I'd let Daemon kiss me back there. Because if I was going to disappear, then at least my last memory would've given me some sort of completion.

I forced myself to breathe slowly as I raised my hand, wiggling my fingers at him before the woman shut the door.

She climbed into the passenger seat and twisted around. "Seat belt?"

Hands shaking and sweaty, I fastened myself in. The man behind the wheel said nothing, but the hairs on his mustache kept blowing as if he were breathing heavily. "Um, thanks for the ride."

"It's no problem. My name is Nancy Husher," she said, and then nodded at the driver. "This is Brian Vaughn. He's known Daemon's family for several years. I'm just along for the ride."

I'm sure you are. "Oh…that's really nice."

Nancy nodded. "Daemon is like one of Brian's own, isn't he?"

"Yes," agreed Brian. "It's not often that we see him with a girl. He must think a lot of you to help look for your cell phone."

My eyes darted between the two. "I guess so. He and his sister are really nice."

"Dee is a doll. How close are you with them?" Brian asked.

I was being interrogated. Great. "Well, since we're the only ones who live on the same street, we're kind of close."

Nancy glanced out the front window. Luckily, I recognized that we were heading back toward Ketterman. "And Daemon? How close are you with him?"

My mouth dried. "I'm not sure I'm following the question."

"I thought you said he was dating someone, Brian?"

"Ash Thompson," he answered.

Like they didn't know her name, but hey, I could play along. "Yeah, I think they broke up during the summer, but that doesn't have anything to do with us."

"It doesn't?" Nancy asked.

I shook my head, deciding a little bit of the truth couldn't hurt. "We're just friends. Most of the time we don't really even get along."

"But you just said he was nice."

Shit. Face blank, I shrugged. "He can be nice when he wants."

A single pale eyebrow arched. "And what about Dee?"

"She's awesome." I glanced out the window. This was the longest trip ever. I was going to have a heart attack before it was over. There was something about Nancy, more than just the obvious, that made me squirm.

"And what do you think of their parents?"

I frowned. These were really weird questions to be asking, given the fact they didn't know I knew anything. "I don't know. They're parents."

Brian laughed. Was this dude real? It sounded a bit mechanical.

"What I meant is, do you like them?" she asked.

"I don't see them often. Just coming and going. I really haven't talked to them." I met her eyes, willing her to believe me. "I don't hang out at their house often, so I don't run into them."

She held my stare a few more moments and then turned around in her seat. No one spoke after that. Sweat gathered along my brow. When Brian turned onto my road, I almost cried in relief. The car coasted to a stop, and I was already unbuckling my seat belt.

"Thanks for the ride," I said hastily.

"No problem," Nancy said. "Take care, Miss Swartz."

The tiny hairs on my body rose. I opened the door and climbed out.

And just then, with the worst case of bad timing in the world, my cell phone went off in my pocket, blaring like an alarm. *Holy crap…* My eyes flicked up to Nancy's.

She smiled.

• • •

"I'm sure he's okay," Dee said again. "Katy, they do this all the time. They stop by, track us down, and act all kinds of weird."

I stopped in front of her TV, wringing my hands. Fear had rooted deep inside my gut from the moment they'd deposited me in front of my house. "You don't understand. He told them we were out there looking for my cell phone and that I'd lost it. And then it rang in front of them."

"I know, but what's the big deal?" Adam sat on the couch, kicking his legs up. "There's no way they'd suspect you know anything."

But they knew we were lying, and they all seemed way too smart to miss that. And it wasn't like I could tell Dee what we'd really been doing out there. Not that she hadn't asked. I'd made up some lame excuse about wanting to see the spot where he'd killed Baruck.

Dee didn't look entirely convinced.

I started pacing again. "But that was hours ago, guys. It's almost ten."

"Honey, he's fine." She got up, clasping my hands. "They were here first and then went looking for him. All they are doing is being annoying and asking questions."

"But why would it take so long with him?"

"Because they like to give him crap and he likes to give it back," Adam said, floating the remote control over to his hand. "It's like a parasitic relationship between the two."

I laughed weakly. "But what if they find out I know? What will they do to him?"

Dee's brows knitted. "They aren't going to find out, Katy. And if they did, you should be more worried about yourself than him."

Nodding, I pulled my hands free and started wearing a path in the carpet again. They didn't understand. I'd seen it in Nancy's eyes. She knew we were lying, but she'd let me go. Why?

"Katy," Dee began slowly. "I'm surprised that you're so concerned about Daemon's welfare."

A flush swept over my cheeks. I didn't want to look too closely at why I was so concerned. "Just because he's...he's Daemon...doesn't mean I want anything bad to happen to him."

Watching me closely, she arched one brow. "Are you sure it's not more than that?"

I halted. "Of course."

"He's been bringing you stuff to school." Adam leaned his head back, eyes narrowed. "I've never seen him act like that with anyone. Not even my sister."

"And you guys have been spending a lot of time together," Dee added.

"So? You've been spending a lot of time with Adam." As soon as it left my mouth, I realized how stupid that was.

Dee smiled, eyes glittering. "Yeah, and we've been having sex. Lots of it."

Adam's eyes went wide. "Wow, Dee, put it all out there like that."

She shrugged. "It's true."

"Oh, geez, that's not what's happening here."

Moving to the couch, she sat beside a red-faced Adam. "Then what is happening?"

Crap. I hated lying to her. "He's been helping me study."

"For what?"

"Trig," I said quickly. "I suck at math."

Dee laughed. "Okay. If you say so, but I hope you know that if you and my brother have something going on, I'm not going to be mad."

I stared at her.

"And part of me understands why you two would keep it hidden. You guys are known for your word war and everything else." She frowned. "But I just want you to know that I'm okay with it. It's crazy and I hope Daemon is prepared for what's going to happen, but I want him happy. And if you make him happy—"

"Okay. I got you." So not a conversation I wanted to have with Dee in front of Adam.

She smiled. "I wish you'd reconsider doing Thanksgiving dinner with us. You know you're welcome."

"I seriously doubt Ash and Andrew would be happy with *me* at the table."

"Who cares what they think?" Adam rolled his eyes. "I don't. Neither does Daemon. And you shouldn't either."

"You guys are like a family. I'm not—"

Tingles spread over my neck. Without thinking, I spun around and raced across the room. Throwing open the door, I rushed out into the cold night air.

I didn't even think.

Daemon had reached the top step when I rushed him, wrapping my arms around his neck, squeezing him tight.

He seemed stunned for a second, and then his arms swept around my waist. For several moments, neither of us spoke. We didn't need to. I just wanted to hold him—for him to hold me. Maybe it was the connection wrapping us together. Maybe it was something infinitely deeper. At that moment, I didn't care.

"Whoa there, Kitten, what's going on?"

Burrowing closer, I drawled in a deep breath. "I thought the DOD carted you off to some lab to keep you in a cage."

"Cage?" He laughed a bit unsteadily. "No. No cages. They just wanted to talk. It took longer than I thought. Everything's okay."

Dee cleared her throat. "Ahem."

Stiffening, I realized what I was doing. Oh, so not cool. Disentangling my arms and wiggling out from his, I backed up and blushed. "I…I was just excited."

"Yeah, I'd say you were," Dee said, grinning like an idiot.

Daemon was staring at me like he'd just won the lottery. "I kind of like this level of excitement. Makes me think of—"

"Daemon!" both of us shouted.

"What?" He grinned, tousling Dee's hair. "I was only suggesting—"

"We know what you were suggesting." Dee darted out from underneath his hand. "And I really want to keep my food down tonight." She smiled at me. "See. I told you. Daemon is fine."

I could see that. He was also smokin' hot, but back to the whole point. "They didn't suspect anything?"

Daemon shook his head. "Nothing out of the norm, but they're always paranoid." He paused, his eyes searching mine in the dim light of the porch. "Really, you don't need to worry. You're safe."

It wasn't me I'd been worried about, and oh boy, that was bad. My sense of self-preservation was messed up. And I honestly needed to get out of here. "All right, I need to go home."

"Kat…"

"No." I waved him off, starting down the steps. "I really need to go home. Blake called and I need to call him back."

"Boris can wait," Daemon said.

"Blake," I said, stopping on the sidewalk. Dee had wisely gone inside, but Daemon had moved to the edge of the porch. My thoughts, my emotions, felt overly exposed when I met his eyes. "They asked me a lot of questions—especially the lady."

"Nancy Husher," he said, frowning. A second later, he was standing before me. "She's apparently a big deal within the DOD. They wanted to know what went down Halloween weekend. I gave them the Daemon-edited-version."

"Did they believe you?"

He nodded. "Hook, line, and sinker."

I shivered. "But it wasn't you, Daemon. It was me. Or it was all of us."

"I know, but they don't know that." His voice lowered as he cupped my cheek. "They won't ever know that."

My eyes closed. The warmth of his hand eased some of the fear. "It's not me I'm worried about. If they think you blew a satellite out of orbit, they could see you as a threat."

"Or they could just think I'm that awesome."

"It's not funny," I whispered.

"I know." Daemon moved closer, and before I knew it, I was in his embrace again. "Don't worry about me or Dee. We can handle the DOD. Trust me."

I let him hold me for a couple of moments, soaking up his warmth, but then I slipped free. "I didn't tell that lady anything. And the damn phone rang as I was getting out of the car. She knew we were lying about why we were there."

"They're not going to care about us lying over the phone. They probably think we were out there getting it on or something. You don't need to worry, Kat."

Anxiety didn't fade. It snaked through me. There had been something about Nancy. Calculating. As if a pop quiz had been sprung on us and we'd failed. I lifted my eyes, meeting his. "I'm glad you're okay."

He smiled. "I know."

I could have stood there staring at his sparkling eyes all night, but something urged me to run as far away from him as quickly as I could. Something bad was going to come from all of this.

I turned and walked away.

Chapter 16

As expected, I spent the better part of Thanksgiving poking around the house alone. Mom really got shafted, pulling a double shift that took her out of the house from around noon Thursday until noon on Friday.

I could've gone next door. Both Dee and Daemon had invited me, but it didn't feel right busting up their alien Thanksgiving. And from the amount of creepy peeping I was doing from my window every time I heard a car door close outside, I knew everyone showing up was secretly an ET. Even Ash arrived with her brothers, looking like she was going to a funeral rather than a dinner party.

Part of me didn't like that she was there. Yeah, I was jealous. Stupid.

But I'd made the right call by not going.

I was an anxious wreck. Today alone, I'd tipped over the coffee table, shattered three glasses, and blew a lightbulb. Being with people probably wasn't a good idea, but it would've been nice to lose myself in the holiday festivities for a little while. The only good thing was the fact my head didn't feel like it was being ripped apart after the shenanigans.

Around six in the evening, I felt that now-oh-so-familiar tingle on the back of my neck right before Daemon knocked. A ball of confusing feelings unfurled inside me as I hurried to the door.

The first thing I noticed was the large box beside him, and then the scent of roasted turkey and yams.

"Hey," he said, holding a stack of covered plates. "Happy Thanksgiving."

I blinked slowly. "Happy Thanksgiving."

"You going to invite me in?" He held up the plates, wiggling them. "I come bearing gifts in the form of food."

I stepped aside.

Still grinning, he came in and waved his free hand. The box lifted off the porch and trailed behind him like a dog. It landed just inside the foyer. As I shut the door, I caught sight of Ash and Andrew climbing into their car. Neither of them looked over.

A lump formed in my throat as I turned to Daemon.

"I brought a little of everything." He headed toward the kitchen. "There's turkey, yams, cranberry sauce, mashed potatoes, green-bean casserole, some kind of apple crisp thing and pumpkin—Kitten? Are you coming?"

Peeling myself away from the front door, I went into the kitchen. He was setting up the table, uncovering the dishes. I...I didn't know what to think.

Daemon raised his hands and two depression glass candleholders Mom never used floated to the table. Candles came next, and with a wave of his hand, their wicks sparked tiny flames.

The lump grew, nearly choking me.

Dinnerware and glasses came from several opened drawers. Mom's wine flew out of the fridge, pouring into two crystal flutes while Daemon stood in the middle of everything. It was like a scene straight out of *Beauty and the Beast*. I kept waiting for a teapot to start singing.

"And after dinner, I have another surprise for you."

"You do?" I whispered.

He nodded. "But you've got to join me for dinner first."

I shuffled to the table and sat, watching him with eyes that were blurry. He made me a plate and then sat beside me. I cleared my throat. "Daemon, I…I don't know what to say, but thank you."

"Thanks aren't necessary," he said. "You didn't want to come over, which I understand, but you shouldn't be alone."

Lowering my gaze before he could see the tears gathering in my eyes, I grabbed the flute and downed the bitter-tasting white wine. When I looked up, his brows were raised.

"Lush," he murmured.

I grinned. "Maybe—for today."

He nudged me with his knee under the table. "Dig in before it gets cold."

The food was divine. Any doubts I had about Dee's cooking abilities vanished. Throughout our little makeshift dinner, I drank another glass of wine. I also ate everything that Daemon put on my plate, including second helpings.

And by the time I stabbed the pumpkin pie with my fork, I was either a little tipsy or I was starting to believe that there was more than just the connection propelling him. That maybe he did care for me, because I was able to fight it—sort of—and I know damn well that Daemon could if he wanted to.

Maybe he just didn't want to.

Cleaning up dinner was a strangely intimate experience. Our elbows brushed several times. Amiable silence descended as we washed the dishes, side by side. My cheeks felt flushed. My thoughts were way too giddy.

Too much wine.

I followed Daemon into the foyer afterward. He moved the large box to the living room without touching it. It sort of jingled. Sitting on the edge of the couch, I folded my hands and waited, having no clue what he was up to.

Daemon opened the box, reached inside, and pulled out a green-needled branch and poked me with it. "I think we have a Christmas tree to put up. I know it's not during the parade, but I think Charlie Brown's

Thanksgiving special is on, and, well, that's not too bad."

That was it. The lump in my throat was back, but there was no stopping it this time. Jumping from the couch, I raced out of the room. Tears formed, then slid down my cheeks. Emotion clogged my throat as I wiped under my eyes.

Daemon appeared in front of me, blocking the staircase. His eyes were wide, pupils luminous. I tried to turn away, but he quickly enveloped me in his strong arms. "I didn't do this to make you cry, Kat."

"I know," I sniffled. "It's just …"

"It's just what?" He cupped my cheeks, his thumbs brushing away the tears. My skin tingled from the contact. "Kitten?"

"I don't think you know how much…something like this means to me." I took a deep breath, but the stupid tears kept falling. "I haven't done this since—since Dad was alive. And I'm sorry to cry, because I'm not sad. I just didn't expect this."

"It's okay." Daemon tugged me forward, and I went. He wrapped his arms around me, holding me close as I buried my face into the front of his shirt. "I get it. Good tears and all."

There was something warm and right about being in his arms. And I wanted to deny it, but for the first time, I stopped—I just *stopped*. Even if Daemon saw me as one giant Rubik's Cube he had to crack or if it was the healing mojo, it didn't matter. Not right now.

I grabbed a handful of his shirt and held on. He may have thought he knew how much this meant to me, but he really didn't. Daemon would never know.

I lifted my head and reached up, clasping his smooth cheeks. With his help, I brought his lips to mine and kissed him. It was a quick and innocent kiss, but I felt the zing all the way to my toes. I pulled back, breathless. "Thank you. I really mean it. Thank you."

He brushed the backs of his fingers over my cheek, smoothing the last of my tears away. "Don't let anyone know about my sweet side. I have a reputation to keep up."

I laughed. "All right, let's do this."

Trimming a Christmas tree with an alien was a different experience. He moved the recliner out from in front of the window with a jerk of his chin. Bulbs hung in the air along with twinkling lights that *weren't* plugged in.

We laughed. A lot. Every so often I'd get choked up when I thought of Mom's face tomorrow afternoon. She'd be happy, I thought.

Daemon dropped silvery tinsel on my head while I plucked a bulb out of the air. "Thanks," I said.

"It kind of fits you."

The scent of artificial pine filled the living room. The holiday spirit woke inside me like a slumbering giant. I grinned at Daemon and held up a bulb that was so green it almost matched his eyes. I decided it was going to be *his* bulb.

I placed it right under the twinkling star.

It was almost midnight by the time we finished. Sitting on the couch, thigh against thigh, we stared at our masterpiece. The tree was a little tinsel-heavy on one side, but it was perfect. A rainbow of colored lights shimmered. Glass bulbs glimmered.

"I love it," I said.

"Yeah, it's pretty good." He leaned in to me, yawning. "Dee put up the tree this morning. She has to have everything the same color, but I think our tree looks better. It's like a disco ball."

Our tree. I smiled, liking the sound of that.

He bumped me with his shoulder. "You know, I had fun doing this."

"I did, too."

Daemon's lashes lowered. Man, I'd kill for a set of those babies. "It's late."

"I know." I hesitated. "You want to stay?"

A single brow arched.

That hadn't come out right. "I don't mean *that*."

"Not that I'd complain if you did." His gaze dropped. "Not at all."

I rolled my eyes, but my tummy was coiling tight. Why had I offered for him to stay? His assumption wasn't too far off. Daemon didn't strike me as the type to dig PG-13 slumber parties. I remembered the last and only time we'd shared a bed. Flushing, I stood. I didn't want him to leave, but I didn't…I didn't know what I wanted.

"I'm going to get changed," I said.

"Need help?"

"Wow. You're so chivalrous, Daemon."

His smile widened, flashing deep dimples. "Well, the experience would be mutually beneficial. I promise."

No doubt it would be.

"Stay," I ordered, then hurried upstairs.

I quickly changed into a pair of sleep shorts and a pink thermal. Not the sexiest sleepwear, but as I washed my face and brushed my teeth, I decided it was the best choice. Anything else would give Daemon ideas. Hell, a paper sack would encourage him.

I left my bathroom and stopped. Daemon had *not* stayed. My smile slipped from my face.

He was standing by the window, his back to me. "I got bored."

"I wasn't even gone five minutes."

"I have a short attention span." He glanced back at me, eyes glittering. "Nice shorts."

I grinned. There were stars on my shorts. "What are you doing up here?"

"You said I could stay." He faced me, his gaze drifting to the bed. The room suddenly seemed too small, the bed even smaller. "I didn't think you meant staying on the couch."

Now I wasn't even sure what I'd meant. I sighed. What was I doing?

Crossing the room, he stopped in front of me. "I'm not going to bite."

"That's good."

"Unless you want me to," he added with a devilish grin.

"Nice," I muttered, side-stepping him. Space was definitely needed. Not that it did much good. Heart pounding, I watched him kick off his shoes and then whip off his shirt. He moved to the button on his jeans.

My eyes widened. "What—what are you doing?"

"Getting ready for bed."

"But you're getting naked!"

He arched his brow. "I do have boxers on. What? Do you expect me to sleep in my jeans?"

"You did last time." I felt the need to fan myself.

Daemon laughed. "Actually, I had pajama bottoms on."

And he'd had a shirt on, but who was keeping track? I could've told him to leave, but I turned away, pretending to be engrossed with a book on my desk. Chills shot straight to my core when I heard the bed groan under his weight. Taking a shallow breath, I turned around. He was in bed, arms folded behind his head, an innocent look on his face. "This was a bad idea," I whispered.

"It was probably the smartest idea you've ever had."

I rubbed my palms on my hips. "It's going to take a lot more than Thanksgiving dinner and a Christmas tree to get laid."

"Damn. There goes my whole plan."

Flustered, infuriated, and thrilled, I stared at him. So many emotions couldn't be possible. My head was spinning as I stalked over to my side of the bed—oh my God, when had we developed *sides*?— and quickly slid under the covers. I did *not* want to know if he'd left the jeans on or not. "Can you turn off the light?" Darkness descended without him moving. Several moments passed. "That's a handy ability."

"It is."

My eyes focused on the pale light peeking through the curtains. "Maybe one day I can be just as lazy as you and turn off lights without moving."

"That's something to aspire to."

I relaxed a fraction of an inch and smiled. "God, you're so modest."

"Modesty is for saints and losers. I'm neither."

"Wow, Daemon, just wow."

He rolled onto his side, his breath stirring the hair along my neck. My heart leaped into my throat. "I can't believe you haven't kicked me out yet."

"Same here," I murmured.

Daemon weaseled his way closer, and, oh yeah, he'd gotten rid of his jeans. His bare legs brushed mine, and my heart rate spiked. "I really didn't mean to make you cry earlier."

I flipped onto my back and stared up at him. He was raised on one elbow. Silky locks fell into his shining eyes. "I know. The whole thing you did, it was sort of amazing."

"I just didn't like the idea of you being alone."

Slow and steady breaths raised my chest. Like when he'd hugged me downstairs and I'd kissed him, I wanted to stop thinking. Impossible when his eyes held the intensity of a thousand suns.

Daemon reached out, brushing a strand of hair off my cheek with the tips of his fingers. Electricity shimmered through me. There was no denying the attraction—the pull that didn't want to let either of us go. My gaze was fixed on his lips like an addict. Memories of the way they'd felt seared me. All of this was crazy. Inviting him to stay, getting in bed with him, and thinking what I was about him. Crazy. Exciting.

I swallowed. "We should go to sleep."

His hand palmed my cheek, and I wanted to touch him. I wanted to be closer. "We should," he agreed.

Lifting my hand, I brushed my fingers over his lips. They were pillowy soft yet firm. Intoxicating. Daemon's eyes flared, and my stomach hollowed. He shifted his head closer and his lips brushed the corner of mine. His hands slid from my face and down my neck, and when he dipped his head again, his lips brushed over the tip of my nose. And then he kissed me. A slow-burning, toe-curling kiss that left me aching for so, so much more. I felt like I was spinning into that kiss, falling into him.

He pulled back with a groan and settled beside me, wrapping an arm around my waist. "Good night, Kitten."

Heart pounding, I let out a long sigh. "That's all?"

Daemon laughed. "That's all...for now."

Biting my lip, I willed my heart to slow down. It seemed to take forever. Then finally, I wiggled closer until he snaked an arm under my head. I turned onto my side, resting my cheek against his upper arm. Our breaths mingled as we lay there, staring at each other silently until his eyes drifted shut. For the second time that night, I admitted that maybe I'd been wrong about Daemon. Maybe I didn't even know myself. And there was no wine to blame this time.

I drifted off to sleep wondering what he meant by "for now."

Chapter 17

When Blake texted me and asked to meet him at the Smoke Hole Diner Friday evening, I didn't know what to do. It seemed…wrong to have an early dinner with him when last night I'd slept in Daemon's arms.

My cheeks flushed. We didn't do anything other than that one kiss, but it was just as intimate, if not more. My feelings for him were all over the place and what he did for me yesterday, with the dinner and the Christmas tree, meant something I couldn't ignore.

But I also couldn't ignore Blake. He was my friend, and after last night, I needed to make sure he didn't expect anything more than that—a friendship. Because somewhere over the course of a day, even though I hadn't figured out things with Daemon, I did realize that he was right about one thing.

I was using Blake.

He was uncomplicated and harmless. Totally a nice guy and dateable, but my feelings were lukewarm for the surfer. Nothing like how I felt for Daemon. And it wasn't right. If Blake did like me, I couldn't string him along anymore.

So I texted him back and said okay, hoping this wouldn't be the most awkward dinner of my life.

The weather had changed the moment the sun went behind the mountains. The comfortable autumn air was replaced by near-frigid winds, and the sky took on a constant gloomy, overcast presence.

I pulled into the closest parking space to the door of the diner. The wind had screamed the whole trip, and I dreaded getting out of my warm car. I couldn't help but notice that the space of glass above the restaurant's business hours held a picture of Simon on it. I grimaced, threw open the door, and hurried into the surprisingly crowded restaurant.

Blake was sitting near the fireplace. He stood and smiled when he saw me. "Hey, glad you made it."

When he reached out as if he wanted to hug me, I pretended not to notice and sat. "I can't believe how cold it is. How was your trip?"

Frowning slightly, he took his seat and methodically straightened his silverware around a pretend plate. "It wasn't bad. Not very exciting." When the cutlery was positioned just so, he glanced up. "How was your break?"

"Not very different than yours." I paused, recognizing a few kids from school. They were clustered together, drinking sodas and eating a large oven pizza. Chad—the boy Lesa was dating—waved at me and I waved back. "But I'm not ready for it to be over."

We paused while a plump waitress took our orders. I got a soda and a basket of fries and he ordered soup.

"Hopefully this doesn't end up all over me," he joked.

I cringed. Not likely, since Daemon wasn't here…yet. "I really am sorry about all that."

Blake tapped his straw off my hand before peeling the paper from around the plastic. "It's not a big deal. Stuff happens."

I nodded, studying the steamed-over windows. He cleared his throat, frowning again as his eyes narrowed on a middle-aged man near the bar who was looking around nervously. "I think that guy's about to skip out on his bill."

"Huh, really?"

Blake nodded. "And he thinks he's getting away with it. He has so many times before."

In stunned silence, I watched the man take one last drink and stand without getting his check.

"Someone is always watching," Blake added with a slight smile.

A couple sitting behind the man, both in flannel shirts and well-worn jeans, were also watching the customer about to flee. The man leaned toward the woman, whispering something. Her heavy face twisted into a scowl, and she slammed her hand down on the table. "No-good bums, always thinking they can get a free meal!"

The outburst caught the attention of the manager who was taking an order by the door. He turned to face the startled man. "Hey! Did you pay for that?"

The man stopped and fumbled in his pockets. He muttered an apology and hastily threw several crumpled bills on the table.

My head snapped back to Blake. "Whoa, that was…uncanny."

He shrugged.

I waited until the waitress returned with our order and left, my unease growing. "How did you know he was going to do that?"

Blake blew on his spoonful of vegetable soup. "A good guess."

"Bullshit," I whispered.

His gaze met mine. "It was just a lucky guess."

Doubt bubbled up. Blake wasn't an alien—at least I assumed he wasn't, and none of the Luxen I knew could read minds or foresee anything, but that was just too weird. It could've been a lucky guess, but every instinct was telling me there was something more.

I munched on the fries. "So do you have lucky guesses a lot?"

He shrugged. "Sometimes. It's just intuition."

"Intuition," I said, nodding. "That's some spot-on intuition."

"Anyway, I heard about that kid going missing. That totally sucks."

The abrupt change of subject was jarring. "Yeah, it does. I think the cops believe he ran away."

Blake twirled his spoon in the soup. "Did they ask Daemon a lot of questions?"

I frowned. "Why would they?"

Blake's hand stilled. "Well…because Daemon did get in a fight with him. I mean, it seems likely they would question him."

Okay, he had a point, and I was being way too twitchy about this. "Yeah, I think they did, but he didn't have anything to do with—" I froze, not believing what I was feeling. Dull heat flared between my breasts.

It couldn't be.

I dropped the fry back into the basket. The obsidian flared under my sweater. Frantically, I reached around my neck, tugging on the chain. When the obsidian slipped free, I wrapped my hand around it, wincing as the stone scorched my palm. Panic clawed up my throat as I lifted my eyes.

Blake was doing something with his wrist, but my eyes latched onto the front door. It swung open. Fallen leaves scattered across the tile. The low hum of conversation continued, the customers unaware a monster was in their mix. Near-scalding heat radiated from the obsidian. Our table started to rattled softly.

In the doorway, a tall and pale woman with dark sunglasses covering half her face scanned the crowded patrons. Her raven-colored hair hung in thick, ropey strands around her cheeks. Her red lips were spread in a serpent's smile.

She was an Arum.

I was starting to stand, seconds away from ripping the obsidian off my neck. Would I really charge her? I wasn't sure, but I couldn't stand here and do nothing. My muscles tensed. Arum always traveled in fours, so if there was one, that meant there were three more somewhere.

Blood pounded in my ears. I was so intent on the female Arum that I hadn't paid attention to Blake until he was in front of me.

He raised one hand.

Everyone stopped. *Everyone.*

Some people had forks of food halfway to their mouths. Others were stopped in mid-conversation, mouths hanging open in silent laughter. A few had even stopped walking with one foot off the ground. A waitress had been lighting a candle with a small lighter. She was frozen but the flame still danced above the lighter. No one talked, no one moved, and no one even seemed to breathe.

Blake? I took a step back from him, unsure of whom I should be more afraid of — the Arum or the harmless surfer boy.

The female Arum hadn't frozen. She was moving her head side to side in slick, fluid motions as she studied the frozen humans and, I assumed, a few Luxen.

"Arum," Blake accused, voice low.

She whipped around, her head still moving. She took off her sunglasses, squinted. "Human?"

Blake laughed. "Not quite."

And then he launched himself at her.

Chapter 18

Blake was a freaking ninja.

Moving lightning fast, he dipped under the Arum's outstretched arm and spun around, delivering a vicious spin kick to her back. She staggered forward a step and whirled. The air around her hand darkened with black energy. She reared back, preparing to deliver a blow.

Dropping down, he spun and knocked her leather-encased legs from underneath her. The dark energy flickered out as they both rose to their feet again, circling each other in the narrow space between the cramped tables and frozen people.

I sort of just stood there, mystified and entranced by the display. There was no expression on Blake's face. It was like a kickass switch had been thrown, and his whole being was focused on the Arum.

Blake darted in, his palm catching the Arum's chin, snapping her head back. Teeth rattled, and when she lowered her head, a dark, oily substance leaked from her lip.

She faded out, taking on her true form. Her shadowy body was thick and smoky as it charged Blake.

He laughed.

And pivoted around so fast that his hand was just a blur as it sunk deep into what appeared to be her chest. His watch…wasn't a normal watch. It was a shred of obsidian currently embedded in the Arum's chest.

Blake jerked his hand back.

As she took on a human form, her face was pale and shocked. A second later, she exploded in a rush of black smoke that blew my hair back and filled the air with a bitter scent.

Not even out of breath, Blake turned to me and pressed something on his watch. He placed it back on his wrist, then ran a hand through his messy hair.

I gaped at him, the obsidian rapidly cooling under my hand. "Are you, like…Jason Bourne or something?"

Striding over to our table, he dropped a twenty and a ten on the plaid tablecloth. "We need to talk somewhere private."

Eyes wide, I took a deep breath. My world just got a little more insane, but if I could deal with aliens, I could deal with ninja Blake. That didn't mean I was going somewhere with him until I knew what the hell he was, though. "My car."

He nodded, and we headed for the door. Blake held it open for me as he faced the frozen diner. With a wave of his hand, everyone started moving. No one seemed to notice that they'd been frozen for minutes.

We were two steps from my car when I realized my hands were shaking and the back of my neck was tingling.

"You have got to be kidding me," Blake muttered and took ahold of my hand.

I didn't even have to look. There was no Infiniti SUV in the parking lot that I could see, but then again, Daemon had his own special method of travel if necessary.

A tall, imposing shadow fell upon us, and I lifted my gaze. Daemon stood there, a black baseball cap pulled low, shielding the upper half of his face.

"What…what are you doing here?" I asked, and then realized Blake was holding my hand. I pulled it free.

Daemon's jaw was so hard it could cut through marble. "I was just about to ask you the same thing."

Oh…oh dear, this didn't look good. Suddenly, the Arum chick and ninja Blake didn't even matter. Only Daemon did and what he must be assuming. "This isn't what—"

"Look, I don't know what's going on between you two or whatever." As Blake spoke, he curved his hand around my elbow. "But Katy and I need to talk—"

One second, Blake was talking, and the next, he was pressed against the window of the Smoke Hole Diner, with a six-foot-and-then-some alien all up in his grille.

Daemon's face was an inch from Blake's, the bill of his baseball cap creasing Blake's forehead. "You touch her again and I will—"

"You'll what?" Blake shot back, his eyes narrowed. "What are you going to do, Daemon?"

I grabbed Daemon's shoulder and pulled. He didn't budge. "Daemon, come on. Let him go."

"You want to know what I'm going to do?" Daemon's entire body tensed under my hand. "You know where your head and ass are? Well, they're about to become well acquainted with each other."

Oh, good Lord. We were starting to gain an audience. People were watching from their cars. No doubt an entire restaurant was witnessing this go down from the inside. I tried again to break the two boys apart, but both of them ignored me.

Blake smirked. "I'd like to see you try."

"You might want to rethink that." Daemon laughed low. "Because you have no idea what I'm capable of, boy."

"See, that's the funny thing." Blake gripped Daemon's wrist. "I know exactly what you're capable of."

A shiver rolled down my spine. Who in the hell was Blake?

Flannel Shirt Guy came out of the diner, hitching up his ragged pants. He spit out a mouthful of chew as he approached us. "Boys, you're gonna wanna break this up right now before someone calls the—"

Blake raised his free hand and Flannel Shirt Guy just stopped. With a sinking feeling, I looked over my shoulder. Everyone in the parking lot was frozen. No doubt they were just as immobile inside the diner.

A whitish-red light crept along the outline of Daemon's body. Tense silence fell. I knew he was seconds away from going all Luxen on Blake.

Daemon's grip must've tightened, because Blake gasped. "I don't care who or what you are, but you better give me a reason not to blast you into your next pathetic life real quickly."

"I know what you are," Blake choked out.

"That's not helping," Daemon growled, and I had to agree. I spared a nervous glance at Flannel Shirt Guy. He was still there, frozen with his mouth hanging open, showing off stained teeth. The light around Daemon was getting stronger. "Try again."

"I just killed an Arum, and even though you're an arrogant prick, we're not enemies." A choke cut off his next words, and I grabbed both of Daemon's shoulders. There was no way I could let him strangle Blake. "I can help Katy," Blake wheezed. "Good enough for you?"

"What?" I demanded, dropping my hands.

"Yeah, see, you saying her name alone makes me want to kill you. So, no, not good enough for me."

Blake's eyes darted to mine. "Katy, I know what you are, what you will become capable of, and I can help you."

Shocked, I stared at him.

Daemon leaned in to Blake. His eyes were pure white and glowing, like diamonds. "Let me ask you a question. If I kill you, will these people unfreeze?"

Blake's eyes widened, and I knew Daemon wasn't kidding around. He didn't like Blake to start off with and the boy—or whatever he was—obviously posed a threat of an unknown kind. He knew a lot, too much, and he knew what I was. *What I was?* Oh, hold up.

I shot forward. "Let him go, Daemon. I need to know what he's talking about."

His glowing eyes were focused on Blake. "Get back, Kat. I mean it; get the hell back."

Like hell. "Stop it." When he didn't respond, I screamed, "Stop! Just freaking stop for a couple of minutes!"

Daemon blinked and his eyes flickered to mine. Taking the distraction, Blake swiped his arm across Daemon's and broke the hold. He scrambled to the side, putting distance between them.

"Jesus." Blake rubbed his throat. "You have anger management problems. It's like a disease."

"There's a cure and it's called kicking your ass."

Blake flipped him off. Daemon started forward, and I barely managed to get in front of him. Placing my hands on his chest, I looked into eyes that were unrecognizable to me. "Stop. You need to stop now."

Daemon's lip curled into a snarl. "He's a—"

"We don't know what he is," I cut in, already knowing what he was going to say. "But he did kill an Arum. And he hasn't hurt me or anyone else, and he's had plenty of opportunity to do so."

Daemon exhaled roughly. "Kat—"

"We need to hear him out, Daemon. *I* need to hear what he has to say." I took a deep breath. "Besides, these people have been frozen, like, twice now. That can't be good for them."

"I don't care." His gaze flicked to Blake, and, dear God, the look on his face should've sent Blake running. But he shook out his broad shoulders and stepped back, turning those diamond eyes on me. *I* shrank back. "He'll talk. And then I'll decide whether or not he gets to see tomorrow."

Well, that was the best we could hope for at this point. I glanced back at Blake, who rolled his eyes. Boy had a death wish. "Can you, um, fix them?" I waved at Flannel Shirt Guy.

"Sure." He flicked his wrist.

"Police," Flannel Shirt Guy finished.

I turned to the guy. "Everything's fine. Thank you." Spinning around, I pushed my windblown hair out of my face. "My car—if you guys can get along in such an enclosed space?"

Without responding, Daemon stalked over and slid into the passenger seat. I let out a ragged breath and headed for the driver's side.

"Is he always so damn touchy?" Blake asked.

I shot him a dark look as I opened the door. Not looking at Daemon, I turned the heat on and then twisted around in my seat, facing Blake in the back. "What are you?"

Staring out the window, his jaw worked. "The same thing I suspect you are."

My breath caught. "And what do you think I am?"

Daemon cracked his neck but said nothing. He was like a grenade that had its tab pulled. We all were just waiting for him to explode.

"I didn't know at first." Blake sat back. "There was something about you that drew me to you, but I didn't understand what it was."

"Proceed with caution when it comes to your next word choices," Daemon growled.

I squirmed in my seat, clutching the obsidian in my hand. "What do you mean by that?"

Blake shook his head and then stared straight ahead. "The first time I saw you, I knew you were different. Then when you stopped the branch and I saw your necklace, I knew. Only those who know to fear the shadows wear obsidian." Seconds ticked by in silence. "Then our date…yeah, that glass and plate didn't just fall into my lap on its own."

A snicker came from the passenger seat. "Good times."

Unease tripled my heart rate. "How much do you know?"

"There are two alien races on Earth: the Luxen and the Arum." He paused as Daemon twisted in his seat. Blake swallowed. "You're capable of moving things without touching them and you can manipulate light. I'm sure you can do more. And you can also heal humans."

The inside of the car was too small. There wasn't enough air. If

Blake knew the truth about the Luxen, wouldn't that mean the DOD did? I dropped the necklace and clenched the steering wheel, my heart racing.

"How do you know this?" Daemon asked, his voice surprisingly even.

There was a pause. "When I was thirteen, I was leaving soccer practice with a friend of mine—Chris Johnson. He was a normal kid like me, except he was super fast, never got sick, and I never saw his parents at any games. But who cares, right? I didn't until I was goofing around and stepped off the curb, right in front of a speeding cab. Chris healed me. Turns out he was an alien." Blake's lips twisted into a wry grin. "I thought it was pretty cool. My best friend was an alien. Who gets to say that? What I didn't know and what he never told me was that he lit my ass up. Five days later, four men entered my house.

"They wanted to know where *they* were," he continued, hands clenching into fists. "I didn't know what they meant. They killed my parents and my little sister right in front of me. And when I still couldn't help them, they beat me within an inch of my life."

"Oh my God," I whispered, horrified. Daemon looked away, jaw working.

"Not sure he really exists," Blake said, letting out a dry laugh. "Anyway, it took me a while to figure out that when you're healed, you take on their abilities. Shit just started flying everywhere after I was sent to live with my uncle. When I realized that my friend had changed me, I researched as much as I could. Not that I needed to. The Arum found me again."

Acid churned in my stomach. "What do you mean?"

"The Arum in the diner, she couldn't sense me because of the beta quartz—yeah, I know about that, too. But if we were outside of the quartz range, we are just like your...*friend* to them. We're actually tastier."

Well, that confirmed one of my fears. My hands slid off the steering wheel. I had no idea what to say. It was like having the carpet pulled out from underneath my feet and face-planting on the floor.

Blake sighed. "When I realized how much danger I was in, I started training physically and working on my abilities. I learned about their weakness through…others. I survived the best I could."

"This is all great, the caring and sharing crap, but how did you end up here of all places?"

He looked at Daemon. "When I learned about the beta quartz, I moved here with my uncle."

"Awful convenient," Daemon murmured.

"Yeah, it is. The mountains. Very convenient for me."

"There are plenty of other places packed with beta quartz." Suspicion clouded Daemon's tone. "Why. Here?"

"Seemed like the least populated area," Blake answered. "I couldn't imagine there being that many Arum here."

"So everything was a lie?" I asked. "Santa Monica, the surfing?"

"No, not everything was a lie. I'm from Santa Monica and I still love surfing," he said. "I've lied as much as you have, Katy."

He had a point.

Blake leaned his head back against the seat and closed his eyes. He sank into the shadows, fatigue weighing his shoulders down. It was obvious his little freeze show earlier had worn him out. "You've been hurt, haven't you? And healed by one of them?"

Daemon stiffened beside me. My loyalty to my friends wouldn't allow me to confirm that. I wouldn't betray them, not even to someone who may be like me.

He sighed again. "You're not going to tell me which one it was?"

"It's not your business," I said. "How did you know I was different?"

"You mean besides the obvious obsidian, the alien entourage, and the branch?" He laughed. "You're full of electricity. See?" He reached between the seats and placed his hand over mine. Static crackled, jolting us both.

Daemon grabbed Blake's hand and threw it back at him. "I do not like you."

"Feeling's mutual, bud." Blake looked at me. "It's the same whenever we touch an Arum or a Luxen, isn't it? You feel their skin hum?"

I remembered the first time we'd touched in biology. "How do you know about the DOD?"

"I met another human like us. She was under the DOD's thumb. Apparently she exposed her abilities and they swooped in. She told me everything about the DOD and what they really want, which isn't the Luxen or the Arum."

Now that had Daemon's full attention. He was practically in the backseat with Blake. "What do you mean?"

"They want people like Katy. They don't give two shits about the aliens. They want us."

Icy fear shot through me as I gaped at him. *"What?"*

"You need to explain that a lot better," Daemon ordered as static built in the tiny car.

Blake leaned forward. "Do you really think the DOD doesn't know what both the Arum and Luxen are capable of, that after studying your kind for decades and decades that they don't know what they're dealing with? And if you really believe not, then you're stupid or naive."

Another jolt of terror shuttled through me, but this time for Daemon and my friends. Even I had my doubts, but they'd seemed so convinced that they'd hidden their talents.

Daemon shook his head. "If the DOD knew about our abilities, they wouldn't let us live free. They'd have us locked up in a heartbeat."

"Really? The DOD knows the Luxen are a peaceful race and they know the Arum aren't the same as your kind. Having the Luxen free takes care of the Arum alien problem. Besides, don't they get rid of any Luxen who causes a problem?" Blake jerked back as Daemon nearly went over the seat, but I grabbed his sweater. Not like I could hold him in place, but he stopped. "Look, all I'm saying is there are bigger fish the DOD wants. And that's the humans the Luxen mutate. We're just as strong as you—even stronger in some cases. The only thing is, we tire out a lot quicker and it takes us longer to recharge, so to speak."

Daemon settled back, his hands clenching and unclenching.

"The only reason why the DOD lets you believe that your big, bad secret is hidden is because they know what you can do to humans," Blake said. "And we're what they care about."

"No," I whispered, my brain rebelling against the idea. "Why would they care about us instead of them?"

"Gee, Katy, why would the government be interested in a bunch of humans who have more powers than the very creatures who created us? I don't know. Maybe because they'd have a superhuman army at their disposal or a group of people who can get rid of the aliens if need be?"

Daemon swore under his breath—a work of art with curse words. And that scared me more than anything, because that meant Daemon was actually starting to listen to what Blake was saying. And believe it.

"But how…how are you stronger than the Luxen?" I asked.

"That's a good question," Daemon admitted softly.

"In the diner, when I knew the guy was going to skip out on his meal? It's because I could pick up on bits of his thoughts. Not all of them, but enough to know what he's planning. I can hear almost any human—any one that's not mutated."

"Mutated?" God, that word brought forth some really gross images.

"You're mutated. Tell me, have you been sick recently? Had a really high fever?"

Apprehension rose so quickly it left me dizzy. From the other seat, Daemon tensed.

"I can tell by your expression you have. Let me guess, you had a fever so bad that it felt like your entire body was on fire? Lasted a couple of days and then you felt fine—better than ever?" He turned to the window again, shaking his head. "And now you can move things without touching them? Probably have no control. The table shaking inside wasn't me. It was *you*. That's just the tip of the iceberg. Soon you'll be able to do a hell of a lot more, and if you don't get control of it, it's going to be really bad. This damn place is swarming with DOD, hidden in plain sight. And they're here looking for hybrids. Far as I know, the Luxen don't typically heal humans, but it happens." He glanced at Daemon. "Obviously."

Hands shaking, I tucked my hair behind my ears. There was no point in lying about what I could do. He'd been right. Jesus. Daemon had *mutated* me. "Then why are you here if it's such a risk now?"

"You," he said, ignoring Daemon's barely audible growl. "Honestly, I thought about not coming back. Moving on, but there's my uncle… and you. That's not many like us who haven't been caught by the DOD. You need to know what kind of danger you're in."

"But you don't even know me." It seemed absurd that he'd risk so much.

"And we don't know you," Daemon added, eyes narrowed.

He shrugged. "I like you. Not you, Daemon." He smiled. "But Katy."

"I really, really do not like you at all."

My stomach twisted. This wasn't the time to get into that mess. My brain was on overload. "Blake…"

"That wasn't said to make you say you like me or not. I'm just stating the fact. I like you." He glanced at me, eyes shuttered. "And you don't know what you've stepped in. I can help you."

"Bullshit," Daemon said. "If she needs help controlling her abilities, then I can do it."

"Can you? What you do is second nature to you. Not to Katy. I had to learn how to rein in my abilities. I can teach her. Stabilize her."

"Stabilize me?" My laugh sounded a bit choked. "What's going to happen? I'm going to explode or something?"

He looked at me. "You can seriously end up hurting yourself or others. I've heard things, Katy. Some mutated humans… Well, let's just say it doesn't end pretty."

"You don't need to scare her."

"I'm not trying to. It's just the truth," Blake responded. "And if the DOD finds out about you, they're going to take you in. And if you can't control your abilities, they will put you down."

I gasped, turning away. Put me down? Like a feral animal? All of this was happening way too fast. Just last night I'd been having a good, *normal* time with Daemon. The very thing I'd wanted from Blake, who turned out not to be normal at all. And the whole time I believed Blake was attracted to me because he wanted to be, he was drawn to me because we were both X-Men wannabes.

Ha. Irony was such a bitch.

"Katy, I know this is a lot. But you have to be prepared. You leave this town, the Arum are going to be on you. That is, if you can slide by the DOD."

"You're right. This is a lot." I faced him. "I thought you were normal. And you're not. You're telling me that I have the DOD gunning for me. That if I ever decide to leave this place, I'm going to be a Snack Pack for an Arum. And better yet, I may lose complete control of whatever powers I have and wipe out a family of four, then be *put down*! All I wanted to do today was eat some goddamn fries and *be normal*!"

Daemon let out a low whistle and Blake winced. "You're never going to be normal, Katy. Never again."

"No shit," I snapped. I wanted to hit something, but I needed to pull it together. If I'd learned anything from my dad's sickness, it was that things couldn't be changed. But I could change how I dealt with them. Since I moved here—since I met Daemon and Dee—I'd changed.

Taking a deep breath, I pulled in the anger, fear, and frustration. Perspective was needed. "What are we going to do?"

"We don't need his help," Daemon said.

"But you do," Blake whispered. "I heard about the window thing with Simon."

I glanced at Daemon, and he shook his head.

"What do you think will happen next time? Simon ran off, doing God knows what. You won't get so lucky again."

Simon's disappearance wasn't luck. I didn't want to look at it that way. Tipping my head back, I closed my eyes. Ice settled in my limbs. It was no longer a fear of exposing the Luxen, but myself now, too. And my mom.

"How do you know so much about them?" I asked, voice small.

"The girl I was telling you about? She told me everything. I wanted to help her…to get away, but she wouldn't leave. The DOD had something or someone that meant a lot to her."

God. The DOD was like the mafia. They'd use any means necessary. I shivered. "Who was she?"

"Liz something," he said. "Don't know her last name."

The walls of the car seemed to shift even closer. Trapped. I felt trapped.

Daemon was boiling over in the seat next to me. "You know," he said to Blake, "there's nothing stopping me from killing you. Right now."

"Yes, there is." Blake's voice was even. "There's Katy and the fact I doubt you're a cold-blooded killer."

Daemon stiffened. "I don't trust you."

"You don't have to. Only Katy does."

And that was the thing. I wasn't sure I did trust him, but he was like me. And if he could help me not expose Daemon and my friends, I'd do anything. It was just that simple. Everything else would have to be played by ear.

I looked at Daemon. He was staring ahead now, hand on the dashboard as if the plastic was grounding him somehow. Did he feel as helpless as I did? It didn't matter. I couldn't—wouldn't risk him.

"When do we start?" I asked.

"Tomorrow if you can," Blake said.

"My mom leaves for work after five." I swallowed.

Blake agreed and Daemon said, "I'll be there."

"Not necessary," Blake shot back.

"And I don't care. You aren't doing a damn thing with Katy without me being there." He faced the boy again. "I don't trust you. Just so we're clear."

"Whatever." Blake climbed out of the car. Cold air rushed in, and I called out his name. He stopped with his hand on the door. "What?"

"How did you get away from the Arum when they attacked you?" I asked.

Blake looked away, eyes squinting at the sky. "That's not something I'm ready to talk about, Katy." He shut the door and jogged off toward his car.

I sat there for several minutes, staring out the window, not really seeing anything. Daemon muttered something under his breath and then opened his door, disappearing into the shadows surrounding the diner. He'd left me.

I didn't even remember the trip home. Pulling into the driveway, I killed the engine and sat back, closing my eyes. Night seeped into my silent car. I got out, took a step, and heard my porch steps groan.

Daemon had beaten me home. He came down the steps, his baseball cap hiding his eyes.

I shook my head. "Daemon…"

"I don't trust him. I don't trust a damn thing about him, Kat." He took off his hat, thrust his fingers through his hair, and then slammed the cap back down. "He comes out of nowhere and knows *everything*. Every instinct is telling me he can't be trusted. He could be anyone, working for any organization. We don't know anything about him."

"I know." Suddenly, I was just so freaking tired. All I wanted to do was lay down. "But at least this way we can keep an eye on him. Right?"

He gave a short, dry laugh. "There are other ways of dealing with him."

"What?" My voice rose and was carried away by the wind. "Daemon, you can't be thinking…"

"I don't even know what I'm thinking." He took a step back. "And dammit, my head is so not in the right place at this moment." There was a pause. "Why were you with him in the first place?"

My heart lurched. "We were grabbing something to eat and I was—"

"You were what?"

Somehow I felt like I'd walked into an even bigger trap. Unsure of how to answer, I didn't say anything. That was my biggest mistake.

Understanding dawned, and he tipped his chin up. For an instant, the green of his eyes darkened with raw emotion. "You went to Bryon after…"

After I'd spent the night with him…wrapped in *his* arms. I shook my head, needing him to understand why I went to see Blake. "Daemon—"

"You know, I'm not really surprised." His smile was half knowing and half bitter. "We kissed. Twice. You spent the night using me as your own body pillow…and liking it. I'm sure that had you freaking out the moment I left. You ran straight to Boris, because he really doesn't make you feel anything. And feeling something for me scares the hell out of you."

My mouth snapped close. "I did not run straight to *Blake*. He texted me about getting something to eat, and it wasn't even a date, Daemon. I went to tell him—"

"Then what was it, Kitten?" He stepped forward, peering down at me. "He obviously likes you. You've kissed him before. He's willing to risk his own safety to *train* you."

"It's not what you think. If you'd let me explain…"

"You don't know what I think," he snapped.

Something awful unfurled in my stomach. "Daemon—"

"You know, you're unbelievable."

I was sure he didn't mean that in a good way.

"The night of your party, when you thought I was messing around with Ash? You were so pissed that you went outside and blew up windows, exposing yourself."

I flinched. All true.

"And now you're doing—what? Messing around with *him* in between kissing me?"

But I like you. The words wouldn't leave my lips. I didn't know why, but I couldn't say them. Not when he was looking at me, full of anger and distrust and, worse yet, disappointment. "I'm not messing around with him, Daemon! We're just friends. That's all."

Skepticism drew his lips into a tight line. "I'm not stupid, Kat."

"I didn't say that you were!" Irritation spiked, overshadowing the deep ache in my chest. "You're not giving me a chance to explain anything. As usual, you're acting like a freaking know-it-all and you keep cutting me off!"

"And as usual, you're a bigger problem than I could've ever imagined."

Flinching as though I'd been slapped, I took a step back. "I'm not your problem." My voice cracked. "Not anymore."

Regret seeped through his anger. "Kat—"

"No. I was never your problem in the first place." Anger sped through me like an out-of-control forest fire. "And I'm sure as hell not your problem now."

The windows in his eyes to all those emotions slammed shut, leaving me trembling in the dark. And I knew. I knew I'd hurt him more than I thought possible. I'd hurt him in a way much worse than he'd ever hurt me.

"Hell. This"—he waved his hand around me—"isn't even important right now. Just forget it."

He was gone before I could even finish my sentence. Stunned, I turned around, but he was nowhere. A pang hit me in the chest and tears filled my eyes as I turned back to my door.

The sudden realization smacked me upside the head.

This whole time, I'd been so busy pushing him away, telling him whatever was between us wasn't real. And now that I'd realized the depth of what he felt for me—what I felt for him—he was gone.

Chapter 19

All morning and part of the afternoon, I poked around the house like a zombie. There was this weird throbbing in my chest. My eyes ached as if they were filled with tears that wouldn't fall. It reminded me of the months after Dad's death.

With my heart not really in it, I did a quick review on this dystopian novel I'd read last week and closed my laptop. Lying down, I stared at the spider web of cracks in my bedroom ceiling. The truth was hard to face. I'd been trying to deny it all morning. A jumbled knot of clogged emotions had formed under my ribs last night and it was still there. Every so often it seemed heavier, more intense.

I liked Daemon—really, *really* liked him.

I'd been so caught up nursing my hurt over the way he'd acted when we first met that I'd been blind to my growing feelings, to what I wanted, and to how he felt. And now what? Daemon, who never backed down from anything, had walked away before allowing me to explain anything.

There was no escaping it. I'd hurt him.

Rolling over, I shoved my face into the pillow. His scent was still there. I clutched it tightly and closed my eyes. How had things gotten so tangled up? At what point had my life turned into some bizarre science fiction soap opera?

"Honey, are you feeling okay?"

I opened my eyes and focused on my mom, who was wearing scrubs with little hearts and swirls on them. Where did she get those things? "Yeah, I'm just tired."

"You sure?" She sat on the edge of the bed, placing her hand against my forehead. When she determined I wasn't sick, she smiled a little. "The Christmas tree is beautiful, honey."

A rush of swirling emotions crashed into me. "Yeah," I said, voice hoarse. "It is."

"Who helped you with it?"

I bit the inside of my cheek. "Daemon."

Mom smoothed my hair back with her hand. "That's really sweet of him."

"I know." I paused. "Mom?"

"Yes, honey?"

I didn't even know what I was going to tell her. Everything was too…complicated, too jumbled up in the truth of what my friends were. I shook my head. "Nothing. Just that I love you."

Smiling, she bent over and kissed my forehead. "I love you, too." She got up and stopped at the door. "I was thinking about having Will over for dinner this week. What do you think?"

It was great my mom had a stellar love life. "Cool with me."

After Mom left for work, I forced myself to get up. Blake would be here soon. So would Daemon, if he still showed.

I went into the kitchen and grabbed a Coke out of the fridge. Passing time, I collected all the books I had duplicate copies of and placed them on my desk. A book giveaway would make me feel better. When I went downstairs to find my Coke—because apparently it had run away from me at some point—a familiar warmth spread along my neck.

I froze on the bottom step, hand gripping the banister.

There was a knock on the door.

Hopping from the step to the floor, I rushed to the door and threw it open. Out of breath, I clenched the knob. "Hey."

Daemon arched a dark eyebrow. "It sounded like you were going to come straight through the door."

I flushed. "I, uh, was…looking for my drink."

"Looking for your drink?"

"I lost it."

He glanced over my shoulder, a small smile playing on his lips. "It's right there, on the table."

Turning around, I saw the red-and-white can laughing at me from a corner table. "Oh. Well, thank you."

Daemon stepped inside, brushing my arm as he passed. Oddly, the fact he just invited himself in didn't upset me anymore. He shoved his hands into his pockets and leaned against the wall. "Kitten…"

A thrill went through me. "Daemon…?"

The half smile was there, but it lacked its usual smugness. "You look tired."

I crept closer. "I didn't sleep well last night."

"Thinking about me?" he asked in a hushed voice.

There wasn't a moment of hesitation. "Yes."

His eyes widened slightly with surprise. "Well, I was preparing this whole speech about how you need to stop denying that I consume your every waking thought and haunt your dreams. Now I'm not sure what to say."

Leaning against the wall beside him, I could feel his body heat. "You, speechless? That's one for the record books."

Daemon lowered his head, his eyes as deep and endless as the forests outside. "I didn't sleep well last night, either."

I moved closer until my arm brushed his. He stiffened ever so slightly. "Last night—"

"I wanted to apologize," he said, and I was stunned yet again. He turned so that he was facing me completely, and I found his hand without looking. His fingers threaded through mine. "I'm sorry—"

Someone cleared his throat.

Surprise flitted through me. Before I could turn, Daemon's eyes narrowed, glinting with anger. He dropped my hand and took a step back. *Crap.* I'd forgotten about Blake. And I'd forgotten to close the door behind me.

"Am I interrupting?" Blake asked.

"Yes, Bart, you are always interrupting," Daemon responded.

I turned around, my heart deflating as if someone had popped it. The entire length of my back burned under Daemon's stare.

Blake opened the storm door and stepped inside. "Sorry it took me so long to get over here."

"Too bad it didn't take longer." Daemon stretched idly, like a cat. "And too bad you didn't get lost or—"

"Eaten by wild boars or killed in a horrific ten-car pile-up. I get it." Blake interrupted and sauntered past us. "You don't need to be here, Daemon. No one is forcing you."

Daemon pivoted on his heel, following Blake. "There's no other place I'd rather be."

My head was already starting to throb. Training with Daemon present wasn't going to be easy. I slowly made my way into the living room. They were in an epic stare down.

I cleared my throat. "So, um, how are we going to do this?"

Daemon opened his mouth, and the good Lord only knows what he was about to say, but Blake beat him to it. "What we need to do first is figure out what you can already do."

I tucked my hair back, uncomfortable with both of them staring at me like…like I didn't even know what. "Uh, I'm not sure there's much I can do."

Blake's lips pursed. "Well, you stopped the branch. And the time with the windows. That's two things."

"But I didn't do them on purpose." At Blake's confused expression, I looked over at Daemon. He appeared bored, sprawled on the couch. "What I mean is, it wasn't a conscious effort, you know."

"Oh." His brows lowered. "Well, that's disappointing."

Gee. Thanks. My hands fell to my sides.

Daemon's bright gaze slid to Blake. "What a great motivator you are."

Blake ignored him. "So these have been random outbursts of power?" When I nodded, he pinched the bridge of his nose.

"Maybe it will just fade?" I said, hopeful.

"It would've already done that by now. See, one of four things happens after a mutation, from what I could learn." He started moving around the living room, giving me a wide berth. "A human can be healed, and then it fades after a few weeks, even months. Or a human can be mutated and it sticks, and they develop the same abilities as a Luxen—or more. Then there are the ones who kind of…self-destruct. But you're out of that stage."

Thank God, I thought wryly. "And?"

"Well, and then there are humans who are mutated beyond what would be expected, I guess."

"What does that mean?" Daemon tapped his fingers on the arm of the couch. I glared at them.

Blake folded his arms and rocked back. "Like in the freakish-mutant-looks department and in the head, and it's different for everyone."

"Am I going to turn into a mutant?" I squeaked.

He laughed. "I don't think so."

I don't think so wasn't high on the reassurance scale.

Daemon's fingers stopped their annoying tapping. "And how do you really know all of this, Flake?"

"Blake," he corrected. "Like I said, I've known others like Katy who have been sucked into the DOD."

"Uh huh." Daemon smirked.

Blake shook his head. "Anyway, back to the important stuff. We need to see if you can control it. If not…"

Before I even had a chance to respond, Daemon was on his feet and in Blake's face. "Or what, Hank? What if she can't?"

"Daemon." I sighed. "First off, his name is *Blake*. B-L-A-K-E. And really, can we do this without any macho-man moments? Because if not, this is going to take forever."

He spun around, pinning me with a dark look that made me roll my eyes. "Okay, so what do you suggest?"

"The best thing to start with is to see if you can move anything on command." Blake paused. "And I guess we can go from there."

"Move what?"

Blake looked around the room. "How about a book?"

A book? Hell, which one? Shaking my head, I focused on the one that had a cover of a girl whose dress turned into rose petals. So pretty. It was about reincarnation and had a male main character who was swoon-worthy and then some. God, I'd so want to date—

"Focus," Blake said.

I made a face, but okay, I wasn't really focusing. I pictured the book lifting into the air and coming to my hand like I'd seen Daemon and Dee do so many times.

Nothing happened.

I tried harder. Waited longer. But the book remained on the back of the couch…as did the pillows, the remote control, and Mom's *Good Housekeeping* magazine.

Three hours later and the best I'd done was cause the coffee table to tremble and Daemon to doze off on the couch.

I fail.

Tired and cranky, I ended practice and woke up Daemon by kicking the leg of the coffee table. "I'm hungry. I'm tired. And I'm done."

Blake's brows shot up. "Okay. We can pick up tomorrow. No biggie."

I glared at him.

Stretching his arms, Daemon yawned. "Wow, Brad, you are such a great trainer. I'm amazed."

"Shut up," I said, and then ushered Blake out the front door. On the porch, I apologized. "I'm sorry for being so bitchy, but I feel like an epic fail right now. Like I'm the captain of my own personal failboat."

He smiled. "You're not a failboat, Katy. This can take a while, but the frustration is worth it in the end. The last thing you want is the DOD knowing you're mutated and coming for whoever was responsible."

I shivered. Causing something like that to happen would kill me. "I know. And…thank you for wanting to help." I bit my lip and peeked at him. Maybe Daemon was right last night. Blake was risking a lot even being around me. Wouldn't most people bail if they knew the DOD was heavily entrenched here? I just didn't want to believe it was because he had feelings for me.

"Blake, I know this is dangerous for you and I don't—"

"Katy, it's okay." He placed his hand on my shoulder and squeezed. He also let go pretty quickly; probably he was afraid Daemon would appear out of nowhere and break his hand. "I don't expect anything from you."

A little bit of relief flooded me. "I don't know what to say."

"You don't have to say anything."

Didn't I, though? Trusting Blake took a leap of faith, but he had plenty of opportunity to turn Daemon and me over and he hadn't. I wrapped my arms around my waist against the cold. "What you're doing by helping me is pretty amazing. I just wanted to say that."

Blake's grin grew into a smile that caused his hazel eyes to dance. "Well, it does mean I get to spend more time with you." The tips of his cheeks flushed, and he looked away, clearing his throat. "Anyway, I'll see you tomorrow. Okay?"

I nodded. Blake gave me a weird sort of smile and then left. Feeling all kinds of whacked out, I went back in.

Daemon wasn't on the couch, of course. Going on instinct, I shuffled into the kitchen. He was there. Bread, lunch meat, and mayo were spread out on the counter.

"What are you doing?"

He waved a knife around. "You said you were hungry."

My heart did a back handspring. "You...didn't have to make me anything, but thank you."

"I was also hungry." Daemon plopped mayo on the bread, spreading it out evenly. He made two ham and cheese sandwiches quickly. Turning, he handed me mine as he leaned against the counter. "Eat."

I stared at him.

He smiled and then took a huge bite of his. Chewing slowly, he watched me eat, and the silence seemed to stretch on forever. After he went round two with the ham and cheese, which really was just cheese and mayo, I cleaned up. I finished washing my hands and turned off the faucet when Daemon placed his hands on either side of my hips, his fingers curving over the counter. Heat rolled up and down my back, and I didn't dare move. He was way, way too close.

"So, you had a very interesting conversation with Butler on the porch." His breath danced over my neck.

I fought the shiver and failed. "His name is Blake and were you eavesdropping, Daemon?"

"I was keeping an eye on things." The tip of his nose brushed the side of my neck and my fingers spasmed against the stainless steel sink. "So, his helping you is amazing?"

Closing my eyes, I cursed under my breath. "He's putting himself at risk, Daemon. Whether you like him or not, you have to give him props for that."

"I don't have to give him anything other than the ass-kicking he deserves." He rested his chin on my shoulder. "I don't want you doing this."

"Daemon—"

"And it has nothing to do with my raging dislike of the boy." His hands left the counter and found my hips. "Or the fact that—"

"That you're jealous?" I said, turning my cheek so that it was daringly close to his lips.

"Me? Jealous of him? No. What I was going to say was, or the fact that he has a stupid name. Blake? It rhymes with flake. Come on."

I rolled my eyes, but then he straightened and tugged me against him. With my back flush against his front, he wrapped his arms around my waist. Dizzying warmth zinged through my veins. Why, oh why, did he always have to be so damn close?

"Kitten, I don't trust him. Everything about him is too convenient."

To me, Daemon's reasons for not trusting him were too obvious. I wiggled free, managing to get myself turned around so I faced him. His hands fell back to the sink. "I don't want to talk about Blake."

One dark brow arched. "What do you want to talk about?"

"Last night."

He stared at me a moment, then backed off. Retreated all the way to the other side of the kitchen table as if he were suddenly afraid of me. I folded my arms. "Actually, I wanted to finish the conversation we were having before Blake came over."

"Which is about last night."

"Yeah," I said slowly, dragging out the word.

Daemon scratched the five o'clock shadow on his chin. "I don't even know what I was going to say to you."

My brows flew up. What a disappointment.

"Look, last night I was mad. I was also a little caught off guard with…with everything." He closed his eyes briefly. "Anyway, that's not important. This thing with Bart is."

I opened my mouth, but he went on. "Part of me just wants to snatch him up and get rid of him. It would be easy." My mouth hit the floor this time, and his smile was cold. "I'm being serious, Kitten. He's not just a danger to you, but if he's playing us, he's a danger to Dee. So I want her kept as far away from this as possible."

"Of course," I murmured. There was no way I'd involve her.

His muscled arms folded, and he became all business. "And going along with everything will keep tabs on him. So, you were right last night about that."

This wasn't the part of last night's conversation I wanted to talk about. After seeing how affected he was when he'd thought I'd gone out on a date with Blake—even though he seemed to have gotten over that pretty quickly—and spending all day feeling heartsick and shattered, I wanted to talk to him about us. About what I'd realized as I moped around the house all day.

"I don't like this, but..." He paused. "But I'll ask you one more time to not do this with him. Trust that I can find something out that can help you—help us."

I wanted to tell him yes, but how was Daemon going to ask anyone without arousing suspicion? If the DOD was everywhere, who could say there weren't Luxen working for them? Anything was possible.

Since I didn't answer right away, he seemed to know what my decision was, because he made this laugh/inhale sound and nodded. A splinter pierced my heart.

"Okay. You need to get some rest. Tomorrow is a big day. More Butler. Yay."

And then he walked out. Actually walked out of the kitchen instead of doing that super-fast thing he usually did. And I stood there, wondering what the hell just went down and why I never stopped him and told him what I was thinking.

What I was feeling.

Courage—I really needed to find the courage to tell him how I felt tomorrow, before things went further south between us.

Chapter 20

Days and then weeks went by. Each morning started the same as the one before. I'd wake up dizzy, feeling like I hadn't slept at all. Every day the dark smudges under my eyes grew more prominent.

I didn't speak to my mom most mornings, which blew, because that was the only time we really got to see each other. She was busy with work and Will, and I was busy with school; Blake; and a distant, closed-off Daemon. Who spent most of the practices watching Blake like a hawk does when searching for prey.

A frosty air had developed between Daemon and me, and no matter how many times I tried to start up a conversation about our relationship, he was quick to shut me down. My heart ached.

Even though he didn't stop the training sessions and rarely missed them, he was still dead set against them. Most of our time alone consisted of him trying to convince me that Blake was no good. That there was something inherently wrong with the boy, other than the fact he was a hybrid. Like me.

But as the weeks passed and the DOD didn't storm the house for me, I chalked it up to Daemon's rightful paranoia. He had reason not to trust the guy. Given what happened with Dawson and Bethany, he was leery of all humans.

And Blake did his best to handle Daemon. I had to give it to him. Not many people would keep coming back, especially considering I sucked butt at the whole ability thing and Daemon made him feel less than welcome. Blake was patient and supportive, while Daemon was the pissy pink elephant in the room with the bad attitude.

All the training after school affected any and all social life. Everyone knew that Blake and I were hanging out. No one, not even Dee, realized that Daemon was there, too. Since she was spending all of her time over at Adam's, she didn't know where Daemon was or what he was doing. So Carissa and Lesa believed that Blake and I were dating, and I'd given up on trying to convince them otherwise. And it blew, because they thought I was so wrapped up in him that nothing else mattered. Without even doing it, I'd turned into one of *those girls* whose life ceases to exist outside of her boyfriend.

And I didn't even have a boyfriend.

Their detailed attempts to draw me back into their world were incessant, but each time Dee wanted to take a shopping trip or Lesa wanted to grab something to eat after school, I had to turn them down.

My evenings were all about training. There was no time for reading. No time for my blog. Those things I once spent all my free time doing were now pushed to the side.

I always asked Blake the same question before we got started. "Have you seen any Arum?"

The answer was always the same. "No."

And then Daemon would show up and things usually got crazy at some point. Blake would try to teach me while ignoring the homicidal alien taking up way too much room.

"Technically, whenever we use our abilities, we are sending a piece of ourselves," he explained. "Like if I want to pick something up, a part of me is doing that as an extension of me. It's why using our powers weakens us."

That really made no sense to me, but I nodded. Daemon rolled his eyes.

Blake laughed. "You have no idea what I'm talking about."

"Nope." I smiled.

"All right, back to the arms, then." His fingers slipped over the curve of my shoulders, and the crazy began.

Daemon was up and off the couch in a nanosecond, forcing Blake to back away. I took a deep, patient breath and faced the alien.

He glared Blake into submission. "I think I can help her with this."

Sitting on the arm of the couch, Blake waved his hand. "Sure. Whatever. She's all yours."

Daemon grinned. "That she is."

My hand was itching to connect with his face. "I am not yours." A small part of me wanted him to deny my words, though.

"Shush it," he said, walking up to me.

"How about I shush it right up your—"

"Kitten, your language is so unladylike." He stepped behind me, placing his hands on my shoulders. Admittedly, the static charge from his touch was much more powerful...and tempting. He leaned in, his cheek against my hair. "Ben over there is on to something. Whenever we use our ability—tap into the Source—we are sending a part of us to do it. It's like an extension of our physical form."

Daemon was making just as much sense as Blake, but I went along with it.

"Picture having hundreds of arms."

I did as he instructed. In my head, I imagined I looked like that Hindu goddess. I giggled.

"Katy." Blake sighed.

"Sorry."

"Now take those arms and make them transparent in your mind." Daemon paused. "You can see those arms; see the books all over the living room. Can you? I know you know where each and every one is placed."

Knowing that if I spoke, I'd break my concentration, I nodded.

"Okay. Good." His fingers tightened. "Now I want you to turn those arms into light. An intense, bright light."

"Like…your light?"

"Yes."

I took another breath and pictured my Hindu arms as long, slender ribbons of light. Yeah, I looked ridiculous.

"Do you see it?" he asked softly. "And do you believe it?"

Pausing before I answered, I worked really hard to believe what I was seeing. The arms of blinding white light *were* mine. Like Daemon and Blake had said, they were extensions of my being. I imagined each of those hands picking up the books scattered about.

"Open your eyes," Blake instructed.

When I did, books floated around the room. I moved them to the coffee table, stacking them in alphabetic order without laying a finger on, them. A heady thrill went through me. Finally! Ecstatic, I almost started jumping and squealing.

Daemon let go, his smile an odd mixture of pride and something much more. It tugged at my heart. So much so that I had to look away, and my gaze collided with Blake's.

He grinned at me, and I grinned back. "I actually did something."

"You did." He stood. "And it was pretty damn good. Nice work."

I turned to say something to Daemon, but there was a rush of warm air and I realized the spot where Daemon had stood was empty. A door opened and then closed.

Surprised, I turned to Blake. "I…"

"He sure can move fast," he said, shaking his head. "I can move fast, but damn. Not as fast as him."

I nodded, blinking back hot tears. The one time I actually did something right, Daemon bailed. How freaking typical.

"Katy," Blake said softly, wrapping his hand around my arm. "Are you okay?"

"Yeah." I pulled free, dragging in deep breaths.

He followed me into the living room. "Do you want to talk about it?"

I choked out a laugh, embarrassed. "No."

Blake was silent for several moments. "It's probably better this way."

"It is?" I folded my arms, willing my tears to go away. Crying fixed nothing.

He nodded. "From what I've gathered, relationships between the Luxen and humans don't work out. And before you tell me there's nothing between you two, I know better. I can see the way you look at each other. But it's not going to work out."

If this was supposed to be a motivational speech, it was *so* not working. Blake picked up the first book, smoothing his hands over the glossy purple cover. "It's better if you cut ties. Or he does, before someone gets hurt."

My stomach hollowed. "Hurt?"

He nodded solemnly. "Look at it this way. If he thought the DOD was onto you, what do you think he'd do? Risk his life, right? And if the DOD does find out you've been mutated, they're going to want to know who did it. Their first guess is going to be him."

I started to tell Blake that it wasn't Daemon, but that would just sound suspicious, and damn if he didn't have a point. Daemon was the obvious suspect. I sat down, rubbing the heel of my hand over my forehead. "I don't want anyone to get hurt," I said finally.

Blake sat beside me. "Do we ever? But what we want rarely changes the outcome, Katy."

. . .

In trig the following day, Daemon tapped his pen off my back. "I'm not going to be at your training today," he said in a low voice.

Disappointment swelled inside me. Even though Daemon usually wasn't the most helpful person during these sessions, I truly believed the reason I'd been able to move the books was because of him.

And yeah, I also looked forward to seeing him. Sigh.

I forced a shrug, playing it cool. "Okay."

His emerald-colored eyes met mine for a brief moment and then he sat back, scribbling along his notebook. Feeling as if I'd been dismissed, I faced the front of the class and exhaled slowly.

Carissa tossed a folded-up note on my desk. Curious, I spread it open.

Why the :(face?

Gosh, was I that obvious? I scribbled a quick message:

Just tired, heart your new glasses,

And I did. They were a rocking zebra print. I managed to toss the note back to her. We weren't worried about our teacher—it was doubtful he could see all the way to the back of the classroom. The guy made Santa look young.

A few seconds later, the note was back on my desk. I grinned as I unfolded it.

Thank you. Lesa wants me to tell you: "Daemon looks hot today." I have to agree.

I laughed under my breath and wrote back,

Daemon always looks hot!!!

Stretching into the aisle, I went to drop the note back on Carissa's desk. Before it could leave my fingertips, it was snatched from my hand. Son of a donkey butt! My mouth dropped open and my cheeks burned. Twisting around in my seat, I glared at Daemon.

He held the note close to his chest and grinned. "Passing notes is bad," he murmured.

"Give it back," I hissed.

Shaking his head, he unfolded the note much to my—and I'm sure, to Lesa's and Carissa's—horror. I wanted to die as I watched those vibrant eyes quickly scan the note. I knew when he got to my part, because his dark brows shot up his forehead.

He grinned, used his mouth to pop off the cap on his pen, and wrote something on the page. Groaning, I glanced at Lesa and Carissa. Lesa's mouth was hanging open and Carissa's cheeks matched mine. God, he was taking enough time.

Daemon finally folded the note and handed it back. "There you go, Kitten."

"I hate you." I snapped around—just in time, because the teach was scanning the classroom. When he went back to the chalkboard, I handled the note like it was a bomb. Slowly and carefully, I unfolded the damn thing.

And I died a little more.

That note would never, ever see the light of day again. I refolded the paper and shoved it in my bookbag, my movements stiff and my entire body enflamed.

Daemon chuckled.

• • •

For several days, Blake and I worked alone. Unsurprisingly, things were a lot smoother without Daemon's threatening presence. With Blake's coaching, I went from being able to move small objects for short periods of time to rearranging the entire living room with a single thought. Each time I was successful, Blake got all kinds of happy, and I tried to join in the revelry—because this was good—but there was always an edge of disappointment riding each accomplishment.

I wanted to share my successes with Daemon, and he wasn't there.

Blake eventually moved on to harder stuff, attempting to teach me how to control the more powerful things through a horrible series of trial-and-error experiments. The first time I'd attempted to control fire ended up with what I swore were second-degree burns on my fingers.

He'd presented me with a series of white candles and my goal was to light all of them at once through concentration. I was allowed to touch each of them, and after several hours of staring at them with a seriously empty stomach, I'd managed to light one by picturing the flame in my mind and holding the image.

Once I had mastered that, I could no longer touch the candle. Instead I had to create the fire just by looking at it. Blake waved his hand over the candles, and all the wicks sparked a tiny flame.

"Easy peasy," he said, and then ran his hand over them again. The flames went out.

"How did you do that—putting them out? Can the Luxen do that?"

He smiled at me. "They can only control things related to some form of light, right? So moving, stopping things, and fire are all right up their alley. They can generate enough energy to create electricity and fuel a storm."

I nodded, remembering how it had stormed that day Daemon had returned from the lake and Mr. Garrison had been waiting for him.

"And it's like pulling atoms from the air around us, so yes, they can create wind. We're just stronger than they are at it."

"You keep saying that, but I don't understand how."

He shrugged. "They have only one kind of DNA." He paused, frowning. "*If* they have DNA. But let's say they do for argument's sake. We have two different sets of DNA in us. Like the best of both worlds."

Not very scientific.

"Anyway, try it." He prodded me with his knee.

I did exactly what I had done while holding the candle, but something went wrong.

My fingers lit up like the Fourth of July.

"Holy shit!" Blake jumped out of the way, pulling me along with him. Shock had set in as he dragged me into the kitchen and shoved my hands under a rush of cool water. It was the first time I'd heard Blake swear.

"Katy, I asked you to light the candle, not your damn fingers! It's really not that hard. Jesus."

"Sorry," I mumbled as I watched my skin turn an ugly shade of pink and then red. It didn't take long before the skin puckered and blistered.

"You may not be able to control fire or start it," he commented, gently wrapping my fingers in a towel. "If you could, it shouldn't have burned you. The fire would have been *a part* of you. But what that was? That was real honest-to-God fire."

I frowned as my fingers throbbed. "Wait a sec. There's a chance I can't work with fire and you let me do that?"

"How else am I going to figure out your limitations?"

"What the hell!" I pulled my hand free, furious. "That's not cool, Blake. What's next? Trying to stop a moving vehicle by standing in front of it, but whoops, I can't do that and now I'm dead?"

Blake rolled his eyes. "You should be able to do that. At least, I hope so."

Disgusted with him, I went back to the candles. Needing to prove myself, I tried again and again. I couldn't light the fire without touching the candles no matter how hard I tried.

The following morning I had to come up with a good excuse for my mom. It involved something stupid like placing my hand on a lit burner, but she believed me, and I even scored some weak pain pills.

Later that night, Blake explained that he'd never been able to heal anyone. When I asked when and why he'd been presented with the opportunity, he didn't get a chance to answer. Warmth tingled over my neck and then a few seconds later there was a knock on my door.

I shot up. "Daemon."

"Woo hoo." Blake exuded so much false enthusiasm he could've been an actor.

Ignoring him, I rushed to the front door. "Hey," I gasped, feeling hot and dizzy when I saw him. It never failed to amaze me how striking Daemon really was. "Are you helping tonight?"

Daemon's gaze dropped to my bandaged fingers and nodded. "Yeah. Where's Bilbo?"

"Blake," I corrected. "He's in the living room."

He shut the door behind him. "About your hand…"

When Daemon had asked me about it in class earlier, I'd avoided answering, because I seriously doubted he would think how it happened was kosher. The last thing any of us needed was for him to kill Blake over my own ineptitude.

"I burned it on the stove last night." I shrugged, looking down at the tips of his black boots peeking out from his denim jeans.

"That…is…"

I sighed. "Lame?"

"Yeah, really lame, Kat. Maybe you should stay away from the stove for a little while?"

He sidled past me and headed for the living room. I trailed behind, knowing I couldn't leave him alone with Blake for any amount of time.

Blake gave him a halfhearted wave. "Nice of you to join us again."

Grinning, Daemon plopped down next to Blake and spread his arm over the back of the couch, crowding the other boy. "I know you've missed me. It's all right, I'm here."

"Yeah," Blake said, sounding real genuine.

We got started with moving stuff around for a little while and Daemon didn't say much, not even a "Wow" or a "Congratulations," but he watched me. Constantly.

"Moving stuff is just a parlor trick, really." Blake's arms were pinned to his chest.

"Wow." Daemon cocked his head to the side. "You're just now figuring that out?"

Blake ignored him. "The good news is you can do it on command now, but that doesn't mean you have control. I hope it does, but we really don't know."

Damn. Blake was such a downer sometimes.

"I have an idea. You're going to need to completely trust me. If I ask you to do something, you can't fire back with a thousand questions." He paused while Daemon's eyes narrowed. "We need to see something amazing."

Amazing? I was moving stuff without touching it! That's pretty amazing in my book. But then again, there was the fire hoopla. "I'm doing my best."

"Your best isn't good enough." He exhaled loudly. "Okay. Stay here."

I glanced at Daemon as Blake disappeared into the foyer. "I have no idea what he's up to."

Daemon arched a brow. "I'm guessing it's going to be something I don't like."

Like there was much Blake could do that Daemon would like. What he didn't know or get was that Blake hadn't put the moves on me. Not once since he'd tried to hug me that day in the diner. But maybe it was just plain old dislike.

While we waited, I heard drawers opening in the kitchen. There was a *clank* of silverware. Oh goodie, more glassware to destroy.

Blake returned and stopped in the doorway, one hand behind his back. "You ready?"

"Sure."

He smiled and then cocked his arm back. Light reflected off the sharp edge of metal. A knife? And then the *butcher knife* was flying straight at my chest.

A scream caught in my throat. I threw up my hand, horrified and panicked. The knife stopped in midair. Frozen inches from my chest, pointy end facing toward me. It just stayed there, suspended.

Blake clapped. "I knew it!"

I stared at him as my critical-thinking skills slowly trickled back in. "What the hell, Blake?"

Several things happened all at once. Now that my concentration was broken, the knife fell out of the air, smacking off the floor harmlessly. Blake was still clapping. I let loose several curses that would've caused my mom to cry and Daemon, who'd appeared to have been knocked into a stupor by what Blake had done, snapped out of it.

Daemon shot off that couch like a rocket, simultaneously flipping into his true form. A heartbeat later, he had Blake pinned halfway up the wall, swathed in an intense whitish-red light that lit up the entire living room.

I craned my neck and whispered, "Holy smokes."

"Whoa! Whoa!" Blake yelled, arms flailing in the light. "You need to check yourself. Katy wasn't in any danger."

There was no response from Daemon, not one that Blake could hear, anyway, but I did. Loud and clear. *That's it. I'm going to kill him.*

Windows began to shake and walls trembled. The flat-screen on the TV stand rattled. All around, little puffs of plaster filled the air. Daemon's light flared, swallowing Blake whole, and for a horrible moment, I really thought he had killed Blake.

"Daemon!" I shrieked, darting around the coffee table. "Stop!"

But then there was a crackling sound, like air heated and charged after a lightning strike. Still in his Luxen form, Daemon jerked back and let Blake go. The boy landed on his feet and staggered to the side as he rose.

Daemon hummed and started toward Blake, but I got in the middle. "Okay. You two need to freaking stop."

Blake ran both his hands down his shirt, straightening it. "I'm not doing anything."

"You did throw a freaking knife at me," I shot back. Wrong thing to say, because I heard Daemon promise, *I will break him in two.* "Stop."

An arm appeared in the light and fingers brushed along my cheek. The touch was soft as silk and brief, lasting only half of a second and so quick that I doubted Blake even saw it. Then his light flickered out. He stood in his human form, trembling with barely restrained rage, his eyes white and sharp like icicles. "What the hell were you thinking?"

"She wasn't in any danger! If I thought for a second she couldn't do it, I wouldn't have thrown it at her!"

Daemon sidestepped me, his large hand curled into a fist. Human or alien, Daemon could do some real damage. "But there was no way you would've known she could do it! Not a hundred percent!"

Turning wide, pleading eyes to me, Blake shook his head. "I swear you were never in any danger, Katy. If I thought you couldn't stop it, I wouldn't have done it."

Daemon cursed again and I moved, blocking him. "Who does that?" Daemon demanded. Heat rolled off his body.

"Actually, Kiefer Sutherland did. In the original Buffy movie," he explained. When I continued to gape at him, he grimaced. "It was on TV a few nights ago. He threw one at Buffy and she caught it."

"That was Donald Sutherland—the dad," Daemon corrected, much to my surprise.

Blake shrugged. "Same difference."

"I'm not Buffy!" I yelled.

A slow grin pulled at his lips. "You are definitely cuter than Buffy."

And that wasn't the right thing to say. Daemon growled low in his throat. "You got a death wish? Because you're really pushing it tonight, buddy. I'm dead serious. Really pushing it. I can hold you up against that wall until you run out of juice. Can you hold me off forever? No? I didn't think so."

Blake's jaw jutted out. "Okay. I'm sorry. But if she hadn't been able to catch it, I would've stopped it. Just like you would've. No harm. No foul."

A whirlwind of rage was building inside Daemon and I doubted I could stop him again if he went after Blake. I tensed. "I think that's enough for tonight."

"But—"

"Blake, I *really* think you should leave," I said meaningfully. "Okay? I think you need to go."

Blake looked over my shoulder and seemed to get it, because he nodded. "All right." He started toward the door and stopped. "But you did great, Katy. I don't think you realize how awesome that was."

A low hum rattled the floors and Blake took his cue, hightailing his behind out of the house. Only when I heard the rumbling of his truck's engine did I relax.

"No more," Daemon said, voice low. "Absolutely no more."

Slowly, I turned around. His eyes were still doing the glow thing. Up close, they were sort of beautiful—odd but really striking.

"He could have killed you, Kat. I'm not okay with that. I won't be okay with that."

"Daemon, he wasn't trying to kill me."

He looked incredulous. "Are you insane?"

"No." Tired, I bent and picked up the huge serial-killer knife. As I held it, it sunk in that I had stopped a knife whizzing toward my chest. I faced Daemon, swallowing.

He was still ranting. "I don't want you doing any more training with him. I don't even want you near him. That boy's got a few screws loose."

Freezing anything was a huge deal. It was one of the most powerful uses of the Source, Blake and Daemon had both said, with the exception of using it as a weapon.

"I'm going to give him back-alley plastic surgery. I can't—"

"Daemon," I whispered.

"—believe he did that." All of a sudden, he was wrapping his arms around me, hauling me against his chest. By some miracle, I didn't stab him. "Jesus, Kat, he could have hurt you."

Somewhat shocked by the close contact that he'd avoided since the evening he made me a sandwich, I didn't move at first. His entire body hummed. The hand that came up, wrapping around the back of my head, shook slightly.

"Look, you've obviously got some control. I can help you work on it," he said, resting his chin against the top of my head, and God, his arms, his body was so warm and so perfect. "This can't happen again."

"Daemon." My voice was muffled against his chest.

"What?" He pulled back a little, lowering his chin.

"I froze it."

His brows knitted. "Huh?"

"I *froze* the knife." I wiggled free, waving the thing around. "I didn't just stop it, but I froze it. The thing was just hovering in air."

It seemed to hit him, too. "Holy…"

I laughed. "God, that's pretty huge, isn't it?"

Daemon nodded. "It is. That's…that's a big deal."

Excitement thrummed through me. "We can't stop training."

"Kat—"

"We can't! Look, throwing a knife at me isn't cool. And God knows, I'm not exactly thrilled that he did it, but it worked. It really worked. We're getting somewhere—"

"What part of 'He could've killed you' don't you understand?" Daemon backed off, which usually meant he was really, really angry. "I don't want you training with him. Not when he's putting your life in danger."

"He's not putting my life in danger." Besides catching my fingers on fire and the knife incident—but still, the risks were worth it. If I could control these abilities and actually use them to protect Daemon and Dee, then I wouldn't be just a human—or just a mutated human one step away from exposing them to the world.

"We can't stop," I reasoned. "I'll be able to control it and use the Source, just like you and Dee can. I can help you—"

"Help me with what?" Daemon stared at me, then laughed. "Help me to fight Arum?"

Okay. I wasn't going that far, but now that he mentioned it, why not? According to Blake, I had potential to be stronger than Daemon. Crossing my arms over my chest, I tapped the edge of the knife on my arm. "Yeah, what if I wanted to?"

He laughed again, and I wanted to kick him. "Kitten, you're not helping me fight Arum."

"Why not? If I can control the Source and help, why not? I could fight."

"I think the reasons are pretty huge," he yelled, all the humor vanishing. "First off, you're a human."

"Not really."

His eyes narrowed. "Granted, you're a mutated human, but a human who's a hell of a lot weaker and more vulnerable than a Luxen."

I exhaled slowly. "You don't know how weak or vulnerable I'll be fully trained."

"Whatever. Secondly, you have no business going up against the Arum. That will never happen."

"Daemon—"

"It won't if I'm still alive. Do you understand that? You will never go after an Arum. I don't care if you can stop the world from spinning."

I tried to push down my anger. One thing I hated more than Daemon's douche-nozzle side was him telling me what to do. "You don't own me, Daemon."

"It's not about ownership, you little nut."

"Nut?" I glared at him. "I wouldn't call me names when I have a knife in my hand."

He ignored that. "Thirdly, there is something off about Blake. You can't tell me you don't see or sense that."

"Oh, don't—"

"You know nothing about him—nothing deeper than that he likes to surf and blog. Big deal."

"These aren't good enough reasons."

"Because I don't want you in danger—how about that? Is that damn good enough for you?" he shouted, and I jumped. He looked away, drawing in several deep breaths.

I hadn't realized that could've been the real reason behind it all. About every part of me softened, and my temper slipped away like a snowflake melting. "Daemon, you can't stop me just to protect me."

His head swung back to me. "I *need* to protect you."

Need was such a strong word that it stole my breath and my heart.

"Daemon, I'm flattered—I am, but your job is not to protect me. I'm not Dee. I'm not another one of your responsibilities."

"Damn right you're not Dee! But you are my responsibility. I got you into this mess. And I will not be dragging you further into it!"

My head was spinning. His reasons for wanting me to stop training with Blake were right but all wrong. I needed to prove to him that I wasn't a liability or something to be constantly watched over. If he felt that way and did keep putting himself in jeopardy because of me, he could lose his own life or Dee's.

"I'm not stopping," I said.

Daemon stared at me. "Does it even matter that I don't want you in that kind of danger? That I won't facilitate something as idiotic as you gearing up to go against the Arum?"

I flinched. Ouch, that stung. "Wanting to help you and your kind is idiotic?"

His jaw tightened. "Yeah, it is."

"Daemon," I whispered. "I get that you care—"

"You don't get it. That's the problem!" He stopped, pulling it all back in, sucking the air right out of the room with it. "I won't be a part of this. I mean it, Katy. You chose this, then…whatever. I won't have this hanging over my head like I do every freaking day with Dawson. I won't make another mistake and condone this."

I sucked in a sharp breath. My chest ached at the thought of him carrying that kind of guilt—guilt that didn't belong to him. "Daemon—"

"What will it be, Katy?" He looked at me dead-on. "Tell me now."

"I don't know what to tell you," I whispered, tears burning my eyes. Didn't he see? Going through with this would give me a better chance of not turning out like Bethany and Dawson, of being able to take care of myself and protect him, because one day, he'd need it.

Daemon took a step back as though I'd hit him. "That was the wrong thing to say." His face turned hard, his eyes like glaciers. The coldness radiating from him chilled me to the bone. He'd never looked more detached. "I'm done."

Chapter 21

Part of me wanted to skip classes the next day, but it wasn't like I could hide forever. Unexpectedly, Daemon was a no-show. I didn't see him in the halls, either, or when I grabbed my stuff out of my locker before lunch. He never showed.

I'd chased him right out of the damn school.

"Hey," Blake said, strolling up to me. "You don't look any better."

Through the duration of bio, I'd pretty much had my face stuck in my textbook. I sighed, closing the door. "Yeah, not feeling it today."

"Hungry?" When I shook my head, he tugged on my backpack. "Me neither. I know a place to go, no food and no people."

Sounded good to me, because the last thing I could stomach right now was watching Adam and Dee go to second base at the lunch table. Turned out, the place Blake had in mind was the empty auditorium. Perfect.

We sat in the back, propping our feet up on the seats in front of us. Blake pulled an apple from his bag. "Did Daemon ever calm down last night?"

I groaned inwardly. "Yeah…not really."

"I was afraid of that." There was a pause as he bit into the shiny red fruit. "You really weren't in any danger. If you didn't stop it, one of us would've."

"I know." I scooted down and laid my head on the back of my seat. "He just doesn't want to see me hurt." And that actually hurt to say, because I knew there was a mile-long road of good intentions behind what he had been saying last night, but he needed to see me as an equal. Not someone who was weak and needed rescuing.

"That's admirable." Blake grinned around his apple. "You know I don't like the tool, but he cares about you. And I'm sorry. I didn't mean to cause trouble between you two."

"It's not your fault." I patted his knee, not surprised when I got a little shock. "Everything will be okay."

Blake nodded. "Can I ask you something?"

"Sure."

He took another bite before he continued. "Is Daemon the one who healed you? I ask, because it may give me a better understanding of your power to know who changed you."

Anxiousness blossomed. "Why would you think it was him?"

Blake gave me a pointed look. "It would explain how close you two are. My friend and I were close afterward. I almost always knew when he was around. We were like two halves of the same whole after he healed me. It was a strong…bond."

Healing me was so forbidden that even an army of Arum couldn't get me to admit that it had been Daemon. "That's good to know, but that's not the case." Curiosity did get the best of me, though. "You say you two were close. Did it make you…attracted to him?"

"What?" He laughed. "No. We were like brothers, but the connection—whatever it is that they do to us—doesn't force us to feel anything. It just makes us close to who healed us. It's stronger than a familial bond, but not sexual or even emotional on that kind of level."

I lowered my lashes before he could see the rush of fresh tears that burned my eyes. Great. I was the biggest asshat alive. This whole time

I'd kept throwing the alien connection in Daemon's face and it hadn't been what was propelling him.

"Well, that's good to know." My own voice sounded strange to me. "Anyway...why is it so important who healed me?"

He looked at me like he doubted my IQ as he finished off his apple. "Because I hear that how strong the Luxen is who heals you is an indication of how much stronger you'll be. At least, that's what I've picked up from Liz. Her power and limitations were linked to who healed her. Same as me."

"Oh." Well, that explained how I blasted a satellite into outer space. Daemon's ego would go through the charts if he knew. I started to grin, but thinking of him renewed the ache in my chest.

"Which is why I thought it was Daemon, but he's pretty damn powerful. No offense, but you really haven't done anything extraordinary, so…"

"Gee, thanks?" I laughed at his chagrined look. "Anyway, it's not anyone you'd ever expect, and that's all I'm willing to say about it, okay?"

"All right." He held up the core of his apple, frowning. "You don't trust me, do you?"

I was quick to tell him that I did, I stopped. Someone at least deserved my honesty. "Don't take it personally, but right now, I think trust is something not easily given, considering."

Blake glanced at me sideways and smiled. "Good idea."

• • •

If I saw another knife in the next ten years, I'd need long-term psychiatric care. Spending time with a knife being thrown at me wasn't my idea of fun.

Thankfully, I'd been able to stop them all. And without Daemon there, Blake stayed in one piece.

He moved onto throwing non-deadly stuff at my head, like pillows and books, by the end of the week. After several hours, I'd mastered the art of not eating fabric. I never let the books hit me or the floor, though. That just seemed sacrilegious.

It seemed ass backward to start off with the knives and end with the pillow, but I understood his master plan. My ability was also tied to my emotions—like fear. I needed to be able to tap into those strong feelings and use them when I wasn't freaking out. I also needed to be able to control them when I was spazzing.

I groaned as I picked up all of the pillows off the floor and the books off the coffee table, putting them each back where they belonged.

"Tired?" Blake commented, lounging against the wall.

"Yeah." I yawned.

"You know how the Luxen get tired from using their powers?" Blake grabbed the last book, placing it where he'd gotten it: the TV stand.

"Yeah, and I remember you saying something about us tiring out faster than they do."

"We are just like the Luxen in that sense. They use up energy to do things—the whole sending-a-piece-of-them thing? We're the same way, but they can go a lot longer than we can. I don't know why. Has something to do with the fact that we only have half-alien DNA, but we have to be careful, Katy. The more abilities we use, the weaker we get. And faster."

"Great," I muttered. "So Daemon could've really held you against the wall all night?"

"Yep." He stopped beside me. "Sugar helps. But so does the Melody Stone."

"The what?" I rubbed the back of my neck as I dropped onto the couch.

"It's a type of crystal—a very rare opal." He sat beside me, so close that his thigh pressed against mine. I scooted away.

"What does it do?"

He rested his head back on the cushion and gave me a lopsided shrug. "From what I've learned, it can help increase our powers. Possibly even stabilize them so we don't grow tired like the Luxen do."

The whole crystal business didn't make sense to me. It sounded like a bunch of New Age crap, but then again, what did I know? "Do you have one?"

Blake laughed. "No. They're hard to get."

Grabbing an abused pillow, I placed it under my head and closed my eyes, snuggling against the arm of the couch. "Well, then I guess it's just me and sugar."

There was a pause. "You did really well, though. You're a fast learner."

"Ha! You weren't saying that the first week of training." I yawned. "Maybe this won't be so hard. I'll get control of my abilities...and everything will go back to normal."

"Things won't ever be normal, Katy. Once you step outside the range of the beta quartz, the Arum will find you." The couch dipped on my side, but I was too tired to open my eyes. "But if you can really control this, you'll be able to defend yourself."

And that's what I wanted. To stand beside Daemon, not cower behind him. "You're such a bearer of great news. You know that?"

"I don't mean to."

The cushion under me shifted even more, and I felt Blake's fingers brushing my hair aside. My eyes snapped open, and I jerked up, twisting around to face him. "Blake."

He sat back, placing his hand on his thigh. "I'm sorry. I didn't mean to startle you. I just wanted to make sure you were okay over there."

Was that all? Or more? Oh, man, this was so awkward. "Things are really complicated right now."

"Understandable," he said, sitting back. "You like him, don't you?"

I clutched the pillow to my chest, not sure what to say.

"Don't lie." He laughed when I frowned. "You always blush when you lie."

"I don't know why people keep saying that. My cheeks are not a human lie detector." I toyed with a frayed thread, knowing we needed to have *that* conversation, especially since we were working together. "I'm sorry. Just right now—"

"Katy, it's okay." He placed his hand on mine, squeezing reassuringly. "For real. I like you. I do. Obviously. But you have a lot going on, and probably some of that was before I even came here. So it's okay. Really."

The first real smile in two days turned up my lips. "Thanks for being so…understanding."

Blake pushed off the couch, running his hand through his hair. "Well, I have the time to be patient. I'm not going anywhere."

• • •

I sat in class, trying to focus on what Carissa and Lesa were talking about. My skin was alternating between hot and cold flashes.

"So, Katy, you've been hanging out with surfer boy a lot." Lesa cocked an eyebrow. "Care to share the details on that?"

I shrank in my seat. "No. We're just hanging out."

"Just hanging out," Lesa repeated slyly, "is like code for having sex."

Carissa's mouth dropped open. "No, it's not!"

"You obviously haven't dated a lot of guys around here." Lesa sat back in her chair, pulling on a tight curl. "Actually, pretty much everything with guys around here is code for sex."

"I'm going to have to go with Carissa on this one. Hanging out does not equal sex the last time I—"

Tingles shot across my neck and my heart rate spiked. I caught a glimpse of Daemon coming through the doorway and I focused on Lesa's face as though she were my lifeline.

Daemon glided past my seat and took his behind me. I clenched the edges of my notebook, hoping our teacher wouldn't take his sweet time getting to class.

A pen poked me in the back.

An unbelievably giddy rush swept through me. I turned slowly. I couldn't pick up anything from his guarded expression.

"I see you've been…busy," he said, lashes lowered.

Sucky part about living next to Daemon was the fact he pretty much saw everything I did. And that meant he knew I was still training with Blake. "Yeah, kind of."

Daemon's elbows scooted over the desk as he cupped his chin in his hands. "So what is Bobo doing?"

"It's *Blake*," I said, voice low. "And you know what we've been doing. You're more—"

"Not going to happen." He then laughed under his breath, but there was no humor to it as he inched a little closer. His irises deepened. "I really wish you'd think about this."

"And I wish *you*'d think about this."

Daemon didn't respond. He pulled his elbows back toward him, crossing his arms. Our conversation was obviously over. I twisted around, feeling icky.

Morning classes dragged. Lesa was waiting for me outside of bio, stopping me from going in. "Can I ask you a question?" she said, glancing around.

I sighed. "Sure."

She pulled me against an unoccupied locker. "What's going on? You kissed Daemon before Halloween, went out with Blake once, and now you went out with him again, but you and Daemon undeniably have something going on."

I made a face. "Gee, it sounds like I'm a ho-bag or something."

Lesa made a face. "I'm so not the one who's going to slut shame. Trust me. I'm just curious. Do you have any idea what you're doing?"

One of the reasons I liked Lesa? She didn't beat around the bush. She spoke what she thought, and because of that, I was more open with her than anyone. "I honestly don't know. I mean, I do. I'm not…dating Blake. And I'm not dating Daemon."

"You're not?"

I leaned against the cool steel and sighed. "It's complicated."

"Can't be that complicated," she said. "Who do you like?"

Closing my eyes, I finally put voice to it. "Daemon."

"Ah-ha!" She bumped me with her hip. "Wait. How is it complicated? Daemon's got it for you big time. Everyone can see that, even when you guys are at each other's throats. And you like him. What's the deal?"

How could I explain how messed up everything was? "It's just really complicated. Trust me."

Lesa frowned. "I'm going to have to take your word for it, because Blake is coming down the hall." She whipped around so quickly it was like she'd been caught peeping down my shirt.

Bio was uneventful. Blake typically acted like we weren't mutants or anything while we were in school, and I appreciated him for that. Here, I could be normal, as odd as that was.

I discovered they were serving cold lasagna and salad that smelled funny for lunch. Yum. I slopped some on my plate while craving a strawberry smoothie. Doubtful I'd get that delivered today. Daemon had stopped bringing me treats about the time training had started. I missed it. I missed him.

Dee and Adam were joined at the mouth when I sat down. I glanced at Carissa. She rolled her eyes, but I smiled. My sucky love life aside, I was still on Team Love Rocks. The only thing I honestly couldn't deal with was my mom and Will making out, which I'd gotten an eyeful of yesterday before she left for work. Ew.

"You going to eat that salad?" Dee asked.

"It's cute how you stopped kissing for food." I laughed, pushing my tray toward her. "Hey, Adam."

His cheeks were flushed. "Hey, Katy."

"Sorry. I worked up an appetite." Dee grinned.

"And I lost mine," Carissa muttered.

Blake never arrived at the cafeteria, but Daemon had. He'd taken his seat beside Andrew and Ash. Against my will, I watched him.

Daemon glanced up, holding a smoothie. He smirked.

Bastard.

I shifted my gaze to Dee. "How can you eat that? I swear the edges of the lettuce are brown. It's gross."

Adam laughed. "Dee can eat anything."

"So can you." She offered him the tomato on her fork. "Want some?"

"Okay." I sat back. "If you feed him, I'm going to have to find a new table."

"I second that," Carissa added.

Dee rolled her eyes but relented. "I like to share. What's wrong with that?" Then she looked at me, her expression hopeful. "I'm glad you're eating with us…alone today."

Uncomfortable, I nodded and focused on pulling apart my lasagna. I hated layered food, unless those layers involved chocolate and peanut butter.

Lunch and the afternoon classes finally ended, and I swung by the post office to pick up the mail before Blake came over.

As I was placing the junk and packages on the backseat, I caught sight of one of the black Expeditions parked at the edge of the parking lot, as if they'd pulled over abruptly and left the engine running.

It could be any Expedition, I told myself as I closed the door, but a shiver danced down my spine and all the tiny hairs rose on my arms. Maybe I'd developed some kind of wicked sixth sense along with my alien mojo?

Going to the driver's side, I kept an eye on the Expedition. Smoke plumed out of the muffler, choking the air.

Suddenly, the passenger door jerked open and I saw two people. Brian Vaughn, the DOD officer who owned the creepiest laugh ever, was leaning over the passenger, grabbing for the door. His mouth was a thin, angry slash as he groped for the door with one hand while his arm braced a girl against the seat.

Squinting, I took another look at the girl when I should've been climbing into my car and getting the hell out of there. The last thing I needed was for Vaughn to catch me peeping at him, but...I *knew* this girl.

I'd seen her face on a flyer, taped on the glass windows of FOOLAND. Her brown hair was pulled back tightly from her pale, elfin face. Her eyes weren't dancing with laughter when she turned to the door, watching Vaughn pull it shut, closing her in...closing me out.

Her eyes were empty.

But it was her.

It was Bethany.

Chapter 22

Bethany—Dawson's girlfriend—was alive. And she was with the DOD. It sounded insane, and I went through every stage of denial as I made my way home, but it was *her*. That face had been burned into my memory. I paced the house until Blake showed up, stunned by what this could mean.

He took one look at me and frowned. "You look like you've seen a ghost."

"I think I have." My hands opened and closed at my sides. "I think I saw Bethany today with this guy from the DOD."

Blake frowned. "Who's Bethany?"

It felt wrong telling Blake about this, but I needed to tell *someone*. "Bethany was Dawson's girlfriend. And Dawson was Daemon and Dee's brother. They were supposedly attacked by an Arum and killed, but their bodies were taken away by the DOD before Daemon or Dee could see them."

Understanding dawned in his eyes. "Man, I was curious. Every Luxen comes in threes."

I nodded. "But if it's really her—and I'm pretty sure it's her—what does that mean?"

Blake sat on the arm of the recliner, turning the TV remote over and over above his hands...without touching it. "How close were Dawson and Bethany?"

Then it hit me. It all seemed so clear. The walls tilted a little as panic punched a hole in my chest. "Oh my God, Dawson had healed Bethany. That's what everyone thinks. That she got hurt somehow and he healed her. And he could've changed—mutated—her, right?"

Blake nodded. "Oh, man…"

"And I bet Bethany is a nickname for Elizabeth and… And what did that girl look like—the one who told you about the DOD named Liz?"

His brows rose. "She had brown hair, a little darker than yours. Kind of sharp features, but really pretty."

It all started to click together. "This is insane. How would the DOD have known about her? She and Dawson disappeared just a couple of days after whatever happened between them, unless...unless someone who suspected that Bethany had been healed told the DOD." My stomach tumbled over as I pulled my hair back into a messy twist. "Who would do that? One of the Luxen?"

"I don't know. I wouldn't put it past the DOD to have Luxen who are the eyes and ears for them," he said, rubbing his brow. "Man, that sucks."

Suck didn't even cover it. That meant someone close to the Blacks had most likely betrayed them in the worst way. Anger whipped through me. I turned just as the curtains billowed out as if a rush of air had entered the room. A small cyclone of books and magazines moved through the living room, spinning and spinning.

"Whoa, simmer down, Storm."

I blinked and the cyclone fell apart. Sighing, I picked up the books and magazines now scattered around the room. My pulse thrummed in my ears as my mind raced through what I'd discovered. "If the DOD has Beth, then what did they do with Dawson? Do you think he's still alive?"

Hope sparked with that idea. If Dawson was alive, that would… It would be like my father still being alive. My life would change. Daemon's and Dee's lives would change for the better. They'd be a family again…

Blake grasped my arm gently, turning me toward him. "I know what you're thinking. How wonderful it would be for him to still be alive, but Katy, the DOD doesn't want Dawson. They wanted Bethany. And they'd do *anything* to get control of mutated humans. If the DOD told his family he was dead…"

"But you don't know if they told the truth," I protested.

"Why would they keep him alive, Katy? If that really is Liz—Beth—then they have what they want. Dawson would be dead."

I couldn't believe that. There was a chance he was alive, and there was no way I could live with myself without telling Daemon and Dee.

"Katy, he can't be alive. They are ruthless," he persisted, and his grip tightened on my arm. "You do understand that, right?" He shook my arm. Hard. "Do you?"

Surprised by his doggedness, I lifted my chin. My eyes met his, and there was something wrong in his, a quality that was slightly off and scary, like when he'd smiled and threw the knife at my head. Ice trickled through my veins.

"Yeah, I understand. It probably wasn't even her." I swallowed, forcing a smile. "Blake, can you let go of my arm? You're hurting me."

He blinked and then seemed to realize he'd been squeezing my arm. He let go and choked out a laugh. "I'm sorry. I just don't want you getting your hopes up and being let down. Or doing something crazy."

"No, my hopes aren't up." Rubbing my arm, I backed up. "And what could I do, anyway? I'd never tell Daemon or Dee if I wasn't sure."

Relieved, he smiled. "Good. Let's start training."

Nodding, I dropped the subject and hoped Blake forgot about it. Our training consisted of freezing things, and as soon as he left, I rushed to grab my cell. It was near midnight, but I texted Daemon anyway.

Can u come over?

I waited ten minutes before I texted him again.

This is important!!!

Another ten minutes went by, and I was starting to feel like I was one of those psychotic girlfriends who texted the crap out of guys until they responded. Damn him. Cursing, I sent him one more text.

Its abt Dawson.

Not even a minute later, I felt the rush of warmth on my neck. Stomach tumbling and twisting, I answered the door. "Daemon..." My words died off and my eyes widened. I must've woken him up, because...

No shirt. Again.

It had to be below thirty degrees outside, but he was standing in front of me in flannel pajama bottoms and nothing else but glorious, perfectly formed skin stretched taut over hard muscle. I hadn't forgotten what he'd looked like shirtless, but my memory had not served him one bit of justice.

Daemon stepped inside, eyes wide and luminous. "What about Dawson?"

I shut the door, heart racing. What if telling him was a mistake? What if Dawson was dead? I'd just be screwing up Daemon's life even more. Maybe I should've listened to Blake.

"Kat," Daemon snapped, impatient.

"Sorry." I moved past him, careful not to touch any of his exposed skin, and went into the living room. Popping in front of me, he planted his hands on his hips. I took a deep breath. "I saw Bethany today."

Daemon's head jerked to the side and he blinked once, then twice. *"What?"*

"Dawson's girl—"

"I know what you said," he interrupted me, dragging both hands through his tousled hair. For a moment I was a bit distracted by the way the muscles in his arms and shoulders rippled. *Focus*. "How can you be sure it was her, Kat? You've never seen her."

"I've seen her missing person's flyer. It's a face I can't forget." I sat down, rubbing my hands over my knees. "It was her."

"Holy shit..." Daemon sat beside me on the couch, dropping his hands between his legs. "Where did you see her?"

I watched the confusion lining his face and I wanted nothing more than to comfort him somehow. "At the post office after school."

"And you waited until now to tell me?" Before I could answer, he laughed under his breath. "Because you were training with Bilbo Baggins and you had to wait until he left to talk to me?"

Squeezing my knees, I jerked my chin. Daemon should've been the first person I went to. Being shocked by what I saw and the training sessions weren't nearly as important or a good enough excuse. "I'm sorry, but I'm telling you now."

He nodded curtly and returned to staring at the Christmas tree. It seemed like forever ago that we'd put it up. "Man, I don't...I don't even know what to say. Beth's alive?"

I nodded, pressing my lips together. "Daemon, I saw her with Brian Vaughn. She's with the DOD. They'd pulled over on the side of the road and the car door had opened. That's how I saw them. He was closing the door and he looked angry."

Daemon slowly twisted his head toward me, and our gazes locked. Time stretched. An array of emotions went through his eyes, turning them from a bright green to a dark, stormy color. I saw the moment he knew what I was getting at—the second that his entire world came crumbling down and was rebuilt within seconds.

Suspecting that Dawson had healed Bethany, and then jumping to Dawson and Bethany disappearing because of the DOD rather than the Arum wasn't a hard leap to make. Not after discovering that by healing me, Daemon had also changed me. Then you throw Blake into the mix, plus everything he'd told us about the DOD and their search for mutated humans.

Daemon was smart.

He shot to his feet and within seconds, he was out of his human form and blinding me. His light flared a shade of red-white as he pinged across the room. Wind picked up, stirring the bulbs on the Christmas tree. *She was with the DOD?* His voice whispered to me, tight with fury. *The DOD is responsible for this?*

Hearing Daemon's voice in my head always took me a few seconds to get accustomed to, and out of habit I answered verbally. "I don't know, Daemon, but that's not the worst part of this. How would the DOD know what happened between Dawson and Bethany unless…?"

Unless someone told them? His light pulsed and a blast of heat filled the room. *But Dawson didn't even tell me he'd healed her or that anything happened. How would anyone know? Unless someone had seen them other than me, suspected what happened, and betrayed us…*

I nodded, not even sure if he was looking at me or not. All I could see was his form, no features, no eyes. "That's what I've been thinking. It had to be someone who knew, and that probably really limits the pool of suspects."

Several moments passed and the temperature in the room continued to rise. *I need to know who betrayed us. Then I'll make them wish they'd never landed on this planet.*

Eyes wide, I stood and pushed up the sleeves of my sweater. Swallowing, I took a chance. *Daemon?*

His light flickered. *I hear you.*

More proof that our connection hadn't gone anywhere. *I know you're hell-bent on revenge, but most importantly, what if Dawson is still alive?*

Daemon drifted over to me, and tiny beads of sweat broke out on my forehead. *Then I don't know if I should be happy or sad. He'd be alive, but where? The DOD has him, and if that's the case, what kind of life has he had? For two years?* His next words sounded choked, even within my mind. *What have they been doing to him?*

Tears filled my eyes, blurring his light. *I'm sorry, Daemon. I'm really sorry. But if he's alive, then he's alive.* I reached out, placing my hand through the light, touching his chest. The light pulsed erratically then calmed. My fingers hummed. *That's got to mean something, right?*

Yes, yes it does. Then he stepped back, and a second later he was in his human form. "I need to find out if my brother is alive—and if he's not…" He looked away, jaw working. "I need to know how and why he died. It's obvious why they would want Beth, but my brother?"

I sat back down, wiping my palm over my forehead. "I don't know—" Daemon grasped my hand so quickly, I gasped. "What are you doing?"

He turned my hand over, his brows furrowing. "What is this?"

"Huh?" I glanced down, and my heart stuttered. A deep, purplish bruise circled my wrist, right where Blake had grabbed me earlier. "It's nothing," I said quickly. "I banged my arm into the counter earlier."

His eyes lifted, piercing mine. "Are you sure that's what happened, because I swear if it's not, you tell me and *that problem* will be solved."

I forced a laugh and an eye roll for extra benefit. There was no doubt in my mind that Daemon would do something terrible to Blake even though it was an accident. There were no shades of gray with him. "Yes, Daemon, that's all that happened. Geez."

Studying me, he backed up and sat on the couch. Several moments passed. "Don't tell Dee about this, okay? Not until we get some leads or something. I don't want her knowing anything until we know for sure."

Great. One more lie, but I could understand why. "How are you going to get leads?"

"You said you saw Bethany with Vaughn, right?"

I nodded.

"Well, I happen to know where he lives. And he probably knows where Beth is and what happened to Dawson."

"How do you know where he lives?"

He smiled, a bit evilly. "I have my ways."

A new panic dug in with icy fingers. "Wait. Oh no, you can't go after him. That's insane and dangerous!"

Daemon arched a coal-black brow. "As if you care what happens to me, Kitten."

My mouth dropped open. "I do care, jerk-face! Promise me you won't do anything stupid."

Watching me a few seconds, his smile turned sad. "I won't make promises I know I'll break."

"Argh! You're so freaking frustrating. I didn't tell you so you'd go off and do something stupid."

"I'm not going to do anything stupid. And even if what I plan is risky and insane, it's a well-thought-out level of stupidity."

I rolled my eyes. "That's reassuring. Anyway, how do you know where he lives?"

"Since we're surrounded by people who potentially want to do my family harm, I tend to keep tabs on them like they keep tabs on me." He leaned back, stretched his arms until his back bowed. Good God, I had to look away. But not before I caught the gleam of satisfaction in his eyes. "He's been staying at a rental in Moorefield, but I'm not sure which one it is."

I shifted on the couch, yawning. "What are you going to do? Stake out his block?"

"Yes."

"What? Do you have a James Bond fetish?"

"Possibly," he replied. "I just need a car not easily recognizable. Does your mom work tomorrow?"

My brows rose. "No, she's off in the evening and will probably be sleeping, but—"

"Her car would be perfect." He shifted his weight on the couch and was now so close, his bare arm pressed into mine. "Even if Vaughn has seen her car, he won't suspect it belongs to her."

I scooted over. "I'm not letting you take my mom's car."

"Why not?" He inched over, grinning. A charming smile—the

same he'd used on my mom the first time they'd met. "I'm a good driver."

"That's not the point." I moved against the arm of the couch. "I can't just let you take her car without me."

He frowned. "You're not getting involved in this."

But I wanted to be involved in this, because it did involve me. I shook my head. "You want my mom's car, then you get me along with it. It's a two-for-one special."

Daemon tipped his chin now, peering up through thick lashes. "Get you? Now that sounds way more interesting of a deal."

My cheeks flushed. Daemon already had me, but he just didn't know. "As in a partnership, Daemon."

"Hmm." Daemon flickered to the door. "Be ready after school tomorrow. Ditch Bartholomew by any means necessary. And do not speak a word of this to him. You and I will be playing spy alone."

Chapter 23

Making up some lame excuse about having to spend time with my mom, I successfully ditched a very pouty Blake. Getting the keys from my mom wasn't too difficult, either. She'd crashed from a double shift as soon as she got home, and I knew she wouldn't be awake to notice her car was gone. We'd waited until darkness fell, which clocked in around five thirty.

Daemon met me outside and tried to take the keys. "Nope. My mom's car means I'm driving."

He glared at me but got into the passenger seat. His long legs were no match for the cramped seating. He looked like he'd outgrown the car. I laughed. Daemon scowled.

I turned on a rock station, and he changed it to an oldies station. Moorefield was only fifteen minutes away, but it would be the longest damn drive of my life.

"So how did you drop Butter-face?" he asked before we even pulled out of the driveway.

I shot him a dirty look. "I told him I have plans with my mom. It's not like I spend every waking minute with Blake."

Daemon snorted.

"What?" I glanced at him. He stared out the window, one hand on the oh-shit handle. As if my driving was *that* bad. "What?" I repeated. "You know what I'm doing with him. It's not like we're hanging out and watching movies."

"Do I really know what you're doing with him?" he asked softly.

My hands tightened on the wheel. "Yes."

The muscle worked in his jaw, and then he turned, angling his body toward me the best he could given the limited space. "You know, your whole life doesn't have to involve training with Bradley. You can take time off."

"You could also join us. I liked it…when you helped out, when you were there," I admitted, feeling my cheeks burn.

There was a pause. "You know my stance on that, but you need to stop avoiding Dee. She misses you. And that's just messed up."

Guilt chewed at me with small, razor-sharp teeth. "I'm sorry."

"You're sorry?" he said. "What for? For being a crappy friend?"

In a second, anger flashed through me, wild and hot like a fireball. "I'm not trying to be a *crappy* friend, Daemon. You know what I'm doing. *You're* the one who told me to keep her out of this. Just tell Dee I'm sorry, okay?"

The familiar challenge was in his voice. "No."

"Can we not talk?"

"And that would also be a no."

But he didn't say anything else while he gave me directions to the subdivision where Vaughn lived. I parked the car halfway between the suspected six houses, grateful that my mom tinted the windows of her car.

Then Daemon started in again. "How has your training been going?"

"If you got over yourself, you'd know."

He smirked. "Are you still able to freeze things? Move objects around?" When I nodded, his eyes narrowed. "Have you had any unexpected outbursts of power?"

Besides the whole mini cyclone in my living room after seeing Bethany, I hadn't. "No."

"Then why are you still training? The whole purpose was for you to get control. You have."

Wanting to bang my head against the steering wheel, I groaned. "That's not the only reason, Daemon. And you know that."

"Obviously I don't," he retorted, pushing back against his seat.

"God, I love how you're all up in my personal business but don't want to be involved in it."

"I like talking about your personal business. It's usually entertaining and always good for a laugh."

"Well, I don't," I snapped.

Daemon sighed as he twisted in his seat and tried to get comfortable. "This car sucks."

"It was your idea. I, on the other hand, think the car is a perfect size. But that might be because I'm not the size of a mountain."

He snickered. "You're the size of a little, itty bitty doll."

"If you say a vacant doll, I will hurt you." I wound the necklace chain around my fingers. "Got that?"

"Yes, ma'am."

I stared out the windshield, caught between wanting to just be angry with him—because that was easy—and wanting to explain myself. So much bubbled up in me that nothing would come out.

He sighed. "You're worn down. Dee's worried. She won't stop bugging me to check on you and see what's wrong, since you won't hang out with her anymore."

"Oh, so we're back to you doing things to make your sister happy? Are you getting bonus points for asking?" I asked before I could stop myself.

"No." He reached out, catching my chin in a gentle grasp, forcing me to look at him. And when I did, I couldn't breathe. His eyes churned. "I'm worried. I'm worried for a thousand different reasons and I hate this—I hate feeling like I can't do anything about it. That history is on repeat and even though I can see it as clear as day, I can't stop it."

His words opened up a hole in my chest and suddenly I thought of Dad. When I was little and would get upset, usually over something stupid like a toy I wanted, I could never really put my frustration into words. Instead, I'd throw a fit or pout. And Dad…he always said the same thing.

Use your words, Kitty-cat. Use your words.

Words were the most powerful tool. Simple and so often underestimated. They could heal. They could destroy. And I needed to use my words now. I wrapped my fingers around his wrist, welcoming the jolt that touching him gave me.

"I'm sorry," I whispered.

Daemon looked confused. "About what?"

"About everything—about not hanging out with Dee and being a terrible friend to Lesa and Carissa." I took a deep breath and gently pulled his hand away. I looked out the windshield, blinking back tears. "And I'm sorry about not being able to stop training. I get why you don't want me to. I really do. I understand that you don't want me in danger and that you don't trust Blake."

Daemon sat back against the seat and I forced myself to continue. "Most of all, I do know you fear that I'm going to end up like Bethany and Dawson—whatever really did happen to them—and you want to protect me from that. I understand. And it…it kills me knowing that it hurts you, but you've got to understand why I need to be able to control and use my abilities."

"Kat—"

"Let me finish, okay?" I glanced at him and when he nodded, I took another breath. "This isn't just about you and what you want. Or what you're afraid of. This is about me—my future and my life. Granted, I didn't know what I wanted to do with my life when it came to college, but now I face a future where if I step out of the range of the beta quartz, I'm going to be hunted. Like you. My *mom* will be in danger if an Arum sees and follows me home. And then there's this whole DOD mess."

I squeezed my hand around the obsidian. "I have to be able to defend myself and the people I care about. Because I can't expect you to always be there to protect me. It's not right or fair to either of us. That's why I'm training with Blake. Not to piss you off. Not to get with him. I'm doing it so that I can stand beside you, as your equal, and not be someone you need to protect. And I'm doing this for myself, so that I don't have to rely on anyone to save me."

Daemon's lashes lowered, shielding his eyes. Seconds passed in silence and then he said, "I know. I know why you want to do this. And I respect that. I do." There was a "but" coming. I could feel it in my bones. "But it's hard to stand back and let this happen."

"You don't know what's going to happen, Daemon."

He nodded and then turned to the passenger window. One hand came up, rubbing along his jaw. "It's hard. That's all I can say about this. I'll respect what you want to do, but it's hard."

I released the breath I hadn't realized I was holding on a soft sigh and nodded. I knew he wasn't going to say anything more about this. Respecting my decision was better than an apology. At least now, we were on the same page, and that was important.

I peeked at him. "Anyway, what are we going to do if we see Vaughn?"

"Haven't thought that far ahead yet."

"Wow. This was a good plan." I paused. "I really doubt Bethany is in one of these houses. That would just be too dangerous."

"I agree, but why did they have her out in public like that?" He'd asked the million-dollar question. "Where anyone could see her?"

I shook my head. "I got the distinct impression that Vaughn wasn't too happy. Maybe she escaped."

He looked at me. "That would make sense. But Vaughn, well, he's always been a punk."

"You know him?"

"Not extremely well, but he started working with Lane a few months before Dawson *disappeared*." The last word seemed to get stuck on his tongue, as if he were still getting acquainted with the possibility that Dawson wasn't dead. "Lane had been our handler for God knows how long, and then Vaughn showed up with him. He was there when they told us about Dawson and Bethany."

Daemon's throat worked. "Lane seemed genuinely upset. Like Dawson wasn't just a *thing* that had died, but a person. Maybe he grew attached to Dawson over the years. See"—he cleared his throat—"Dawson had that kind of effect on people. Even when he was being a smartass, you couldn't help but like him. Anyway, Vaughn couldn't have cared less."

I didn't know what to say. So I reached over the small space between us and squeezed his arm. He looked at me, his eyes bright. Beyond him, several large snowflakes fell with a quiet hush.

Daemon placed his hand on mine for the briefest moment. Something infinite flared between us—stronger than physical, which was weird because it really fueled all that physical stuff in me. Then he pulled back, watching the snow. "You know what I've been thinking?"

Why I hadn't crawled over the center console and into his lap yet? Because damn if I was wondering that very thing, but the car was way too small for those kinds of shenanigans. I cleared my throat. "What?"

Daemon leaned back against the seat, watching the snow just like I was. "If the DOD knows what we can do, then none of us are really safe. Not that we've ever been safe, but this changes everything." He turned his head toward me. "I don't think I said thank you."

"For what?"

"For telling me about Bethany." He paused, a tight smile pulling at his lips.

"You needed to know. I would—*wait*." Two headlights turned onto the street. It was at least the fifth one, but it was from an SUV. "We've got one."

Daemon's eyes narrowed. "It's an Expedition."

We watched the black Expedition slow down and pull into the driveway of a single-story home two houses in. Even though the windows in our car were tinted, I wanted to slide down in the seat and hide my face. The driver's door opened and Vaughn stepped out, frowning at the sky as if it dared to annoy him by snowing. Another car door closed and a figure moved into the light.

"Dammit," Daemon said. "Nancy's with him."

"Well, you weren't really planning on talking to him, were you?"

"Yeah, I kind of was."

Dumbfounded, I shook my head. "That's insane. What were you going to do? Bust up in his house and demand answers?" When he nodded, I gaped. "Then what next?"

"Another thing I hadn't fully worked out yet."

"Geez," I muttered. "You suck at this whole spy thing."

Daemon chuckled. "Well, we can't do anything tonight. If one of them went missing it probably wouldn't be such a huge deal, but two of them would raise too many questions."

My stomach churned as I watched the agents disappear into the house. A light turned on inside, and a slender figure moved in front of the window, drawing the curtains closed. "Huh. Private bunch, aren't they?"

"Maybe they're getting some bow-chicka-pow-wow."

I looked at him. "Ew."

He flashed his teeth. "She's definitely not my type." His gaze dropped to my lips, and parts of me quivered in response to the heat in his gaze. "But now I totally have that on my mind."

I was breathless. "You're a dog."

"If you pet me, I'll—"

"Don't even finish that sentence," I said, fighting a grin. Smiling only encouraged him, and he needed no extra reason to be a terror. "And knock the innocent look off your face. I so know—"

The obsidian flared quickly, heating up my sweater and chest like someone placed a hot coal against my skin. I yelped and jerked in my seat, banging my head on the roof.

"What?"

"An Arum," I gasped. "An Arum is nearby! You don't have any obsidian on you?"

Alert and tense, he scanned the dark road. "No. I left it in my car."

I stared at him, shocked. "Seriously? You left the one thing that kills your enemy in your *car*?"

"It's not like I need it to kill them. Stay here." He started to open the door, but I grabbed his arm. "What?"

"You can't get out of the car. We're right in front of their house! They'll see you." I ignored the rising fear that always came with the Arum. "Are we still close enough to the Rocks?"

"Yes," he growled. "They protect us for about fifty miles in every direction."

"Then just sit still."

He looked like he didn't understand the concept, but he took his hand off the door and sat back. A few seconds later, a shadow moved up the street, darker than the night itself. It glided to the curb, drifting over the lawns coated with a thin layer of snow, stopping in front of Vaughn's house.

"What the hell?" Daemon placed his hands on the dashboard.

The Arum took form, right there, out in the open. He was dressed like the ones we'd faced in the past: dark pants, black jacket, but no sunglasses. His pale blond hair moved slightly as he stepped up to the front door and pressed his finger on the doorbell.

Vaughn answered the door and grimaced. His mouth moved, but I couldn't make out what he said. Then he stepped to the side, letting the Arum enter his house.

"Holy monkey balls," I said, eyes wide. "That did not just happen."

Daemon sat back, his voice tight with fury when he spoke. "That did. And I think we've discovered how the DOD knows what we're capable of."

Mind reeling, I stared at him. "The DOD and the Arum are

working together? Sweet alien baby… Why?"

His brows puckered, and he shook his head. "Vaughn said a name—Residon. Read his lips."

This new development was so not good. "What do we do now?"

"What I want to do is blow up their house, but that would draw too much attention."

I pursed my lips. "No doubt."

"We need to go see Matthew. Now."

• • •

Matthew lived farther out in the boondocks than we did, and if the snow kept coming down, I had no idea how I was going to get Mom's car home. His house was a large cabin built into the side of a mountain. I carefully made my way up his steep, graveled driveway that my mom's Prius wouldn't dare conquer.

"If you fall and break something, I'm going to be irritated." Daemon grabbed my arm as I started to slip.

"Sorry, not all of us can be as awesome—" I squealed as he slid an arm around my back and lifted me into his arms. Daemon zipped us up the driveway, wind and snow blowing at my face. He put me down, and I stumbled to the side, dizzy. "Could you give me a warning next time?"

He grinned as he knocked on the door. "And miss that look on your face? Never."

Sometimes I seriously wanted to just punch him in the face, but it made me warm in all the right places to see this side of him again, too. "You're insufferable."

"You like my kind of suffering."

Before I could answer, Mr. Garrison opened the door. His eyes narrowed when he saw me standing next to Daemon, shivering. "This is…unexpected."

"We need to talk," Daemon said.

Eyeing me, Mr. Garrison led us into a very sparsely decorated living room. The walls were bare log and a fire in the fireplace crackled, throwing off heat and the scent of pine. There wasn't a single Christmas decoration. Needing to thaw out, I sat close to the fire.

"What's going on?" Mr. Garrison asked, picking up a small glass full of red liquid. "I'm assuming it's something I don't want to know, considering she's with you."

I checked myself before I said something back. The man was an alien, but he was also in control of my bio grade.

Daemon sat beside me. On the way up here, we agreed not to tell Mr. Garrison I'd been healed, much to my relief. "I guess we should start from the beginning, and you're probably going to want to sit."

He moved his hand, swirling the ruby liquid in his glass. "Oh, this is starting out good."

"Katy saw Bethany yesterday with Vaughn."

Mr. Garrison's brows shot up. He didn't move for a long breath, and then he took a drink. "That's not what I was expecting you to say. Katy, are you sure that's who you saw?"

I nodded. "It was her, Mr. Garrison."

"Matthew, call me Matthew." He took a step back, shaking his head. I felt like I just completed some major task to move to a first-name basis with him. Matthew cleared his throat. "I really don't know what to say."

"It gets worse," I said, rubbing my hands together.

"I know where one of the DOD officers lives, and we went there tonight."

"What?" Matthew lowered his glass. "Are you insane?"

Daemon shrugged. "While we were watching his house, Nancy Husher showed up and guess who else did?"

"Santa?" Matthew said dryly.

I laughed out loud. Wow, he did have a sense of humor.

Daemon ignored that. "An Arum showed up and they let him in. Even greeted him *by name*—Residon."

Matthew downed the entire drink and set the glass on the mantel above the fireplace. "This isn't good, Daemon. I know you want to rush up there and find out how Bethany is still alive, but you can't. This is too dangerous."

"Do you understand what this means?" Daemon stepped forward, holding his hands out, palms up. "The DOD has Bethany. Vaughn was one of the Officers who came and told us that they were both dead. So they lied about her. And that means they could've lied about Dawson."

"Why would they have Dawson? They told us he was dead. Obviously Bethany isn't, but that doesn't mean he's alive. So get that out of your head, Daemon."

Anger flashed in Daemon's deep green eyes. "If it was one of your siblings, would you 'get it out of your head'?"

"All my siblings are dead." Matthew stalked across the room, stopping in front of us. "You guys are all I have left, and I will not stand by and humor false hope that will get you killed or worse!"

Daemon sat down beside me, taking a deep breath. "You're family to us, too. And Dawson also considered you family, Matthew."

Pain flashed in Matthew's ultra-bright eyes, and he looked away. "I know. I know." He moved over to his recliner and sat down heavily, shaking his head. "Honestly, it would be best if he weren't alive, and you know that. I can't even imagine…"

"But if he is, we need to do something about it." Daemon paused. "And if he's truly dead, then…"

Then what kind of closure would that be? They'd already believed he was dead, and finding out that it wasn't the Arum would rip open old wounds and dump salt on them.

"You don't understand, Daemon. The DOD would have no interest in Bethany unless…unless Dawson healed her."

Blake had been saying this all along. The confirmation relieved me.

"What are you saying, Matthew?" Daemon asked, keeping up with the cluelessness.

Matthew rubbed his brow, wincing. "The elders…they don't talk about why we're not allowed to heal humans, and they have good reason. It's forbidden, not only because of the risk of exposure on our end, but because of what it does to a human. They know. So do I."

"What?" Daemon glanced at me. "Do you know what happens?"

He nodded. "It alters the human, splicing his or her DNA with ours. There has to be a true *want* for it to work, though. The human takes on our abilities, but it doesn't always stick. Sometimes it fades. Sometimes the human dies from it or the change backfires. But if successful, it forms a connection between the two."

As Matthew went on, Daemon grew more agitated, and rightfully so. "The connection between a human and a Luxen after a massive healing is unbreakable at a cellular level. It marries the two together. One cannot survive if the other perishes."

My mouth dropped open. Blake had *so* not told me that, but that meant...

Daemon was on his feet, chest rising with every rough, painful breath. "Then if Bethany is alive..."

"Then Dawson would have to be alive," Matthew finished, sounding weary. "If he had in fact healed her."

He had to have. There was no other reason why the DOD would be interested in Bethany.

Daemon just stared at the fire, twisting and curling on itself. Once again, I wanted to do something to comfort him, but what could I really do to make any of this better?

I shook my head. "But you just said he couldn't be alive."

"That was my weakest attempt to persuade this one from getting himself killed."

"Did you...did you know this the entire time?" Raw emotion filled Daemon's voice. His form started to fade, as if he were losing all control. "Did you?"

Matthew shook his head. "No. No! I believed both of them to be dead, but if he did heal her—did change her—and she's alive, then he has to be alive. That's a big if—an if based on whether or not Katy really did recognize someone she's never met."

Daemon sat down, eyes glittering in the firelight. "My brother's alive. He's…he's alive." He sounded numb, lost, even.

Wanting to cry for Daemon, I dragged in a shallow breath. "What do you think they're doing to him?"

"I don't know." Matthew stood unsteadily, and I wondered how much he'd been drinking before we arrived. "Whatever it is, it can't be…"

It couldn't be good. And I had a sinking suspicion. According to Blake, the DOD was interested in acquiring more mutated humans. What better way to achieve that goal than capturing a Luxen and forcing him to do it? Bile rose. But if it took a true want to successfully change a human, how could Dawson truly want to heal them when forced? Was he failing, and if so, what was happening to those humans? Matthew had already said it. If the change didn't stick, they were horribly mutated, or they died. My God, what could that do to a person—to Dawson?

"The DOD knows, Matthew. They know what we can do," Daemon said finally. "They've probably known since the beginning."

Matthew's lashes swept up, and he met Daemon's stare. "I've never truly believed they didn't, to be honest. The only reason I never voiced my belief is because I didn't want any of you to worry."

"And the elders—do they know this, too?"

"The elders are just grateful to have a place to live in peace and be basically separated from the human race. Stick their heads in the sand kind of thing, Daemon. If anything, they probably choose to not believe our secrets aren't safe." Matthew glanced at his empty glass. "It's… easier for them."

That sounded incredibly stupid and I said so. Matthew smiled wryly in response. "Dear girl, you do not know what it is like to be a guest, do you? Imagine living with the knowledge that your home and everything could be whipped out from under you at any moment? But you have to lead people, keep them calm and happy—safe. The worst thing would be to voice the darkest of your concerns to the masses." He paused, eyeing that glass again. "Tell me, what would humans do if they knew aliens lived among them?"

My cheeks flamed. "Uh, they'd probably riot and go nuts."

"Exactly," he murmured. "Our kinds are not that different."

Nothing was really said after that. We all sat there, lost in our own troubles. My heart was cracking into a million pieces because I knew Daemon wanted to rush Vaughn and Nancy right now, but he wasn't that reckless. There was Dee, and any action he took would affect her.

And apparently it would also affect me. If he died, then I'd die. I couldn't even fully wrap my head around that. Not right now with everything else going on. I decided to leave that until later to freak out over.

"What about the Arum thing?" I asked.

"I don't know." Matthew refilled his glass. "I can't even fathom a reason why the DOD would be working with them—what they could even gain. The Arum absorb our powers, but never healing—nothing of that magnitude. They have a different heat signature than we do, so with the right tools, the DOD would know they weren't dealing with us, but to walk up to an Arum or a Luxen on the street, there would be no way to tell us apart."

"Wait." I tucked my hair back, glancing at a silent Daemon. "What if the DOD captured an Arum, believing it to be a Luxen, and you guys were studied, too, right? Forced to assimilate into the human world? I don't know what assimilation entails, but I'm sure it was some kind of observation, so wouldn't they have noticed eventually, especially with the heat-signature thing?"

Matthew got up, went to a cabinet in the far corner. Opening it, he pulled out a square bottle and poured himself a glass. "When we were being assimilated, they never saw our abilities. So, if we work off the theory that they've known for some time, they studied our abilities on Luxen who could never tell us that the DOD is aware what we can do."

Nausea rose sharply. "You're saying that those Luxen would be…"

"Dead," he said, turning around and taking a drink. "I'm not sure how much Daemon has told you, but there were Luxen who didn't assimilate. They were put down…like feral animals. No stretch of the imagination to believe that they used some Luxen to study their abilities, to learn about us, and then got rid of them."

Or sent them back as spies—ones who could keep an eye on the others, report back to the DOD with any suspicious activity. Seemed paranoid, but this *was* the government we were talking about.

"But that doesn't explain why the Arum would work with the DOD."

"It doesn't." Matthew moved to the fireplace. He propped his elbow on the mantel, swirling the ruby liquid with his other hand. "I am afraid to theorize over what that could mean."

"Part of me doesn't even care about that right now." Daemon finally spoke again, sounding tired. "Someone betrayed Dawson. Someone had to tell the DOD."

"It could be anyone," Matthew said wearily. "Dawson didn't try to hide his relationship with Bethany. And if anyone was watching them closely, they could've suspected something happened. We all watched them when they first got together. I'm sure some of us didn't stop."

That did nothing to really calm Daemon. Not that I expected it to. We left Matthew's house shortly after that, silent and stuck somewhere between hope and despair.

At my mom's car, I handed him the keys when he asked for them. I started toward the passenger side, then stopped. Turning around, I went back to him and snaked my arms around his taut body.

"I'm sorry," I whispered, squeezing him tight. "We'll figure out something. We'll get him back."

After a moment of hesitation, his arms wrapped around me and held me so tightly I could've molded to him. "I know," he said against the top of my head, his voice firm and strong. "I'll get him back if it's the last thing I do."

And part of me already knew and was afraid of what Daemon was willing to sacrifice for his brother.

Chapter 24

Daemon didn't want his sister to know Dawson was most likely alive. I promised, mainly because I understood that imagining what was being done to Dawson right now was probably worse than thinking he was dead. Daemon didn't want to share that helplessness with his sister.

He was that kind of guy, and I respected him for it.

But there was a rising tide of sorrow for his brother I wished I could take away.

During the next couple of days, I did my training with Blake and then after he left, Daemon and I would drive to Moorefield. Brian hadn't returned home since the night we'd seen him and Nancy with the Arum. I had no idea what Daemon planned, but whatever it was, I wasn't letting him do it alone, and for once he wasn't hell-bent on doing everything alone.

On the Thursday before Christmas break, Blake and I worked on manipulating light. It was harder than freezing an object. I had to pull from within me, to tap into an ability I had no real understanding of.

Frustrated after hours of me not being able to produce even a spark of the deadly light, Blake looked like he wanted to run his head into a wall. "It's not that hard, Katy. You have it in you."

My foot tapped the floor. "I'm trying."

Blake sat on the arm of the recliner, rubbing his brow. "You can move things easily now. This shouldn't be that much harder."

He was doing wonders for my self-confidence.

"Look at it this way. Every cell in your body is encased in light. Picture in your mind pulling all those cells together and feel the light. It's warm. It should vibrate and hum. It's like lightning in your veins. Think of something that feels that way."

I yawned. "I've tried—"

He shot off the chair, moving faster than I'd ever seen him. Grabbing my wrist until his thumb and forefinger met, he stared into my wide eyes. "You're not trying hard enough, Katy. If you can't manipulate light, then…"

"Then what?" I demanded.

Blake drew in a deep breath. "It's just that…if you can't control the strongest part of you, there's a chance you'll never really be under control. And you'll never be able to defend yourself."

I wondered if it had been this hard for Bethany. "I'm trying. I promise."

He let go of my wrist and ran a hand through his spiky hair. Then he smiled. "I have an idea."

"Oh, no." I shook my head. "I don't like your ideas at all."

He cast a grin over his shoulder as he pulled his keys out of his pocket. "You said you'd trust me, right?"

"Yeah, but that's before you threw a knife at my chest and caught my fingers on fire."

Blake laughed, and I scowled. None of that was funny. "I'm not doing anything like that. I think we just need to get out of here. Go grab something to eat."

Wary, I shuffled from one foot to the next. "Really? That…doesn't sound like a bad idea."

"Yeah, why don't you grab a jacket and we'll get some food."

Lately, I was always hungry, so the prospect of greasy food sealed the deal. Grabbing my chunky sweater, I slipped it on and followed Blake out to his truck. It wasn't as huge as the ones the guys drove around here, but it was nice and brand spanking new.

"What are you in the mood for?" He clapped his hands together, warming them up as the engine roared to life.

"Anything that will cause me to gain ten pounds." I buckled myself in.

Blake laughed. "I know just the place."

Pressing against the seat, I decided to ask the question that had been plaguing me since Daemon and I talked to Matthew. "What happened to the Luxen who healed you?"

His hand clenched the steering wheel until his knuckles bleached. "I…I don't know. And not knowing kills me, Katy. I'd do anything to find out."

I stared at him as sadness crept into me. Since Blake was here, his friend had to be alive. Most likely the DOD had him. I started to say something about it but stopped.

Lately, I'd started to feel more and more weird around Blake. I couldn't put my finger on it, and maybe it was just a matter of Daemon repeating it every chance he got, but I didn't trust Blake as much anymore.

"Why do you ask?" He glanced at me, face drawn tight.

I shrugged. "I was just curious. I'm sorry about what happened."

He nodded, and neither of us said anything for a while. It wasn't until we passed the exit for Moorefield that I started to get nervous. "Is it safe for us to go this far? The Rocks only have a fifty-mile radius, right?"

"That's just a guesstimate. We'll be fine."

I nodded, unable to shake the sudden dread curling around my insides. Each mile farther Blake took me from home, I started to get antsy. The Arum were obviously around, could even know who we were, since it looked like they might be in cahoots with the DOD. This was reckless, even stupid. Running my hands over my jeans, I stared out the window as Blake hummed along to a rock song.

I reached into my purse and pulled out my cell. If we were really within the shelter of the beta quartz, Blake should be cool with me letting Daemon know.

"You're not one of those girls who has to tell her boyfriend every move she makes, are you, Katy?" Blake nodded at my phone and smiled, but the humor never reached his eyes. "Besides, we're here anyway."

I wasn't one of those girls, but...

He pulled into the parking lot of a little joint that boasted the best wings in West Virginia. Christmas lights decorated their pitch-black windows. There was a giant mountaineer statue guarding the entrance.

It all looked incredibly normal.

I silently blamed Daemon for making me doubt Blake, shoved my phone back in my purse, and headed into the restaurant.

Dinner was oddly strained. Nothing like the first two times Blake and I had gone out. Trying to get him to even talk about surfing was like squeezing glass—painful and pointless. I talked about how much I missed blogging and reading while he texted away on his phone. Or played a game—I couldn't be sure. Once I thought I heard a pig oink. Eventually I stopped talking and focused on ripping the skin off my wings.

It was past six, and we'd been sitting at the little table, going on our third soda refill, when I couldn't deal with this anymore. "Are you ready?"

"Just a few more minutes."

This was the second set of "Just a few more minutes." I sat back, blowing out a long breath, and started counting the red squares on some dude's flannel jacket. I'd already memorized the Christmas song they'd been playing over and over.

I glanced at Blake. "I'm *really* ready to go home."

Annoyance flared in his hazel eyes, turning the flecks of brown dark. "I thought you'd enjoy getting out and just chilling."

"I am, but we're sitting here, not even talking to each other, while you play some pig-poking game on your phone. Seriously not a fun time for me."

He propped his elbows on the table and rested his chin in his hands. "What do you want to talk about, Katy?"

My irritation rose at his tone. "I've been trying to talk to you about all kinds of topics for over an hour."

"So, doing anything for Christmas?" he asked.

Taking a deep breath, I reined in my temper. "Yeah, Mom is actually off for once. We're doing something with Will."

"The doctor? Sounds like they're getting pretty serious."

"They are." I pulled my sweater closer, shivering as the door opened. "I'm pretty sure that's the only reason why—"

Blake's phone dinged, and he immediately checked it out. Annoyed, I clamped my mouth shut and stared at the empty table behind him. "You ready?" he asked.

Thank freaking God. I grabbed my purse and stood, walking out without waiting for him to pick up the check. My boots crunched over the packed snow and ice. As soon as November had rolled around, all it did was snow an inch or two every few days. It was like one giant prelude to a blizzard.

Blake joined me a couple minutes later, frowning. "Way to wait."

I rolled my eyes but said nothing as I climbed into his truck. We headed back onto the road in silence. Arms folded tightly across my chest, I felt like a pissy girlfriend, which was so wrong. We weren't like that, but it was as if we'd just had the date from hell.

And to make everything worse, he was driving at the speed of Grandma. My leg bounced with annoyance and impatience. I just wanted to go home. There would be no training tonight. I was going to pick up an effin' book, and I was going to read for *fun*. Then I would blog. I would forget about Blake and this stupid, craptastic alien power. My gaze dropped to my boot. There was something on the floor, hard and slender under the thin soles of my boot. Moving my foot to the side, the passing highway lights reflected off something gold and shiny. Curious, I started to bend down.

The obsidian flared under my sweater without any warning at the same moment Blake swerved the truck off the road and into a ditch.

Swinging toward him, my heart raced as the heat from the obsidian seared my skin. "There's an Arum nearby."

"I know." He killed the engine, jaw tight. "Get out of the truck, Katy."

"What?" I shrieked.

"Get out of the truck!" He reached over, unhooking my seat belt. "We're training."

Realization set in, hard and frightening. I let out a shaky breath as the obsidian continued to increase in heat. "You brought me out of the safety of the beta quartz on purpose!"

"If your strongest abilities are attached to your emotions, then we need to find out how to tap into them when you're feeling all emotional to see what you can do, then practice with less excitement. Like we did with the knife and then pillows." He stretched over farther and opened my car door. "Arum can sense us better than they can the Luxen. It's the DNA thing. Luxen have a built-in cloaking in their DNA. We don't."

My chest rose and fell quickly. "You never told me that before."

"You were safe within the beta quartz. It wasn't an issue."

I stared at him, horrified. What if I had left with my mom to go shopping out of the radius without knowing this? We would've been attacked. Did Blake even care about my safety?

"Now get out," he said.

Obviously not. "No! No way am I going out there with an Arum! You're a crazy—"

"You're going to be okay." He sounded as if he were telling me to give a speech in front of a class and not face a murderous alien. "I'm not going to let anything happen to you."

Then he got out of the car, disappearing into the thick tree line and leaving me alone in the truck. Too stunned to move, I stared at the encroaching darkness. I couldn't believe he'd done this.

If I survived tonight, I was going to kill Blake.

An inky shadow glided over the road and followed the trail Blake has walked into the woods. A burst of light exploded, filling up the sky, but was quickly snuffed out as I heard Blake's pained scream.

Scrambling out of the truck, I slammed the door shut and squinted into the darkness. "Blake?" After several moments of no answer, panic clawed up my throat. "Blake!"

I stopped at the edge of the woods, wary to enter them. Clutching my sweater close, I shivered as an unnatural silence settled around me. Screw this. Turning around, I headed back to the truck. I'd call my mom. I'd even call Daemon. There was no—

A shadow pooled in front of the passenger door before I could take another step. Dark and oily, it built onto itself until an outline of a man blocked my path.

"Crap," I whispered.

It took the form of a human male, a startling resemblance to the one we'd seen outside of Vaughn's house. "Hello, little one. Aren't you something...special?"

Spinning around, my sweater flapped like wings behind me as I took off. I ran fast—faster than I'd ever run before. So fast that the little flakes of snow the biting wind pelted against my cheeks felt like tiny pebbles. I wasn't even sure my feet were touching the ground.

But no matter how fast I ran, the Arum was faster.

A dark, murky shade appeared beside me and then in front of me. Sliding across snow and ice, I grabbed for my obsidian. Ready to shove the point into whatever part my hand landed on.

Anticipating the move, an arm took form and swung out. It caught me in the stomach. Up in the air I went, landing on my side. Jarring pain shot through my bones. I rolled onto my back, blinking snow from my lashes.

Now I knew why Daemon was so adamant against me running out

and fighting the Arum. I'd just got my ass kicked and the fight hadn't even started.

A dark, insidious shadow crept into my vision. Out of human form, when he spoke his voice was a menacing murmur among my own thoughts. *You're not a Luxen, but you're sssomething unique. What powersss do you have?*

Powers? The powers Daemon had given me when he mutated me. The Arum would take them by killing me. But I'd killed an Arum before by tapping into Daemon and Dee. Blake believed that ability—that Source—still existed in me. It had to, and if it didn't, I would die.

And I wanted to be able to defend myself. Not lay here. Not wait on someone to save me.

What had Blake said to picture? Lightning in the veins and cells surrounded in light?

The Arum leaned over me; the tendrils of black smoke were thick and colder than the hard ground. A smoky, transparent smile appeared. *Easssier than I thought.*

I squeezed my eyes shut and pictured every weird cell I'd ever seen in bio class surrounded by light, and I thought about that one moment—that first time I'd ever felt lightning in my veins. I held onto the image as the first brush of the Arum's cold fingers swept over my cheek. I latched onto the swamping, red-hot lava coursing through my veins.

It started with a crackle—a small light burned behind my eyelids. A strange feeling spread down my arm, scalding hot. The light behind my eyes was red-white; the source of the power was utterly destructive, shattering in its complexity.

I could feel it burning through my veins, whispering a hundred promises. It called to me, welcomed me home. It had been waiting, wondering when I would heed its call.

Wind whipped the snow out from underneath me as I rose. When I opened my eyes, the Arum was gliding back, shifting between human and Arum.

I was on my feet now, barely breathing. I could feel *it*, and it was exciting and terrifying. Every nerve in my body came alive and tingled in anticipation. *It* wanted to be used, this power. It seemed like the most natural of all things. My fingers curved inward. The world around me was lit in red and white.

Destroy.

The Arum shifted back into its true form, spreading out and endless like the night sky.

There was a snapping sound coming from inside me, and the Source rushed from my fingertips, slamming into the Arum at an alarming speed.

He spun into the air, but the Source followed him. Or I made it follow him. But he was shifting forms so quickly it was dizzying. He froze and then shattered into a million thin shreds of glassy shadows.

The obsidian cooled against my skin.

"Perfect," Blake said, clapping his hands together. "That was freaking unbelievable. You killed an Arum with one shot!"

Waves of electricity returned to me, and the red-white haze faded away. When the Source left, so did most of my energy. I turned to Blake, feeling something else replace the void the Source had left behind. "You…you left me alone with an Arum."

"Yeah, but look at what you did." He strode forward, grinning at me like I was the prized pupil. "You killed an Arum, Katy. You did it all by yourself."

I took a breath and it *hurt*. Everything hurt. "What if I hadn't been able to kill the Arum?"

Confusion marked his expression. "But you did."

I stepped back, winced, and realized my pants were soaked and clinging to my chilled, chafed skin. "What if I couldn't do it?"

Blake shook his head. "Then…"

"Then I would've died." My hand shook as I placed it on my hip. My entire backside throbbed from the fall. "Do you even care?"

"Of course I do!" He moved forward, placing his hand on my

shoulder.

I yelped as sparks of pain shot straight down my arm. "Don't... don't touch me."

In a flash, the confusion was gone and replaced by anger. "You're overreacting when you should be celebrating. You did something... amazing. Don't you understand that? No one kills an Arum in one blast."

"I don't care." I started limping back toward the car. "I want to go home."

"Katy! Don't act like this. Everything's fine. You did—"

"Just take me home!" I screamed, close to tears, close to completely shutting down. Because there was something wrong with him. "I just want to go home."

Chapter 25

Running late to trig on the last day of classes before break, I eased into my seat and winced. There was a good chance that I'd broken my butt last night. Sitting was extremely painful. Lesa raised a brow as she watched me struggle to get comfortable.

"Are you okay?" Daemon asked, causing me to jump a little.

"Yeah," I breathed out as I carefully turned halfway, surprised that he hadn't poked me. "Just slept wrong."

His eyes were sharp. "Did you sleep on the floor or something?"

I laughed dryly. "Feels like it."

Daemon stopped me from turning around. "Kat…"

"What?" Unease crept through me. When he looked at me like that I felt exposed to the core.

"Never mind." He sat back, eyes narrowed as he folded his arms. "You still on for tonight?"

Biting my lip, I nodded and made a mental note to pick up some energy drinks on the way home. When I'd gotten back last night, I brutalized Mom's secret chocolate stash. It did nothing to help replenish my energy. Easing back around, I gritted my teeth and ignored the flare of pain. It could be worse. I could be dead right now.

Sitting in the seat during class sucked to the nth degree. My body ached from hitting the cold, hard ground last night. The only reprieve I had was that Blake wasn't in bio, and I wasn't sure how to feel about that. I'd lain awake last night, replaying everything that had happened. Would Blake have let me get seriously hurt or die if I hadn't been able to use the Source to take out the Arum? I didn't have an answer, and that troubled me.

Walking out of bio, Matthew called out to me. He waited until the class was empty before speaking. "How are you feeling, Katy?"

"Good," I said, surprised. "You?"

Matthew smiled tightly as he leaned against the corner of his desk. "You looked like you were in pain during class. Hopefully my lecture wasn't that bad."

I flushed. "No, it's not your lecture. I slept wrong last night. Now I'm all achy."

He looked away. "I don't want to keep you, but how is…"

Now I understood why he'd really stopped me. I glanced at the open door. "Daemon's okay. I mean, he's as okay as he can be, I guess."

Matthew closed his eyes briefly. "That boy is like a son to me—both he and Dee are. I don't want to see him doing anything crazy."

"He won't," I told him, wanting to reassure the man. And I also didn't want Matthew knowing that Daemon was stalking Vaughn. Doubted that would go over well.

"I hope so." Matthew looked at me, eyes bloodshot. "Some things are best left…unknown, you know? People search for answers and they don't always like what they get. Sometimes the truth is worse than the lie." He turned back to his desk, messing with a stack of papers. "I hope you sleep better, Katy."

Realizing I'd been dismissed, I left the class weirded out to the max. Was Matthew drinking while at work? Because that was the strangest conversation I'd ever had with him. And it was the longest conversation alone with him.

At lunch, I joined my friends and tried to forget about last night. Watching Dee and Adam make out was a good distraction. During the rare moments her mouth wasn't attached to his, she talked about this weekend and Christmas. Whenever she looked at me, though, there was a sadness in her eyes. A gulf had developed between us, and I missed her. I missed my friends so much.

When classes were over, I headed to my locker to grab my English book, since there was a paper due once school started back up. Just as I shoved it into my backpack, I heard my name.

I looked up, tensing when I saw Blake. "Hey…you weren't in bio."

"I came in late today," he said, leaning against the locker beside me. "I'm not going to be able to do any practice tonight or during Christmas break. I'm visiting some family with my uncle."

Sweet relief flooded my system, leaving me dizzy. After last night, I wasn't sure I wanted to continue training with Blake, despite my need to be able to defend myself. Now just wasn't the time to talk about any of that. "That's okay. I hope you have fun." There was a distant, closed-off look in his eyes as he nodded. I cleared my throat. "Well, I'm going to get going. See you when—"

"Wait." He stepped closer. "I wanted to talk to you about last night."

I closed my locker door when I wanted to slam it shut. "What about it?"

"I know you're pissed."

"Yeah, I am." I faced him. Could he really not understand why I was mad? "You risked my life last night. What if I didn't use the Source? I'd be dead now."

"I wouldn't have let him hurt you." Sincerity filled his words and eyes. "You were safe."

"The bruises up and down the side of my body are telling me I got hurt."

He blew out an exasperated breath. "I still don't get why you're not happier about this. The power you showed—it's amazing."

I shifted the bag off my bruised backside. "Look, can we talk about training when you get back?"

He looked like he wanted to argue, because those green flecks in his eyes deepened and churned, but he turned his cheek and let out a harsh breath. I wanted to be out of this school, to be home in my bed, and to be away from *him*. Away from this boy I'd once believed was normal, once believed wanted to help me because we were alike, and now I wasn't sure if he really cared if I survived any of his training techniques at all.

• • •

Changing into a pair of loose sweats and a thermal when I got home, the first thing I did after that was take a nap, and I slept most of the evening away. Mom was gone when I got up, and I scrounged together a sandwich and then gathered all the books I'd gotten in the last month.

I stacked them beside my laptop and was in the process of getting my webcam to not zoom up my nose when I felt the familiar tingles like a warm breath on the back of my neck. I glanced at the clock. It wasn't even ten o'clock yet.

Sighing, I got up and went to the front door, opening it before Daemon could knock. He stood there, his hand raised in midair. "I'm really beginning to dislike the fact that you know when I'm coming," he said, frowning.

"I thought you loved it. It enables you to be such a great stalker."

"I've already told you. I don't *stalk* you." He followed me into the living room. "I use it to keep an eye on you."

"There's a difference?" I sat on the couch.

Daemon sat right beside me, his thigh pressing against mine. "There is a difference."

"Sometimes your logic scares me." I wished I'd changed into something else. He was just in jeans and a sweater, but he looked good. And my thermal had little strawberries on it. Embarrassing. "So what are you doing over here so early?"

Leaning back against the cushions, he was even closer than before, smelling of a crisp autumn morning. Why, oh why, did he have to always get so close? "Bill didn't come by tonight?"

I tucked my hair back behind my ear, ignoring the mad rush of the desire to climb into his arms. "No. He had something to do with family."

His eyes narrowed on the laptop. "What are you doing? Making another one of those videos?"

"I was planning to. I haven't done one in a while, but then you showed up. Plan ruined."

He grinned. "You still can film one. I promise I'll behave."

"Yeah, not going to happen."

"Why not?" He raised his hand, and the book on the top of the pile shot toward him. "Hey, I have an idea. I could pretend to be him."

"What?" I frowned as he showed me the blond guy on the cover. "Wait. You don't mean—"

Daemon shimmered out, and in his place was the exact replica of the cover model, right down to the curly lock of blond hair, baby blue eyes, and brooding stare. *Wow, such a pretty boy.* "Hello there…"

"Oh my God." I poked his golden cheek. Real. I laughed. "You can't do that. People would freak."

"But it would definitely get a lot of attention." He winked. "It would be fun."

"But this cover model"—I took the book from him and waved it around—"is a real person somewhere. He'd probably be curious how he ended up in my In My Mailbox video."

His full lips pouted. "You do have a point." The cover model faded out, and Daemon reappeared. "But don't let that stop you. Go ahead and film. I'll be like your assistant."

Trying to determine if he was being serious or not, I stared at him. "I don't know about this."

"I'll be completely quiet. I'll just hold books for you."

"I don't think you have the ability to be completely quiet. Ever."

"I promise," he said, grinning.

This would probably end up disastrous, but the idea of him being in the video had me all giddy and amused. I adjusted the webcam so he was included in the picture and pressed record.

Taking a deep breath, I started to do my vlog. "Hi, this is Katy from Katy's Krazy Obsession. Sorry for such a long absence. School and… "—my eyes darted to Daemon for a fraction of a second—"stuff have gotten in the way, but anyway, I have a guest. This is—"

"Daemon Black," he answered for me. "I'm the guy she lays awake at night and fantasizes about."

My cheeks flushed as I elbowed him back. "And that is *so* not the truth. He's my neighbor—"

"And the guy she's completely obsessed with."

I forced a weak smile. "He's very egotistical and likes to hear his voice, but he's promised to stay quiet. Right?"

He nodded and smiled angelically for the camera, but his eyes stirred with amusement. Yep, this was a bad idea. "I think reading is sexy." Daemon smiled at himself.

My brows inched up my forehead. "Do you now?"

"Oh, yes, and you know what else I think is sexy?" He leaned forward so his entire face filled the picture and nodded his head toward me. "Bloggers like this. Hot."

Rolling my eyes, I smacked his arm. "Get back," I whispered.

Daemon sat back and *tried* to stay quiet for the next five minutes. He handed me each book, unable to refrain from making a comment and taking my whole recording hostage. Like, "This guy looks stupid," or "What's the obsession with fallen angels?" And my favorite was when he held the book *in front* of my face and said, "This reaper dude sounds like my kind of guy. He gets to kill people for a living."

At the end of the recording, I couldn't even hide the stupid grin plastered on my face. "And that's it for today. Thanks for watching!"

Daemon practically knocked me over to get in one last comment. "Don't forget. There are cooler things out there than fallen angels and dead guys. Just saying." He winked.

I pictured an entire legion of females swooning. Pushing him aside, I winced and clicked the off button on the webcam page. "You like seeing yourself being recorded."

He shrugged. "That was fun. When do you do another?"

"Next week if I get more books."

"More books." His eyes went wide. "You have, like, ten books you just said you haven't read."

"Doesn't mean I won't get more books." I smiled at his incredulous expression. "I haven't been able to read a lot lately, but I will, and then I won't be out of anything new to read."

"You haven't had time because of *him* and that's ridiculous." He looked away, jaw working. "Reading is something you love. So is blogging, and you've completely dumped those things."

"I have not!"

"You're such a little liar," he shot back. "I've checked out your blog. You've done five posts in the last month."

My jaw hit the floor. "You've been stalking my blog, too?"

"Like I said before, I'm not stalking. I'm just *keeping an eye* on you."

"And like I said before, your reasoning is faulty." I bent forward, closing my laptop. "You know what I've been doing. It pretty much soaks up my time —"

"What the hell?" he exploded, grabbing the back of my thermal and tugging it up.

"Hey." I twisted around, ignoring the fresh spike of pain. "What are you doing? Hands off, mofo."

He looked up, eyes glowing with a hint of desperation and vengeance. "Tell me why your back looks like you fell out of a two-story window."

Oh, crap. Standing, I headed toward the kitchen to get some space. Daemon was right behind me as I grabbed a Coke out of the fridge. "I…I fell in training with Blake. It's not a big deal, though." Sounded believable, and the truth would send him into a murderous rage that right now no one wanted. And Daemon didn't need something else to stress over. "I told you I slept wrong, because I figured you'd make fun of me."

"Yeah, I would've made fun of you…a little bit, but Jesus, Kat, you sure you didn't break something?"

Not really. "I'm fine."

Concern etched into the lines of his face as he followed me around the table, eyes unflinching. "You've been hurting yourself a lot lately."

"Not really."

"You're not clumsy, Kitten. So how does this keep happening?" He advanced forward, moving like a predator about to pounce. Suddenly I wasn't sure what was worse: him moving at the speed of light or with slow, calculated steps that sent a shiver down my spine.

"I tripped in the woods the night I first found out about you," I reminded him.

"Nice try." He shook his head. "You were running full-out in the middle of pitch-black woods. Even I'd…" He winked. "Well, maybe not me, but *normal* people would trip then. I'm just too awesome."

"Well…" God he was full of himself.

"It looks like it hurts."

"It does a little."

"Then let me fix it." He reached out, fingers blurring.

"Wait." I backed up. "Should you be doing that?"

"Healing you can't hurt. Not at this point." He tried to touch me again, but I knocked his hand away. "I'm just trying to help!"

I'd cornered myself. "I don't need you to help me."

The muscle in his jaw started working as he turned his head. It appeared as if he'd given up, but then his arm went around my hips and a second later he was sitting on the couch in the living room, and I was in his lap.

Stunned, I stared at him. "That's not fair!"

"I wouldn't have had to do it if you would just stop being so freaking stubborn and let me help you." Daemon held me still, ignoring my protests as he slipped his hand under my thermal, flatting it against my lower back. I jerked at the zing his touch produced. "I can make you feel better. It's ridiculous that you won't let me."

"We have stuff to do, people to stalk, Daemon. Just let me up." I wiggled, trying to get free, and groaned in pain. I don't know why I didn't want him to heal me; we'd already proven I didn't develop a trace from being near him anymore. But he already had too many people counting on him.

"No," he said. Heat flared against my back, pleasant and heady, threatening to consume me whole. His lips turned up at one corner when he heard my soft intake of breath. "I can't be around you when I know you're in pain, okay?"

My mouth opened, but I didn't say anything. Daemon looked away, focusing on a blank spot on the wall. "Does it really bother you, me hurting?" I asked.

"I don't feel it, if that's what you're asking." He paused, exhaling softly. "Just knowing you're hurt is enough for it to bother me."

I lowered my gaze and stopped struggling. Only one hand was on me, but I could feel it in every cell. When Blake had said to think of something that felt like lightning heat, I'd thought of Daemon's touch— the way he kissed. That was what I felt when I tapped into the Source and destroyed the Arum.

The whole healing thing had a lulling effect. It was like lying out in the sun or snuggling under cozy blankets. Lack of sleep and his touch lapped at me in steady, comforting waves. Relaxing in his loose embrace, I placed my head on his shoulder and closed my eyes. His touch—the healing warmth sunk deep into my skin, through bruised muscle and bone.

After some time, I realized nothing ached, but he was still holding me. Then Daemon stood, cradling me in his arms. I stirred. "What are you doing?"

"Taking you to bed."

My body flushed at those words. "I can walk."

"I can get you there faster." And he did. One second we were in the living room, surrounded by the twinkling lights on the Christmas tree, and then the next we were in my bedroom. "See?"

I was half transfixed by him as he placed me on the bed, moving the covers back without touching them. Such a handy ability when the hands were full.

Daemon tugged the comforter up, hesitating as he stared down at me. "Do you feel better?"

"Yeah," I whispered, unable to look away. With him standing over me, his eyes such a stark contrast with the darkness, he looked like something straight out of my dreams...or the books I read.

His throat worked slowly. "Can I...?" There was a pause and my heart stuttered. "Can I just hold you? That's all...that's all I want."

A knot formed in my throat and my chest tightened, cutting off my voice. I didn't want him to leave, so I nodded.

Relief flickered across his stoic face, softening the hard lines, and then he walked around to *his* side, kicked off his shoes, and slid into bed beside me. He moved closer, extending an arm, and I went, curling against his body, my head nestled in the space between his shoulder and chest.

"I kind of like being your body pillow," he admitted, a smile in his voice. "Even if you drool on me."

"I do *not* drool." I smiled, placing my hand over his heart. "What about tailing Vaughn?"

"That can wait until tomorrow." He tilted his head to the side, his lips moving against my hair as he spoke. "Get some rest, Kitten. I'll be gone before morning."

Under my hand, the steady beat of his heart matched my own, slightly accelerated. Was it the healing or just being this close? I didn't know. But before I knew it, I'd drifted into the deepest, calmest sleep I'd had in weeks.

Chapter 26

The irate sound of "KATY ANN SWARTZ!" being yelled, followed by a husky male laugh was what roused me from the satisfying haze of deep sleep. My eyes fluttered open, and I tried to remember the last time Mom had used my full name. Oh yeah, it had been years ago, when I'd tried to pet a baby opossum that had gotten on our balcony somehow.

Mom stood in my bedroom doorway, dressed in her robe, her mouth hanging open. Will stood behind her, one a strange, satisfied smile on his face.

"What?" I mumbled. My hard pillow moved. Glancing down, I felt my cheeks burn hot. Daemon was still in my bed. And I was half lying on him. One of his hands was wrapped around mine, pinning it against his chest. *OhmyGodno…*

Mortified on an epic level, I pulled my hand free. "This isn't what it looks like."

"It's not?" Mom folded her arms.

"They're just kids," Will said, grinning. "At least they're fully clothed."

"Not helping," she shot back.

I started to sit up, but Daemon's arm tightened around my waist as he rolled into me, nuzzling my neck. Wanting to die a thousand deaths, I pushed at him. He didn't budge.

His eyes opened into thin slits. "Mmm, what's your problem?" I stared meaningfully at the doorway. Frowning, he turned his head and froze. "Oh, wow, awkward." He cleared his throat as he removed his arm from my waist. "Good morning, Ms. Swartz."

Mom smiled tightly. "Good morning, Daemon. I think it's time for you to go home."

Daemon left as fast as humanly possible after that. Mom went downstairs without saying a word. Knowing I was in trouble, I passed Will in the hallway. He was barefoot. Apparently, I wasn't the only female in the house to have had a guy in my bed.

I found her shoving the coffee pot into the maker. "Mom, it's not what you think. I promise."

She turned around, planting her hands on her hips. "You had a boy in your bedroom, in your bed. What am I supposed to think?"

"Looks like you had a sleepover, too." I fixed the pot so it wasn't half out of the maker.

"I'm the adult here. I can have whomever I want in my bed, young lady."

Will laughed form the doorway. "I have to disagree with that. I'm hoping I'm the only one in your bed."

"Ew," I groaned, going to the fridge to get juice.

Mom's eyes narrowed on her boyfriend. "Is this what you're doing when I'm working nights, Katy?"

I sighed. "No, Mom, I swear it's not. We were…studying, and we fell asleep."

"You were studying in your bedroom?" She smoothed some of the mussed hair back from her face. "I've never had to set rules with you before, but I see there need to be some established."

"Mom," I groaned, glancing at Will. "Come on…"

"There will be no boys in your bedroom. Ever." She pulled the creamer out. "There will be no boys staying the night in any part of this house."

Sitting down, I sipped my OJ. "Can you stop referring to boys in the plural? Geez."

She poured herself a cup of coffee. "Blake is here all the time. And then there is Daemon. So, yes, it's boys in the plural sense."

I bristled. "Neither of them is my boyfriend."

"Is that supposed to make me feel better about one of them being in *your* bed?" She took a drink of her coffee and then scrunched up her nose in distaste. "Honey, I've never had to worry about you doing anything stupid."

I stood and handed her the sugar she forgot. "I'm not doing anything stupid. Nothing is happening with either of them. We're just friends."

She ignored the last statement. "I can't be here a lot, and I have to trust you. Please tell me that you're being…safe."

"Oh my God, Mom, I'm not having sex."

Her look told me she wasn't entirely convinced. "Just make sure you'll be careful. You don't want to be a young mother."

"Oh, dear God," I whispered, hiding my face behind my hands.

"And I am concerned," she continued. "First it was Daemon, then you seemed to have started seeing Blake, but now…"

"I'm not seeing either of them," I said for what felt like the hundredth time.

"You two did look very close." Will propped a hip against the sink, watching us. "You and Daemon."

"This really isn't any of your business," I said, angry that he was here for such a private and excruciatingly embarrassing conversation.

"Katy," Mom snapped.

Will laughed it off. "No. It's okay, Kell. She's right. This isn't my business. But there does seem to be some history between you two."

For a moment, his smile reminded me of someone. Fake. Plastic.

Nancy Husher. I shuddered. God, I was paranoid. "We're just friends."

"Friends who hold hands while sleeping?"

I glanced at my mom, but she was busy studying the inside of her chipped cup. Feeling overly exposed, I folded my arms around me. "I'm sorry, Mom, for upsetting you. It won't happen again."

"I hope not." She washed out her coffee cup, wearing a slight frown. "The last thing I want right now is a grandchild."

Done with this conversation, I squeezed past Will and went into the living room. Gah, my mom thought I was making babies. Even I was disturbed by that thought.

Grabbing my backpack off the floor, I dragged it to the couch. When I looked up, I saw Mom and Will in the hallway. He was whispering something to her, and she laughed softly. Before I could look away, he kissed her…but *our* eyes locked.

· · ·

Hours later, Will was still in the house—my house. Not his. Was this how my Saturdays would be when Mom was off? Watching the two of them working on crossword puzzles in between making out? I wanted to claw my eyes out.

The way he stared at me made my skin feel like a thousand dirty roaches were crawling under it. It had to be my paranoia, but I couldn't shake the ugh factor.

I checked my blog real quickly and found that I had over twenty comments on my IMM. Curious for the sudden comment love, I scrolled through them. Some of them gushed over the books I had. Others gushed over the boy who'd been sitting beside me.

Dammit. He'd hijacked my blog.

Putting in earbuds, I listened to some tunes while reading my English assignment. Mom appeared sometime later, and I tugged out the buds, hoping we weren't going to have another sex conversation. Especially when I knew Will was right in the kitchen, making himself at home.

"Honey, Dee is here to see you." Then she walked over and flipped my textbook shut. "And before you say you're busy or have plans with a boy, you need to get up and go talk to her."

I took the last bite of my cold Pop-Tart and frowned. "Oookay…"

She pushed back her side-swept bangs. "You can't spend every waking second studying and hanging out with Blake or whomever."

Or whomever? Like I had this long list of boys. I sighed as I stood. Before I left the room, I caught her staring at the Christmas tree, and I wondered what she was thinking.

Dee was waiting outside, a vision in white. It took me a few seconds to realize the white sweater she wore had blended into the background. It was snowing heavily, so much so I could barely see the tree line a few yards away.

"Hey," I said lamely.

She blinked and her eyes immediately darted from my face. "Hey," she responded with forced enthusiasm. "I hope I'm not bothering you."

I leaned against the door. "Well, I just started my English paper. Wanted to kind of get that out of the way."

"Oh." Her pink lips turned down. "Well, it's going to have to wait. We're going to watch a movie."

I stepped back. With everything that was going on and all the lies, being around Dee was hard. "Maybe some other time, because I'm really busy. How about next weekend?" I didn't wait for an answer. I started to shut the door.

Dee did the super-speed crap and pushed the door back open. She looked like an angry little pixie. "That was extremely rude, Katy."

I flushed. I couldn't deny that and still, it obviously hadn't driven her away. "I'm sorry. I'm just so swamped with schoolwork."

"I understand that." She pushed the door farther open. "But you're going to the movies with Adam and me."

"Dee—"

"You're not backing out of it." Her eyes met mine, and I saw the hurt in them. I swallowed, looking away. "I know you and Daemon are...well, whatever's going on between you two, and you're doing whatever with Blake and I've been spending a lot of time with Adam, but that doesn't mean we can't be friends."

She rocked back on her heels, clasping her hands under her chin. "Just put your shoes on, Katy, and go to the movies with me. Please. I miss you. *Please*."

How could I say no? I turned slightly, spying my mom standing in the doorway to the kitchen. The look on her face pleaded with me, too. I was caught between the two, and neither knew that I was trying to stay away from Dee for her own good.

"Please," Dee whispered.

I remembered Daemon telling me I was being a shitty friend. I wasn't trying to be, and Dee didn't deserve that. I nodded. "Let me grab my hoodie and shoes."

She jumped forward and gave me a quick, tight hug. "I'll be waiting right here."

Just in case I tried to sneak out of it, I supposed. Passing my mom a look, I grabbed my hoodie off the back of the recliner and slipped into a pair of knee-high, fake-sheepskin boots. Pocketing money in my jeans, I headed out into the brisk December afternoon.

Snow covered the ground, making it slick under my boots. Dee skipped beside me and then took off, throwing herself into Adam's arms. Giggling, she kissed the top of his blond head and then wiggled free.

I hung back, my hands shoved into my hoodie. "Hey, Adam."

He looked surprised to see me. "Hey, you're actually coming with us?"

I nodded.

"Awesome." He glanced at Dee. "What about...?"

Dee dashed around the front of Adam's SUV, shooting her boyfriend a look.

I slid into the backseat. "Did you invite...someone else?"

Buckling herself in, she twisted around to face me. "Ah, yeah, but it's cool. You'll see."

Adam turned around in the driveway, and I felt the warmth tingling along my neck. Unable to stop myself, I twisted in the seat, eager to see him.

Daemon stood on the porch, dressed in only jeans, even though it was too cold for that. A towel was flung over his shoulder. Impossible, but I'd swear our gazes sought the other's out. I watched until the house disappeared from view, positive that he'd waited until he could no longer see the car.

• • •

Color me annoyed when I realized *who* Dee had invited. Ash Thompson was waiting at the movie theater. She gave me her typical bitch look and walked in ahead of us, somehow managing to sway her hips in skintight jeans and four-inch heels across the ice-covered pavement.

I would've broken my neck.

Lucky me, I ended up sitting between Ash and Dee. I sunk in my seat, ignoring Ash as we waited for the lights to go down and the movie to start.

"Whose idea was it to pick a zombie flick?" Ash demanded, cradling a bucket of popcorn bigger than her head. "Was it Katy? They kind of share the same appearance."

"Ha ha," I muttered, eyeing her popcorn. Bet there wasn't much between her ears for a zombie to survive on.

On my other side, Dee and Adam had cleaned out the candy counter. She dipped a chocolate bar in her cheese sauce, and I gagged behind my hand. "That is so gross."

"Don't knock it," she said, taking a huge bit. "It's the best of both worlds. Chocolate and cheese, which is why the letter *C* is my favorite in the alphabet."

"You know," Ash said, wrinkling her nose, "I'm actually going to have to agree with living dead girl here. That is disgusting."

I frowned. "Do I look that bad or something?"

Ash said, "Yes," at the same time Dee said, "No." I folded my arms and kicked my feet onto the empty seat in front of me. "Whatever," I muttered.

"So," Adam said, drawing the word out, "things going well between you and Blake?"

Sinking down farther in my seat, I bit back a string of curses. "Yeah, things are dandy."

Ash snorted.

"Well, you've been spending a lot of time with him." Dee watched me as she dipped another bar of chocolate. "Things must be going great."

"Look, I'm just going to be honest here." Ash flicked a buttery kernel in her mouth. "You had Daemon—*Daemon*. And I know how good that is. Trust me."

A surge of jealousy rose so quickly, I wanted to slam the popcorn down her throat. "I'm sure he is."

She snickered. "Anyway, I have no idea why you'd give him up for *Blake*. He's cute and all, but he can't be as good as—"

"Ew!" Dee's face scrunched up. "Can we not talk about how good he is at anything that will force me into therapy later? Thank you."

Ash chuckled as she shook her bucket of popcorn. "I'm just saying—"

"I don't care what you're saying." I grabbed a handful of her popcorn partly to see her eyes narrow. "I don't want to talk about Daemon. And Blake and I aren't dating."

"Friends with benefits?" Adam asked.

I groaned. How did today end up being all about my non-existent sex life? "There are no benefits at all."

They stopped questioning me about Daemon and Blake after that. Halfway through the movie, the three aliens got up and came back with more food. I did try the chocolate dipped in cheese, and it was as gross as expected. And even though I was stuck next to Ash, I was having fun. The time I spent watching zombie after zombie eat various parts of humans, I forgot about everything that was going on. Things felt normal. I was smiling, joking with Dee as we left the movie theater. The sun had already set, and the parking lot was awash in the soft glow of streetlamps and Christmas lights.

We hung back from Ash and Adam, arm and arm. "I'm glad you came," she said in a hushed voice. "I had fun."

"I did, too. I'm...I'm sorry I haven't been around a lot."

The breeze played with her curls, tossing them across her face. "Is everything...okay with you? I mean, I know a lot has happened since you moved here. And I'm so afraid that you've decided you don't want to be friends with me anymore because of what I am and everything that entails."

"No. No way." I rushed to reassure her. "I wouldn't care if you were a were-llama. You're still my best friend, Dee."

"It hasn't felt like that in so long." She smiled weakly. "What's a were-llama, by the way?"

I laughed. "It's like a llama and a human, like a werewolf."

Her nose wrinkled. "That is bizarre."

"Yeah, it is."

We'd stopped at Adam's car. Ash was fiddling with her keys as she inspected her nails. Snow was already beginning to fall again, each flake fatter than the one before. I closed my eyes for a second, and when I reopened them, the snow had stalled. Over just like that, in the blink of an eye.

Chapter 27

I loved Christmas when Dad was alive. Both of us were those people who digressed several years on Christmas morning. I'd scamper down the stairs at the crack of dawn to sit alone in front of the Christmas tree, spending the early hours of Christmas morning waiting for my parents to wake. A ritual only broken when Dad died.

The last three years, I'd made cinnamon buns alone, filling the air with their sweet scent, and when Mom came home from work, we'd exchange gifts.

This year was different.

When I woke up, the scent of cinnamon already permeated the air and Will was downstairs, wearing a checkered robe and sharing a cup of coffee with Mom. He'd stayed the night. Again. Upon seeing me standing in the doorway, he got up and hugged me.

I froze, my arms hanging awkwardly at my sides.

"Merry Christmas," he said, patting me on the back.

I mumbled the same back to him, aware of my mom beaming from the couch. We opened gifts, like we used to with Dad. Maybe that's what put me in a weird mood that lingered all morning, dogging every step I took, determined to ruin the holiday.

Mom had gone upstairs to shower after putting Will and me to work on dinner. He pulled a glazed ham out of the oven. His attempts at small talk had been vastly ignored until he went *there*.

"Any more overnight visits?" he asked with a sly, conspiratorial smile.

I beat the mashed potatoes harder, wondering if he were trying to be the good guy in the picture so I wouldn't give Mom crap about him. "No."

"Not like you'd tell me, right?" He dropped the oven mitts on the counter, facing me.

Honestly, I hadn't seen Daemon since Saturday morning. Two days had gone by without a word from him.

"That boy does seem like a nice kid," Will went on, pulling out one of the knives Blake had thrown at my head. "He's a little intense, though." He paused, brows drawing in a slant as he held the knife up. "Well, so was his brother."

I almost dropped the spatula. "You're talking about Dawson?"

Will nodded. "He was the more outgoing of the two, but just as intense. Acted like the whole world could end any minute and each second had to be lived to the fullest. I never got that impression from Daemon. He's a bit more reserved, eh?"

Reserved? At first I wanted to deny that, but Daemon had always been…restrained. As if he were holding back the most important part of himself.

Cutting into the steaming ham, Will chuckled. "All of them were really tight. I guess that comes with being triplets. Like the Thompson kids."

My pulse was jumping all over the place for no reason. I went to work on the potatoes again. "You sound like you know them pretty well."

He shrugged, moving several thick slices onto one of Mom's fancy porcelain platters that hadn't seen the light of day in years. "It's a small town. Pretty much know everyone around here."

"None of them has ever mentioned you." I sat the bowl on the counter and grabbed for the milk.

"Don't know why they would." He angled toward me, smiling. "I don't think they even realize that Bethany was my niece."

The carton of milk slipped from my fingers, knocking off the counter and hitting the floor. Frothy white liquid pulsed across the tile. Yet I stood frozen. Bethany was his niece?

Will set the knife down and grabbed several paper towels. "Slippery bugger, isn't it?"

Snapping out of it, I bent down and grabbed the carton. "Bethany was your niece?"

"Yeah, such a sad story, and I'm sure you've heard it."

"I have." I placed the milk back on the counter and helped him mop up my mess. "I'm sorry about…what happened."

"So am I." He tossed the towels in the trash. "It destroyed my sister and her husband. They moved away just a month or so ago. I guess they couldn't stand living here, being reminded of her. Then that Cutters boy disappears, just like with Bethany and Dawson. It's a damn shame so many young people disappeared."

Never once had Daemon or Dee said a word about Will being related to Bethany, but they also didn't talk about her often. Troubled by the relation Will had and the mention of Simon, I finished making my potatoes in silence. He liked them country style—skin on. Yuck.

"There's something I wanted to make sure you understood, Katy." Will laced his fingers in front of him. "I'm not trying to take the place of your father."

Surprised by the turn in the conversation, I stared at him.

He stared back, pale eyes steady and fixed on mine. "I know it's hard when one parent moves on, but I'm not here to replace him."

Before I could respond, he patted me on the shoulder and left the kitchen. The ham had cooled on the counter. The mashed potatoes were finished and so was the macaroni casserole. Up to that moment, I'd been starving, but with the mention of my father, all my appetite vanished.

Deep down I knew Will wasn't trying to take his place. No man could ever take my father's place, but two fat tears rolled down my cheeks. I'd cried the first Christmas without him, but the last two I hadn't. Maybe I was crying now because this was the first real holiday I'd had with my mom that involved someone other than my dad.

My elbow caught the edge of the bowl as I turned, and it spun toward off the counter. Without thinking, I froze the bowl so all my hard work wouldn't end up on the floor. I grabbed it out of the air, placing it back on the counter. Turning around, I caught sight of a shadow in the hallway, right outside the kitchen door. My breath froze in my throat as two footsteps heavier than my mom's crossed the hall and started up the steps. *Will.*

Had he seen me?

And if he had, why hadn't he busted in here demanding how I froze a bowl in midair?

• • •

When I woke up the day after Christmas, Will had already taken down the tree. That alone earned him serious negative points. That wasn't his tree to take down. And I'd wanted to keep that green bulb, and now it was packed away in an attic I wouldn't dare venture into. Add that to my growing dislike of the man, and I foresaw some serious problems in the future.

Had he seen me stop the bowl? I didn't know. Could it be a coincidence that the uncle of the girl who had mutated just like me was now putting the moves on my mom? Seemed unlikely. But I had no evidence and who could I really go to? Well, there *was* one person.

It was hours after Mom had left for work and moments before I headed upstairs that I felt warmth prickle my neck. Stopping in the hallway, I waited with my breath in my throat.

There was a knock on my door.

Daemon waited on the porch, hands in his pockets and a black baseball cap pulled low, hiding the upper part of his face. The look accentuated his sensual lips that were tipped in a crooked grin. "You busy?"

I shook my head.

"Wanna go for a ride?"

"Sure. Let me grab something warmer to put on." I hurried to find my boots and hoodie, then joined him outside. "Are we going to check on Vaughn?"

"Not really. There's something I've discovered." He led me to his SUV and waited until we both climbed in before he continued. "But first, did you have a good Christmas? I was going to stop over, but I saw your mom was home."

"It was good. Will spent the day with us. That was weird. What about you?"

"It was okay. Dee nearly burned the house down trying to make a turkey. Other than that, not very entertaining." He pulled out of the driveway. "So, how much trouble were you in after Saturday?"

I flushed, thankful for the darkness. "I got a lecture about not making my mom a grandmother." Daemon laughed, and I sighed. "Now I have rules to follow, but nothing serious."

"Sorry about that." He grinned as he slid me a sideways look. "I didn't mean to fall asleep."

"It's okay. So where are we going? What have you found out?"

"Vaughn came home Sunday night for about ten minutes. I followed him to just outside of Petersburg to this warehouse in an industrial park that hasn't been used in years. He stayed there for a few hours and then left, but there were two officers who remained." He slowed down as a deer dashed across the highway. "They're keeping something there."

Excitement hummed through me. "You think they're keeping Bethany…or Dawson?"

He glanced at me, lips pressed into a tight line. "I don't know, but I need to get in there and someone needs to keep an eye on the outside while I go."

Feeling useful, I nodded. "What if the guards are still keeping watch?"

"They weren't doing anything until Vaughn showed up. He's home right now. With Nancy." His lip curled. "I think the two really have something going on."

It was like Will and my mom. Gross. Thinking of that reminded me of something I needed to ask. "Did you know my mom's boyfriend is Bethany's uncle?"

"No." His brows pinched as he focused on the road. "I didn't really try to get to know her. Hell, I didn't really try to get to know any human girl."

There was a weird flutter in my belly. "So you've never...dated a human girl before?"

"Dated? No." He glanced at me quickly, seeming to decide what to say next. "Hang out with? Yes."

The flutter turned into a red-hot snake coiling around my insides. Hung out—*hung out* in the way everyone thought Blake and I were? I wanted to hit something.

"Anyway, I didn't know they were related."

I pushed away the jealousy. Now wasn't the time. "Do you think that's weird? I mean, he's related to Bethany, who's sort of like me now, and he's messing around with my mom. We know that someone had to have betrayed Dawson and Bethany."

"It's weird, but how would he know what had happened? He would've needed to have some inside knowledge of the whole healing process to know what to look for."

"Maybe he's an implant."

Daemon looked at me sharply but didn't say anything. The possibility was disturbing. Will could be using my mom to keep an eye on me. Gaining her trust, sleeping in her bed... I'd kill him.

After a few moments, Daemon cleared his throat. "I've been

thinking about what Matthew told us—the whole marrying DNA thing."

Every muscle in my body tensed, and I stared straight ahead. "Yeah…?"

"I talked to him later and I asked him about the connection, if it could make someone feel anything. He said no. But I already knew that. Thought you should know."

Closing my eyes, I nodded. Of course, I already knew that. I squeezed my hands into tight balls. I almost told him I knew, but bringing up Blake would really mar the moment. "What about the whole you die, I die thing?"

"What about it?" he responded, eyes on the road. "There isn't anything we can do about that other than not getting ourselves killed."

"There's more to it than that," I said, watching the rolling white-tipped hills go by. "We're really joined together, you know. Like, forever…"

"I know," he said quietly.

There really wasn't anything I could add to that.

We arrived at the abandoned industrial park near midnight, driving past it first to make sure there were no cars around. There were three buildings clustered together near a field covered in white. One was a squat, one-story brick building and one in the middle was several stories high, large enough to store a jumbo jet.

Daemon pulled behind one of the buildings, parking the SUV between two large sheds with the front facing the only entrance. He turned to me, killing the engine. "I need to get in that building." He gestured at the tall one. "But you need to stay in the car while I do this. I need eyes on the road and I don't know what's waiting in there."

Fear pinched my stomach. "What if someone is in there? I want to go with you."

"I can take care of myself. You need to stay in here, where it's safe."

"But—"

"No, Kat, stay here. Text me if anyone comes in." He reached for the door. "Please."

Given no other choice, I did nothing as Daemon slid out of the car. Twisting in my seat, I watched him disappear around the side of the building. I let out a breath I didn't know I'd been holding and faced the front, keeping my eyes trained on the main road.

What if Bethany was in there? Hell, what if *Dawson* was in there? I couldn't even wrap my brain around that and what it would mean. Everything would change. Rubbing my hands together, I leaned forward and watched the road. My thoughts kept going back to Will. If he was the implant, then I was so screwed. He'd most likely seen me use my abilities, but if he was the implant, then why hadn't he contacted the DOD immediately?

Something didn't add up with that theory.

My breath started to make little puffs of clouds in the rapidly cooling interior. Only ten minutes had passed, but it felt like forever. What was Daemon doing in there? Sightseeing?

I shifted, trying to keep warm. Off in the distance, I saw two headlights piercing the dark. My breath held.

Please go by. Please go by.

The vehicle slowed as it neared the entrance to the industrial park. My heart raced as I realized it was a black Expedition.

"Crap." I pulled my phone out of my pocket and sent Daemon a quick text. *Company*.

When he didn't respond and I didn't see him heading out of the warehouse, I started to get anxious. The Expedition had disappeared from view, most likely parking in the front. I turned in the seat, gripping the leather until my fingers ached.

No Daemon.

I wasn't about to let fear or his misguided attempt to keep me safe stop me from helping Daemon. Dragging in a cold breath of air, I opened the door and quietly shut it behind me. Keeping to the shadows, I crept to the corner of the building, passing padlocked bay doors. There were no windows, just a steel door I had no hope of getting open after

I tried the lock. Above the door, there was something embedded in the brick, round and glossy in the moonlight, but too dark to make out the color. Glancing back at the bay doors, which were perfect for unloading cargo, it also had a round object embedded over the doors.

I crouched at the edge of the building, craning my neck to see around the side. The path was clear. Not quite relieved, I continued around the corner, keeping close to the side. Up ahead, I saw another door. Was that where Daemon had gone? Biting my lip, I crept closer to the entrance.

Out of the corner of my eye, I saw movement. Holding my breath, I flattened myself against the building as two men dressed in all black came around the front, talking softly. The orange glow of a cigarette flared and then it flickered through the air, fading out when it hit the ground.

I was trapped.

Stark terror forced the air out of my lungs so quickly it left me dizzy. My muscles locked as I turned my head to the side. The taller man—the smoker—looked up. I knew the second he saw me.

"Hey!" Smoker yelled. "Stop right there!"

Like hell. Pushing off the wall, I sprinted away. I made it a couple of feet before he yelled out again. "Stop! Or I'll shoot!"

I stopped, throwing my hands up. Each breath I took sawed painfully in and out of my lungs. *Crap. Crap. Crap.*

"Keep your hands up and turn around," Smoker ordered. "Now."

Doing as instructed, I pivoted in place. They were a few steps away, sleek black guns drawn and pointed directly at me. They were dressed like paramilitary or something, in full combat gear. Jesus, what had Daemon stumbled upon?

"Just stay right there," the shorter one said, approaching me cautiously. "What are you doing here?"

I clamped my mouth shut and felt the heady rush of Source pooling in my veins, provoked by fear. Static built under my clothing, raising the tiny hairs on my body. It demanded to be called upon, used.

But tapping into it would seriously expose what I was.

"What are you doing here?" the shorter one demanded again, now just a foot away.

"I'm…lost. I was looking for the interstate."

Smoker glanced at the shorter officer. "Bullshit."

My heart was pounding so hard I felt like it was going to jump out of my chest, but I kept the Source locked inside. "I'm serious. I was hoping this was, like, a visitor's center or something. I got off at the wrong exit."

The closest one lowered the gun by a fraction of an inch. "The highway is several miles from here. You must've taken the wrong exit by a long shot."

I nodded eagerly. "I'm not from around here. And all the roads and signs look the same. Like the towns all sound the same," I rambled on, playing the dumb girl. "I'm trying to get to Moorefield."

"She's lying," Smoker spat.

Any hope that had sparked in me died in a fiery crash. Smoker came closer, keeping the gun trained on me. With one hand, he reached out and placed his palm against my cheek. His hand smelled of cigarettes and disinfectant.

"See," the shorter one said, starting to put his gun back into the holster attached to his thigh. "She's just lost. You're getting paranoid. Go ahead, honey, get out of here."

Smoker grunted and grasped my other cheek, ignoring his partner. Something warm and sharp was in his palm. Fear spiked my heart rate. Was it a knife?

"I'm lost. I swear—"

Red-hot, needle-sharp pain streaked across my cheek, slicing down my neck and over my shoulder. I opened my mouth to scream, but no sound came out.

The pain rushed at me in waves. Blackness inched across my vision, and I doubled over, breaking contact with whatever he held in his hand.

"Christ," the shorter one said. "You're right. She's one of *them*."

I dropped to my knees as the pain ebbed, leaving a dull ache throbbing deep in my skin. Gulping in air, I placed my hand against my cheek, expecting to find my skin split open, but it was only warm.

"Told you." Smoker grasped my arm, yanking me forward. When I lifted my head, he had a gun pressed between my eyes. "What's in this barrel will do far worse. So you better think carefully before you answer the next question. Who are you?"

Speechless, fear held me paralyzed.

He shook me. "Answer me."

"I...I..."

"What's going on out here?" a new voice asked, coming up from behind the two men.

Smoker stepped to the side, and my heart dropped. It was Vaughn.

"We found her sneaking around back here," Smoker said, sounding like he'd just caught the biggest catfish to date. "She's one of them."

Vaughn frowned as he moved closer, his bushy mustache blowing as he breathed heavily. "Good job. I'll take this one."

I couldn't breathe. Vaughn had been inside, where Daemon was. Had he caught Daemon, done something to him? If so, it was entirely my fault. I'd started this by telling him I'd seen Bethany. I may not have controlled where the rock went, but I'd pushed it down the hill.

"Are you sure?" asked the shorter officer.

Vaughn nodded, reaching down and grasping my other arm, hauling me to my feet. "I've had my eye on this one for a while."

"The cages should be prepped," Smoker said, letting go of my other arm reluctantly. "It took a while for it to work on her. You might want to double it up."

Cages? My mouth dried up.

The shorter officer looked me over, eyes narrowing. "Since we caught this one, shouldn't we get a reward?"

"Reward?" asked Vaughn, voice low.

Smoker laughed. "Yeah, like with the other one. That was one hell of a reward. Husher won't know any different as long as we don't mess her up."

Before my brain could come to terms with what he meant, Vaughn pushed me to the side hard enough I lost my balance and hit the ground. He threw up his hand. Lightning crackled around his arm, flaring red-white as it enveloped his body until he was nothing more than light.

I gasped, realizing Vaughn was…Daemon.

"Dammit!" yelled Smoker, reaching for his gun. "It's a trick!"

Pulsing with light and power, he released the energy. It struck Smoker first, sending him several feet back. The light arched, smacking into the shorter officer. He too went flying into the side of the building. There was a sickening crunch, and he fell to the ground, skin and clothing smoking. The man shuddered once, and then his face turned to…*ash*.

"Oh my God," I whispered.

A slight breeze moved down the building, stirring the fallen man. Pieces of him flicked up into the air, floating away until nothing remained. It was the same where Smoker had fallen. There was nothing left of them.

Daemon's light dimmed, and when I looked at him, he was in his human form. I expected him to flip out about my not staying in the car, but all he did was reach down and take my hand, gently pulling me to my feet. The baseball cap hid his eyes, but his lips were pressed in that hard, unyielding line.

"We need to get out of here," he said.

I agreed.

Chapter 28

Back at my house, we sat on the couch, facing each other with our legs crossed. I held a steaming cup of hot cocoa that he'd placed between my hands, but I couldn't get warm enough. I kept running down everything that had happened, ending with the men turning into ash. It reminded me of the videos of the atomic bomb being dropped on Hiroshima. The blast of heat had been so intense it had turned people to ash and permanently implanted their shadows into buildings.

We'd driven their car into the woods, and Daemon had then fried it, burning it until there wasn't much of anything left. Any evidence of us being there had been removed, but eventually people would miss the two men and questions would start getting tossed around, especially from their families. Because they had families…

The baseball cap had been tossed onto the coffee table, but I couldn't read anything in Daemon's eyes. He'd been quiet the whole way back.

I squeezed the warm mug. "Daemon…are you okay?"

He nodded. "Yeah."

Taking a sip, I watched him from under my lashes. "What was

inside the building?"

He rubbed the back of his neck as he closed his eyes briefly. "There wasn't anything in the first couple of rooms. Just empty office space, but it's obvious the place is used a lot. There were empty coffee cups, filled ashtrays everywhere. The farther I got in, there were...cages. About ten of them; one looked like it was used recently."

Nausea rolled inside me. "Do you really think they were keeping people in there?"

"Luxen? Yes. And maybe others like you." He dropped his hands on his legs. "One of the cages had dried blood in it. All of them had chains and manacles encased in this dark red stone I've never seen before."

"I saw something outside the building, above the doors. It was shiny, looked black to me because it was dark." I set my cup aside. "And he put something against my cheek, and God, that hurt like hell. I wonder if it was the same thing you saw."

His poetic lips tipped down at the corners. "How are you feeling now?"

"Perfectly fine." I waved it off. "Did you see anything else?"

"I didn't have time to go upstairs, but I had this feeling that something...something was up there." He stood with fluid grace, clasping his arms behind his head. "I need to get back in there."

My eyes followed him. "Daemon, it's too dangerous. People are going to realize that the officers are missing. You can't go back there."

He whirled around, facing me. "My brother could be in there or something that will tell me where my brother is. I can't just walk away because it's too dangerous."

"I understand that." I stood, clenching my hands. "But what good are you to Dawson—or to Dee—if you get caught?"

Daemon stared at me for several long moments. "I have to do something."

"I know, but it needs to be more thought out than any of your plans have been so far." I ignored the flash of temper in his bright gaze.

"Because you could've been captured tonight."

"I'm not worried about myself, Kat."

"Then that's a problem!"

His eyes narrowed. "I wouldn't have involved you in this if I knew you were going to wimp out."

"Wimp out?" The events of the night heightened everything I was feeling and I was on overload, seconds from breaking down, sitting in the corner somewhere. Maybe rocking in that corner, too. "*I'm* the one who involved *you*. I saw Bethany."

"And I agreed to let you come with me the first time." He ran his hand through his messy hair, exhaling roughly. "If you'd stayed in that car, I could've had time to check the floors above."

My mouth dropped open. "You would've been caught inside. I got out of the car because you didn't respond to my text! If I stayed in there, we'd both be in those cages."

The tips of his cheeks flushed as he looked away. "Okay. Both of us are aggravated right now. We should just let it drop for tonight. Get some rest. Whatever."

I didn't want to let it drop, but he had a point. I crossed my arms. "Fine."

With one last look, he grabbed his cap from the table and turned to leave, stopping at the end of the couch. His shoulders shuddered and his voice came out a whisper. "I've never killed a human before."

Suddenly, his aggravation made more sense. It wasn't just the helpless feeling of not being able to do anything. The need to comfort him, to touch him, turned physical. I reached out, placing my hand on his arm. "It's okay."

Daemon shrugged off my hand, scowling. "It's not okay, *Katy*. I killed two humans. And don't—just don't do anything."

I flinched, more from the use of my real name than his action. Daemon blinked out, and the front door slammed shut. Running both my hands over my head, I bit down on my lip hard enough for a metallic taste to spring into my mouth.

Daemon wouldn't go back to that warehouse. Never in a million years.

Even I couldn't convince myself of that.

· · ·

Sleep didn't come easily that night, and I spent the better part of the next day strung tight as a bow pulled too hard. I kept checking the driveway next door, making sure Daemon's car was there. He could just zip his way back to the warehouse without his SUV, but seeing the car gave me some relief.

The next couple days of winter break crept by. Most of the time I expected SWAT to bust up in my house, demanding to know what happened to the officers. But nothing happened. The day before New Year's Eve, Dee stopped by.

"Like my new boots?" She stuck out one slender leg. Black leather boots ended just below her knees. The heel was killer. "Daemon got them for me."

"They're awesome. What size are you?"

She giggled, then popped a lollipop back in her mouth. "Okay, before you tell me no, I already cleared it with Ash."

I frowned. "Cleared what?"

"Ash is throwing a little New Year's Eve party at her house. It's just going to be a few of us. Daemon is going."

"Uh, I doubt Ash is okay with me going to her party."

"No, she is." Dee pinged around the living room like a captured butterfly. "She promised she'd be cool with it. I think you're growing on her."

"Like mold," I muttered. Watching Dee made me dizzy. "I don't know."

"Oh, come on, Katy. You can even invite Blake if you want to."

I made a face. "I'm not inviting him."

She came to a sudden halt, the lollipop dangling from her fingers.

"Are you guys having problems?" she asked hopefully.

"You know, if I were actually dating him, I'd have a problem with how happy you sounded there, but since I'm *not* dating him, I'm okay."

Her eyes narrowed suspiciously. "What's going on with you two, then?"

"Nothing." I sighed.

She sucked on her lollipop for a few moments as she watched me. "And nothing is going on with my brother. Right? He's just slinking around the house for no reason."

My lips pursed. "Dee…"

"He's my brother, Katy. I love him. And you're my best friend, even though you haven't really acted like it recently." She flashed a quick grin before continuing. "So I feel like I'm stuck in the middle of you two. And I know neither of you is putting me there, but I want…both of you happy."

Wondering how we ended up on this conversation, I sat down with a sigh. "Dee, it's really complicated."

"It can't be that complicated," she replied, sounding like Lesa. "You guys like each other, and I know Daemon would be risking a lot by pursuing a relationship with you, but that's his risk to take." Dee sat beside me, her body humming with energy. "Anyway, I think you guys need to talk or…I don't know. Cave to your passions."

I busted out laughing. "Oh my God, are you serious?"

She grinned. "So are you going to go with us tomorrow night?"

As much as I wanted to see the Thompsons' house, because I bet it was super posh and cool, I was still undecided. "I'll think about it."

"You promise?" She nudged me with her elbow. "It would make me really happy if you did."

Partying with them did sound better than what I had planned, which was nothing. Dee stayed for a little while, borrowing a couple of books, and then left. Then, around suppertime, Will showed up with Chinese takeout. I didn't turn the food down, but I wasn't much for conversation. Mom practically floated around the kitchen, buzzing on a good-boyfriend high.

When they left, I spent the rest of the evening reading, finishing a book for a blog tour, and starting a new one I wasn't scheduled to read. Having time to read was nice and relaxing. I could feel a little bit of my old self creeping back. Not the timid Katy, but the one who did what she wanted because she enjoyed it.

When it got close to ten, I put the book down and considered checking in with Daemon. Was he going back to that warehouse without me? There was a good chance he was. Trying to distract myself, I logged into one of the local news websites and searched for any mention of the two officers going missing. I'd checked each night with no results.

But tonight was different.

The headline on the Charleston Gazette read:

TWO DEPARTMENT OF DEFENSE OFFICERS MISSING AFTER LAST
SEEN NEAR PETERSBURG.

My breath caught as I scanned the article. *Officer Robert McConnell and Officer James Richardson were last seen near Petersburg on December 26th and have not been heard from since. Authorities are not saying the nature of their dealings in Grant County but are asking anyone who may have seen the officers or may know anything to please contact their tip line.*

Below the article were two pictures. I recognized them immediately. Clicking off the webpage, I immediately brought up a new web search screen. First, I Googled Nancy Husher and came up with nothing. Smoker had mentioned her by last name, saying she wouldn't be mad if I wasn't…messed up.

I shuddered.

I'd thought there'd at least be something in relation to the DOD, but it wasn't like the woman existed on the Internet. My next search victim was my mom's boyfriend. There were quite a few sites linking to numerous awards won in the medical community, but nothing showing a connection to Bethany.

But there was something that left a bad taste in my mouth about him.

One article's headline read:

LOCAL DOCTOR OVERCOMES LEUKEMIA, BACKS FUNDING FOR NEW
CANCER TREATMENT CENTER IN GRANT COUNTY.

My eyes scanned the article. It was Will. There was a picture of him, most likely taken during rounds of treatment, because I recognized that bone-haggard look.

I couldn't believe it. Did Mom know this? I mean, cancer wasn't a reason not to date someone, but after everything she went through with Dad? Could she go through something like that again if the cancer came back?

And if I actually grew to like the dude, if he wasn't an implant, could I deal with that again? I went back to the search page, unable to wrap my brain around this new fact.

Stopping to grab a cup of cocoa, I returned to my amateurish investigation. My fingers hovered over the keyboard while a sense of guilt flushed my cheeks. Then, with a cringe, I Googled Blake Saunders, telling myself I only wanted to see his old blog, since he never did tell me its name.

The first searches linked to some college athlete, but down toward the bottom of the first page, I saw a news report about his parents' murders. Clicking on the link, I read the sad, sad write-up on the deaths of his parents and sister. It was called a brutal break-in.

There were a couple more articles stating the same, and then I found the obituary for his parents, which took me to a funeral home site in Santa Monica. Sunny Acres. Who in the hell named a funeral home Sunny Acres? Shaking my head, I took a sip of my cocoa and clicked the pictures the website had of the family. The younger Blake was cute, and so was his sister. My gut clenched when I looked at the pictures of him and his little sister playing on a swing set. The kid was way too young, and her death was probably horrific. I blinked back hot tears, moved by someone I'd never even met. It just wasn't fair or right. Death usually was never those two things but this…this was wrong.

I kept going through the pictures, stopping on an older one of Blake's father. I could see the resemblance in the easy smile and hazel eyes. The man next to his father looked oddly familiar. He shared some of the same features as Blake's dad, but his face was rounder. Some of the pictures had captions below, but this one didn't. I went through the next couple of pictures greedily, and then I stopped on one that looked like a family reunion taken around the holidays.

Leaning closer, I set the cup down before I dropped it. A sharp pang sliced my breath as I got a real good look at the guy who'd been in the picture with Blake's father.

The man had his hand clamped on the younger Blake's shoulder and was smiling at the camera from beneath a wiry, light brown mustache. The caption below listed him as Brian Vaughn.

Thoughts warred in my head as I quickly clicked on the obituary again, skimming for surviving family members. Brian Vaughn was listed as a stepbrother of the deceased—of Blake's dad.

My surprised laugh came out strangled, and I stood, looking around the room expectantly, although I wasn't sure what I was looking for. Shock beat at me, struggling to keep the rising tide of anger at bay.

Blake was related to a DOD officer.

How…coincidental.

I started to pace the length of the living room, my breath coming out harsh and fast. The illogical part of my brain was trying to convince myself that it was just a coincidence, that it was *another* Brian Vaughn who looked like the DOD officer. But the harsh reality of being fooled…of allowing myself to be played right into the DOD's hands beat at me.

His relation to the DOD explained how Blake knew so much about the Luxen and mutated humans. Why he'd asked so many times about who had healed me. How reckless and dangerous he'd grown in his training sessions. I didn't even know where Blake lived.

But I knew where Vaughn lived.

I stopped myself before I reached for my car keys. There was no way I was going to Vaughn's house. What would I do? Bust up in there? That was worse than Daemon's typical plans.

Torn between wanting to talk to Daemon and letting the issue drop until I knew what I was dealing with, I sat back and pulled my knees to my chest. Could I have been fooled this badly? This entire time working with someone who was tied to the DOD?

Anger and fear kept alternating, gripping me for several minutes, then letting go and allowing the other emotion to take hold.

My eyes found my car keys. Vaughn hadn't been home, and Blake *claimed* he'd be out of town until school picked up, visiting family with his...*uncle*. And this would be the perfect opportunity to see if I could find any undisputable evidence that would point to Blake working with the DOD.

"Dammit!" I exploded, jumping to my feet.

Fury became a living, breathing entity inside me, coloring everything in a reddish-white light. Some of it was directed at me, but most of it had a target. Blake had been in *my house*, talked to *my mom*, earned *my trust*, and *kissed me*. That kind of betrayal ran so deep it left a permanent mark on my soul.

Daemon was the last person I needed to go to right now. If Blake was working for the DOD, I needed to keep Daemon far away from this. At least until I knew he wouldn't fly off and do something even dumber than what I was about to do.

Done thinking, I snatched my hoodie and tugged it on over my head. Grabbing my keys and my cell phone, I left the house.

I'd done an incredible amount of stupid things in my life. Petting the baby opossum was one of them, walking out in front of the MAC truck was another. I'd even gotten pissy once about the pirating of books and had posted this manifesto on my blog that hardly made any sense.

This, though, probably topped the list.

But as I hit the highway, hands clenching the steering wheel, I was a much different person now. I could kick major ass if need be, and I wouldn't let Blake get away with this.

I parked my car two roads down from where Vaughn lived and stepped out into the frigid air that smelled of snow. Tugging the hood up over my head, I shoved my hands into the middle pocket and hoofed it back toward Vaughn's house. The irony of bitching out Daemon due to his lack of plans didn't pass me by, but now I understood that sometimes certain situations called for well-thought-out stupidity.

This was one of them.

Vaughn's house looked empty as I approached from the rear. Luckily, the two houses closest to his were spaced out. One had a foreclosure sign, and the other was just as dark. Little flakes of snow started to fall as I crept around to the front. My breath came out in puffs, hanging in the air like clouds.

The driveway was empty.

Knowing that didn't mean the house was completely devoid of people, I debated what to do. I didn't come all the way here to stare at the outside of the house. I wanted in there. I wanted to find evidence linking Blake to Vaughn, and I wanted to see if there was anything on the location of Dawson and Bethany.

I went to the back of the house and tried the door. It was locked as expected, but I remembered both Daemon and Blake mentioning how easy locks were to manipulate. It should be a piece of cake.

An alarm system would be a whole different story.

Pressing against the door, I closed my eyes and pictured the lock. The rush of static crept down my arms, jumping from the tips of my fingers through the wood. The click of the lock turning sounded like a nuclear bomb going off in my head.

I took a moment to prepare myself for what could be waiting on the other side of the door. If someone were in there, I'd have to defend myself. The idea of hurting someone, possibly killing him or her, sickened me, but I knew whoever it was wouldn't stop twice from locking me up in a cage.

Telling myself I could do this, I opened the door and slowly stepped into the kitchen. A light was on above the stove, casting the room in soft light. I shut the door behind me and drew in a deep breath. *This is insane.* I crept forward, grateful for the thin soles on my boots.

Timid Katy no more…I'd moved onto good old B&E.

Balling my hands up under the sleeves of my hoodie, I moved down the hallway. The dining room was empty with the exception of a rolled-up sleeping bag on the floor. Two couches were pressed against the wall in the living room. There wasn't a TV. It reminded me of a model home where everything was fake.

It gave me the creeps.

Holding a breath, I went upstairs slowly. Nothing about this house seemed real. It had no homey smells like leftover food or perfume. It smelled vacant. At the top of the stairs, there was a bathroom that had clearly been in use. There were hair products on the sink—gel and two toothbrushes.

My stomach tightened as I left the bathroom. All the bedroom doors were open. Each of them just had a bed and a dresser. All were empty.

The last room at the end of the hall was an office of sorts. A large desk sat in the middle of the otherwise empty room. There was a monitor on the top, but no hard drive. Moving around the desk, I pulled out the center drawer. Nothing. I checked the side drawers, becoming frustrated when they were all empty. I yanked open the last one.

"Jackpot," I whispered.

I pulled out a file folder that was thick and heavy at the bottom. Lifting the file out carefully, I laid it on the desk and flipped it opened. There were pictures, hundreds of pictures.

My hands shook as I went through them. A buzzing filled my ears as I turned over picture after picture.

One of me walking from my car to the front of school in short sleeves. There were several from outside the Smoke Hole Diner, and

I could just make out Dee and me sitting in front of the window, then one of us walking out the door, my arm in a splint and Dee laughing. Several more photos showed us together, at school, on *my front porch*, and in her car. There was one of us hugging in front of the FOOLAND, the first day I'd met her.

Then there were pictures of Daemon, eyes narrowed and face drawn tight as he was snapped walking around his SUV, keys clenched in his hand. Another was him standing on his porch, shirtless and in jeans, with me on his steps, glaring at him.

I picked up one, holding it in the light that came through the window. I was in my red two-piece bathing suit, standing on the bank of the lake. I'd been looking off to the side, and Daemon had been watching me, smiling—really smiling—unbeknownst to me. I hadn't known he ever smiled around me at that time.

I dropped the picture as if it burned my skin. And it did on a surreal level.

There were more. Photos chronicling from the time I arrived in this place up until a few days ago. There were pictures of my mom heading to work, some with her and Will. There were no pictures of Blake and me together.

But the worst picture, the one that almost dropped me to my knees was one of Daemon carrying me back from the lake the night I'd been sick. The photo was dark and grainy, but I could make out the white sleep shirt, the way my arm hung limp, the look of pure concentration on Daemon's face as he had one foot on the porch step.

Hell, could they be watching me now? I couldn't let myself think about it.

The sense of violation sliced through skin and bone. They'd been watching us from the beginning. I wanted to take all these pictures. I wanted to burn them. Where there should've been fear, there was only anger. Who gave them the right to do this? With an anger so potent I could taste it, I gathered up the photos and placed them back in the file. I knew I couldn't take them. Shoving them back into the drawer, I stood with hands trembling.

The bottom of the drawer poked up at the corner. Shoving the file back, I reached down and felt around until I got a grip on the edge. Peeling the contact paper back, I saw several sheets of paper. Most of them were receipts, which seemed odd to hide, considering everything. There were bank slips, too, showing money transfers. My eyes bugged at the amounts. Another slip of paper had an address with the letters *DB* written under it.

Dawson Black? Dee Black? Daemon Black?

Shoving the slip of paper into my pocket, I pressed the contact paper back down and put the file away. I closed the door, feeling numb as I started to stand.

"What are you doing in here?" a voice demanded.

Chapter 29

My heart leaped in my throat at the question. I jerked up, letting the rush of energy move along my skin, but the moment I locked eyes with the person standing in the doorway, I gasped.

Moonlight coming in from the window washed over Bethany's pale face as she stepped into the room. Jeans and a T-shirt hung off her slender body. Her dirty hair fell in clumps. "What are you doing in here?"

"Bethany?" I croaked.

She cocked her head to the side. "Katy?" Her voice mimicked mine.

Taken aback by the fact she knew my name, I stared at her. "How do you know who I am?"

An eerie, faint smile tugged at her lips. "Everyone knows who you are," she said in a singsong voice that reminded me of a child. "And so do I."

I swallowed. "You mean the DOD?"

"I mean whoever is watching knows. They always know. They always hope, too. Whenever we get close." She paused, closing her eyes, sighing. "They hope we get close."

Oh, boy, this chick was cracked like Humpty Dumpty. "Beth, is the DOD keeping you?"

"Keeping me?" She giggled. "I can no longer be kept. He knows that. He keeps catching me, though. It's almost like a game. A never-ending game where no one really wins. I come here…my family. My family is no longer here."

She sighed. "You really shouldn't be here. They will see you. They will take you."

"I know." I wiped my sweaty palms on my jeans. "Beth, we can —"

"Don't trust him," she whispered, glancing around the room. "I did. I trusted him with my life, and look what happened."

"Who? Blake?" Not like she needed to tell me that. "Look, you can come with me. We can keep you safe."

She straightened, shaking her head. "You can't do anything for me now."

"But we can." I took a step forward, reaching out to her. "We can help you, protect you. We can get Dawson back."

"Dawson?" she said, eyes going wide.

I nodded, hoping I'd found the key to make her listen to me. "Yes, Dawson! We know he's alive —"

Bethany threw up her hand, and a burst of hurricane-strength winds slammed into my chest, lifting me off my feet. I hit the wall with enough force I swore I heard plaster crack. And I stayed there, pinned several feet off the ground, my hands and legs planted against the wall.

Apparently bringing up Dawson's name was not the right thing to do.

She moved so fast I didn't see her until she was standing below me. Long, stringy strands of hair lifted off her shoulders, spreading out around her like a modern-day Medusa. Her feet came off the ground as the outline of her body blurred, swathed in a bluish light. Within seconds, she was eye level with me.

Holy crap…I'd never seen Blake do anything like that.

"There is no hope for me," she said, dropping the kid voice. "I'm not even sure there is any hope for *you*. So you should leave here, take your chances with the Arum, or you'll end up like me."

Icy fear trickled down my spine. "Bethany…"

"Listen to me and listen closely." She was now above me, looking down as her head nearly touched the vaulted ceilings. "*Everyone* is a liar. The DOD?" She laughed, a high-pitched giggle. "They don't even know what they plan. They are coming."

"What are you talking about?" I tried to peel my head off the wall, but she wouldn't let me budge. "Beth, who is coming!"

The blue light enveloped her completely. "You need to go NOW!"

I suddenly dropped from the wall, hitting the floor in front of the door with a loud grunt. Scrambling to my feet, I whipped around.

Bethany looked just like a Luxen, except her light was blue and less intense. She floated over the ceiling, her voice picking up in my head. *Go. Go before it's too late. GO!*

A pulse of energy nudged me out the door and down the hall. She wasn't giving me much of a choice. At the top of the stairs, I spun around and tried one more time. "Bethany, we can—"

She slid down the wall and lifted both hands. Before I could scream, I tipped over the top step and fell backward down the steep stairs. I stopped a foot above the landing, bouncing in air as if I were hooked to a bungee cord.

My feet swung down onto the landing, and I was suddenly standing. *Go,* her voice urged. *Get far away from here.*

I went.

• • •

My hands were cold and shaking by the time I turned the ignition in my sedan. Snow was falling steadily, coating the streets. I needed to get home before I got stuck. I had bad tires, no match for more than an inch of snow. And I really didn't want to break down out here. These were the things I was busy thinking about. I had to keep everything else at bay until I could get home and successfully freak out. Now I just needed to get there without running off the road and smacking into a tree.

Halfway to my house, two approaching headlights sped up in the other lane, going in the direction I'd just come from. As the car neared me, the back of my neck tingled. The SUV's tires squealed as it spun around, rushing up behind me.

"Dammit," I whispered, glancing at the dashboard. It was close to midnight.

Daemon tailed me the whole way home, repeatedly calling me. I ignored the calls, focusing on the ever-increasing lack of visibility due to the snow. The moment I parked in my driveway, he was at the side of my car, throwing open the door.

"Where in the hell were you coming back from?" he demanded.

I climbed out of the car. "Where were you going?"

He glared down at me. "I have a feeling it was the same place you were coming back from, but I'm telling myself that you can't be that stupid."

My look matched his as I stomped up my steps. "Well, since that's where you were going, I guess that means you're stupid, too."

"You seriously went there, didn't you?" He sounded incredulous as he followed me inside. "Please tell me that's not where you were. That you were just out for a midnight drive."

I shot him a bland look over my shoulder. "I went to Vaughn's."

Several moments went by as he stared at me. Flakes of snow melted, dampening the locks of hair clinging to his cheeks. "You're insane."

I tugged off my wet hoodie and tossed it aside. With only a tank top underneath, tiny bumps spread over my skin. "So are you."

His full lips twisted into a grimace. "I can take care of myself, Kitten."

"And I can, too." I tugged my hair back. "I'm not helpless, Daemon."

He stood still for a moment, and then a shudder rolled through his body. Next second he was in front of me, grasping my chilled cheeks. "I know you aren't helpless, but there are things I would do that you won't. Things I know you could never live with, but I can. What would you have done if someone saw you? What would *I* have done if you were captured or…"

Daemon didn't finish, but I knew what he was getting at. I could've been captured tonight or worse, and he wasn't worried about how the connection would have caused his own death. He was worried about me.

I don't know why I did what I did next. Maybe it was everything that had happened tonight. Or maybe it was the tone of his voice—the fear behind his words. Too many emotions were building in me. I felt slippery inside, tipping in one direction and then the next.

I clasped his cheeks. They were warm, like always—a touch of sunlight. His skin was smooth and hummed under my hands. I leaned in, and he didn't move…or breathe. Like, at all. Knowing that I could do that to him filled me with a heady rush of power. Closing my eyes, I brushed my lips over his.

"Kitten," he growled roughly.

I kissed him softly, sliding my hands into his silky locks, letting the pieces slide through my fingers. I tasted in him my own rising desire, my own need and heartache. Thrilling. Frightening. I pulled back.

"Kitten," he said again, voice strained. "You don't get to do that and then stop. That's not how it works."

I stared at him, my breath stalling in my lungs.

"Not when you're mine." Daemon backed us up and slid down the wall, pulling me onto his lap so I was straddling him. "And you're mine."

I placed my hands on his shoulders as he brought my mouth to his. This kiss was lazy, exploratory…and sensual. For once, I wasn't fighting the depth of my response. I welcomed it, thrived in the warmth rippling through me. *I* deepened the kiss. He made a sound in the back of his throat, and his arms wrapped around me, pinning me to him.

My fingers found the strands of hair curling at the back of his neck and dug in. I couldn't get enough of him—never could. I couldn't remember feeling this way about anyone else. I couldn't remember being kissed like this by anyone else. I'm not sure how long we kissed, but it seemed like forever, and at the same time, it wasn't long enough.

"Wait. Wait," I breathed, pulling back slightly. I closed my eyes, dragging in a deep breath. "Important stuff."

His hands dropped on my hips, pulling me down and against him. "This is important."

"I know." I gasped as his hands slid under the hem of my tank top, teasing the edges of my rib cage. "But this is really important. I found something in Vaughn's house."

Daemon stilled, opening his eyes. They were luminous. Beautiful. Mine. "You went *inside* Vaughn's house?"

I nodded. "Yeah, I went into his house."

"Are you a career criminal?" he asked quietly. When I shook my head, his lips turned down at the corners. "I'm curious how you got into his house, Kitten."

Biting my lip, I prepared myself. "I unlocked the door."

"With what…?"

"The same way you would."

A muscle popped in his jaw. "You shouldn't be doing things like that."

Growing uncomfortable, I wiggled around. His hold tightened. If we started arguing about what I was and wasn't supposed to be doing, we'd never get through this. "I found stuff. And I also met someone." I tried to get up, but his arms clamped around me. "Are you going to let me go?"

He gave me a tight smile. "Nope."

I sighed, folding my hands primly in the small space between us. "They've been watching us, Daemon. From the moment I moved here." The way his eyes flared, I could tell all of this was going to go over real well. I told him about the pictures, the receipts, and the money transfers. "But that's not all. Bethany showed up."

"What?" Suddenly we both were standing. He backed off, needing space. "Did she talk to you about Dawson?"

"Ah, see, she's not…well, she didn't respond well to his name."

He gave me a cool, measured look. "Explain."

"She kind of went alien ninja on my butt." Feeling too warm, I grabbed a hair tie and twisted my hair up. "She threw me against the wall."

His eyebrows shot up in interest.

I rolled my eyes. "Not in that way, you perv. She's like a suped-up freakin' mutant. She even did the whole glowworm thing, too."

Daemon rubbed his chin. "Did she tell you anything useful?"

I told him what she'd said, elaborating on the fact that most of it didn't make sense. "I think she's cracked. And she flipped out when I mentioned Dawson. She didn't give me much of a choice to push the questioning. She removed me from the house."

"Dammit," he said under his breath, turning away. "Besides getting ahold of one of the DOD officers, she was my last hope to find out where Dawson could be."

"I did find something else." I dug into my pocket, pulling out the scrap of paper. "I found this."

Daemon took it, his eyes widening.

"Do you think DB stands for Dawson Black?"

"It could." He clenched the paper tight. "Can I use your laptop? I want to see where this address goes."

"Sure." I moved over to the coffee table, opening up the computer and quickly shutting down the website I'd been looking at. I didn't want to tell him about Blake's potential involvement in all of this. Not when Daemon was looking incredibly scary and I had no idea how deep Blake was involved.

Daemon sat beside me and quickly typed the address in Google Maps. Modern technology was frightening. Not only did it give us directions right to the doorstep, but he was able to pull it up on the satellite and see that it was an office building in Moorefield.

I chewed on my fingernail as he scribbled down the directions. "Are you going?"

"I want to, right now, but I need to scope out the place first. Tomorrow I'll check it out, then go back later." He shoved the piece of notebook paper in his pocket and faced me. Hope sparked in his eyes. "Thank you, Kat."

"I kind of owed you something, right?" I rubbed my arms, shivering. "You've saved my butt a lot."

"And what a lovely butt it is, but you risked too much by doing this." He reached behind me, tugging the quilt off, draping it over my shoulders. He held the edges together, searching my face intently. "Why did you do this?"

I lowered my eyes. "I just was thinking about everything, and I wanted to see what was in there."

"It was crazy dangerous, Kitten. You can't do anything like that again. Promise me."

"Okay."

He caught the edge of my chin, tilting my face up to him. "Promise me."

My shoulders slumped. "I won't. Okay. I promise. But you've got to promise me the same thing. I know you can't drop this. I understand that, but you have to be careful, and you can't sneak off without me, either."

Daemon scowled. "This shouldn't involve you."

"But it does," I insisted. "And I'm not a fragile human, Daemon. We're in this together."

"Together?" He mulled over the word, then a slow smile played on his lips. "Okay."

I gave him a tentative smile. "So, that means I go when you check out the address."

He nodded with a resigned smile. We talked about the photos, and how much the DOD had to know. He was taking the violation of privacy a lot better than I had, but I discovered he was accustomed to them being all up in his business. "What do you think Bethany meant by 'They are coming'?" I asked.

He was sprawled against the back of the couch, the picture of ease and lazy arrogance, but I knew he was coiled tight. "I don't know."

"I guess it might not mean anything. I mean, she was kind of whacked out."

Daemon nodded, staring straight ahead. Many seconds passed before he spoke again. "I can't help but wonder what my brother is like right now. Is he like that? Whacked out? I don't think I could...deal with that."

My chest ached from the desperation in his voice. Tomorrow could bring anything, and things were really up in the air between us, but he... he needed me.

I inched toward him. My confidence wavered with the near-feral look he shot my way. Pushing forward, I crawled up against him, wiggling down so that my head was against his shoulder. He inhaled sharply, and I squeezed my eyes shut. "Even if he is...whacked out, you can deal with it. You can deal with anything. I don't doubt that at all."

"You don't?"

"No."

Very slowly, he draped his arm around my shoulders. I felt his chin rest on top of my head. "What are we going to do, Kitten?"

My toes curled at the deep octave of his voice. "I don't know."

"I have a few ideas."

I cracked a grin. "I'm sure you do."

"Wanna hear about them? Although, I'm much better at the show part rather than the tell."

"Somehow, I believe you."

"If you didn't, I could always give you a teaser." He paused, and I could hear the smile in his voice. "You bookish people love teasers, don't you?"

I laughed. "You've been doing your research on my blog."

"Maybe," he replied. "Like I said, I've got to keep an eye on you, Kitten."

Chapter 30

Daemon and I checked out the office building in Moorefield the following morning. We'd thought it would be empty, considering it was sort of a holiday, but the whole plaza of offices was packed with cars.

Pulling the cap over his face, he jumped from the car and checked out the office on the street. When he returned, he grinned at me and quickly pulled out of the plaza. "It appears to be a lawyer's office. Has at least two floors above the main one. They're closed for New Year's and obviously on Sunday. Bad news is they are outfitted with an alarm system."

"Crap. Know a way around that?'

"Fry their systems. If I do it quickly enough, I shouldn't trigger an alarm. But that's not all. Above the entrances and windows is that same damn blackish-red gemstone." His lips tipped up higher. "This is good, though. Whatever those stones are, they have to mean something."

It did. Dawson could be in there right now. "What if it's guarded?"

He didn't answer.

I knew what that meant. He'd do anything to get his brother. Some people might think that's wrong, but I understood. If that were my mom or something, no one would be safe. "When are you going back?"

Again, he was silent. And I knew that meant he didn't want to tell me because he was planning to do this on his own. I pushed the issue the entire way home, but he didn't cave.

"So are you going to Ash's party?" he asked, changing the subject eventually.

"I don't know." I fiddled with the button on my sweater. "I can't imagine her wanting me there, but back to—"

"I want you there."

I glanced at him, my chest swelling to the point of bursting. Way to knock me off track in such a deliciously tender way.

Daemon's eyes slid toward me. "Kitten?"

"Okay. I'll go." At least I'd be able to keep an eye on him there, because I knew he wouldn't wait past tonight to check out the offices. Or at least that's what I was telling myself. The fact he wanted me there didn't outweigh the importance of my keeping an eye on *him*.

The party wasn't starting until nine, and he was heading over early to help Adam with a few things. I was supposed to drive over with Dee, and with a sly wink, he said he was taking me home.

When I got back, I chatted with Mom before she left for work. She appeared happy to hear that I was spending New Year's Eve with Dee. Of course, I left the part out about Daemon taking me home.

Grabbing a book off the counter, I headed upstairs to unwind. Surprisingly, I passed out about twenty-five pages into the urban fantasy novel.

Some time later, the sound of my bedroom door closing woke me up. I rolled onto my side, frowning as my eyes drifted from my door, then across my dresser, past the closet door, and over the silent, stiff form of Blake.

Blake?

I jerked up, but in a burst of alarming speed, he shot forward and clamped his hand over my arm. Fear dug in with razor-sharp barbs. Rearing up, I knocked his hand away and twisted, scrambling across the bed.

"Whoa! Whoa, calm down, Katy." Blake darted around the bed, hands raised in a harmless gesture. "I didn't mean to scare you."

My pulse was all over the place as I backed up against my desk, heart pounding. Seeing him in my bedroom was unexpected, terrifying. "How…how did you get in here?"

He winced as he ran a hand through his spiky hair. "I knocked for a couple of minutes, but you didn't answer. I…sort of let myself in."

The same way I'd let myself into Vaughn's house. My eyes darted to the door behind him, and all I could think about was who his uncle was, how deeply involved he must be with the DOD…and how dangerous he could be.

"Katy, I'm sorry. I didn't mean to scare you." He crept closer, and I felt the rush of static moving up my arms in response to the perceived threat. Somehow, he sensed it and blanched. "Okay. What is your deal? I'm not going to hurt you."

"You already have," I said, swallowing.

He looked wounded as he lowered his hands. "That's why I came here as soon as I got back into town. I've had this whole week to think about what happened with the Arum, and I'm sorry. I understand why you're upset." He paused, looking contrite. "That's why I'm here. I just wanted to talk things out with you."

Was he telling the truth? My hands opened and closed at my sides. I felt like a caged animal with no way out.

"Obviously coming into your house like this wasn't a good idea." Blake smiled. "I just wanted to talk to you."

I forced myself to calm down. "Okay. Um, can you give me a few seconds?"

Blake nodded as he backed out of the room, and I slumped against my desk, dizzy with adrenaline. He didn't know that I'd discovered his relationship with Vaughn, and that meant I had the upper hand. And if he really was working with the DOD, I needed to calm the hell down. He wasn't nearly as dangerous believing I didn't have a clue about anything than if he did know.

I quickly changed into a pair of skinny jeans and a turtleneck. The whole way downstairs, I took deep, even breaths. Blake waited in the living room, sitting on the couch. I gave him a smile I didn't feel. "Sorry. You just caught me off guard. I don't like when people…just show up in my bedroom like that."

"Understandable." He rose slowly, and I noticed then a pallor clung to his skin, heightening the shadows under his eyes. "I won't do it again."

My eyes went to my laptop, and I suddenly wished I'd cleared the search history. I moved into the room, feeling like I was stepping into quicksand. I didn't know how to talk to him, to even look at him. He was a stranger to me now. Someone that, no matter how harmless he looked right this second, I couldn't trust. Part of me wanted to rage at him and the other wanted to run.

"We need to talk," he said awkwardly. "Maybe it would be better if we went to get something to eat?"

My distrust spiked.

He laughed grimly. "I was thinking the Smoke Hole Diner."

I hesitated, not wanting to go anywhere with him, but I also didn't want to be in the house alone with him, and being out in public had to be a better choice. I glanced at the clock on the wall. It was near seven. "I have to be back here in an hour."

"Doable." He grinned.

I slid on my boots and snatched my phone. It was still snowing, so we opted for his truck. I glanced next door as I climbed in. Daemon's SUV was gone and so was Dee's car. She'd mentioned something about getting party favors.

"Did you have a good Christmas?" he asked, sliding the key into the ignition.

"Yeah, you?" My seat belt was stuck, as usual, and I tugged on it. "Do anything exciting?" *Like go on a covert mission for the DOD?*

"I spent some time with my uncle. Really boring."

I froze at the mention of Vaughn, and the strap slipped away from my fingers, snapping back into the holder.

"Are you okay, Katy?"

"Yeah," I said, taking a deep breath. "This damn seat belt is stuck. I don't know why I have so many problems with seat belts, but they are always giving me crap." I tugged on it, cursing under my breath. Finally I got it unstuck and twisted around. My gaze drifted over the dashboard and dipped to the floor.

Something gleamed under the exterior light, peeking out from the corner of the mat. I let go of the strap and bent, grabbing the cool metal off the floor while he fiddled with the wipers, brushing a thin coating of snow from the windshield.

I stared down at the strip of goldish blue metal, struck by the familiarity of it. I'd seen it before on someone. Turning it over, I saw the engraved shape of the state. A flakey reddish substance, kind of like rust, covered half of the state and the lettering. I smoothed my finger over it, revealing the name engraved on the band. Comprehension crept in slowly, mainly out of disbelief, because I knew who half this watch belonged to.

Simon…Simon Cutters…

I'd seen him wear this before. And…and the stuff on the band wasn't rust. My stomach tilted and a violent shudder rolled through me. It was blood. Simon's blood, most likely. My heart leaped into my throat, and I squeezed my hand over the band, hoping Blake hadn't seen me pick it up.

My breath halted in my chest as I glanced at him.

Blake was staring back at me. His gaze dropped to my hand and then flicked up, meeting my eyes again. Our gazes locked. Pure, raw fear dug at me.

"Shit," I whispered.

A small, weak smile crawled across his lips. "Dammit, Katy…"

I spun around in my seat, reaching for the door handle with my free hand. I threw it open and got half of my body out of the truck before his hand clamped down on my arm.

"Katy! Wait! I can explain."

There was nothing to explain. The bloodied watch belonged to Simon—Simon who'd been missing. Add that onto everything else, and I was so out of there. I threw my weight forward, breaking his hold. Scrambling to my feet, I darted around the front of the truck.

Blake was fast, on me before I even reached the first step of the porch. He grabbed my shoulders and whirled me around. I went, swinging at him. He dodged the blows, catching my arms, pinning them to my sides in a brutal bear hug.

"Let me go!" I screamed, knowing there was no one who would hear me. I only had myself to get out of this mess. "Let me go, Blake!"

"I can explain." He grunted as I managed to jab an elbow into his stomach, but he held on. "I didn't kill Simon!"

I struggled, throwing my weight from one side to the next. Of course he'd lie. "Let go!"

"You don't understand."

Static rushed over my skin in response to the threat. Red-white light clouded the corners of my vision. Blake's eyes widened slightly. "Don't do it, Katy."

"Let me go," I growled, feeling the explosion of heated lightning zinging through my veins.

"I don't want to hurt you, but I will," he warned.

"So will I." And I would—*I could.*

Blake let go, pushing me back. My boots slipped over the ice and snow, and my arms flailed wildly. Then he charged me. A flash of intense blue light blinded me. Pain reverberated off my skull, tearing through me, splintering my grasp on the Source. I screamed out, feeling my legs go out from underneath me.

He swooped in, catching me before I fell, half dragging me up the stairs. "I told you not to do it. You didn't listen to me."

Something was wrong with my motor function skills. I opened my mouth, but nothing came out except soft moans. My legs wouldn't work.

I couldn't feel my feet. A metallic taste was in the back of my mouth; blood leaked out of my nose and, I think, my ears, too.

The door swung open in front of us, and he dragged me in. It slammed shut, shaking the pictures on the walls. I kept trying to talk, but only garbled words came out. What did he do to me?

"It'll wear off," he said, as if reading my mind. "Hurts, doesn't it? One of the first things they teach us is to control a concentrated blast of Source so it's like getting hit with a super-charged Taser. We all have to take a hit, just to know how bad it feels."

He dropped me on the couch, and my head lolled to the side as I blinked slowly. His face blurred in and out, and then steadied. He looked grim as he leaned over me, brushing the strands of hair off my face. I tried to knock his hand away, but my arm wouldn't cooperate.

"I know you can hear me. Just give it a couple more minutes, and it will wear off." He sat back, one hand moving up my leg that was off the couch. He positioned it beside the other. My heart pounded, and I whimpered.

Shaking his head, he slipped his hand into my front pocket and slid out my cell phone. Holding it up between us, the Source flared in his hand, obliterating the fragile piece of electronics. He tossed the remains to the floor. "Now, listen to me, Katy."

I squeezed my eyes shut against the rush of tears. That quickly, he had subdued me. And I'd been planning on training and fighting Arum—plus the DOD? I was so foolish.

"I didn't kill Simon. I don't know what happened to him, but you—*you* left me no other choice," he said, voice grave. "I had to clean up after you, make sure you didn't expose yourself before they knew what to do with you. If you hadn't busted those windows in front of him, he'd still be hanging around here and dreaming about college. You didn't leave me a choice."

"No," I croaked out, horrified at what he was saying.

"Yes! He would've told the world."

"You're…you're insane. You…didn't need to kill him."

"Listen to me!" he yelled, dragging his fingers through his hair, eyes bugging. "After I left the party, I stayed and I saw him leave once you broke the windows. I followed him home, and he was so drunk he pulled over on the side of the road. He was going crazy about it and I had to turn him over. I don't know what they did with him."

"There…there was blood on his watch."

"Simon fought back, but he was alive when I last saw him."

But those who discovered the truth about the Luxen *disappeared*. Simon…Simon wasn't coming back. And there wasn't enough air in the house. My chest was rising and falling, but I felt like I couldn't breathe. Tears built in my eyes as I stared up at him.

"Listen to me, Katy. This is bigger than you think." He grasped my cheeks, forcing me to look at him. "You have no idea who this involves, the lies, and what people will do for power. I *didn't* have a choice."

I could feel my strength sliding back into me. A few more moments… "You've lied to me."

"Not everything is a lie!" His grip dug in painfully, bruising my skin until a strangled cry escaped. He drew in a ragged breath. "You know, this wasn't how it was supposed to go down. I was supposed to get you ready, to make sure you are a viable subject. And then I turn you in. If I don't, they'll kill Chris. I can't—I won't let that happen."

Chris? Brain cells must've been damaged because it took a few seconds to remember who Chris was. "Your friend—the one who healed you?"

Blake closed his eyes, nodding. "They have Chris. And if I don't perform, they'll hurt him. They'll kill him. And I can't let that happen. Not because of what it means for me, because I know—I *know* if they kill him I die, but there are things they do…"

They knew… One couldn't survive without the other. Oh my God, they knew. The kind of power that knowledge wielded was horrific.

"I know you understand how strong that bond is." Blake opened his eyes. "You won't tell me who healed you, but you'd do anything to protect that Luxen, wouldn't you? Anything. Chris… He's the only real family I have left. And I don't care about what they do to me, but him?"

As I stared into Blake's eyes, a thin tendril of sympathy wiggled free. If the DOD was holding Chris, using him to force Blake to do things for them, then he was trapped. There was a moment of stark clarity. Were Dawson and Bethany in the same position?

But there was something else. Blake and I did have something in common. He'd do anything for Chris. And I'd do anything for Daemon.

With a burst of energy, I buckled under him, trying to throw him off. He captured my hands and yanked me off the couch. I hit the floor on my side, knocking the air out of me. Rolling me over, he straddled my hips, lifting my joined wrists so they were above my head.

He pressed his weight down. "I didn't want to do this. I never wanted anything to do with this."

I clung to the anger boiling inside me, knowing if I caved to the fear—or worse yet, the compassion—I'd be useless. "Do what, exactly? Lie to me? Work for the DOD—for your uncle?"

Blake blinked. "You know about Brian? Since when?"

I didn't give him the benefit of my answer.

His grip on my wrists tightened until I could feel the bones rubbing together. "Tell me!"

"I saw the obituary for your parents! I put two and two together."

"When?" He shook me, snapping my head back. "How long have you known? Who have you told?"

"No one!" I screamed, dizzy and faint. "I haven't told anyone."

For several seconds, he stared at me, and then his grip loosened. "I hope so, for their sake. Things are bigger than you realize. Not everything I told you is a lie. The DOD does want humans like us. That's their ultimate plan." He eased up a little, but I still felt like I was being smothered by his weight. "I know what you're doing, Katy. Don't call upon the Source. I'm stronger than you. Next time you won't recover so quickly. I will hurt you."

"I already know that," I spat.

"I like you. I really do. And I wish things were different. You have no idea how badly I wish things were different, Katy." He closed his eyes briefly, and when he opened them, they glistened with tears. "Everything I told you about my friend was true, but I grew up knowing about the Luxen. My dad worked as liaison to the DOD, on genetic engineering. And, well, you know who my uncle is. I'm not even sure if the whole accident that changed me wasn't staged." He laughed grimly. "They knew how close Chris and I were, so maybe they expected him to heal me. And the Arum did find my family. None of that is a lie."

"But after that? Everything else is a lie."

"My family was gone, Katy. All I had was my uncle. They trained me and since I'm young, they sent me to areas where they suspected a human around my age had been mutated."

"Oh my God..." I felt sick, and I wanted him off me. I wanted him to be gone. "So this is what you do? Go around, pretending to be someone's friend? Setting up others?"

"My job is to discover if they are salvageable."

"Salvageable?" I whispered, knowing what he meant. "And if they're not, they get put down."

He nodded. "Or worse, Katy... There are worse things than death."

I shuddered. It made sense, his obsession with me being able to control the Source, his escalating recklessness.

"I came here to see if you could control the Source. If you would be an asset to the DOD or a waste, but they already checked you out before I arrived, watching you, following how close you are with the Blacks. I heard they even engineered the Arum attacks on you, hoping one of the Blacks would step in and save you, heal you."

I gasped. Everything that happened to me had been some sort of *experiment*? What if I'd died? "What if no one had survived the Arum attack to heal me?"

Blake laughed. "What's one more dead Luxen to these people? But when they suspected that you'd been healed, they made the necessary calls, and I was brought in." He lowered his head, voice dropping. "They also want to know which one healed you. No guesses. No assumptions. You're going to have to tell them."

My heart tumbled over. "I'll never tell."

A sad smile appeared on his lips. "Oh, you will. They have ways of making you talk. They already have their suspicions. My guess is Daemon. It's so obvious, but they want proof. And if you don't play their games, they'll find ways to make you play." The smile faded from his lips, eyes growing dark and haunted. "Just like they found a way to make me play."

I swallowed, unnerved by the pain in his eyes. "Like with Bethany and Dawson?"

Blake's lashes lowered, and he nodded. "There are more, Katy. You...you have no idea...but it doesn't matter. You'll probably be seeing him soon enough. All I need to do is make one call, and Uncle Brian and Nancy will come. Nancy will be ecstatic." He grunted out an ugly laugh. "Uncle Brian has kept her out of the loop. She has no idea how well you're doing. And they're going to take you away. They take care of you...as long as you behave. You just have to behave."

For a moment, my brain emptied and panic replaced any calm I'd gained. I struggled wildly under him, but he held me down easily.

"I'm sorry," he whispered hoarsely, and God, I believed that he was. "But if I don't do this, they will hurt Chris and I can't..." He swallowed thickly.

My fear knew no limits at that point. Blake really had no choice. It was his life and his friend's or mine. No. No, that wasn't right. He did have a choice, because I would never give up someone else for my survival.

But would I for Daemon?

My heart turned over heavily, and I knew the answer to that. Shades of gray...one big, giant gray area I couldn't think about right now.

"No. You do have a choice," I insisted. "You can go against them. Escape! We can find a way to free—"

"We?" He laughed again. "Who is *we*, Katy? Daemon? Dee? You and me? Hell, every one of us could try to go against the DOD and we'd fail. And the Blacks are going to want to help me? Knowing that I work for the people who took their brother?"

My stomach twisted. "You still have a choice. You don't have to do this. Please, Blake, you don't have to do this."

He looked away, jaw clenching. "But I do. And one day, you'll be in the same position as I am. You'll understand then."

"No." I shook my head. "I'd never do this to someone. I'd find a way out."

His eyes met mine. They were empty, vast. "You'll see."

"Blake—"

A knock on the front door cut off my words. My heart tripled in beat, and Blake froze above me, eyes narrowed, breathing heavy. He pressed his hand over my mouth.

"Katy?" Dee called out. "It's time to par-tay. Hurry up! Adam is waiting for us in the car."

"What is she doing here?" he asked in a hushed voice.

I trembled, staring up at him with wide eyes. How was I supposed to answer with his hand over my mouth?

Dee banged on the front door again. "Katy, I know you're in there. Answer the door."

"Tell her you've changed your mind." His hand pressed harder against my mouth. "Tell her or I swear to God, I'll blow her into the Milky Way. I don't want to do it, but I will."

I nodded and very slowly, Blake lifted his fingers and hauled me to my feet. He pushed me out of the living room and toward the door.

"Come on," Dee whined. "You're not even answering your phone. Tell Blake you've got to go. I know he's in there. His truck's out front." She giggled then. "So, yeah, hi, Blake!"

I squeezed my eyes against the tears. "I've changed my mind."

"What?"

"I've changed my mind," I repeated through the door. "I don't want to go out tonight. I just want to stay home."

Please, I begged silently. *Please just go. I don't want to drag you into this. Please.*

There was a heavy pause, and then Dee banged on the door harder. "Don't be a douche, Katy; you're coming tonight. So open this goddamn door!"

Blake glared at me, and I knew she'd come through that door. I took a deep breath and I choked on a dry, hoarse sob. "I don't want to go with you! I don't want to even hang out with you, Dee. Go and leave me the hell alone."

"Damn," whispered Blake.

"Katy…?" Dee said, voice rough. "What's going on? This…this doesn't sound like you."

I pressed my forehead against the door. Tears rolled down my cheeks. "It is me. It's why I haven't been hanging out with you. Okay? I don't want to be friends with you anymore. So please leave me alone. Go bother someone else. I don't have time for this."

The only sound was her heels rapping off the porch. Blake moved to the window, watching them climb into Adam's SUV. When he heard the sound of tires peeling, he marched over and gripped my arm. He pulled me back into the living room, forcing me to sit on the couch.

"She'll get over it," he said, pulling his cell out of his pocket.

"No," I whispered, watching him type away on his phone. "She won't."

Since Blake was distracted by his phone, I saw my only chance. As I tapped into the Source, there wasn't a single part of me that doubted my next actions, not even for a second. Rage clouded my sense of moral code. Everything was twisted now. There was no right, no wrong.

A fierce wind howled throughout the house. Pictures from the hallway shook and fell to the floor, shattering. The cupboards rattled, doors swung open, and books toppled over.

Blake whirled on me, lowering the phone, eyes filled with awe. "You really are sort of amazing."

Strands of hair whipped around me, my fingers ached with energy that crackled all through me. I felt the tips of my feet leave the floor.

He snapped the phone shut and threw out his hand. The wind I was stirring kicked back on me, sending me into the wall. Stunned, I fought the force holding me back, but like with Beth, I couldn't break it.

"You haven't been fully trained." Blake advanced on me, smiling wryly. "There's a lot of potential, don't get me wrong, but you can't fight me."

"Screw you," I spat.

"I would've been game for that." He brought his hand back toward him, and it was like an invisible string had been attached to me. Against my will, my body went right to him, and I was suspended there, kicking and thrashing at nothing but air. "Tire yourself out. It doesn't matter."

"I'm going to kill you," I promised, welcoming the rising tide of fury building in me.

"You don't have it in you." He paused, cocking his head to the side. "Not yet, at least."

His phone dinged, and he flipped it open, smiling. "Uncle Brian's on his way. It's almost over."

I screamed, feeling the energy pulse around me. My vision clouded once again, and I *felt* each one of my cells warming. Anger fueled the alien part of me, giving it strength. I zeroed in on Blake.

He backed up, brows raised. "Give it your best shot. I'll just throw it back on you."

A window shattered upstairs, the sound explosive and jarring. I lifted my head as Blake spun around. Two streaks of light shot down the stairs, breaking apart and heading straight for Blake. One smaller and less powerful form drew up short.

The light flickered out, and Dee took shape, her mouth hanging open as she stared at me. "You're…you're glowing."

The other light crashed into Blake, sending him several feet back. I turned, feeling myself lower to the floor. Blake roared as he pushed the light off him, and he, too, started to glow, much like Bethany had.

An intense blue light surrounded him as he reared back and released a pulse of light.

Dee shot forward, flickering out as she grabbed for Adam. The pulse hit them and they froze. Both took on their human forms for a brief second. An iridescent stream of light leaked from Dee's nose and spilled from her mouth.

I staggered forward, screaming her name. Blake grabbed me from behind, thrusting me down onto the floor.

She was the first to collapse. Blinking in and out, she crumpled, eyes closed. I struggled under Blake, managing to rise up on my elbows. I screamed again, but it didn't even sound like me.

Adam...Adam was much worse. A river of light came from his mouth, his eyes, and his ears. His human body shuddered. Liquid radiance dripped onto the floor. He was swathed in light, but it flickered erratically. He took a step forward, raising his hand.

"No!" I screamed.

Blake reared off me, hitting Adam with another blast.

Adam went down.

Pushing on the back of my head, he forced my face into the wooden floor, pressing his knee into the center of my back. "Dammit," he said hoarsely. "Dammit!"

I couldn't breathe.

"I didn't... I didn't want that to happen," he said, bending over me. His head pressed into my shoulder and his body shuddered. "Oh God, I didn't want to hurt anyone." He trembled, lifting his head. He croaked out a broken laugh. "Well, at least I know it wasn't either of them who healed you. I'm pretty sure they're both dead."

Chapter 31

The last time I'd cried this hard was when the hospice worker forced me away from my dad's bed during his final moments. They weren't pretty as he struggled to take his last breath.

"She's not dead," Blake said, sounding relieved. "She's still alive."

Blood and tears mixed on my face. Sobs clogged my throat, rendering me speechless. Dee was alive. Barely. Her light continued to flicker softly, but Adam... Oh, God. Adam's light had dulled, no stronger than a weak and faded lightbulb. I could see the shape of his hands and legs. His face wasn't shapeless, and neither was the rest of his body. It was like a pale, translucent shell of a human. A network of silvery veins existed under the semi-transparent shell. It reminded me of a jellyfish.

Adam was dead.

Quiet sobs raked my throat until it was so hoarse and raw I could hardly breathe. This was my fault. I'd trusted Blake when Daemon practically begged me not to. I'd befriended Dee, and she'd known something was wrong because *she knew me*. I hadn't killed Adam, but I'd led him right into this. He'd died trying to protect me.

"Shh," Blake crooned, lifting me off the floor, turning me over. "You've got to calm down." He wiped a hand along my cheek. "You're going to make yourself sick."

"Don't touch me," I croaked, scrambling away from him. "Don't... come. Near. Me."

He crouched, watching as I crawled to Dee's side. I wanted to help her, but I didn't know how. My gaze flickered over to Adam, and I choked on my breath. Not knowing what else to do, I blocked Adam from her view. It was all I could do.

No more than five minutes later, a car door shut outside. Blake stood fluidly, stalking toward me. He placed his hand on my shoulder, and then his phone beeped. I shuddered, knowing what waited beyond the door.

But what I wasn't expecting was the flare of heat that radiated off my obsidian. I lifted my head. "Arum..."

His fingers dug in. "Just sit still."

Oh, God... I glanced down at Dee. She was vulnerable, easy pickings. My front door opened. Heavy feet filled the hallway, and the obsidian scalded my skin. I reached up, hands trembling, and dug the rock out.

Vaughn was the first to enter. His eyebrows rose as his gaze landed beside me. "Blake, what happened here?"

I felt Blake stiffen, but I kept my eyes on the two Arum behind Brian. One was Residon and the other male looked a lot like him. Their greedy eyes were bare and went straight to Dee. I turned, feeling the hair on the back of my neck raise.

"They surprised me. I had to fight back or they would've taken me out. I didn't have a choice." Blake cleared his throat, sounding confused when he spoke again. "Where's Nancy?"

"This has nothing to do with Nancy." Vaughn rubbed a long finger over his brow. "And you say that a lot, Blake. There are always choices. However, you're not really good at making them." He turned to the Arum. "Take the dead one. See if you can get anything off him."

"The dead one?" Residon scuffed. "We want the one who is still alive."

"No." My voice came out harsh and ragged. "No! They can't have either of them. They can't touch them."

Residon laughed.

Vaughn knelt down in front of me, and as close as we were, I could see the resemblance now. "This can go one of two ways. You come with us of your own free will or I will hand over both of them to these guys. Do you understand?"

My eyes darted to the Arum. "I want them gone first."

"You're negotiating?" Vaughn laughed as he glanced up at his nephew. "See, that's what you do when you're presented with the unexpected."

Blake looked away, jaw clenching. "What do you mean this isn't about Nancy?"

"Just what it sounds like."

A shudder racked Blake's taut body. "If we don't turn her over, they'll kill—"

"Do I look like I care? Really?" Vaughn laughed, standing as he turned his attention to me. He pushed back his jacket, flashing his gun. "Residon, take the dead one. Dispose of him."

Take his body, so Ash and Andrew would face what Dee and Daemon had? No body. No closure. My brain clicked off. What rose in me, replacing the sorrow and helplessness, was primal and ancient. Not just alien in origin, but a combination of both foreign and organic. I sucked in air, but there was something...*more*. Particles all around us—tiny atoms, but powerful, too small to see with the naked eye—lit up as they danced in the air and then froze. Like a thousand twinkling stars, they gleamed a dazzling white.

I sucked in and they came toward me, rushing, falling like shooting stars. They built and swirled, surrounding my body and those on the floor. I stood as they pieced together, settling on my skin, soaking through until they bonded with my cells. My entire body warmed, mixing with the roaring tide of emotions gathering in me.

I was no longer just Katy. Something—someone else—moved inside me. Another part of me that had been split months ago, on Halloween, had returned.

The Arum sensed it first. They shifted into their true forms, tall, imposing shadows thick and muddled like midnight oil. They would die.

"Don't kill her," Vaughn yelled, pulling out his gun, leveling it at me. "Now, little girl, you don't want to do anything rash. Think this through."

He would die, too.

Backing up, Blake glanced between his uncle and me. "Christ…"

In the back of my mind, I knew there was something else fueling this power—s*omeone else* from the outside. It was like the night in the clearing. What was in me was fully joining with my other half. I lifted into the air, no longer seeing them in color, but only in white, tinged with red.

"Shit," Vaughn muttered. His finger twitched. "Don't make me do this, Katy. You're worth a lot of money."

Money? What did this have to do with money? But I was beyond caring. I welcomed the feeling encroaching upon me. My vision shifted, blurred, and tingled. My head cocked to the side. Static filled the air, devouring oxygen. Blake gagged, dropping to his knees.

The Arum rose up, spinning around and rushing the door. Their black tendrils reached out, knocking off furniture and sending picture frames to the floor. They drew up short.

"Leaving so soon?" a deep, furious voice said from the doorway. "I'm offended."

Daemon shifted into his true form and took out the first Arum with one blast followed by another…and then another. Pieces of it broke away and floated up and up, disappearing into thin wisps before they reached the ceiling.

I drew Residon, the one who'd wanted Dee, back to me. He was caught between Daemon and me, like a ping-pong ball. My light pulsed.

Daemon's flared.

Residon roared.

Tell me what has happened, Daemon's voice whispered among my thoughts.

I told him everything about Blake and Vaughn while we worked on Residon, tearing him down. But movement caught my attention. Vaughn was trying to work the window open. When he got nowhere with that, he grabbed the floor lamp and swung it toward the glass.

I froze the lamp and then whipped it out of his hands. Vaughn spun around, dashing behind Daemon. In the chaos, Blake had made it outside somehow. So had Daemon and Residon. Three forms streaked into my house. I heard a wailing sound, and it drove deep inside me, darkening a part of me. There was a crack and one of the large oaks came down, landing near the driveway.

Ash was in her human form, tugging on her brother's lifeless body, pulling him into her lap. Her head was tipped back, her mouth open as she keened and wept. Dee was moving beside her, growing stronger and stronger. And I knew her wail would soon join Ash's.

Vaughn? Blake? They wouldn't escape this. I glided out of the living room, my feet on the ground, but I didn't feel the steps. I passed Matthew as he rushed into the living room; the startled cry he let out splintered my heart.

Daemon burned brighter than I'd ever seen. A pure, concentrated white light tinged in red as he darted down the driveway toward the mass of shadows gathering. His light flared intensely, and I threw up my arm, shielding my eyes. I thought of the DOD officers he'd turned to ash…and again I thought of an atomic bomb.

The light had turned that bright.

A bolt of lightning shot from Daemon and slammed into Residon, spinning him into the air. Suspended, the Arum flickered from shadows to human form and then froze, his upper body human and his lower body nothing more than smoke.

And he broke into a thousand shards with a loud *crack* that sounded like thunder.

The snow fell heavier.

Out of the corner of my eye, I saw Vaughn leaping from behind my car—the spot he had been *cowering* in. Gun in hand, he rushed toward his Expedition at the same moment Blake spun toward the woods.

Before I could even move, Daemon threw out a light-encased arm and the Expedition lurched into the air, flipping over Vaughn, exposing him. The roof gave with a crunch. Glass exploded in every which direction as metal snapped.

In awe of such power, I froze.

Daemon whipped toward Blake, catching him by the throat. A heartbeat later, he had the boy against the hood of my car, and in his human form, he was no less frightening or powerful.

"You have no idea how painful I'm going to make this for you," Daemon said, eyes like orbs of white light. "For every bruise you gave Kat, I'm going to return to you tenfold." He lifted Blake off my hood. The boy's feet dangled in the air. "And I'm going to seriously enjoy this."

Vaughn made his move then. Rushing forward, he raised the gun.

"Daemon!" I shot toward them.

Vaughn pulled the trigger. Once. Twice. Three times.

Daemon's head jerked around and he smiled—he actually smiled. And the bullets…they stopped inches from Daemon's face. They just hovered there, as if someone had pressed pause.

"You really shouldn't have done that," Daemon growled.

Comprehension showed in Vaughn's pale face. "No—no!"

The bullets flipped over and returned to the sender with an alarming speed. They hit Vaughn in the chest and that was that. There was no chance for any more reactions. The man's legs crumpled and he was nothing but a lifeless heap beside the twisted metal of the Expedition.

Red spread across the snow in a stream of scarlet.

Blake tore free, hitting the side of my bumper, and then he was up, running toward the woods. He was fast.

Not as fast as Daemon, and not as fast as me. Wind and snow blew back at me as I gave chase. Blood didn't pump. Light did.

I caught up to Blake by a pine tree. He spun around, sending a blast of light at me. It struck my chest, knocking me back a few steps. Pain shimmied down my body, but I straightened…and I tracked forward.

He threw another pulse of light.

It ricocheted off my shoulder. Liquid warmth cascaded down my arm, but I pressed on, stalking him, taunting him. Another took my leg out from underneath me, but I picked myself back up.

His hands were shaking. "I'm sorry…" he said. "Katy, I'm sorry. I didn't have a choice."

There were always choices. I'd made a string of bad ones myself. At least I could admit that. Part of me felt bad for him. He was a product of his family, but he had choices. He just made the wrong ones.

Like me.

Like me…?

Beautiful light approached from behind, moving out to my right. He had gone back to his true form. *What do you want to do with him?* Daemon asked calmly.

He…he killed Adam. My power flickered with that, and I could see skin beneath my hands. They were covered in red. A switch had been thrown inside me. Everything left me, and I swayed on the ground, my boots sinking through snow. I couldn't do this anymore. "He killed him. And hurt Dee."

Daemon's form burned as bright as the sun, and for a moment, I thought that it was for Blake, but he dimmed out, taking human shape. Mutated or not, Daemon would have a problem with killing another human, especially after Vaughn. I knew this. The wound left over from the two officers he'd taken out still festered. Add Blake to the list, and he might never heal. The wound would gape forever.

Taking a breath, I said, "So many have died tonight."

Blake's eyes darted to me. "I'm sorry… I'm so sorry. I never wanted any of this happen. I only wanted to protect Chris." He drew in a ragged breath, wiping at the blood under his nose. "I'm—"

"Shut up," Daemon growled. "Go. Go now before I don't give you a choice."

Shock rippled over Blake's face. "You're letting me go?"

Daemon glanced at me, and I lowered my head, exhausted and shamed. If I'd only listened to Daemon in the beginning, trusted that his instinct regarding Blake had not been off. But I hadn't.

"Go and never, ever come back here," Daemon said, his words carrying on the wind. "If I ever see you again, I will kill you."

Blake hesitated for only a moment, and then he spun and ran. I doubted he would make it very far, because once Nancy—whoever she really was—and the DOD realized he'd failed, they'd kill Chris like Blake feared. And that would be the end of Blake. Maybe that was why Daemon was letting him go. Blake was as good as dead anyway.

Or neither of us could kill anymore. I was done. Daemon was done. Too many had died tonight. My legs folded under me, and I knelt in the snow. Using the Source had weakened me and fighting Blake, the injuries inflicted, caused my thoughts to run together in an endless stream of confusion and regret. I doubted I'd ever feel strong enough again.

Slipping in and out of consciousness, I was vaguely aware of someone holding me. There was this incredible warmth cascading through my veins. When I opened my eyes again, I was bathed in light.

Daemon?

There was a buzzing through the connection and then… *I told you we couldn't trust him.*

The pain I felt couldn't be healed by his touch, couldn't be erased in his light. I squeezed my eyes shut, but the tears leaked out. *I'm sorry. I thought…I thought if I learned how to fight, I could keep you safe, all of you safe.*

His light pulled back and then it was Daemon staring down at me, eyes a brilliant shade of white. His body shook with the force of his anger, which was so at odds compared to the gentleness of his embrace.

"Daemon, I—"

"Don't apologize. Just don't apologize." Daemon lifted me out of his lap and sat me on the cold ground. Climbing to his feet, he drew in a ragged breath. "Did you know he was working with the DOD this entire time?"

"No." I climbed to my feet, swaying to the side as my legs got used to working again. He reached out, cupping my elbow until I stopped moving, then he let go. "I didn't know until a few nights ago. And even then I wasn't sure."

"Dammit," he spat, taking a step back. "Was that the night you went to Vaughn's on your own?"

"Yes, but I wasn't sure." I lifted my hands, surprised to see them covered in blood. Mine? Someone else's? "I should've told you then, but I didn't know for sure, and I didn't want to add anything for you to worry about." My voice cracked. "I didn't know."

He looked away, jaw clenching. "Adam is dead. My sister almost lost her life."

I sucked in a painful breath. "I'm so—"

"Don't! Don't you dare apologize!" he yelled, eyes glowing through the darkness, through me. "Adam's death will *destroy* my sister. I told you we couldn't trust Blake, that if you wanted to learn how to fight, I would've shown you! But you didn't listen. And you've brought the DOD into your life, Kat! Who knows what they know now."

"I didn't tell him anything!" My chest was rising rapidly. My breath came out short. "I never told him you healed me."

Daemon's eyes narrowed. "Do you think he didn't guess?"

I winced, at a loss what to say. "I'm sorry," I whispered.

He flinched. "And those times you were covered in bruises? That was him, wasn't it? He was hurting you during training, wasn't he? And never once did you think there may be something wrong with him? God dammit, Kat! You've lied to me. You didn't trust me!"

"I do trust—"

"Bullshit!" Daemon was in my face. "Don't say you trust me when it's apparent you never did!"

There was nothing I could say.

A burst of energy left him, slamming into an ancient oak. It cracked with a loud snapping sound and then folded into a tree beside it. I jumped, gasping for air.

"All of this could've been prevented. Why couldn't you trust me?" His voice cracked, and the sound reverberated through me like a barb-tailed whip.

I wished I had. My trust should've been placed in the one person I'd always trusted. I'd been fooled. Worse yet, I'd let myself be fooled. Tears streamed down my cheeks, a never-ending river of remorse.

Daemon drew in another harsh breath as he started toward me, but he came up short. "I would've kept you safe."

Then in a flash of red-white light, he was gone. And I was alone in the freezing night, left with my choices, my mistakes…my guilt.

Chapter 32

When I returned to my house, everyone was gone except Matthew, who stayed to help…clean up after everything. Someone had removed Vaughn's body, plus his car and Blake's truck. There were broken picture frames everywhere. The coffee table was scratched all to hell. I had no idea how I was going to explain the broken window in the hallway upstairs.

But the spot where Adam had fallen was worse.

Glistening liquid pooled in two spots. Matthew was trying to clean it up, but his hands were shaking, his jaw working. I grabbed some towels from the linen closet and knelt beside him.

"I have this," I whispered.

Matthew sat back, lifting his head and closing his eyes. He let out a staggered breath. "This should've never happened."

Tears built in my eyes as I sopped up what was left of Adam. "I know."

"They are all like my children. Now I've lost another, and for what? It doesn't make sense." His shoulders shook. "It never makes sense."

"I'm sorry." Wetness gathered on my cheeks, and I wiped at my face with my shoulder. "This is my fault. He was trying to protect me."

Matthew didn't say anything for several minutes. I worked at the spot, drenching two towels before he placed his hand on mine. "It's not just your fault, Katy. This was a world you stumbled into, one filled with treachery and greed. You weren't prepared for it. Neither are any of them."

I lifted my head, blinking back tears. "I trusted Blake when I should've trusted Daemon. I let this happen."

Matthew twisted toward me, grasping my cheeks. "You cannot take on the full responsibility for this. You didn't make the choices Blake did. You didn't force his hand."

I choked on a broken sob as grief tore through me. His words didn't ease the guilt, and he knew it. Then the strangest thing happened. He pulled me into his arms, and I broke. Sobs racked my entire body. I pressed my head against his shoulder, my body shaking his, or maybe he was crying for his loss, too. Time passed, and it became a New Year. I welcomed it with tears streaming down my face and a heart ripped apart. When my tears dried, my eyes were nearly swollen shut.

He pulled back, pushing my hair aside. "This isn't the end of anything for you...for Daemon. This is just the beginning, and now you know what you're truly up against. Don't end up like Dawson and Bethany. Both of you are stronger than that."

• • •

I spent the rest of the night trying to hide what had gone down from my mom. Eventually, I needed to tell her. No doubt the satellites had picked up on what had happened the night before. And there was the issue that some of what Vaughn had said hadn't made sense, a lingering feeling that the worst had yet to pass. I figured in the coming days or weeks, it would. There'd also be questions about Adam.

But she didn't need to know right now.

I convinced her that the wind had thrown a branch into the

window upstairs. Believable, since Daemon had knocked down several outside. The pictures were harder to explain.

Then I slept through New Year's Day, waking the following Sunday morning only to eat sugary Pop-Tarts, and then I went back to sleep to avoid the swamping darkness waiting for me. Guilt ate away at me, even in my sleep. I dreamed of Blake and Adam, even Vaughn. They surrounded me while I swam in the lake, slipping under and pulling me below the surface.

So it was strange that when I did wake that evening, I took a shower, piled on some clothes, and left to go to the place haunting my dreams. Mom was already gone, and I had a vague recollection of hearing Will in the house earlier.

Snow continued to fall, but with the moon out, reflecting off the pristine surface, I found my way to the lake easily. I stood by the frozen, flawless water, huddled down in my sweater and the scarf my mom had bought me for Christmas. I'd even donned the matching gloves.

Things were clearer here. Not less intense, but manageable. Adam was dead, and eventually the DOD would come looking for Vaughn. And when they did, it would come back to me…and to Daemon.

And I'd killed. Not by my own hand, but I had led everyone down this road. People have died—innocent and those not so innocent. Daemon had been right—a life was a life. Enemy or not, there was blood on my hands I couldn't wash away, soaking through my skin and leaving a dark stain.

And every time I closed my eyes, I saw Adam's body. There was a tightness in my chest that would probably never go away.

I wasn't sure about going to school tomorrow. It seemed pointless after everything. I still had no clue who had betrayed Dawson and Bethany, and there were more implants out there, watching me— watching all of us. An invisible clock had appeared, ticking away to my very own personal doomsday, and I had no one to blame but myself.

About a minute later, I felt a warm tingle dancing across my neck. My breath stalled in my chest, and I couldn't will my body to turn around. Why was he here? He had to hate me. So did Dee.

The snow crunched under his footsteps, which I found strange. He could move so quietly when he wanted. His body heat blanketed me as he stopped directly behind me. I couldn't ignore him forever, and I also knew he'd stand there forever if he chose to. Surprised and wary, I faced him.

"I knew you'd be here." He looked away, a muscle popping in his jaw. "It's where I come when I need to think."

I said the first thing that came to mind. "How's Dee?"

"She'll survive," he said, eyes shadowed. "We need to talk." Daemon leaned forward before I could respond. "Are you busy right now? Not sure if I'm interrupting. Staring at the lake can take a lot of concentration."

I couldn't figure out anything from his words or expression. "I'm not busy."

His ultra-bright gaze settled on me. "Then come back with me?"

Anxious energy built inside me. Was he going to kill me and stash my body? Drastic but probable after everything I'd caused. My throat dried as we started back to his house in silence. I followed him inside, hands clammy and trembling.

"Hungry?" he asked. "I haven't eaten all day."

"Yeah, a little."

He moved into the kitchen and pulled out a package of lunch meat. I sat at the table while he made two ham and cheese sandwiches. He doubled up on the mustard on mine, knowing that was how I liked it, and I almost started bawling again right then. We ate in strained silence.

Finally, after he'd cleaned up, I stood. "Daemon, I—"

"Not yet," he said. Drying his hands, he then walked out of the kitchen without answering me. Drawing in a deep breath, I trailed after him. When he started up the steps, my pulse skyrocketed.

"Why are we going upstairs?"

Daemon glanced over his shoulder, hand on the mahogany-colored rail. "Why not?"

"I don't know. It's just seems…"

He went up the stairs, leaving me no other choice. We passed Dee's empty bedroom. It looked like Pepto-Bismol threw up in there. There was another bedroom with the door closed. I figured it had been Dawson's, probably untouched since he'd disappeared. Months had passed before Mom and I had moved any of Dad's stuff.

"Where's Dee?" I asked.

"She's with Ash and Andrew. I think being with them is helping her…"

I nodded. More than anything, I wanted to go back in time, to ask more questions, to not be so damn stupid.

Daemon opened a door, and my heart flip-flopped. Stepping aside, he let me brush past him. "Your room?"

"Yep. The best spot in the whole house."

His room was large, surprisingly clean and organized. A few band posters hung on the walls, which were painted a deep blue. All the blinds were down, curtains drawn. With a wave of his hand, a bedside lamp clicked on.

There were a lot of expensive electronics: a flat-screen TV, a Mac that sent a dose of envy through me, a stereo system, and even a desktop. My gaze went to his bed.

It was big.

And the blue down comforter looked comfy and inviting. Lots of room to roll around…or just to sleep. Nothing like my little-girl bed. I forced my gaze away from his bed and walked over to his Mac. "Nice computer."

"It is." Daemon kicked off his shoes.

I could barely breathe. "Daemon—" The bed springs creaked under his weight as I ran my fingers over the lid of the Mac. "I am so sorry about everything. I shouldn't have trusted him—I should've listened to you. I didn't want anyone to get hurt."

"Adam didn't get hurt. He died, Kat."

A lump formed in my throat as I turned to him. His eyes glittered.

"I… If I could go back, I'd change everything."

Daemon shook his head as his gaze dropped to his open hands. He curled them into fists. "I know we don't always get along, and I know the whole connection thing freaked you out, but you knew you could always trust me. The moment you suspected Blake was with the DOD, you should've come to me." Helplessness cracked his voice. "I could've prevented this."

"I *do* trust you. With my life," I said, inching closer. "But once I thought he could possibly be involved with them, I didn't want you involved. Blake knew and suspected too much already."

He shook his head, as if he didn't hear me. "I should've done more. When he threw that damn knife at you, I should've stepped in then and not backed down, but I was just so damn angry."

Tears built in my eyes. How could I still cry or think it would make any of this better? Some papers on his desk stirred restlessly behind me. "I was trying to protect you."

He lifted his eyes, and they pierced straight through me. "You wanted to keep me safe?"

"Yes." I swallowed past the lump in my throat. "Not that it turned out that way in the end, but when I found out Blake and Vaughn were related, all I could think was that he played me—I let myself be played. And he knew how close we were. They'd do to you what they did to Dawson. There is no way I could have lived with that."

Closing his eyes, he turned his head. "When did you know definitely that Blake was working with the DOD?"

It was the second time he'd ever said his name. That's how serious things were. "On New Year's Eve—Friday. Blake showed up while I was sleeping, and I saw Simon's watch in his car. He says Simon's still alive, that the DOD took him, but there…there was blood on his watch."

Daemon cursed and then asked, "While you were sleeping? Did he do this often?"

I shook my head. "Not that I know of."

"You should've never been worried about me getting hurt." He stood, running both hands through his hair. "You know I can take care of myself. You know I can handle my own."

"I know," I said. "But I wasn't going to knowingly put you at risk. You mean too much to me."

His head swung toward me, eyes suddenly sharp. "And what does that mean, exactly?"

"I…" I shook my head. "It doesn't matter now."

"The hell it doesn't!" he said. "You nearly destroyed my family, Kat. You almost got both of us killed, and none of this is over. Who knows how much time any of us have before the DOD comes? I let that dickhead go. He's still out there, and as terrible as this sounds, I hope he gets what's coming to him before he can report back to anyone."

Daemon swore. "You lied to me! Are you telling me all of this is because I mean something to you?"

Heated blood crept across my face. Why was he making me do this? How I felt didn't matter now. "Daemon…"

"Answer me!"

"Fine!" I threw my hands up in the air. "Yes, you mean something to me. What you did for me on Thanksgiving—that made me…" My voice cracked. "That made me *happy*. You made me *happy*. And I still care about you. Okay? You mean something to me—something I can't really even put into words because everything seems too lame in comparison. I've always wanted you, even when I hated you. I want you even though you drive me freaking insane. And I know I screwed everything up. Not just for you and me, but for Dee."

My breath caught on a sob. The words rushed from me, one after another. "And I never felt this way with anyone else. Like I'm falling every time I'm around you, like I can't catch my breath, and I feel *alive*—not just standing around and letting my life walk past me. There's been nothing like that with anyone else." Tears pricked my eyes as I stepped back. My chest was swelling so fast it hurt. "But none of this matters, because I know you really hate me now. I understand that. I just wish I could go back and change everything! I—"

Daemon was suddenly in front of me, clasping my cheeks in his warm hands. "I never hated you."

I blinked back the wetness gathering in my eyes. "But—"

"I don't hate you now, Kat." He stared intently into my eyes. "I'm mad at you—at myself. I'm so angry, I can taste it. I want to find Blake and rearrange parts of his body. But do you know what I thought about all day yesterday? All night? The one single thought I couldn't escape, no matter how pissed off I am at you?"

"No," I whispered.

"That I'm lucky, because the person I can't get out of my head, the person who means more to me than I can stand, is still alive. She's still there. And that's you."

A tear trailed down my cheek. Hope spread through me so fast it left me dizzy and breathless. The feeling was like taking a step off the edge of a cliff without seeing how far the fall would be. Dangerous. Exhilarating. "What...what does that mean?"

"I really don't know." His thumb chased after a tear on my cheek as he smiled slightly. "I don't know what tomorrow is going to bring, what a year from now is going to be like. Hell, we may end up killing each other over something stupid next week. It's a possibility. But all I do know is what I feel for you isn't going anywhere."

Hearing that only made me cry harder. He bent his head, kissing the tears away until he caught each of them with his breath. Then his lips found mine and the room fell away. The whole world disappeared for those precious moments. I wanted to throw myself into the kiss, but I couldn't. I pulled away, dragging in air.

"How can you still want me?" I said.

Daemon pressed his forehead against mine. "Oh, I still want to strangle you. But I'm insane. You're crazy. Maybe that's why. We just make crazy together."

"That makes no sense."

"It kind of does, to me at least." He kissed me again. "It might have to do with the fact you finally admitted you're deeply and irrevocably in love with me."

I let out a weak, shaky laugh. "I *so* did not admit that."

"Not in so many words, but we both know it's true. And I'm okay with it."

"You are?" I closed my eyes, breathing in what felt like the first real breath in months. Maybe years. "It's the same for you?"

His answer was to kiss me...and to kiss me again. When he finally lifted his head, we were on his bed and I was in his arms. I had no recollection of moving. That was how good his kisses were. I had to wait until my heart slowed down. "This doesn't change anything I've done. All of this is still my fault."

Daemon was on his side beside me, his hand on the material covering my stomach. "It's not all your fault. It's all of ours. And we're in this together. We'll face whatever is waiting for us together."

My heart did a wild dance at those words. "Us?"

He nodded, working on the buttons of my sweater, laughing softly when he came to where they were buttoned incorrectly. "If there is anything, there is *us*."

I lifted my shoulders, and he helped me shrug out of the sweater. "And what does 'us' really mean?"

"You and me." Daemon moved down, tugging off my boots. "No one else."

Blood pounded as I yanked off my socks and lay back down. "I...I kind of like the sound of that."

"Kind of?" His hand was on my stomach, slipping down, moving under the hem of my shirt. "Kind of isn't good enough."

"Okay." I jerked when his fingers splayed across my skin. "I do like that."

"So do I." He lowered his head, kissing me softly. "I bet you love that."

My lips curved into a smile against his. "I do."

Making a deep sound in the back of his throat, Daemon trailed kisses over my still-damp cheek that scalded my skin and lit a fire. We whispered to each other, the words slowly stitching together the aching hole in my chest. I think they were doing the same for him. I told him everything Blake had said and done. He told me how angry he'd been just seeing me around Blake, confused and even hurt. The truths he admitted, I kept them close to my heart.

The fear he'd felt when he saw the Arum and Blake this weekend was in every slight, delicate touch of his fingers. Those precious words may not have been spoken up until then, but love was in every touch, every soft moan. I didn't need him to say it, because I was surrounded in his love for me.

Time stopped for us. The world and everything I'd been part of only existed outside the closed bedroom door, but in here, it was only us. And for the first time, there was nothing between us. We were open, vulnerable to each other. Pieces of our clothing disappeared. His shirt. Mine. A button came undone on his jeans...and on mine, too.

"You have no idea how badly I want this." His voice was rough against my cheek. Raw. "I think I've actually dreamed about it." The tips of his fingers drifted over my chest, down my stomach. "Crazy, huh?"

Everything felt crazy. Being in his arms like this when I'd truly believed he'd never forgive me. I lifted my hand, running my fingers down his cheek. He turned to the touch, pressing his lips against the palm of my hand. And when his head lowered to mine again, I sparked alive under him, only for him.

As our kisses deepened and our explorations grew, we got lost in how our bodies moved against each other, how we couldn't get close enough. The clothes that we still wore were a hindrance I wanted to be rid of, because I was ready to take that next step and I could feel that Daemon was, too. Tomorrow or next week wasn't guaranteed. Not that it ever was, but for us, things really weren't looking in our favor. There really was only now, and I wanted to seize the moment and live in it. I wanted to share the moment with Daemon—to share everything with him.

His hands…his kisses were completely undoing me. And when his hand moved down my stomach, slipping even farther down, I opened my eyes, his name barely a whisper. A faint whitish-red glow outlined his body, throwing shadows along the walls of his bedroom. There was something soul-burningly beautiful about being on the brink of losing control, tumbling over into the unknown, and I wanted to fall and never resurface.

But Daemon stopped.

I stared up at him, running my hands over the hard planes of his stomach. "What?"

"You…you're not going to believe me." He pressed another sweet and tender kiss against my lips. "But I want to do this right."

I started to smile. "I doubt you could do this wrong."

Daemon's lips stretched into a smug half grin. "Yeah, I'm not talking about *that*. That I will do perfectly, but I want to… I want us to have what normal couples have."

Stupid, damnable tears rushed to my eyes, and I blinked them back. Oh dear God, I was going to bawl like a baby.

Cupping my cheek, he let out a strangled sound. "And the last thing I want to do is stop, but I want to take you out—go on a date or something. I don't want what we're about to do to be overshadowed by everything else."

With what looked like a great amount of effort, Daemon lifted off me and eased down on his side. He wrapped an arm around my waist and pulled me back against him. His lips grazed my temple. "Okay?"

Tipping my head back, I looked into his bottle-green eyes. This… this was more than okay. And it took me several tries to speak, because my throat was burning with emotion. "I think I might love you."

Daemon's arm tightened around me as he kissed my flushed cheek. "Told you."

Not what I expected as a response.

He chuckled, rolling onto his side—onto me, really. "My bet—I won. I told you that you'd tell me you loved me on New Year's Day."

Looping my arms around his neck, I shook my head. "No. You lost."

Daemon frowned. "How do you figure?"

"Look at the time." I tipped my chin toward the clock. "It's past midnight. It's January second. You lost."

For several moments he stared at the clock like it was an Arum he was about to blast into the next county, and then his eyes found mine. Daemon smiled. "No. I didn't lose. I still won."

Chapter 33

I crept back into my house right before six in the morning, feeling airy and…happy. I needed to shower and get ready for school. There was a part of me that felt wrong for the smile on my face. Should I be content after everything? I wasn't sure. It didn't seem fair.

And I needed to see Dee.

After I stepped out of the steamy bathroom wrapped in my robe, I wasn't startled when I saw Daemon lounging on my bed, freshly showered and changed. At some point, I'd felt him.

I made my way over to the bed. "What are you doing?"

He patted the spot beside him, and I crawled onto my knees. "We need to stick close together over the next couple of weeks. I wouldn't be surprised if the DOD shows. We're safer together."

"Is that the only reason?"

A lazy, indulgent grin played across his lips as he tugged on the belt of my robe. "Not the only reason. Probably the smartest, but definitely not the most pressing."

Things had changed between us in a matter of hours. We talked more last night…and kissed some more before falling asleep in each other's arms. Now, there was an openness, a partnership in things. He was still a total smartass. And yeah, that smug grin still irked me.

But I loved him.

And the jerk loved me, too.

Daemon sat up and pulled me into his lap. He kissed my forehead. "What are you thinking?"

I burrowed my head into the space between his shoulder and neck. "A lot of things. Do…do you think it's wrong to be happy right now?"

His arms tightened. "Well, I wouldn't send out a mass text message or anything."

I rolled my eyes.

"And I'm not entirely happy. I don't think I've really come to terms with everything. Adam was…" He trailed off, his throat working.

"I liked him," I whispered. "I don't expect Dee to ever forgive me, but I want to see her. I need to make sure she's okay."

"She'll forgive you. She needs time." His lips moved against my temple, and my heart squeezed. "Dee knew you tried to warn her off. She called me when you told her to leave, and I told her and Adam to stay out of there, but they parked the car down the street and came back. They made that choice, and I know she'd do it again."

My throat tightened. "There are so many things I wouldn't do again."

"I know." He placed two fingers under my chin, tipping my head back. "We can't focus on that now. It's not going to do any good."

I stretched up, kissing his lips. "I want to see Dee after school."

"What are you doing for lunch?"

"Other than eating? Nothing."

"Good. We're skipping."

"Going to see Dee, right?"

His smile turned wicked. "Yeah, but first, there are things I want to do, and we don't have nearly enough time for that now."

I arched a brow. "Are you going to try to squeeze in dinner and a movie then?"

"Kitten, your mind is a terrible and dirty place. I was thinking we could go for a stroll or something."

"Tease," I murmured and started to stand, but he held me there.

"Say it."

"Say what?" I asked.

"Tell me what you told me earlier."

My heart leaped into my throat. I'd told him a lot of things, but I knew what he wanted to hear. "I love you."

His eyes darkened a second before he kissed me until I was ready to say screw the whole doing-right-by-me thing. "That's all I ever need to hear."

"Those three words?"

"Always those three words."

• • •

News of Adam's passing hadn't hit the school yet, and I wasn't telling anyone other than Lesa and Carissa. The story was he had died in a car accident. Police would back it up if questions were asked. My friends took it like expected. There were a lot of tears, and again I was surprised that my eyes could still fill with them.

Daemon poked me once in class to remind me of our lunch plans, and then one more time because he felt like it. Layers of guilt followed me through most of morning classes, alternating with brief moments of exhilaration. I knew that even if Dee forgave me, it wouldn't change anything. I needed to come to terms with the role I'd played.

But I also knew I couldn't stop living.

When I entered bio, I met Matthew's eyes. There was a twitch to his lips before he opened up his grade book. Lesa was abnormally subdued due to what I'd told her. Halfway through class, the intercom kicked on.

The school secretary's voice rang out. "Katy Swartz is needed in the principal's office, Mr. Garrison."

A jolt of unease pierced my stomach as I grabbed my bag.

Shrugging at Lesa's look, I passed Matthew a near-panicked one as I headed out. I sent Daemon a quick text from my mom's cell that she'd given me that morning, letting him know I was being called to the office. I didn't expect him to respond back. I wasn't even sure he had his cell with him.

The gray-haired secretary was rocking a Brigitte Bardot hairstyle and a bright pink sweater. I leaned against the counter, waiting for her to look up. When she did, she squinted through her spectacles. "Can I help you?"

"I'm Katy. I was called to the office?"

"Oh! Oh, yes, come on, dear." There was compassion in her tone as she stood. She hobbled toward Principal Plummer's office. "Right this way."

I couldn't see through the glass windows, so I had no idea what was waiting for me when she threw all her weight behind opening the door. I marked off any job in the school system in my future if she hadn't been able to retire at her age.

Principal Plummer sat behind his desk, smiling at whoever was seated on the other side. My gaze followed his, and I was shocked to see Will.

"What's going on?" I asked, twisting my backpack's strap against my shoulder.

Will came to his feet quickly and rushed to my side. He clasped my free hand. "Kellie's been in an accident."

"No," I think I gasped. Alarm pounded at my sides as I stared at him. "What do you mean? Is she okay?"

His expression was pained and haggard as he avoided meeting my eyes. "She left work this morning, and they think she hit a patch of ice."

"How bad is it?" My voice wobbled. All I could see was Dad— Dad in a hospital bed, pale and frail, the smell of death that clung to the walls and the hushed voices of the nurses…and then the mannequin in the coffin that sort of resembled Dad but couldn't have been him. Now all those memories were replaced with Mom. *This can't be happening.*

Will curved a hand over my shoulders, gently turning me around. We were walking out of the office, but I wasn't conscious of any of it. "She's in the ER. That's all I know."

"You have to know more than that." I didn't recognize my own voice. "Is she awake? Talking? Does she need to have surgery?"

He shook his head, opening the door. Outside the snow had stopped, and plows were clearing the parking lot. The air was frigid, but I didn't feel it. I was numb. Will led me to a tan Yukon I didn't recognize. Unease trickled in, and a horrible thought struck me. I halted a few feet from the passenger side.

"Did you get a new car?" I asked.

He frowned as he opened the car door. "No. I use this during the winter. Perfect for snowy roads. I tried to tell your mother to get something like this other than that damn matchbox she drives."

Feeling stupid and paranoid, I nodded. It made sense. A lot of people had their "winter" vehicle around here. And with everything that had happened, I'd forgotten about what I'd discovered about Will—his sickness.

I climbed in, clutching my bag to my chest after I buckled my seat belt. Then I remembered Daemon. I checked the phone and saw there wasn't a reply yet. I sent him another quick text, telling him that Mom was in an accident. I'd call him and leave a more detailed message once I knew how…how bad things were.

I choked on a breath when I thought about losing her.

Will rubbed his hands together before he turned the key. The radio came on immediately. It was a weather broadcast. The man's voice coming from the speakers was cheery. I hated him. Meteorologists were watching a Nor'easter forming in the South, slated to slam into West Virginia early next week.

"What hospital is she at?" I asked.

"Winchester," he said, twisting around as he reached for something in the backseat.

I stared straight ahead, trying to keep the panic at bay. *She's going to be okay. She has to be. She'll be okay.* My lips trembled. Why weren't we already on the damn road?

"Katy?"

I faced him. "What?"

"I'm really sorry about this," he said, his face expressionless.

"She's going to be okay, right?" My breath caught again. Maybe he wasn't telling me the worse of it. Maybe she was...

"Your mom is going to be fine."

There wasn't time for me to feel relief or to question what he said. He leaned forward, and I saw a long, scary-looking needle. I jerked back in the seat, but I wasn't fast enough. Will pushed the needle into the side of my neck. There was a pinch, and then coolness rushed through my veins, followed by a faint burning sensation.

I knocked his hand away, or I thought I did. Either way, the needle was gone from his hand, and he was watching me curiously. My hand fluttered to my neck. I couldn't feel my pulse, but it beat through me wildly. "What...what did you do?"

Hands on the steering wheel, he pulled out of the school parking lot without answering. I asked him again. At least I think I did, but I wasn't sure. The road up ahead blurred in a kaleidoscope of white and gray. My fingers slipped over the door handle. I couldn't will them to work, and then I couldn't keep my eyes open.

Calling upon the Source was out of the question. Darkness crept into the corners of my eyes, and I fought it with every ounce of the strength I had left. If I lost consciousness I knew it was all over, but I couldn't keep my head from listing to the side.

My last thought was, *Implants are everywhere.*

Chapter 34

When I came to, it felt like a drummer had taken up residency in my head and my mouth was dry. I'd felt like this once before, when a friend and I had drunk an entire bottle of cheap wine during a sleepover. Except then I'd been hot and sweaty, and now I was freezing.

I lifted my head off the coarse blanket my cheek rested on, prying my eyes open. Shapes were blurry and indistinguishable for several minutes. Flattening out my hands, I pushed up, and a wave of dizziness assaulted me.

My arms and feet were bare. Someone had taken off my sweater, shoes, and socks, leaving me in my tank top and jeans. Goose bumps pimpled my skin in response to the near-freezing temperature of wherever I was. I knew I was inside somewhere. The steady hum of lights and distant voices told me that much.

Eventually my eyes cleared, and I almost wished they'd stayed out of focus.

I was in a cage that resembled a large kennel used for dogs. The thick black metal was spaced enough that I could fit a hand through it. Maybe. I looked up, realizing there was no way I could stand or even lie down completely straight without touching the bars. Manacles and chains hung from the top. Two of them were hooked to my numb, chilled ankles.

Panic clawed through me, forcing my breath in and out as my gaze darted around at a frantic pace. Cages surrounded me. A gleaming reddish-black substance coated the insides of the bars closest to me and on top of the manacles around my ankles.

I kept telling myself to keep it together, but it wasn't working. I scooted onto my backside, sitting up as far as I could and reaching down, wanting to pull the things off my ankles. The moment my fingers touched the top of the metal, red-hot pain swept up my arms, straight to my head. I yelped, jerking my hands back.

Terror consumed me, swallowing me like a rising tide. I reached for the bars, and the same barbed pain sliced through me, throwing me back. A scream tore from my throat as I shuddered, bringing my hands close to my chest. I recognized the pain now. It was what I'd felt when Smoker had placed that object against my cheek.

I tried to call on the power that was in me. I could blow these cages apart without touching them. But there was nothing inside me. It was like I was empty or detached from the Source. Helpless. Trapped.

A lump of material stirred in the cage nearest to me, rising up. It wasn't a lump, but a person—a girl. My heart pounded against my ribs as she sat up, pushing greasy strands of long blond hair off her pale face.

She turned to me. The girl was my age, give or take a year. A wicked red-blue bruise spread out from her hairline, across her left cheek. She would've been pretty if she weren't so thin and unkempt.

She sighed, lowering her face. "I *was* really pretty once."

Had she read my thoughts? "I…"

"Yes, I read your thoughts." Her voice was hoarse, thick. She glanced away, scanning the empty cages and then settling on the double doors. "You're like me, I guess—owned by the Daedalus. Know any aliens?" She laughed then, lowering her pointy chin to her bent knees. "You have no idea why you're here."

Daedalus? What the hell was that? "No. I don't even know where I am."

She started to rock a little. "You're in a warehouse. It's like a transportation pod. I don't know what state. I was out of it when they brought me in." She gestured at the bruise with a flick of tiny fingers. "I wasn't *assimilating*."

I swallowed. "You're human, right?"

Another choked, grim laugh sounded. "I'm not really sure anymore."

"The DOD is involved in this?" I asked. Keep talking. I wouldn't flip out completely if I could keep talking.

She nodded. "Yes and no. The Daedalus is, but they are a part of the DOD. And they are involved in me, but you..." Her eyes narrowed. They were a dark brown, almost black. "I could only pick up fragmented thoughts from the guys when they brought you in. You're here for a different purpose."

That was reassuring. "What's your name?"

"Mo," she croaked, touching her dry lips. "Everyone calls me Mo... or used to. Yours?"

"Katy." I crawled closer to her, careful not to touch the cage. "What were you not assimilating to?"

"I wasn't cooperating." Mo lowered her head, hiding her face behind stringy hair. "I don't even think they believe what they're doing is wrong. It's like one big gray area with them." She lifted her chin. "They had another one here. A boy, but he's not like us. They moved him out right after they brought you in."

"What did he look like?" I asked, thinking of Dawson.

Before she could answer, a door shut somewhere outside of the large, cold room. Mo scrambled back, wrapping her thin arms around her bent knees. "Pretend to be asleep when they come up here. The one who brought you in isn't as bad as the rest. You don't want to provoke them."

I thought of Smoker and his partner. My stomach roiled. "Wh—"

"Shh," she hissed. "They're coming. Pretend to be asleep!"

Not knowing what else to do, I moved to the back of the pen and laid down, throwing my arm over my face so I could peek under it without being seen.

The door opened and I saw two sets of legs encased in black pants enter the room. They were silent as they moved toward our two cages. My heart was racing again, increasing the ache in my head. They stopped in front of Mo's cage.

"Are you going to behave today?" one of the men asked. There was laughter in his voice. "Or are we going to have to make this hard?"

"What do you think?" Mo spat back.

The man laughed and bent down. Black handcuffs dangled from his hands. "We don't want to mess up the other side of your face, sweetie."

"Speak for yourself," the second man groused. "Bitch nearly ended any chances of me having kids."

"Touch me again," Mo said, "and you won't."

He opened the cage, and she immediately went after them. But she was no match for them. They grabbed her legs, pulling her out of the cage until she was lying on the cold cement floor. The one who called her a name rolled her over roughly, slamming her face into the floor. She grunted as he put his knee into her back, pulling her arms behind her. She let out another soft cry as he wrenched her arms.

I couldn't sit still and watch this. I pushed up, ignoring the nausea. "Stop it! You're hurting her!"

The one on her back looked over, frowning as he saw me. "Look at this, Ramirez. This one's awake."

"And that one needs to be left alone," Ramirez replied. "We're getting paid enough money to pretend she ain't here, Williams. Get the stuff on her, and let's get out of here."

Williams climbed off Mo and approached my cage, kneeling down so he was eye-level with me. He wasn't very old—maybe mid-twenties. The look in his dissipated blue eyes scared me more than the cages. Put what on me? "She's a pretty one."

I scooted back, wanting to cross my hands over the thin material of my tank top. "Why am I here?" My voice wavered even though I met his gaze.

Williams laughed as he glanced over his shoulder. "Listen to this one, asking questions."

"Leave her alone." Ramirez hauled the silent girl to her feet. Her head hung low, face shielded by hair. "We've got to get this one back to the center. Come on."

"We could always Windex her brain. Have a little fun."

I shrank back from the suggestion. Could they do that? Wipe away my memories? All I had were my memories. My eyes darted between the two men.

Ramirez swore under his breath. "Just do it, Williams."

When Williams started to stand, I scrambled backward. "Wait. Wait! Why am I here?"

Williams opened the cage door with a small key and grabbed the chains. He yanked hard, and I fell backward. "I really don't know what he wants with you, and I really don't care." He pulled on the chain again. "Now be a good girl."

Showing how much I appreciated his suggestion, I kicked. If I could just get past him... My foot caught him under the chin, snapping his head back. Williams retaliated with a punch in my stomach, doubling me in half. I wheezed as he grabbed my wrists while he retrieved the handcuffs from the top of the cage, pulling so the chain attached to them reached the floor.

"No!" screamed Mo. "No!"

The fear in her voice increased my own, and my struggles renewed. It was no use. Williams clamped the handcuffs around my wrists, and the world exploded in pain. I started screaming.

And I didn't stop.

• • •

My screams only died off when I could no longer make anything louder than a raspy whisper. My throat felt scraped raw. Only uncontrollable whimpers or moans escaped me now.

It had been hours since the men left with Mo. Hours of nothing but scalding, blistering pain that shot down my arms, bounced off my skull. It felt like my skin was continuously being flayed, torn apart to get to *something* underneath.

I faded in and out. Those moments of nothing were pure bliss, a short reprieve that ended too soon. I'd wake, thrust into a world where pain threatened to fray my sanity. Many times over I thought I'd die from it. That there had to be an end somewhere in sight, but the waves of hurt just kept coming, rolling over me, suffocating me.

My tears had also ended when my screams stopped. I tried to not move or jerk when the pain spiked. It only made it worse. I was no longer cold. Maybe it was because I couldn't feel anything other than the hurting that was inflicted by whatever was encased on those handcuffs.

But through it all, I didn't want to die. I wanted to live through this.

At some point, the doors opened. Too exhausted to lift my head, I stared blindly at the metal beams through the bars. Would they take the handcuffs off? I wasn't holding my breath.

"Katy..."

My gaze lowered, taking in the salt and pepper hair, the handsome face, and the smile that had charmed his way into my life and right into my mom's bed. My mom's boyfriend—the first man she'd even paid attention to after my dad's death. I think she loved him. That was what made all of this so much worse. I didn't care about what it meant for me. I had my suspicions before, and there was the general dislike of the fact he had been taking Dad's place, but Mom... This would kill her.

"How you hanging in there?" he asked, as if he truly cared. "I hear it's painful—the coating—to those like you and the Luxen. It's pretty much the only thing that can completely incapacitate both the Luxen and those they mutate. Onyx mixed with a few other stones, like rubies, inflects such a strange reaction. It's like two photons bouncing off each other, looking for a way out. That's what it's doing to your mutated cells."

He adjusted his tie, loosening it around his neck. "I'm what the DOD calls an implant, but I'm sure you've figured that out by now. You're a smart cookie, but you're probably wondering how I knew? The night you were brought into the ER after you were attacked, you were recovering way too fast. And the DOD was already keeping an eye on you because of your proximity to the Blacks."

And being a doctor—wow, he'd know right off the bat if someone healed abnormally fast. Disgust seeped through me like a disease. It took me several tries to get the next raspy words out. "You started… to date my…mom, just to keep…an eye on me?" When he winked, I wanted to vomit. "You son…of a bitch."

"Well, dating your mom did have its benefits. Don't get me wrong. I do care about her. She's a lovely woman, but…"

I wanted to hurt him. Badly. "You…told them about…Dawson and Bethany?"

He flashed a smile, showing off perfect white teeth. "The DOD was already monitoring them. Any time a Luxen gets close to a human, they do, hoping the Luxen will mutate the human. I was staying with her parents when she returned from hiking. I had my suspicions, and I was right."

"You…you were sick."

Something dark flashed in his eyes. "Hmm, haven't you been doing your research?" When I said nothing, he smirked. "And I won't ever be sick again."

I blinked. He'd sold out his only family.

"I brought them in first…and, well, we know what happened from there." He knelt down, head tilted to the side. "But you're different. Your fever ran higher, you responded to the serum miraculously, and you're stronger than Bethany."

"Serum?"

"Yes. It's called Daedalus, named after the division within the DOD that oversees mutated humans. They've been working on it for years—a mixture of human and alien DNA. I injected you with it when you first became ill." Will laughed. "Come on, did you think you'd survive a mutation of that kind of magnitude without help?"

Oh my God...

"You see, not all mutated humans survive the change or the booster shot developed to enhance your abilities. That's what the Daedalus is trying to find out. Why only some—some like you, Bethany, and Blake—react approvingly to the mutation and others do not. And you, you I hear are quite amazing in that department."

He'd shot me up with something? I felt violated on a whole new level. Anger continued to build inside me, overshadowing the pain.

"Why?" I croaked.

Will looked pleased. Excited. "It's rather simple. Daemon has something I want, and you will ensure he behaves long enough so this meeting ends beneficially for all parties involved. And I do have something, besides you, that he will do *anything* for."

"He'll...kill you," I rasped, wincing.

"Doubtful. And you really shouldn't talk," he said conversationally. "I think you've done some permanent damage to your vocal chords. I've been downstairs for a while, waiting for you to stop screaming."

Downstairs? I realized then that we were most likely in the warehouse that Daemon had attempted to investigate the night we ran into the officers. Moving restlessly, I moaned as he brought the handcuffs more into contact with my skin. I may've faded out for a few seconds, because when I opened my eyes, Will was leaning closer.

"Did you know the Luxen healing power is at its strongest when a person is wounded and the effects weaken the longer the gap is between the injury and the healing? So I'm thinking he won't be able to fix the voice thing."

I drew in a ragged, painful breath that scorched my throat. "Fuck... you."

Will laughed. "Don't be angry, Katy. I don't mean him any harm. You, either. I just need you compliant while Daemon and I negotiate. And if he plays along, both of you will walk out of this building alive."

An unexpected jolt of pain rocked me, and my body went stiff as I gasped. It felt like my cells really were bouncing off one another, trying to escape.

He stood, hands clenching at his sides. "I almost thought I lost it all this weekend. You can imagine how pissed I was when I learned that Vaughn was dead. He was supposed to bring you to me then. That poor boy had no idea that his own uncle was working to undermine what Nancy had him doing." He laughed, trailing his fingers over the bars. "Kind of messed up, if you think about it. Vaughn knew that Nancy would be pissed, most likely would take it out on Blake's little alien friend. Although I shouldn't talk, since I turned over Bethany and Dawson. I should've tried it with them, but I wasn't thinking. Dawson is very much like his brother. He'd have done anything for Bethany."

Anger broke through the pain, burning just as bright. "You…"

He stopped at the front of the cage. "As far as I know, it hasn't worked yet."

I really had no idea what he was talking about, but pieces clicked together. Will had betrayed his own niece. The bank transfer slips made sense. Will had been paying Vaughn off, but for what? I didn't know. Whatever it was, it was enough for Vaughn to go against the DOD, and it also explained why he'd stopped Blake from telling Nancy any of my progress.

"Don't worry. Daemon is a smart one." Will turned my old cell over, smiling. "He responded eventually. And let's just say my response will lead him to us."

I focused through the pain, concentrating on what he was saying. "What do you...want from him?"

Will tossed the phone aside and grasped the torturous bars. His eyes met mine, and there was that excitement again, the childlike awe. "I want him to mutate me."

Chapter 35

I'd been expecting a lot of things. Like maybe he wanted Daemon to annihilate an entire town or rob a bank for him, but to mutate him? If pain weren't racking my body, I would've laughed at the absurdity.

Will must've sensed my thoughts, because he scowled. "You have no idea what you're truly capable of. What is money and prestige when you have the kind of power to force people to your will? When you never get sick? When no human and no alien life-form can stop you?" His knuckles bleached. "You don't understand, little girl. Sure, you watched your father succumb to cancer, and I'm sure that was terrible for you, but you still have no idea what it's like when your body turns against you, when every day is a battle to just survive."

He pushed off the bars. "Being sick and close to death changes a person, Katy. I will do anything to never be that weak, that helpless again. And I think your father, if he'd been given the chance, would have felt the same way."

I shuddered. "My father would never…hurt another person…"

Will smiled. "Your naiveté is endearing."

It wasn't naiveté. I knew my dad, what he'd do. Another wave of raw hurt forced my eyes closed. As it ebbed off, a different sensation appeared.

Daemon was here.

My eyes darted to the doorway, and Will turned expectantly, even though there hadn't been a sound. "He's here, isn't he? You can sense him." Relief colored his tone. "All of us suspected him, but we could've been wrong. It wasn't until Blake took out Adam and nearly Dee that we could confirm it was Daemon."

He glanced back at me. "Be grateful that the chain of evidence ends with me. When this is done, we all walk away from this okay. If Nancy knew what we did, neither of you would be leaving here tonight." He glanced over his shoulder. "There's an address you need to remember. 1452 Street of Hopes in Moorefield. There, he'll find what he's looking for. He has until midnight, then he's lost his window of time."

I remembered the address from the slip of paper I'd found, but it was a moot point. I was sure that Daemon was going to blast Will into his next life.

Just then, the double doors opened, slamming off the white cement walls. Daemon came through the entrance, head lowered and eyes like glowing orbs. Even in my state, I could feel the power radiating off him. Not a Luxen power, but a *human* one—one born of desperation and pain.

He looked at Will and quickly dismissed him. His gaze found me and stayed. A multitude of emotions flickered across his face. I wanted to say something, but my body had wanted to move closer to him. It was an unconscious movement, and it caused the onyx on the handcuffs to come into more contact with my skin. Withering on the floor of the pen, my mouth opened in a silent scream.

Daemon shot forward. Not as fast as he normally would. He gripped the bars and then jerked back with a hiss. "What is *this*?" His gaze dropped to his hands and then back to me. Pain fractured the light in his eyes.

"Onyx mixed with ruby and hematite," Will answered. "A nice combination that doesn't sit well with the Luxen or hybrids."

Daemon looked at Will. "I will kill you."

"No, I don't think you will." Will had moved back, though, showing that he wasn't entirely confident in his plans. "Onyx covers every entrance to this building, so I know you can't pull in any power or use the light. I also have the keys to that cage and those handcuffs. And only I can touch any part of that."

Daemon growled low in his throat. "Maybe not now, but I will. You can believe that."

"And you can believe that I'll be ready for that day." Will glanced at me, cocking an eyebrow. "She's been in there for a while. I think you understand what that means. Shall we move this along?"

Ignoring him, Daemon approached the other side of the pen and knelt. I turned my head toward him, and his eyes searched every inch of me intensely. "I'm going to get you out of there, Kitten. I swear to you."

"As sweet as your declaration is, the only way you'll get her out of there is to do as I say, and we only have…" He checked his Rolex. "About thirty minutes before the next round of officers arrive, and while I have every intention of letting you both go, they won't."

Daemon lifted his head, jaw working. "What do you want?"

"I want you to mutate me."

He stared at Will a moment, then laughed grimly. "Are you insane?"

Will's eyes narrowed. "I don't need to explain everything to you. She knows. She can fill you in. I want you to change me." He reached over the cage, wrapping his fingers around the bundle of chains. "I want to become what she is."

"I can't just twitch my nose and make it happen."

"I know how it works." He sneered. "I have to be wounded. You have to heal me, and the rest I can take care of."

Daemon shook his head. "What is the rest?"

Once again, Will looked at me and smiled. "Katy can fill you in on that."

"You'll fill me in right now," he snarled.

"Or not." Will yanked on the chains, and I buckled.

My scream was just a whimper, but Daemon shot up. "Stop it!" he roared. "Let the chains go."

"But you haven't even heard what I'm offering." He held the damn chains up, and I swam in pain.

I faded out for several seconds, returning to see Daemon at the front of the cage, his eyes wide and frantic. "Let the chains go," he said. *"Please."*

My heart cracked. Daemon never begged.

Will released the chains, and I slumped against the pen. The pain was still there, but it was nothing like it had been seconds ago.

"That's much better." Will stepped closer to the cage Mo had been in. "This is my deal. Mutate me, and I'll give you the key to the cage, but I'm not stupid, Daemon."

"You're not?" Daemon snickered.

The older man's lip twitched. "I need to make sure you don't come after me as soon as I leave here, which I know you will once she's removed from that cage."

"Am I that predictable?" He smiled smugly, and his stance changed, taking on the arrogant swagger he was famous for, but I knew he was coiled tight. "I may have to change up my game."

Will let out an exasperated breath. "When I leave here, you will not follow me. We have less than twenty minutes to do this, and then you'll have only thirty minutes, give or take a few, to go to the address I've given to Katy."

Daemon glanced at me quickly. "Is this a scavenger hunt? I so do love them."

Always a smartass, I thought, *even in the worst situations*. I think I kind of loved him just for that.

"Possibly." Will slowly approached him, pulling out a gun from his back. Daemon just arched a brow while my heart tumbled over. "You'll have a choice to make after you let her out of the cage. You can come after me or you can get the one thing you've always wanted."

"What? A tattoo of your face on my ass?"

Will's cheeks flushed with anger. "Your brother."

All of Daemon's arrogance vanished. He took a step back. "What?"

"I've paid a lot of money to get him in a position where he could've 'escaped.' Besides, I doubt they'll really be searching for him." Will smiled coldly. "He's proven to be quite useless. But you—you, on the other hand, are stronger. You'll succeed where he's failed time and time again."

I wet my dry lips. "Failed…at what?"

Daemon's head jerked toward me, his eyes narrowing at the sound of my voice, but Will spoke up. "They've been forcing him to mutate humans for years. It hasn't been working. He's not as strong as you, Daemon. You are different."

Daemon drew in a breath. Will was offering Daemon everything he'd wanted—his brother. There was no way he'd turn that down. And he was fighting not to show any emotion. To Will, he was expressionless, but I recognized the minute ticking in his jaw, the way his eyes flickered, and the tight line of his mouth. He was caught between excitement and the knowledge that he was creating someone who could ultimately destroy the ones he loved. And someone who would be tied to him irrevocably—and to me. If Daemon healed Will, their lives would be joined.

"I'd prefer to hunt you down and break every bone in your body for what you've done," Daemon said finally. "Rip your flesh off your body slowly and then feed it to you for hurting Kat. But my brother means more than vengeance."

Visibly shaken by his words, Will paled. "I was hoping that would be your decision."

"You know, you have to be hurt for this to work."

Will nodded, aiming the gun at his leg. "I know."

Daemon looked disappointed. "I was so hoping I was going to get to inflict the damage."

"Yeah, I don't think so."

What happened next was truly macabre. Part of me wanted to look away or cave to the pain, but I didn't. I watched Will cock his arm back and then after a minute, he shot himself in the leg. The man didn't make a sound. Something didn't seem right about that other than the obvious, but then Daemon placed his hand on Will's arm. The onyx didn't block his healing powers. Daemon could've let him bleed out, but he would never get passed the onyx to get me out.

I blacked out again, unable to really fight through the pain anymore. Coming to, I saw Will unlatching the cage door. He moved over me, healthy and whole, unlocking the chains above me. The manacles slipped off my wrists, and I almost cried just for that.

Will's eyes met mine. "I suggest you don't tell your mother about *this*. After all, it would kill her." He smiled, having gotten what he wanted. "Behave, Katy."

Then he was out of the cage, and out of the room. I didn't know how much time we had left. Couldn't be more than ten minutes. I tried to sit up, but my arms gave out. "Daemon…"

"I'm here." And he was. Carefully entering the cage and helping me out. "I've got you, Kitten. It's over."

The healing warmth was in his hands, fueling what strength I had left. By the time he placed me on my feet outside of the cage, I could stand alone, and I gently brushed his hands off me. After healing Will, I knew he wasn't at full strength. And there were officers on their way, limited time to reach Dawson.

"I'm all right," I whispered in a throaty voice.

Making a deep sound in the back of his throat, he clutched my cheeks and placed his lips on mine. I closed my eyes, sinking into his touch. When he pulled away, both of us were gasping for air.

"What did you do?" I asked, wincing at the sound of my voice.

Daemon pressed his forehead against mine, and I felt his half grin against my lips. "For the mutation to work, both parties have to be *willing*, Kitten. Remember what Matthew said? I wasn't entirely into it, if you get my drift. And not to mention, he needed to be dying or close to it. The mutation probably won't work. At least not to the extent he thinks."

I laughed in spite of everything, the sound rasping. "Evil genius."

"You betcha," he replied, his eyes moving over me, his fingers threading through mine. "You sure you're okay? Your voice…"

"Yeah," I whispered. "I'll be okay."

He kissed me again, soft and deep, and he took away most of the hours spent there, even though I was sure they'd linger for some time, creeping up like most dark things do. But for a moment, we weren't in such a terrible place, there wasn't this giant clock ticking over our heads, and I was safe in his arms. Treasured. Loved. We were together. Two halves of the same atom brought back to make one that was infinitely stronger.

Daemon sighed against my mouth, and then I felt his lips curve into a real smile. "Now let's go get my brother."

Chapter 36

My boots and sweater were MIA, so Daemon tugged his sweater on over my head, leaving him in a thin cotton shirt and jeans. There was nothing we could do about the shoes. I'd survive, though. Chilled feet were actually pleasant in comparison to what I'd just experienced.

With no time to waste, Daemon scooped me up and rushed from the warehouse. Once outside and no longer affected by the onyx, I felt the biting wind sting my cheeks as he picked up speed. Seconds later, he was buckling me into his passenger seat.

"I can do it," I mumbled, willing my fingers around the metal.

He hesitated as he saw my hands tremble and then nodded. In a heartbeat, he was behind the steering wheel, turning the key. "Ready?"

When the belt clicked into place, I leaned back against the seat, out of breath. The onyx had done more than block the Source. I felt like I'd climbed Mount Everest while carrying a hundred-pound weight strapped to my back. I couldn't imagine how Daemon was still going full throttle, especially after the admittedly half-assed healing job on Will.

"You could leave me," I realized then. "You'd be faster...without me."

Daemon's brows shot up as he eased the SUV around the Dumpsters. "I'm not leaving you."

I knew how badly he needed to get to the office building—to Dawson. "I'll be fine. I can stay in the car and…you can just do your zippy speed stuff."

He shook his head. "Not going to happen. We have time."

"But—"

"Not going to happen, Kat." He gunned it out of the parking lot. "I'm not leaving you alone. Not for a freaking second, okay? We have time." He brushed the dark waves off his forehead with one hand, his jaw clenching tightly. "When I got your message about your mom and when you didn't respond back to me, I thought maybe you were already at the hospital in Winchester, so I called and when they told me your mom hadn't been admitted…"

Relief coursed through me. Mom was okay.

Daemon shook his head. "I thought the worst—I thought they'd gotten you. And I was ready to tear this whole damn town apart. And then I got the text from Will…so, yeah, I'm not letting you out of my sight."

My chest ached. While I'd been panicking in that cage, I hadn't had a chance to really consider Daemon was aware of what was happening, but now I knew those hours must've been pure hell for him, a flashback to the days after Dawson's supposed death. My heart wept for him.

"I'm okay," I whispered.

He glanced at me sideways as we sped onto the highway heading east. If we didn't get pulled over for speeding, it would be a miracle. "Are you really okay, though?"

I nodded instead of speaking because I had a feeling hearing my damaged voice would probably get to him.

"Onyx," he said, gripping the steering wheel. "It's been years since I saw it."

"Did you know it would do that?" Keeping my voice low took

away most of the raspy sound.

"Back when we were being assimilated, I'd seen it used on those who were causing problems, but I was young. I should've recognized it, though, when I first saw it. I just never saw it in that capacity—on bars and chains. And I didn't know it would affect you the same way."

"It…" I trailed off, taking a deep breath. It had been the worst pain I'd ever experienced. I imagined it was like childbirth plus surgery without anesthesia. Like the mutated cells under my skin were trying to break free, bouncing off one another. Like being ripped apart from the inside—at least that was how it felt.

And the thought of anyone else suffering like that caused my stomach to twist. They controlled Luxen like that, the ones who caused problems? It was inhumane and torturous. No leap of the imagination to think that was how they'd be controlling Dawson…and Blake's friend. And they'd had Dawson for over a year and Chris for how many?

Hours—I only had hours in that cage with the onyx. Hours that would linger with me until I took my last breath, but it was only hours, while others had years, most likely. In those hours, parts of my soul had darkened…hardened. There'd been moments when I would've done *anything* to make it stop. Knowing that, I couldn't even fathom what it had done to others—to Dawson.

Anxiety thrummed through me. I couldn't bear Daemon being in something like that. Caged and in pain with no end in sight—the hopelessness that would eventually creep into him, the pain that would shape him into a different person. I couldn't live with that.

"Kat?" Concern clouded his tone.

Those hours, the knowledge I'd gained from them, had changed me. No. I had been changing before then—going from someone who hated confrontation to someone who wanted to train and gain the power to fight…and to kill. Lying to those I cared about had become second nature when I'd been a pretty honest person before. Sure, it was to protect them, but lying was lying. I was bolder now, braver. Parts of me had changed for the better, too.

And I knew without a doubt I'd kill to protect Daemon and those I loved without a moment of hesitation. Old Katy couldn't fathom that.

Now I was nothing but a shade of gray—my moral compass ambiguous.

There was something I needed him to know. "Blake and I aren't very different."

"What?" Daemon looked at me sharply. "You're nothing like that son—"

"No. I am." I twisted toward him. "He did everything to protect Chris. He betrayed people. He lied. He killed. And I get that now. Doesn't make anything he did okay, but I get that now. I…I would do *anything* to protect you."

He stared at me as what I didn't say hung in the air between us and then sunk in. I wasn't sure if what I'd become was a better version of me or not. And I also wasn't sure if that was going to change how Daemon looked at me, but he had to know.

Daemon reached over with one hand, threading his fingers through mine. He remained focused on the dark road as he pressed our hands to his thigh, keeping them there. "You're still nothing like him, because in the end, you wouldn't hurt someone who was innocent. You'd make the right call."

I wasn't so sure about that, but his faith in me brought tears to my weary eyes. I blinked them back and squeezed his hand. Daemon didn't say it, but I knew he wouldn't make the "right call" if someone he loved was in danger. He hadn't made the "right call" when the two DOD officers caught us at the warehouse.

"About Will? What…what do you think will happen with him?"

Daemon growled. "God, I do want to hunt him down, but here's the deal. Worst-case scenario, he's pissed when the mutation fades, and he comes back after us. If so, I'll take care of him."

My brows arched. Worst-case scenario to me was if he came back in any form—normal, mutated, or whatever—and got anywhere near my mom again. "And you think there was no way the mutation stuck?"

"Not if Matthew is right. I mean, I wanted to do it to get you out of there, but it wasn't this true and deep want. He nicked an artery, but he wasn't dying." He cast me a look. "I know what you're thinking. That if it did, we're connected to him."

Healing Will without really knowing what the outcome would be was a huge risk and sacrifice for Daemon. "Yeah," I admitted.

"There's nothing we can do about that now but wait and see."

"Thank you." I cleared my throat, but it didn't help. "Thank you for getting me out of there."

Daemon didn't respond, but his fingers tightening around mine grounded me in reality. I told him about the Daedalus, but as expected, he hadn't heard of them. The little talking we did on the way to the office building weakened my voice further, and each time my words ended on a raspy note, Daemon flinched. I pressed my head against the backseat, forcing my eyes to stay open.

"Are you okay?" Daemon asked as we neared Street of Hopes.

My smile felt wobbly. "Yeah, I'm okay. Don't worry about me right now. Everything…"

"Everything is about to change." He pulled along the back of the plaza, hitting the brakes. Pulling his hand free, he cut the engine. He took a deep breath as he glanced at the clock in the dashboard. We had five minutes.

Five minutes to get Dawson out of there if what Will had said was true. Five minutes wasn't nearly enough time to prepare for this.

I took off the seat belt, ignoring the weariness sinking into my bones. "Let's do this."

Daemon blinked. "You don't have to come in with me. I know… you're tired."

No way in hell was I letting Daemon face this alone. Neither of us had any clue what waited inside, what kind of condition Dawson was in. I opened the door, wincing as pins and needles shot across my feet.

Daemon was beside me in a second, taking my hand as he looked down, meeting my eyes. "Thank you."

I smiled even though my insides were twisting and turning. As we walked up to the front doors, I started a mini prayer in my head for whoever was listening. *Please don't let this end badly. Please don't let this end badly.* Because in reality, this could go wrong on so many different levels it was frightening.

Daemon reached for the handle on the double glass doors and surprise, surprise, the door was unlocked. Suspicion blossomed. Too easy, but we'd come this far.

Looking up, I saw a circular piece of onyx embedded in the brick. Once inside, we'd be powerless, with the exception of healing. If this were a trap, we were so screwed.

We went inside. To the right, the alarm system shone green, meaning it wasn't set. How much money did Will invest in this? The guards at the warehouse, Vaughn, and all the people he had to pay off to just leave the office building...unlocked?

Money would've been of no real hindrance to him. Hell, he'd turned over his own niece.

The lobby looked like any office-building lobby. Half-circle desk, fake plants, and cheap tile floors. There was a door leading to a stairwell that had been conveniently left open. Glancing at Daemon, I squeezed his hand. I'd never see him so pale, his face so hard it could've been made of marble.

His destiny waited upstairs, in a way. His future.

Squaring his shoulders, he started toward the door and we went, climbing the stairs as fast as we could. When we reached the top, my legs were shaking from exhaustion, but fear and excitement spiked my blood with adrenaline.

At the top landing, there was a closed door. Above it, there was more onyx—a sure sign. Daemon let go of my hand and wrapped his fingers around the handle, a slight tremor running up his arm.

My breath caught in my throat as he opened the door. Images of the impending reunion flitted through my thoughts. Would there be tears and shouts of joy? Would Dawson be in any shape to recognize his brother? Or was there a trap waiting to be sprung on us?

The room was dark, lit only by the moonlight streaming in through one window. There were a couple of folding chairs propped against the wall, a TV in the corner, and a large kennel-like cage in the middle of the room, outfitted with the same kind of manacles that had hung from mine.

Daemon stepped into the room slowly, his hands falling to his sides. Heat blasted off his body as his spine stiffened.

The cage…the cage was empty.

Part of me didn't want to process what that meant, couldn't let the thought sink in and take root. My stomach cramped, and tears burned the back of my sore throat.

"Daemon," I croaked.

He stalked to the cage, stood there a moment, and then knelt, pressing his forehead against his hand. A shudder racked his body. I hurried to his side and placed my hand on his rigid back. Muscles bunched under my touch.

"He…he lied to me," Daemon said, voice ragged. "He lied to us."

To come this close, to come seconds from seeing his brother again, was heartbreaking. The kind of shattering there was no coming back from. There was nothing I could say. No words could make this better. The emptiness tearing open inside me was nothing compared with what I knew Daemon was feeling.

Choking back a sob, I knelt behind him and rested my cheek on his back. Had Dawson ever been here? There was a good chance he'd been at the warehouse because of what Mo had said, but if he'd been here, he was gone now.

Gone again.

Daemon jerked up. Caught off guard, I started to tip over, but he whipped around, catching me before I hit the floor and pulling me to my feet.

My heart stuttered and then accelerated. "Daemon…"

"Sorry." His voice was rough. "We…we need to get out of here."

I nodded, stepping back. "I…I'm so sorry."

He pressed his lips into a thin line. "It's not your fault. You had nothing to do with this. He tricked us. He lied."

I honestly wanted to sit down and cry. This was so wrong.

Daemon took my hand, and we headed back to the car. I climbed in, buckling the seat belt with numb fingers and a heavy heart. We pulled out of the plaza, hitting the road in silence. Several miles later two Ford Expeditions sped past us. I twisted in my seat, expecting the vehicles to do a one-eighty in the middle of the road, but they kept going.

Turning around, I glanced at Daemon. His jaw was carved out of ice right now. His eyes glowing like diamonds from the moment we stepped out of the office building. I wanted to say something, but there really weren't words that could do the loss any justice.

Daemon had lost Dawson all over again. The injustice of it ate away at me.

I reached between us, placing my hand on his arm. He glanced at me briefly but said nothing. Settling back against the seat, I watched the scenery blur by in a mesh of shadows. I kept my hand on his arm, though, hoping it brought him comfort like he'd given me earlier.

By the time we reached the main route leading to our road, I could barely keep my eyes open. It was late, past midnight, and the only good thing I had going was my mom was in fact at work and not wondering where in the hell I'd been all day. There had probably been texts from her, and she wasn't going to be happy when I responded with some lame excuse.

Mom and I were going to have to talk. Not now, but soon.

We pulled into Daemon's driveway and the SUV idled to a stop. Dee's Jetta was in the driveway, along with Matthew's car. "Did you call them, tell them what happened to…me?"

He took a breath and I realized he hadn't been breathing this whole time. "They wanted to help find you, but I had them stay here in case…"

In case things had gone badly. A very smart move. At least Dee hadn't experienced the piercing hope that turned into bottomless despair like Daemon had.

"If the mutation doesn't hold, I will find Will," he said, "and I'm going to kill him."

I was probably going to help, but before I could respond, Daemon leaned over the center console and kissed me. The tender touch was so at odds with what he'd just said. Deadly and sweet—that was what Daemon was; two very different kinds of souls rested in him, fused together.

Daemon pulled back with a shudder. "I can't…I can't face Dee right now."

"But won't she worry?"

"I'll text her as soon as you're settled."

"Okay. You can stay with me." *Always*, I wanted to add.

A wry grin appeared on his lips. "I'll get out before your mom comes home. Swear."

That would be a good idea. He asked me to wait while he got out and came around the front of the SUV, slower than he normally moved. Tonight had taken its toll. He opened the door and reached in for me.

"What are you doing?"

He arched a brow. "You haven't had shoes on this entire time, so no more walking."

I wanted to tell him that I could walk, but some inherent instinct told me not to push it. Daemon needed this, needed to take care of someone right now. I relented and scooted to the edge of the seat.

The front door to his house swung open, slamming against the clapboard like a gunshot. I froze, but Daemon spun around, his hands closing into fists, preparing to face anything and expecting the worst.

Dee rushed out. Strands of dark curly hair streamed behind her. Even from where I was, I could see the tears glistening on her pale cheeks, under her swollen eyes. But she was laughing. She was smiling, babbling nonsense, but she was *smiling*.

I slipped out of the seat, wincing as coldness bit deep into my flesh. Daemon took a step forward as the front door started to swing shut but stopped. A tall and thin form filled the doorway, swaying like a reed. As the form drifted forward, Daemon stumbled.

Oh God, Daemon never stumbled.

The why sunk in slowly, and I blinked—too scared to believe what I was seeing. It all seemed surreal. Like maybe I'd fallen asleep on the way back, and I was dreaming something too perfect.

Because under the glow of the porch light was a boy with dark wavy hair curling around broad cheekbones, lips that were wide and expressive, and eyes that were dull but still such a striking shade of green. An exact replica of Daemon stood on the porch. Gaunt and pale, but it was like seeing Daemon in two spots.

"Dawson," Daemon croaked out.

Then he broke into a dead run, feet pounding over frozen ground and up the steps. Wetness gathered in my eyes, spilling down my cheeks as Daemon threw his arms out, his broader body blocking his brother's.

Somehow, someway, Dawson was home.

Daemon pulled his brother to him, but Dawson… He was just standing there, arms limp against his sides, his face as beautiful as his brother's but painfully empty.

"Dawson…?" Uncertainty carried in Daemon's voice as he pulled back, twisting my insides into raw, nervous little knots that traveled up my throat, getting stuck and stealing my breath.

As the two brothers stared at each other, with the wind blowing loose flakes of snow on the ground, sending them swirling into the night sky, I remembered what Daemon had said earlier. He had been right. In that moment, everything did change…for the better and for the worse.

Acknowledgments

Writing acknowledgments is probably the hardest part of the book-making business. Every time, I feel like I forgot someone terribly important, and like Katy would say, that would make me a douche canoe.

I want to thank my family and friends for not hating me when I ignore them for days to finish a book. A huge shout-out and a big thank-you to the book lovers and bloggers out there. Your love for the Lux series…and Daemon awes me.

A big thank-you to Liz Pelletier, the editor behind the Lux Series and the one who demanded that I put more Daemon into *Onyx*. Yeah, thank her. Thank you to my awesome publicist, Misa, and the rest of the crew at Entangled. And, of course, I can't forget my awesome agent, Kevan Lyon, and foreign rights agent, Rebecca Mancini, and all the hard work they do.

Also, thank you Wendy Higgins!

Thanks to Cindy, Carissa, Lesa, and Angela for actually reading this before the red pen got a hold of it.

Bonus Material

Read one of your favorite ONYX scenes from Daemon's point of view, and then catch a sneak peek of one of Entangled Teen's hottest new YA releases...

Do This the Right Way

Daemon

The entire world was crashing down on us. That son of a bitch Blake—I should've killed him the moment I first saw him. I should've killed him now. Kat had *lied* to me. Adam was dead. Dee was destroyed. The DOD would be knocking on our doors any damn second, I still had no idea where Dawson was, and the only thing I could think about—cared about—was what Kat was telling me. That she had never felt this way about anyone before. That she couldn't catch her breath and that she felt alive.

And she was talking about how she felt about *me*.

"But none of this matters," she continued, "because I know you really hate me now. I understand that. I just wish I could go back and change everything! I—"

I moved too fast for her to track and clasped her cheeks. "I never hated you."

She blinked, and God, I couldn't stand it if she cried. "But—"

"I don't hate you now, Kat." My gaze locked with her watery one.

"I'm mad at you—at myself. I'm so angry, I can taste it. I want to find Blake and rearrange parts of his body. But do you know what I thought about all day yesterday? All night? The one single thought I couldn't escape, no matter how pissed off I am at you?"

"No," she whispered.

My chest constricted. "That I'm lucky, because the person I can't get out of my head, the person who means more to me than I can stand, is still alive. She's still there. And that's you."

A tear trailed down her cheek. "What…what does that mean?"

"I really don't know." I chased after the tear with my thumb. "I don't know what tomorrow is going to bring, what a year from now is going to be like. Hell, we may end up killing each other over something stupid next week. It's a possibility. But all I do know is what I feel for you isn't going anywhere."

She started to cry harder, and it made me weak in the knees. I bent my head, kissing the tears away until that wasn't enough and I *needed* a taste of her. I kissed her, growling at the way her lips felt against mine.

But Kat pulled back. "How can you still want me?"

I pressed my forehead against hers. "Oh, I still want to strangle you. But I'm insane. You're crazy. Maybe that's why. Maybe we're meant to be together."

"That makes no sense."

"It kind of does, to me at least." I kissed her again. I had to. "It might have to do with the fact you finally admitted you're deeply and irrevocably in love with me."

She let out a weak, shaky laugh. "I *so* did not admit that."

"Not in so many words, but we both know it's true. And I'm okay with it."

"You are?" She closed those beautiful, heather-gray eyes, and all I could think was how grateful I was she was still breathing.

Man, I was turning into a pansy.

But I didn't care. Not when it came to her.

"It's the same for you?" she asked.

My answer was to bring our mouths together again…and again. The touch was like tapping into the Source, sending lightning straight to the soul. The kiss deepened until there was no me, no her. It was just us, and it wasn't enough—could never be enough.

I was moving without realizing it, and the next thing I knew we were on the bed and she was right where I wanted her—in my lap. And then she was beside me on the bed, and my heart was doing crazy crap in my chest. Such a human thing, but it was happening.

Kat breathed heavily. "This doesn't change anything I've done. All of this is still my fault."

Placing my hand on her stomach, I moved so close I was practically attached to her. And I wanted to be in so many different ways. "It's not all your fault. It's all of ours. And we're in this together. We'll face whatever is waiting for us together."

"Us?"

I nodded, working on the buttons of her sweater. Some of them were buttoned incorrectly, and I laughed. Only Kat could have trouble putting clothes on correctly and somehow make it sexy. "If there is anything, there is *us*."

Kat lifted her shoulders, and helped me get her out of the damn thing. Good. She was on board with where this was heading. "And what does 'us' really mean?"

"You and me." I moved down, tugging off her boots.

"No one else."

Her cheeks flushed as she pulled off her socks and lay back down. Jesus, she still had on way too many clothes. "I…I kind of like the sound of that."

"Kind of?" Bull. Shit. I slipped my hand down her stomach, to the hem of her shirt and underneath. I bit down on the inside of my cheek. The minor burn of pain did nothing. I loved the way her skin felt like satin. "Kind of isn't good enough."

"Okay. I do like that."

"So do I." I lowered my head, kissing her slowly. "I bet you love that."

Her lips curved into a smile against mine. "I do."

There was that damn constriction again, like I'd been punched in the chest, but in a good way. How you could be punched in a chest in a good way was beyond me, but damn, I sort of loved that feeling.

The sound that came from deep in my throat was more animal than Luxen or human. I kissed her still damp cheeks as she told me everything Blake had said and done, and I wanted to kill him all over again, but right now, I was with her and Kat was the only thing that mattered.

In between the kisses that unraveled me and then pieced me back together, I spoke things I never told anyone. How crazy I had felt after hearing Dawson was dead, and the hope I felt learning he had to be alive. I told her how badly I wished my parents were here, how sometimes I hated being the one who had to take care of things, and I admitted how jealous I had been when I saw her around Blake.

Everything I felt was in every touch and even what I didn't see was in the way my fingers brushed over the fragile bones of her ribcage. And with every breathy, soft moan that escaped her lips, I was snared in her web a little more.

My hands shook as they moved up, and I hoped she didn't notice. I was blown away, shattered by what she allowed me to do. Pieces of our clothing disappeared. My shirt. Hers. Kat's hand drifted down my stomach, and I clenched my jaw so hard I was sure I was going to be paying a visit to a dentist soon.

When her fingers found the button on my jeans, I was completely lost to her, but in a way I never, ever expected.

"You have no idea how badly I want this," I told her, bringing the tips of my fingers down her chest and over her stomach. So beautiful. "I think I've actually dreamed about it. Crazy, huh?"

She lifted a small hand, running the pads of her fingers down my cheek. I turned into the touch, pressing a kiss against the palm of her hand, and then I found her mouth again. This kiss was different, more intense, and Kat—aw, God—Kat came alive. Hips rocking together, our bodies fitted so tightly there was a good chance I would slip into my true form and knock out the power in the entire state.

Our explorations grew. Her hands were everywhere, and I urged her with words and touches to go further. Her leg curled around my hips—sweet, baby Jesus—I was nearly undone.

With my name on her lips and with barely anything separating us, I felt the last of my control slipping. Whitish-red light radiated off of me, bathing Kat in the warm glow. There was nowhere that my hands didn't explore, and the way her body arched into the slightest touch, I was awed and consumed. Kissing her and drawing her deep inside me, I never wanted this to end. She was perfect to me. She was *mine,* and I wanted her more than I wanted anything in my life.

But I stopped.

Everything that had happened flipped through my head like a photo album I wanted to burn. Both our emotions were all over the place. There had been death, discovery, and so much more. And we were rushing headfirst into not turning back.

I didn't want our first time to be like this—to be because of what happened.

My God, I *was* a mushy pansy ass, but I stopped.

Kat stared up at me, running her hands over my stomach and making it really hard to slam on the brakes. "What?" she asked.

"You…you're not going to believe me." Hell, I didn't believe it. In a couple of seconds, I was really going to regret this. "But I want to do this right."

She started to smile. "I doubt you could do this wrong."

Ha. "Yeah, I'm not talking about *that.* That I will do perfectly, but I want to…" Break out the subscription to the Hallmark Channel and Lifetime Movie Network. "I want us to have what normal couples have."

Kat looked like she was going to cry again. I'd probably be crying soon, but for a totally different reason.

I cupped her cheek, exhaling roughly. "And the last thing I want to do is stop, but I want to take you out—go on a date or something." I sounded like an idiot. "I don't want what we're about to do to be overshadowed by everything else."

I think I might have blushed. Damn me.

Calling on every ounce of self-control I had, I did the unthinkable and lifted off her, easing down on my side. I wrapped an arm around her waist and tugged her close. I brushed my lips across her temple. "Okay?"

Kat tipped her head back, meeting my stare. Her throat worked on her next words. "I think I might love you."

Air punched out of my lungs. I held her tight, and I knew right then I would burn down the whole universe for her if I had to. I would do anything to keep her safe. Kill. Heal. Die. Anything. Because she was my everything.

And I wanted to tell her so, but I didn't want to tempt the universe. Bad things happened to the people I loved.

I kissed her cheek. "Told you."

Kat stared at me.

I chuckled, and although it didn't seem possible, I moved closer. "My bet—I won. I told you that you'd tell me you love me on New Year's Day."

Looping her arms around my neck, she shook my head. "No. You lost."

I frowned. "How do you figure?"

"Look at the time." She tipped her chin toward the clock on the wall. "It's past midnight. It's January second. You lost."

For several moments I stared at the clock, wishing it into a black hole, but then my gaze found hers and I smiled—really smiled. "No. I didn't lose. I still won."

Keep reading for a sneak peek of Tara Fuller's

inbetween

*"A captivating whirlwind of death, revenge, and true love.
I want a reaper of my own!!"* - Jena from Shortie Says

Since the car crash that took her father's life two years ago, Emma's life has been a freaky—and unending—lesson in caution. Surviving "accidents" has taken priority over being a normal seventeen-year-old, so Emma spends her days taking pictures of life instead of living it. Falling in love with a boy was never part of the plan. Falling for a reaper who makes her chest ache and her head spin? Not an option.

It's not easy being dead, especially for a reaper in love with a girl fate has put on his list not once, but twice. Finn's fellow reapers give him hell about spending time with Emma, but Finn couldn't let her die before, and he's not about to let her die now. He *will* protect the girl he loves from the evil he accidentally unleashed, even if it means sacrificing the only thing he has left. His soul.

Prologue

Finn

Two Years Earlier

"Tell me again. How did you miss the mark?" I shoved my hands in my pockets and pressed my lips together to keep from grinning. "I swear, Anaya, this is the last time I follow one of you Heaven reapers anywhere."

Anaya and I walked down a two-lane strip of asphalt that glistened with puddles of leftover rain. Somewhere in the distance, a second round of clouds let out a hungry rumble. Anaya silently kept pace beside me, the gold band around her biceps glinting with each feather-soft footstep.

She turned her nose up into the air. "I never miss a mark."

"Then would you mind explaining why I'm walking up a mountain to get to our reap? We could've just flashed there."

She squinted at her surroundings, hesitating. I knew we were close, but it was way too fun messing with her to let this one go. "It's okay to admit you're losing your touch," I said. "I'd be happy to take the lead on this one."

Anaya held up her hand, ignoring me. "Do you hear that?"

I stopped, listening to the mangled wail of a horn in the distance. As if pulled in by the sound, a black blur, like a cloud of ink, whipped past us before disappearing around the bend.

Shadows. Scavengers from the outskirts of Hell. Souls that weren't chosen to start again, had escaped their reaper, or hadn't earned their way into Heaven, so they'd been left to decay and rot. They were soulless beings that craved the scent of death. The taste of a soul.

I hated them. But I hated the memories they brought back even more.

Every shadow that blurred across my vision was a cold reminder of Allison, the love of my afterlife. What I'd done to her. What I'd almost let her become. Her name tumbling around in my skull made my chest ache.

But I couldn't change it. I'd never be able to change it. I'd pushed her into a world where we'd never be together again and nearly gotten myself banished to Hell in the process. The shadows would never let me forget it. After fifteen years of penance, Balthazar wasn't likely to let me forget it either. A sick feeling started to brew in my gut, so I shook it off and watched another black blur zip past us. At least they always led us to our targets.

"See." Anaya smiled and skipped ahead. "We're here."

Sure enough, around the last bend, a candy-apple-red Camaro lay upside down, crumpled like a discarded Coke can at the tree line. The horn blared, the sound careering off the rock wall and slamming back into the cliffside forest where it splintered into a thousand echoes between the branches. If I had to guess, the car had taken a similar journey. A ringlet of white smoke seeped from under the ruined hood and twirled up into the air.

"Looks like we have a winner." Anaya pulled her pearl-handled scythe from the leather belt she wore around her white dress, and twirled it in her hand. The twelve-inch blade, with its efficient, palm-sized handle, gleamed like it had never been used.

I glanced down at my sad excuse for a scythe with its plain iron handle and dingy blade. Heaven's reapers got all the perks. I may have been a slave to the Inbetween, but I was still a reaper, for God's sake. We were supposed to be the stuff of nightmare and legend. You'd think they'd at least give me a decent scythe. "Hey, what do you think the chances are of me scoring one of those?"

"Keep dreaming, Finn."

I stopped, leaving a few feet of distance between the car and me. Whoever was in there wasn't ready for me. Not yet. A slow warmth, an ache, spread through my chest, and drove sparks through my veins. Not the impatient icy burn I would have expected from a reap at all.

That…was different.

Anaya strolled past me, the shimmery brown plaits that hung down to her waist swaying behind her. "Look at the bright side," she said. "At least they did away with those awful cloaks."

She gripped the scythe and looked to the heavens. Her lips moved around the words to a prayer, one she'd never let me hear. Then, with a graceful sweeping motion, the blade of her scythe sliced through the car. She tugged once, twice, and yanked her glittery prize from the wreckage. Anaya shoved her scythe back into the leather belt at her hip and pulled the man to his feet. The shadows were on him in an instant, hissing and swirling like smoke around his legs and waist, just waiting for us to make a mistake. They were desperate. Hungry. Of course, their reaction wasn't really a surprise. Balthazar had loaded the territories with reapers, cutting off their food supply—souls rarely slipped through the cracks anymore.

Anaya turned around, tucking the soul behind her, and swung out her scythe. The shadows shrank back before dissolving into an oily spot on the pavement. She scowled and shoved her scythe back in its holster. "Vermin."

Vermin. I'd almost doomed Allison to be vermin. I couldn't look away from the dark spot on the pavement.

"Emma?" The soul babbled, rubbing his head. His eyes swam dizzily in his skull as he tried to regain his bearings. "Emma. You have to help Emma. Have you called an ambulance?"

I closed my eyes, trying to block him out. I didn't want to know her name.

"It's going to be fine, sir. She's going to a very…nice place. Don't worry." Anaya looked up at me, her odd golden eyes begging me to back up her lie.

I couldn't give him what he needed. What he needed was to hear that his daughter was going to live a long, happy life. All I offered was death. I wouldn't lie to him. The fact that I was about to take his little girl to the Inbetween was bad enough.

If she ever decided she was ready, that is. I glanced back at the car, waiting for the icy pull to kick in. Something still didn't feel right about this.

"Dad!" a girl's broken voice cried from the inside the crumpled car.

"Help her!" the man cried, trying to scrabble toward the car. Anaya easily held his shimmering form back. "For the love of God, she's only fifteen years old. You should have helped her first."

Now the pull kicked in. Except, *this* pull was dizzying and familiar in an unfamiliar way. And getting stronger by the second. My head spun with the force of it. Something was wrong here. Nothing about this felt like a standard reap. But I'd swear I felt this before. Once…

Memories pulsed through my mind in blinding flashes as I inched toward the vehicle. Soft-as-satin lips, warm whispers against my neck, smiles like the sun… The pull intensified, like a pounding in my chest, and my knees buckled. I knelt down to the broken window. Something like hope surged through me, followed by a cold rush of fear. I could only think of one other time that it had felt like this. Back when I'd peeled the soul from a frail, bloody body, packed in snow. The day that had changed me forever.

No. It couldn't be her. Not again, and not like this. Blond hair lay matted with blood against the girl's cheek. I reached through the window and traced the path of a tear that had fallen from her closed eyelids, my fingers scattering like mist. Her skin was petal-soft, deadly cold. A warm spot pooled in my hand where we touched, then traveled up my arm, down my neck where the heat exploded in my chest. Connection throbbed beneath my ribs. Certainty pounded in my temples.

Allison…

I jerked my hand back and scrambled away from the car. It was her. After all these years…*it was her.*

"What's wrong with you?" Anaya sounded annoyed.

"Dad?" the girl whimpered again, weaker this time. Or maybe that was the gray, gauzy feeling that was suffocating me. Fifteen years. Fifteen years of wondering if I'd done the right thing, and this is what I find? A girl halfway to death, clutching a bloody backpack? *No. No. No!* I shut my eyes and focused, touching my scythe to be certain. It wasn't there. No burning pull. No clawing need to take her soul. She could still be okay. Unless—

"Finn?" Anaya crouched down in front of me. "I don't know what is going on with you, but if you are incapable of handling this, I will."

I blinked until Anaya's blurry face slowly came into focus. I bolted upright. "Is she yours? Are you here for both of them? Because it's not me." A cold, throbbing panic took up residency in my chest. When she just stared at me, confused, I snapped. "Answer the damn question, Anaya!"

Realization slowly replaced the confusion in her eyes. Anaya shook her head and stared up through the spiky treetops where a crow swam across the turbulent lavender sky. "It's her."

It wasn't even a question. I couldn't hide this. Couldn't shove the secret into the dark safety of my pocket and walk away. Anaya knew.

She glanced back at the car, and then her gaze settled on me. "Walk away," she said, her voice just a whisper of breath. "If you have any sense left in you, you'll walk away from this and forget it happened, Finn. Don't screw this up. You've worked too hard to go back now."

I still had *some* sense. I must have, because part of me knew she was right. That I should walk away right now before this went any further. I blinked at the car, trying so hard to ignore the pull tugging me to her, warm and urgent like the need to breathe. The pull telling me I was here for a reason, even if that reason wasn't to take her soul. I didn't admit that to Anaya, though. Instead, I nodded, not trusting the words tumbling around in my mouth.

Anaya wrapped her fingers around her charge's hand and smiled at him. The air behind her rippled like a silk curtain, then erupted with light. His eyes went wide as he glanced at Anaya, then to me.

"I'm…I'm…" He stopped when Anaya patted the back of his hand, the word *dead* hanging among us.

"Yes," she said.

"And my daughter?" His shimmer dimmed as he watched the car teeter ineptly on the cliff's sharp drop-off.

"I'll take care of her," I said. "I swear."

I swallowed, realizing I meant it. What were the odds that I'd find her again like this? What were the odds that out of all of the places in the world she could have been reborn, she'd end up in California? I'd reaped this territory for years, and she'd been right under my nose. There had to be a reason.

Anaya shot me a sharp look, but didn't get a chance to follow through with her usual rant. Glittery tendrils of light reached out and wrapped around her and the soul in tow. A gust of balmy air exploded from the porthole, blowing Anaya's braids in every direction. It fluffed her white skirt until she looked like she was floating on a cotton mushroom top, then spun them around until they were just a swirl of blinding color.

When they were gone, the wind died, and the light dimmed and dissolved into the murky blue twilight.

Something cracked.

The tree that held the wreckage in place swayed. I looked up. A brilliant flash of red bounced on a branch, as if begging it to snap.

Maeve.

The soul whose second chance I'd stolen fifteen years ago when I pushed Allison through the portal in her place.

And all at once, I realized what fate wanted me to do.

"Don't!" I scrambled for the car. It wobbled on the one tire that hadn't gone flat, threatening to go over any second and take the girl inside with it.

"I knew following you around would eventually pay off." Her voice echoed through the treetops, followed by a mocking laugh. "I realize this is bittersweet, so I'll let you say a quick good-bye before I kill her and ruin your sad excuse for an existence."

I wriggled through the window, closed my eyes, and gave into gravity. Cells connected. The air sizzled. I flexed my fingers, only a breath away from being fully corporeal.

No.

I stopped myself, fighting the urge to slip my arms around Allison's limp frame, and pictured Balthazar, the second in command to the Almighty, ruler of reapers. He'd feel me go corporeal and would know I'd found her again. I punched the ceiling and let my skin scatter like sparks against the gray felt. I couldn't afford that kind of hell right now.

She groaned and something like relief flooded me. Yes, definitely still alive. But not for long. The tree swayed again, this time allowing a little of the car to slip through its hold. I glanced out the window and watched a few rocks spring loose from the cliff and roll to the bottom.

"Finn, come out of there," Maeve sang. She bounced again, rocking the car. "Just give in to this and we'll call it a day. She was going to die anyway. You'd just be doing your job."

She was *not* going to die. I wouldn't let her.

"Come on, Allison." I leaned in close and watched her eyelids twitch, then crack open one at a time. Thank God. "I know you're scared, but I need you to trust me."

Her eyes darted back and forth, wide and afraid, before settling on me. "Who are you? Where's my dad?"

When she leaned up to try to see in the front seat I moved in front of her to block her view. "He's fine. Don't worry about him right now," I said, softly. "I need you to get up. See that window?" I pointed to the upside-down broken window and she nodded.

The car lurched again.

"You need to crawl through there. And you need to do it fast."

She tried to sit up, then winced and fell back. "I can't. It hurts."

I plastered a smile on my face and had to force myself not to touch her, to brush the hair out of her face, to grab her arm and pull her the hell out of there. "Yes, you can. You're tough. I can tell."

She shook her head. "No, I'm not. Really. I didn't even make it through one week of softball before I sprained my ankle."

I laughed in spite of myself. "I have a feeling you're a lot tougher than you give yourself credit for. Now come on." The car rocked and I tensed. "Get out of the car."

She looked into my eyes for a long moment, then pushed herself up and inched toward the window. I crawled out first, coaxing her to follow.

The car shifted. Groaned. I heard more rocks break loose from the cliff to tumble over the edge.

"You're making this unbearably complicated, Finn. Really, why not just pull her out of the car and get it over with?" Maeve taunted, a smile behind her words. "You're already dead—what else could Balthazar possibly do? Oh…well I guess there is Hell. But other than that?"

Pushing Maeve's laughter out of my head, I focused on Allison. "Come on, pretty girl," I said, fear thrumming in my chest. "You can do this. You *have* to do this."

The gash bleeding through her blue jeans snagged on the broken window and she sobbed.

"Don't stop. I know it hurts. But you can't stop." We were so close. Another few feet and she'd be free. I kept my eyes on her, trying to figure out a way to distract her from the pain. "You know, one time I broke my leg," I blurted out.

She sniffled and looked up at me.

"I'd climbed this big tree on my dad's farm. I didn't tell anyone where I was going, so when the branch broke, I knew I was in trouble. I had to walk all the way home on that leg just to get there before it got dark."

"Why didn't you wait for somebody to look for you?"

"Coyotes. All I could think about was how I used to hear them howling at night. Our neighbor used to find his cattle torn to shreds."

She scooted a little farther out. "Didn't it hurt?"

The car groaned and tilted underneath us. Allison gripped the seat, her eyes wide.

"It hurt like hell, but it was a lot better than ending up like the cattle."

She squeezed her eyes shut and wiggled the rest of the way through the window, into the pine needles and dirt on the side of the road. She crawled forward a few more feet and collapsed. Her cheek pressed against the wet pavement as she fought to catch her breath.

A loud *crack* split the silence, and the car lurched forward, its weight breaking the tall bone of a tree. Within seconds, it rolled off the side and into the chasm below, a chewed-up red spot swallowed by the dark.

Maeve's scream ripped through the mist that had started to fall, and in it, I heard her cry for revenge. I'd worry about that later. For now, I looked down at Allison.

I watched her breaths make foggy shapes as they puffed erratically into the night. Her lashes blinked away the tears that were running across her cheeks. No. This wasn't Allison anymore.

"Emma," I whispered as a beam of headlights curled around the bend in the road. "You need to flag down the car that's coming around the corner. You're going to have to get up."

"My leg…" She looked up, tears in her eyes. "Why can't you do it? Why aren't you helping me?"

Guilt tied my insides into knots, making it hard to look at the girl reaching up for my help. I couldn't give it to her no matter how badly I wanted to. Balthazar and his damned rules!

"I can't. I'm so sorry." I took a few steps back until she lowered her hand. "But you can do this. You're tough. Remember?"

Her gaze swung to the lights glistening on the pavement and she pushed herself to her knees. I took my chance. I let myself fade. Dissolve into the mist around me that was calling me home.

I watched Emma wave her arms at the slowing car. She was safe. Alive. I closed my eyes, laughing with relief. I'd done it. I'd saved her. Except...

I looked up at the broken tree where Maeve had balanced only minutes ago. There was no way I could walk away now. Not when I'd led Maeve to her.

Damn it. This was bad on so many levels. I watched Emma collapse against the man from the car as he wrapped a jacket around her shivering shoulders. Warmth spread through my chest. Yeah...*bad* wasn't a strong enough word. Disaster was more like it. And I didn't care. She was worth it.

"I'll keep you safe. I swear it." I repeated the promise I'd made to her father, then closed my eyes and let the wind catch me and toss me into the night.

Chapter 1

Finn

Sometimes Emma made me feel so alive, I almost forgot I was dead.

Almost.

I sat on the floor across from her bed listening to her slow, steady breaths. I should have been more alert. I was supposed to be on watch. But it was so hard to concentrate on anything but her when I knew she was remembering.

Emma rolled over, pressing her face into the pillow. "Finn…"

I shut my eyes, trying to hold on to it. I wasn't stupid enough to think she'd remember this when she woke up, but damn it if hearing my name slip through her lips didn't sweep through me like wildfire. Scorching the places where blood used to run. Melting the hollow space where my heart used to beat.

I took a deep, unneeded breath and let the back of my head thump against her overstuffed bookcase. This was never going to get easier. Two years of watching her through the invisible barrier of Balthazar's rules was really starting to suck. Especially when every time I blinked, another piece of Allison was breaking through the surface.

In the pale light of her lamp, I could see the neat row of cookbooks, nestled together like a family, holding all of the secrets Emma created in the kitchen. They smelled like flour and sugar and home. The next orderly row was packed with the worn-out novels she loved, and a new photography book her mom bought her last year. The last shelf belonged to the books her father had written, held in place by gold-framed pictures of him smiling and alive. Emma had so many words inside her. I was surprised they didn't fall out while she was sleeping. Thousands of words about mysteries and romance and life. Things I didn't know anything about.

Things that Allison had known *everything* about.

She whimpered from under the covers and I looked up. What was she remembering this time? What piece of the Inbetween and her time with me was she fighting? There was so much I didn't want her to remember. So much I *needed* her to remember. But that didn't matter. I was here to protect her. That's where it had to end.

I closed my eyes, trying to swallow my own crap lie. She mumbled something in her sleep and began to thrash under the sheets. I groaned and pushed myself up from my safe spot on the carpet, unable to sit there listening to her suffer anymore. I stopped a foot from the bed and knelt down.

"Shh…" I touched the edge of the mattress, forcing myself not to go any closer. "It's going to be okay." She was only a few inches away, but it felt like miles. Miles that left me wanting in so many ways that I ached. Hopefully my presence would be enough. There were times I swore she could feel me.

"What do you think you're doing?" a gravelly voice chided.

I looked up from the edge of Emma's bed just as Easton melted up from the polished hardwood floor beneath the window. Like an oil slick coming to life, he unfolded his long, shadowy legs until he was just an inkblot in front of the splash of lamplight on her wall. His violet eyes pinned me like a kid caught with his hand in the cookie jar.

Which I kind of was.

"Nothing," I lied.

"Yeah, looked like nothing." He strolled across the room accompanied by a wave of sulfur and smoke, the black serpent tattoo on his neck glinting.

"Jesus, Easton." I scrunched up my nose and climbed to my feet. "Don't they have a shower somewhere between here and the afterlife?"

"Screw you. You didn't just have to tow somebody's grandpa to Hell." He brushed something chalky and gray off his long coat, and a shudder worked its way down my spine. God only knows what—or who—it had belonged to. "Besides, I wasn't the one about to feel up a sleeping human."

"I wasn't—"

"Save it." He waved his hand dismissively. "We have work to do. I don't have time for your useless obsession with the human today."

"Will you please stop calling her that?"

"What?" Easton glanced up from Emma's vanity, where he'd been inspecting the various lotions, tubes, and bottles like he was on some alien planet. Then again, Easton had been dead for something like four hundred years and spent most of his life in Hell, so her stuff probably was sort of alien to him.

"'The human.' You make her sound like a freak. It's not like we're a different species, for God's sake. We were humans too, or don't you remember that far back?"

"*Were,*" he said, scowling at me over his shoulder. "Past tense."

Easton's clumsy fingers knocked over the bobblehead zombie on the vanity top and we both froze. Emma shot up from beneath the covers, gasping.

"Mom?" She shoved the tangled blond hair out of her face, her eyes trained on her rumpled reflection in the vanity mirror. "Was that you?"

"Not Mom. Just one of Hell's reapers, at your service." Easton leaned against the bookcase and grinned. "You're right, Finn. This is fun."

"Are you freaking insane?" I hissed.

He rolled his eyes. "Oh calm down, drama queen. It's not like she can hear us."

"You scared her."

"Are you kidding? She's scared of her own reflection. And that has nothing to do with me."

No. But the fact that Emma's life had been a horror movie waiting to happen these last two years had everything to do with me. I'd led a soul that hated my guts and was hell-bent on revenge right to her doorstep.

I turned my attention back to Emma. After she collected herself, she twisted her hair up into a messy ponytail and dug in her nightstand drawer for her journal.

"Dear diary…" Easton nodded at the journal. "What do you think she's going to write?"

I folded my arms across my chest. "Not my business."

He walked over to her bed and plopped down beside her. The mattress didn't creak or groan under his weight. The blankets didn't shift. He peeked over her shoulder at the book. A long tendril of honey-colored hair came loose from Emma's ponytail and fell across her eye. She tucked it behind her ear, but Easton blew on it so that it fell right back down. She swept it out of her face, looking frustrated, and Easton chuckled.

"Will you stop?" I said, feeling uncomfortable with how close he was to her. "This is so screwed up it's not even funny."

He raised a dark brow. "Oh? And what you're doing isn't?"

We could have gone back and forth like that for hours, but the call came. It always did. It started in my bones—a cold so cutting that it sliced through me like a machete. Easton's jaw clenched, his muscles taut and ready. He slowly closed his hand around the handle of his scythe, which burned black and softly smoked at his side. I flexed my fingers as the icy ribbons of death worked their way through each one of my limbs.

"Can you take this one for me?" I asked. "You're already going to be there, and I just got back—"

"No," Easton said. "Hell no. I have my own job to do. I can't keep covering for your sorry ass. Besides, do you have any idea how close you are to being caught? Don't push your luck, Finn. Just keep your nose down, collect your souls, and thank the Almighty that you don't have my job."

"I'm taking a risk every time I leave her. You know that."

"For the love of God. She'll be fine, Finn. It's just one reap."

"How do you know she'll be fine?"

He shrugged. "I don't. But that's the difference between you and me. I don't care."

With that, he vanished, consumed in a flash by the keening wails of the damned. The screams beckoned. Clawed at me from the inside out.

Rule One as a reaper: Death doesn't wait for anyone.

And it sure as hell wasn't waiting for me now.

Like what you've read so far? Pick up

online and in stores everywhere August 2012!